WHEN
UPON LIFE'S
BILLOWS

Sara Powter

ISBN: 9780645783339
Paperback Edition

Pacific Wanderland Publications
ABN 99 768 734 831

Kincumber NSW 2251

saragpowter@gmail.com
www.sarapowter.com.au

1st edition 2025, printed by Kindle and in Paperback by Amazon.
2nd edition 2025 Large Print Paperback Edition, by Amazon.
3rd Edition - Hardcover 2026 by Amazon

Graphic Acknowledgements

Cover
https://collection.sl.nsw.gov.au/record/nmQdrexn
V1/1794+/1

Cover Portrait
Vice-Admiral John Hunter,
c. 1813-15, by William Mineard Bennett
Oil painting DG 394
https://www2.sl.nsw.gov.au/archive/discover_collections/history_nation/
terra_australis/journals/hunter/index.html

Chapter graphics in Public Domain

To my husband, Steve,
Thank you for all your support in my writing.
He's my Alpha reader.

To Roby Aiken
for your patience in correcting my punctuation,
and to my Beta readers
Noreen Robertson, Linda Upcroft, Lee Boehm & Anna Marie Leffew
for doing the final read-throughs and
Anna Marie Leffew for the excellent advertising she does for me.
And…
Rebekah Robinson for my cover.
Cover by Beckon Creative
beck@beckoncreative.biz

Cultural Advice

Aboriginal and Torres Strait Islander people should be aware that this book contains names and
stories of deceased persons.

Acknowledgement of Country:

In the spirit of reconciliation, I acknowledge the Traditional Custodians of country throughout Australia and their
connections to land, sea and community. We pay our respect to their Elders, past and present, and extend that respect to
all Aboriginal and Torres Strait Islander peoples today.

Australian Historical Novels
(All stand-alone books)

A First Fleet Stories (1788+)
Gentle Annie Soames
The Emancipated Potter
Paternity Unknown

The Hunter to Macquarie Collection (1795-1822)
When Upon Life's Billows
The Saddler's Song (2025)
Tuppence to Pass (2025)
His Majesty's Pageboy (2026)
A Fist Full of Holey Dollars (2026)
Far From the Whispering Sheoaks (2026)
Bound Down in Iron Chains (2026)
Buddy's Promise (2027)
Quest for Survival (2027)
Linen Shirts Aplenty (2027)

Unlikely Convict Ladies Trilogy (1792-1840s)
Dancing to her Own Tune
(co-authored by Sheila Hunter & Sara Powter)
Amelia's Tears
A Lady in Irons

The Lockleys of Parramatta (1800-1901)
Unshackled Lives - *Prequel novella - free with newsletter signup*
Hands Upon the Anvil
Out Where the Brolgas Dance
Diamonds in the Dirt
The Earl's Shadow
Once a Jolly Swagman
Jonty's Journey

The Convict Birthstain Collection (1820-1840s)
No More, My Love
The Vine Weaver
Scotch at The Rocks
Waiting at the Sliprails
Convict Shadows of the Past
In Defence of Her Honour
I Can't Stop Tomorrow
Madeline's Boy
Jam or Marmalade for Tea

Shelia Hunter's
Australian Colonial Trilogy (1840-1850s)
Mattie
Ricky
The Heather to the Hawkesbury

Table of Contents

*The grammar and language in this book are
Australian English spelling.*

KEY
~ - Time passing in the same locality

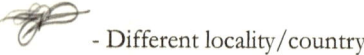 - Different locality/country

Billows - breaking waves
Scuppers - the drain holes on the deck of a ship
Gunnels - railings of a ship

Chapter 1   The *Sirius* Nightmare
September 1795

*T*he sheets twisted around the grey-haired man's waist as he tossed and turned in his sleep. He groaned and occasionally shouted as the memories of the ship running aground tore through his subconscious mind.

His dreams relived the horrific sounds of his vessel, the *HMS Sirius*, crunching on a submerged rock just off Norfolk Island.

Wind bullets had caught the sails, and no matter what he did, he could not steer his vessel to safety. As the wind rose, rather than blow him away from the deadly rocks, an unseen underwater rock caught the wooden vessel, and it crunched as it sheared its way through the hull.

Spots of perspiration beaded on the sleeper's brow and trickled onto his pillow.

Stress!

Panic!

Frustration!

John woke with a start and lay back in relief that it was only another dream. That day haunted him for the past five years, but rarely as bad as this morning. His brow and hair were damp with perspiration.

A long sigh escaped; it was only another nightmare.

The ship was a total loss, but the crew saved most of the stores and the people on board. However, the majority of his personal luggage, along with the possessions of his senior officers and crew, was lost.

He had sent many of his convict passengers back to Sydney Cove on the brig the *Supply*. It remained the only vessel in the colony. He stayed on Norfolk Island for over ten months until other transport could be arranged.

He was now living in Sydney. John rolled over, taking the sheets with him. His bedding was a mess, and his pillow was moist. This morning, his mind would not let go of the episode. On the island, John had lived in one of the small cottages when on Norfolk Island, and helped Phillip Gidley King where possible. Memories of the time on the penal island were not all bad. He would take long walks to the many delightful beaches and bays.

As he had no command, John indulged in his love of fishing, as food in the settlement was needed, and all additions to the meagre rations were good. That was an occupation he did with relish.

John stared blankly at the unseen ceiling above him, remembering the many sunrises and sunsets he had watched. The peace and beauty of the island were soul-cleansing. He could see the pristine beauty of the crystal-clear rock pools and the plethora of fish and birds in his mind's eye.

In the predawn darkness, he closed his eyes, trying to recapture nature's loveliness.

Yet, those on the island were starving; only a miracle could save them. One came. God sent one. An enormous flock of migratory birds arrived just as the food was about to run out. The millions of birds sustained the island residents until the next supply ship arrived.

Thinking back to those days was better than dwelling on what would be ahead of him when he eventually had to get up. He knew that outside was filth, stench and squalor, and his duty was to clean it up. The problem was that he had no idea how to go about it.

This place was not an orderly ship where everyone jumped at his command. No, here, mutiny simmered just below the surface.

As he rested, trying to fall asleep again, his mind returned to four years ago.

The smaller ship, the *Supply*, sailed to Batavia for more food. John was unsure how, but the captain of the *Supply* chartered a Dutch ship while getting food. The *Waakzaamheid* was a brig under Captain Smit's command.

After the *Supply* collected the remainder of the *Sirius* crew from Norfolk Island, they returned to Sydney, bringing John's favourite chair and the few items he had managed to salvage.

When he returned to England later that year, he left the chair with his young friend, Colin, the potter at Parramatta. Colin and Aggie ensured this beloved chair was at his desk when he returned last week.

He smiled. He did love that young couple and their little boy, Jonny.

The arrival of the two laden ships saved Sydney Cove and Norfolk Island from starvation. However, the chartered Dutch ship's existence meant John had to return to England and explain the loss of his beloved leaky tub.

John rolled over and tried to sleep until he dreamed again about the crunch of the ship on the rocks.

It woke him again with a jump.

He groaned.

His pillow was now wet, and sleep fled entirely. He was wide awake.

He flipped onto his back and thanked God that no one died in the shipwreck in March 1790. However, his wrecked vessel had been vital to the infant colony's survival. It supplied food and produce regularly.

John had not long completed a circumnavigation of the globe in the *Sirius* to resupply food for the starving settlements. After some urgent repairs, his ship needed to deliver food to Norfolk Island. He had managed to unload all the food supplies in Sydney and then headed to Norfolk Island. The *Supply* unloaded her convicts and food before moving away for the *Sirius* to take its place. The convicts made it ashore before the storm hit and grounded his ship with its cargo of food.

He threw off the tangled sheets and lay wondering if he should rise. He didn't.

Eighteen months after losing his ship, John returned to London and faced an inquiry there. He had been exonerated of any fault. When a storm appeared almost out of the blue, a sailing vessel in such a situation had little ability to steer away from a reef.

Now, five years later, he, John Hunter, was the newly arrived governor of that same settlement. When he had departed four years ago, Governor Arthur Phillip had the foundations of a decent settlement under construction. Arthur fell ill soon after John departed.

John sighed. The Navy said he would "be a blessing to the colony" when informed of his new command. He was unsure who had made that comment. Still, his friend in the Home Office, Lord Charles Phillimont, informed him that one of the admirals wrote, "his incorruptible integrity, unceasing zeal, thorough knowledge of the country, and steady judgment would bring stability to a difficult situation."

He smiled at that and wondered who had held him in such high esteem. It may have been Lord Howe, as he had served under him on the *HMS Victory*. John accepted the position and arrived in Sydney only days earlier, on September 7th. He took command from Major William Paterson, who had been left in charge when Lieutenant-Governor Francis Grose returned to England ill. He knew he must retain a tough naval persona as he assumed command. He moved into the official residence in Sydney.

This building was erected once the settlement was established. Governor Phillip moved in shortly after his French chef died. The previous dwelling had been a prefabricated timber and canvas structure, which leaked worse than his ship.

After the brick food storeroom was built, this double-storey building was the first substantial construction in the colony. The shingle roof occasionally leaked, but, on the whole, it was comfortable. This substantial dwelling had been enlarged with extra staff rooms on the ground floor. He wished he had room for live-in guards.

On his first sojourn to this desolate shore, he occupied the east-facing room and claimed that room on his return. Arthur's old room was of equal size but faced west over the town.

John had been in the colony for nearly a week and had much thinking to do. He had missed his favourite chair in England; it was now in his office downstairs. Colin Osborne, his protege from his first voyage, had written a lengthy screed from his base in Parramatta. Thankfully, there was nothing there that needed his urgent attention. Richard Johnson returned from a visit to Parramatta last week with the things John left with Colin. This included his chair. His other items and a letter from Colin awaited him when he moved in. It was like a homecoming of sorts.

John was still unused to the bed not moving under him. Although his berth on any vessel was not a hammock, his box bed on the ship rocked him to sleep at night. Here, the sounds were vastly different.

Being September, the first of the bladder cicadas started singing at dusk the night before. He knew from experience that they usually came out at the end of the month. They were early this year.

Bennelong explained that this meant an early and likely hot summer. His native friend had vanished as soon as the ropes were thrown ashore.

John chuckled as he watched Ben disrobe as he moved through town. His hat and coat would be returned when Ben came to visit next.

John knew dawn was at hand as the raucous sounds of the birds made him smile. He had woken before the dawn chorus this morning. Even these were so different from home. Not that he was in England often, but there were no nightingales or larks here. The kookaburras, magpies and other birds seemed to fight over who could make the most noise and welcome in the dawn. Add the screeching white cockatoos to the morning stillness, and he knew sleep would not return.

He looked towards the window and saw that it was now nearly dawn.

Each new day presented a challenge of where to start, what to tackle, and what to do, bringing a new crisis. These ranged from unruly convicts to a lack of food. Often, the latter exacerbated the former. Even so, he missed the sea and the never-ending roll of the deck beneath his feet.

Five years after the grounding of his ship, bad dreams still frequently disturbed his nocturnal slumber.

He hauled himself to sit up, and he watched the sky lighten.

As a child, he and his father were wrecked off the coast of Norway, and it took them time to get back home. This did not make him fear the sea, only respect it. He adored his father, William, and missed him dreadfully.

John sighed. He was to start a new life ashore halfway around the world from his home in Scotland. His thoughts of Leith reminded him again of the lovely walks he used to take. Every day had been an adventure. He and his brothers always found a bird's nest, a flower or something interesting. He did the same during his ten months marooned on Norfolk Island.

He groaned and shook his head to make those memories flee.

Thinking of his travels, he was almost jealous of Matthew Flinders and George Bass. They had a tiny eight-foot boat so small that only one crewman could accompany them. They were about to set off to explore the area, much as he had done in 1788 and for the next couple of years.

On that first trip, they had gone north and discovered an immense river and new bays and harbours. None were comparable with Port Jackson, but still, they were astounding.

John and a crew travelled up the bay from where they had settled and found that the soils further inland were better suited for crops. Six weeks after the first valleys were cleared in Sydney, a Redoubt was constructed in what was then called Barramatta.

Only months after landing, Governor Phillip opened farms in that western area, which were now producing food.

John's mind returned to his nightmare. He hoped being on land would have eased his dreams, but they still haunted him. His nightshirt was drenched in sweat. It was early September; although it was spring, it was balmy weather.

His cheeks blew out in utter frustration at the memories of that day.

As he sat in his bed, he attempted to straighten the sheets and blankets while dwelling on the turmoil the storm had caused.

He wondered if he had called out in his sleep. None of his staff had come to see to his welfare, so he hoped he had not. If he had dogs here, they would have scratched at his door. He had not brought any this time, as the kangaroos killed his greyhounds.

Turning his head, he knew a new day was here.

The cessation of the birds' shrill sounds announced that morning had broken - time to rise.

He flicked back the bedding and eased his feet onto the cool timber floor.

The sky outside was now dark blue rather than black. He would watch the sunrise. Thankfully, his room faced east. Arthur Phillip's room overlooked the town, but he liked this room as he could catch glimpses of the sea.

Sydney was much warmer than England or Scotland. He knew they rarely had a frost here, let alone blizzards or snow. At home in Scotland, his feet would have almost frozen, merely walking to the fire to stir it and add more wood. Here, the fire was not even alight.

Before walking to the window, he straightened his bed so his housekeeper would not realise the torturous state of his dreams.

He was still not used to having maids. He was not used to having women around him at all. He now had a cook, housekeeper, and maid. He only consented to them as the house was large enough to stay well away from them. They would run the official residence and cater for official dinners.

John smiled. His nephew, William, and his wife, Eliza, accompanied him on the voyage and moved to their new home yesterday.

William captained the *Reliance*, the ship that brought him back. Eliza would act as a hostess and First Lady for official functions. It was nice to have a familiar face nearby, and it was even nicer that they were family.

Having tidied his tortured berth - he must think of it as a bed - John wondered if it were too early to dress.

Considering it was springtime, the morning air was cool rather than cold. He donned his woollen dressing gown and walked to the window to watch the sunrise. He chuckled, remembering the penetrating chill of his childhood home; he loved the climate here.

From this vantage point, he could see some of the town slowly waking. Even now, some were in the community garden. Nigel Bray had the fires alight at the salt boilers. Fires were being kindled.

Although he could not see them, there would be smoke puffing from various rickety chimneys of the flimsy wattle and daub structures around town. He knew that if he opened his window, the stench from the filthy Tank Stream would permeate his room.

He sighed and shivered, wondering how to start purging the town of filth. The enormous job was almost overwhelming. He must get it all cleaned.

As reluctant as he was to leave the sea, he had almost had to fight to get this job, and he wondered if leaving the sea for a land office was the correct decision.

Arthur Phillip suggested Phillip Gidley King as his successor. Still, the Navy had given John the position instead. Mayhap, the existence of Phillip Gidley King's mistress, who bore two children, didn't help his friend's cause. John was unmarried, but his nephew William's wife, Eliza Kent, would become the first lady if required.

Although he loved this settlement, John wasn't sure he wanted a land commission. He hadn't thought that through. He was here now and would do what he could. All three men had been on the First Fleet. John had been second in command of the entire fleet on that journey and held a dormant commission to take over the role if something happened to the governor-elect.

When Arthur Phillip sailed ahead, John was left in charge of the remaining nine ships. This did not make much difference, as John had brought the fleet in only two days behind the so-called faster vessels.

John recalled his first view of the desolate bay seven years earlier when they sailed into their designated harbour and its almost barren shore. This stark land was supposed to be their new home. However, the sandy soil in Botany Bay was unsuitable for crops, but they were supposed to farm it anyway.

No sooner did John arrive on the *Sirius* with the remainder of the fleet than Arthur Phillip set off searching for a better area. Before leaving Botany Bay, they traded some items with the natives and left them to their hunting.

Captain James Cook had marked alternate bays to the north when he charted the area twelve years earlier. Phillip and he took longboats and went to investigate.

Port Jackson was the harbour of his dreams; it was near perfect. It was a wonder Cook had not explored this area, but that meant John could.

John remembered hearing about the bullets of wind when trying to leave Botany Bay and the near-wrecking of three vessels as they headed northward.

Meanwhile, two French ships watched on at anchor in Botany Bay. How embarrassing to have nearly grounded one ship and then have two others collide. He was sure the French laughed at that incident.

This morning, as he stood watching the sun rise over the headland to the east, he knew that his red-coated soldiers would be assembling the convicts for the first meal of whatever they could get.

John shivered, not from the cold but from knowing what their rations were like. The convict mess was probably serving some porridge or gruel that tasted revolting. Most of the flour had weevils, and the barrels of salted meat were slimy, but it was food and, for many, better than the convicts had eaten in England. His food at Government House was not much better, but his rations were larger. His new cook, Mrs Peach, could make most food palatable. He wished he had some gardeners who knew how to improve the terrible soil.

On this journey, he brought a decent amount of food with him. The hold of his vessel had been loaded to the brim with supplies. He was fully aware of the privations of the place and knew how precious every beast or sack of grain was. All the fresh food was stored securely, and none had spoiled *en route*.

After the head gardener, Henry Dodd, died from sunstroke, Reverend Richard Johnson was the best farmer in the town, but John did not have much chance to have a long chat with his old friend. On his arrival, Richard passed him a letter from Colin Osborne, the potter at Parramatta, and told him his chair awaited him in his office.

John's nephew, William Kent, had purchased twenty-six Spanish Merino sheep in Cape Town. Henry Waterhouse and William had enough money to buy some of the flock. Belatedly, John realised that he should have bought some as well. Although some sheep had died *en route* to Sydney, half survived.

Even though they had only been in the town a few days, some lambs had already been promised to Reverend Samuel Marsden and Captain John Macarthur.

John sighed; this soldier was already a pain in the neck. He was on record for pushing the rules beyond his due and demanding access to areas set aside for government use only.

In Arthur Phillip's absence, Francis Grose had issued grants in areas decreed closed for allocation. Grose had returned home ill and handed the reins to Captain William Paterson, newly promoted to major. John Macarthur managed to twist his friend's arm for the five hundred acres he now owned, and not only was Macarthur promoted as commandant of

Parramatta, but he held the best farming land discovered so far, so he would farm the land himself. Macarthur stated that the new town needed oversight, so he moved west. Ostensibly, it was to build a residence for his wife, as there were no suitable quarters for a free woman, let alone the commanding officer's wife. *Elizabeth Farm* was now showing productivity, but it set a precedent with which John was unhappy. The die was cast and could not be undone lest he all but cause a civil war.

The first thing he did on arrival was to read the lengthy letter from his friend. Colin outlined the troubles going on out west and the state of health of his growing family. A fifth child was on the way. Thankfully, there was nothing urgent John needed to attend to. A visit there could wait. He trusted Colin's screed over his soldiers' reports.

At least, if reports were correct, the colony now had flourishing farms at Parramatta and a little further beyond; Macarthur had at least been as good as his word with his grant. He reluctantly admired the man's deviousness. Some of these areas had been in the early stages of clearing the land and growing test crops when he left. In the few years that he had been absent, things had changed. Through Grose, the militia, known as the New South Wales Corps, now had a firm foothold in the colony. They had land claims that he now may need to rescind.

John knew it would cause problems, but he had his orders.

Since Arthur Phillip left, Francis Grose had established military rule and abolished civil courts. By the time he departed last year, the Corps was in charge of everything. Captain Paterson was promoted to major and assumed command when Grose returned home ill. Rather than fail to stamp out the practice of paying wages in alcoholic spirits, Grose encouraged it.

The consequence was that public drunkenness and corruption were now rife in the small town. This mess was now his responsibility. John had been sent here because of his upright moral stance, strong faith, and knowledge of the country. He had no idea things had become so corrupt.

John had been absent from the new settlement when the women were landed in 1788. He had been surveying up the river with Colin, William Bradley, Jim Bloodsworth, and others.

John had many discussions with the doctor from the *Lady Penrhyn* about the attacks and molestations that had occurred on their landing. The poor man had been stranded on the ship with no longboats available to go to the aid of the violated women. He had to stand and watch the abuses occur. The following day, Arthur Phillip proclaimed the area for England, read the king's edict and laid strict laws.

Floggings occurred regularly as men were prepared to risk the beatings to while away a moment or two between the legs on one of the many whores on these shores.

John groaned in disgust. What a life those poor wretches chose! He shook his head at the thought of their chosen profession. Were all these women prostitutes, though? He knew some of the young ones, and they certainly were not. Colin's wife, Aggie, Nigel's wife, Connie and their friends were children when transported. The oldest of them was sixteen on arrival.

That thought led him to another; children were a by-product of such activity, and he realised he had to sort out some form of schooling for them. But where to find a good teacher? Mrs Johnson couldn't cope with so many orphaned imps, let alone the free children.

In the newly arrived population of New South Wales, when Grose took over, there were 4,221 settlers, of whom 3,099 were convicts. John had no idea how many of the local tribe members remained, but it was reported that the French had killed some the week they landed. Many more died from both smallpox and measles. The dead bodies floated in the bay for days. Sailors had brought in other diseases.

Of the convicts, less than a third were females. This caused significant problems as the unruly men would take what they wished when they wanted. If the women fought back, they were beaten. That was one thing John had already attempted to fix. When he arrived, he added guards to their sleeping area as he discovered the women's tents were unguarded at night.

The odds were against him succeeding in cleansing the new settlement in this raw land. How the felons had managed to survive this far was astounding. Had it not been for the indigenous men like Bennelong, his friends and other tribal warriors and their women, the settlement would have been sure to have been obliterated.

The new settlers traded fresh fish and local food knowledge with these Aboriginal people. John liked them and learned quickly that although they had no structures, they knew how to live in this wild land.

The settlers were told which foods were safe to consume and, more importantly, how to prepare them. John learned a lot during his eighteen months aboard the *Reliance* with Bennelong. He recorded much of the language, but it was so vastly different to his ears that speaking it was hard.

On one of the early explorations, the crew ate some unknown and unprepared food, and all became violently ill. John learned that these dark-skinned people knew much more than the new arrivals.

Like Arthur Phillip, John was determined to live at peace with them. He knew education was crucial for both sides.

The sun pushed its way up the horizon, and John heard movement from his staff below. He knew it was time to dress and tackle the previous day's problems.

He was about to turn from his window when something caught his eye. An ear-piercing scream followed this. He saw a filthy female struggling in the arms of two convict men.

He threw open the window and shouted at them to release her. However, they did not cease their attention to her. The woman fought valiantly, and he could hear her cries for release.

The bedraggled wench shouted at them. "Get your stinking paws off me, and keep your blooming trousers buttoned! I'm no man's whore, and I never will be."

She tried with everything she had to be released. She managed to kick and scratch her way out of their grasp.

One man caught her arm and twisted it behind her back.

She waited until he moved in front of her, and she kneed him between the legs.

The felon let her go, emitting a cry of agony.

She tried to run before the other convict grabbed her.

John called again, and the convict men must have heard him but ignored his call. John cheered silently as he could see his sentries running towards the affray.

Two more of his guards appeared below his window. He called to them, "Go and make them release her now. Arrest them. I'll deal with them later."

The sleepy soldiers, dozing while on duty, took off toward the affray.

John once again shouted for the convict man to release the petrified and furious woman. He called, "I say, unhand her at once. And you, woman, come to my back door and await me there."

He saw her shrug off her last attacker, but before she moved away from the big house, she turned and gave the remaining man a hefty slap across his unsuspecting face.

He was sent staggering backwards by the forceful blow.

John chuckled. She had spunk. He would be interested in hearing her story.

She stormed away from them, throwing comments over her shoulder as she walked. "No man shall un-maiden me against my will. You are the scum of the earth and not worth the air you breathe."

The slapped man finally retaliated but refrained from touching her. "You think you're so much better than us men, don't you, Hellcat? Well, you wait, you she-cat. You'll get your comeuppance when we're ready. There's nowhere to run here, little kitty-hellcat, and we will find you and have you."

The girl swung around and faced her tormentor. "I'd rather be dead than have your filthy hands on me. I'm only here because I would not lower myself to be sold as a whore. What makes you think I would take you willingly? The only man I will take to my bed will be after I wed him. No one here is likely to fill that role."

She spun around on the spot and stormed off.

John saw that rather than coming to the house as ordered, she was obviously leaving. He called to her. "Hey, you, girl! I'm talking to you."

She froze and reluctantly looked up to see where the voice was coming from above her. The new governor was leaning out the top-floor window and wearing a cosy dressing gown. She gasped but wished she had a nice warm cover like that. The woollen blanket she slept under provided little warmth but was better than nothing. No one would share with her because of her smell. "Me, sir?"

John was thankful she had stopped. He would not have chased her in his night attire, and his soldiers were occupied with her attackers. "Yes, you! I said come to my house on the double. Be at my kitchen door in ten minutes."

Helena froze. Her heart started racing. Why did the new governor wish to see her? She knew he was an unmarried navy man, and if he demanded that she share his bed, she would have no option but to comply. She had been betrayed too often by those who should have protected her. She could not fight him if he wished to use her in such a way.

Overwhelmed, she was distressed that everything she had fought for would possibly have been for nothing.

Her shoulders slumped as she stumbled numbly towards the house.

Two of the New South Wales Corps arrived and marched her attackers towards the lock-up. The other two guards returned to their duty at the front of the house.

The criminals' automatic punishment was flogging, each receiving fifty lashes. No trial was required. That was the law of this raw land, laid out the day after the women landed in 1788.

The soldiers pointed Helena toward the kitchen door.

She barely heard them but walked in the direction they said.

Dust rose as she crossed the dirt road.

John Hunter watched her actions from his window. He would deal with the attempted abusers later. After the violations of the women when they landed on that fateful first day in the colony seven years earlier, there were already rules in place to protect the women, any woman. These two felons would receive the promised fifty lashes each for such treatment of an unwilling female. John had already discovered that the rules had been disregarded since Governor Phillip left. Thankfully, the girl was unharmed this time.

He sighed. How was he supposed to protect them when they could wander freely around the town? Where was she heading? Only the laundry behind his stables was in this direction. Surely, she was too dirty to work there.

With the first order of the day now sorted, John checked to ensure that she was coming to the house before he dressed quickly and went to meet the poor wretch. The first thing he would do was apologise to her. He was determined to keep at least one poor girl safe. Her words that she was still a maiden stunned him. Were there more like her? Maybe he should look deeper into the history of the female convicts.

After reading Colin's lengthy letter, John had hoped to head to Parramatta to see his friends, but that would have to wait.

He huffed with frustration. The Osbornes had three children whom he had not met. The youngest were twins named after his parents, William and Helen. Their eldest lad, Jonny, was named after him. He adored this little chap. He remembered the day the boy first walked unaided. Colin had broken his arm, and Jonny toddled across the hospital compound on his own while he waited for his parents. John had been babysitting the imp and had not realised the little boy was mobile.

With a smile on his lips, he left his room to deal with the girl.

Chapter 2   Helena the Hellcat

*H*elena Rosedale was one of the many women convicted of theft who were transported to the Antipodes. She had been betrayed once too often and trusted no one, let alone a man. After her arrival on the *Surprize* the year earlier, she had been assigned to work in the laundry for the soldiers.

From the day she was arrested, she had fought to remain untouched. Even on board, she needed to fight off the male felons and only survived unscathed as some Scottish male convicts fought to protect her and the fifty-nine other women restrained below decks. Some older female prisoners were happy to satisfy the needs of the male convicts, soldiers and crew, but she remained as distant as possible. However, some of the despicable military guards were the worst offenders. She spread lies about herself to ward off their attention.

The six Scottish convicts she arrived with became known as the Scottish Martyrs. They were, in essence, religious prisoners who fought to protect the rights and dignity of the female convicts. They put their faith into action and protected the women at risk.

Helena sought refuge from abuse by sticking as close to them as she could. She and a few younger ones claimed to have the clap, and the doctor kept their secret. He even painted fake sores around their mouths to fool the soldiers. It had worked. Since she arrived, only one convict had forced her way through Helena's self-imposed seclusion. Connie Bray even hugged her. Having a friend in this hellhole was nice.

Not long after they departed from London, she was informed by the martyrs that half a dozen of the soldiers were deserters from other regiments or captives from the Savoy prison who were given a commission in lieu of imprisonment. She had been told to stay well away from those six guards. One of these soldiers was a mutineer from Quebec. Sergeant Samuel Reddish, an ensign in the New South Wales Corps, led the military guard. Rumours of drunkenness and debauchery preceded them, but this man seemed to try his best to keep the women safe.

As Helena dawdled to the vice-regal back door, she thought back to how she had found herself in this unsavoury situation. She had been seeking honest work to send money to her family. She came from a farm in Lincolnshire, and the large family needed every penny they could find to support the growing number of children. As the eldest daughter, she offered to leave home and find work as her two big brothers had done. Having heard about a job as a laundry maid with a local aristocratic family in London, she willingly accepted it. Leaving her family was hard, but saying goodbye to her dog, Kelly, was the worst. Having been sent the fare by her new employer, she had to travel for days to reach her destination in London. She realised that the one hundred and thirty miles from home meant that returning to see her family would not be possible. Letters home were out of the question as she could not write, and none of her family could read. Each mile the mail coach carried her, the more fearful she became.

Travelling alone at seventeen was not pleasant. Before she had travelled the first ten miles, one man had already placed his hand on her knee and propositioned her. If the fat farmer's wife had not clouted him with one of the big leeks she was taking to market, he might have made himself far more objectionable. The lady demanded that she swap seats to protect Helena. Thankfully, the man alighted at the end of the first day. Sadly, so did the farmer's wife. Helena's next leg of the journey was so bad that she asked to be seated next to the driver. He was not much better, but at least his harassment was mainly verbal, as he had to keep two hands on the reins.

Her arrival in London was equally traumatic. Having fought to keep men's hands from pawing her, she was horrified to find that the position was not with the family but with the young son and heir. He was setting up his own establishment in London, and he was already a drunkard who had been tossed from the family home due to his immoral behaviour. Helena had only been in London for two days when Mr Sylvester made his rounds of the kitchens to see which maid he would have to warm his bed. He dragged away a young girl of sixteen.

Helena later found her in tears and bleeding badly. Their employer had violated her, and her maidenhood had been stolen. She reported it to the housekeeper, who had just laughed. "You are their property; they will use us as they wish, so shut it, girlie."

Helena worked in the laundry, boiling stale urine to clean his linen. She was stomping his sheets in a tub of ammonia urine. As he hated the stench of it, he had stayed away. Her feet stung, and her lungs hurt as she breathed in the fumes, but this was what she had signed up for. She didn't mind hard work; she was used to it. Her mother had warned her about the immorality of the big smoke, as she had called it. She didn't expect it to be going on under her nose. She was the only new maid in the townhouse that week, and she had already caught one of the indoor maids and a groom grunting like pigs in the sleeping loft above the stables. The girl looked very pleased with herself, but Helena was disgusted. This house was corrupt.

At mealtimes, she gobbled her food and went to her room rather than staying to socialise. She knew she could not remain in such an immoral house, so on her third day in London, she was sent to the Domestic Bureau to collect two more maids. While there, she put her name forward for any other position. Unfortunately, one of the new girls overheard her and reported her on their return to the house. She was dismissed on the spot without the few days' pay she was owed. Helena had time to grab her meagre possessions before being told to leave. She returned to the Domestic Bureau with nowhere to go and no money. Unfortunately, it was now closed.

She decided to sleep in the doorway of the office. Hopefully, in the morning, another job would be available somewhere. Helena cuddled her small bag of possessions and tried to get some sleep. She had missed luncheon as she had to collect the two new girls. On return, she had to pack her possessions and tidy the room while dinner was prepared. She left while the staff were in their dining room. The cook managed to sneak her some crusts of bread, two apples, and the ends of the roast meat.

The cook said, "Get out of this den of iniquity while you can, lovey. This man is not fit to have his family name. I can't tell his parents about his behaviour as I would be joining you in the street."

Helena thanked her with a swift hug, took her food parcel and left. Now sitting in the doorway, she decided to nibble at the meat and keep the bread and fruit for tomorrow.

The darkness and smog slowly encompassed her. With no blanket to wrap around her, the chill set in. She could see a few lamplighters lighting oil lamps further down the streets, but those men were few and far between. The dim glow added to the misery of her situation. She dug into her bag and felt around for something to wrap around her shoulders. She pulled out her old dress and used it as a blanket. She tucked the remaining food in the bottom of her bag. Overwhelmed with sadness, Helena felt tears oozing from her eyes. She wiped them away with the sleeve. How could her great adventure have come to this? How could she admit that she had been fired from her first position in the first week she was there? At least the woman in the Domestic Bureau knew what she said was true. Hopefully, she could find another job as a laundry maid or similar. She curled up to sleep, knowing that drunks would be on the prowl later in the evening.

She must have dozed as she woke to someone trying to pull the bag from underneath her arms. She couldn't see if it was man or beast in the inky blackness. She let out a blood-curdling scream, and the person, or whatever it was, took off. Helena's breath was rasping with the cold. She knew that she had received a long scratch on her arm as she could feel the warm blood running down to her hand. To rub insult into injury, she realised that the dress she had used to cover herself was gone.

Hours ticked by. The darkness was absolute as the fog shrouded the lamps. Something ran across her foot, and she discovered a giant rat had taken shelter under her skirt. She hated rats at the best of times, but the size of this beast made her freeze in fear. After a moment or two of near panic, she eased up her gown hem and pushed it away with the fabric. It scurried away. She finally dozed again.

She had no idea what time it was as she could not hear the town crier calling anything. Hopefully, he would come around soon. The bells of the closest church had already rung, but she had not counted them properly. She could not remember if there had been three or four chimes. With the rat gone and her bag devoid of the padding of her gown, she only had a pair of clean drawers and a flannel night rail, other than the food. She would not pull out either item. She nibbled at one of the crusts. Eating would hopefully warm her up. She sat upright with her skirts tucked tightly around her and her bag clasped in her arms. She must have dozed again.

In the pre-dawn light, she was gently shaken awake by a lamplighter.

The tall man leaned over her. He said kindly, "Lassie, if you are found here, Mrs Milroy will not even consider giving you a job. The church has a food kitchen two streets down that way, and you can get some hot porridge. It will fill your tummy. Come back at seven. She should be here by then."

Helena was so tired that hearing someone be kind to her made her weep again. She was also hungry and cold.

The man crouched down in front of her. "Oh, lassie, don't cry. She'll have something for you, I'm sure." He wished he knew her name. She had not stirred when he touched her cheek to see if she was alive. When he found her, the church bells were ringing five chimes. In the dim light, he could see she was beautiful. The name "Bella" came to his mind. It meant beautiful, and she was.

Helena saw that the man was dressed head to foot in black clothing with a floppy cap on his head. He had carried a long ladder, which now rested against the building. It was this that had given his profession away. As he crouched, she realised he was much younger than she had thought. He was so handsome. She realised he was probably only five to ten years older than she was.

Helena smiled at the kind man and said, "I hope so, as I don't think I could spend another night on the step. Someone stole my other dress, and I had a rat decide I was warmer than the river. It crawled under my skirt." She caught sight of the blood that had trickled down her arm and realised it now stained her grey gown. "Whoever took my clothing did this." She held out her cut arm.

The man glanced down the road and stood. He pulled her to her feet. "Miss, you go down to that church, and the minister's young wife, Mrs McGillicuddy, will see you cleaned up. She's a nice lady, and you can trust her. Tell her Crispin sent you." The man pointed her in the right direction. "You had better be off, dear, as Mrs Milroy is on her way. If she catches you on her step, she won't help." He put out his hand to gently push her on the way. "Come on, off you go. She's coming now, so you must leave."

Helena wiped away her tears and said, "Thank you, kind sir." Then she followed the man's direction.

He called, "Two streets down, then turn left at the shop. There will be a long queue of people, so you can't miss it."

She turned to give him a wave. As she did, she saw Mrs Milroy arrive at the corner of the street. The tall woman had her hair coiled into a tight bun. She looked ill, but that may have been how she always looked. Many in London looked sick. When she met her yesterday, she noticed that her eyes were sunk back into her head; she looked almost grey. The woman wore the same black clothing she had worn the day before.

Mrs Milroy noticed Helena but let her walk away.

Helena glanced back and saw the lamplighter in deep conversation with the lady. Then Mrs Milroy called after Helena. "You, girl, come here!"

Helena looked around her and realised no one else was nearby. She retraced her steps to stand before the lady. Her heart was in her mouth with nerves. Helena arrived in front of the stern-looking ma'am. She bobbed a curtsy and said, "Yes, ma'am."

Mrs Milroy motioned for her to spin around. Helena did.

The tall woman sniffed disconcertingly. "I have no positions available; however, my cleaner is sick, and I will need someone to clean my office and make tea for me until she is well. It will probably only be for a week."

Helena gasped. This was not what she expected. "Really, ma'am? I'll do anything except warm the bed of a man. I can't stay in the house of such a person. It's why I asked you to find me something else. However, one of the new maids mentioned that I had left my name with you. I was sacked on the spot, ma'am."

Mrs Milroy frowned. "Where did you stay last night?"

Helena glanced at the lamplighter, who nodded at her. He was still beside Mrs Milroy. "Um, ma'am, I had nowhere else to stay but here. I have only been in London for a few days. In my last job, Mr Sylvester came to the kitchen and took one of the young maids to warm his bed, and no bedpan was taken to heat it, ma'am. He dragged her out and violated her cruelly. I will not be used by any man in such a way. I would rather sleep on the street than be taken so." She stood tall and proud.

Mrs Milroy cupped her cheek. "Dearie, if I had found you on my step when I arrived, I would have shooed you away, but you have a champion in Crispin here. He said you were attacked overnight."

Helena nodded. She lifted her blood-streaked arm for her to see.

The lady's bony, claw-like hand gently took Helena's arm. She turned it over and saw the deep scrape. "Come inside, and I shall clean you up. You can sleep in the storeroom for the week."

Helena noticed the lady's glassy eyes. Tears threatened to overwhelm her. "Thank you! Thank you so much!"

As they walked to the building, Mrs Milroy said, "Do not tell anyone. I don't want to be known as a soft touch. It is because of cases like yours that I started this business." She sniffed. "Come along and get settled."

Helena's face lit up. "Oh, Mrs Milroy, thank you so much." Helena brushed away a tear of her own.

Mrs Milroy turned to the lamplighter and said, "Thank you, Crispin. I shall care for her now." She opened the door for the girl and beckoned her inside. Helena didn't even know Crispin's last name.

Helena shook her head at the memories. Was that over a year and a half ago? She turned into the desolate backyard and walked to the kitchen door of the governor's residence in Sydney Cove. The two doors were similar, and the smells that abounded in this area were equally obnoxious as those in London. However, she knew the odour was from the laundry where she worked. She knocked and waited, looking around her as she did so. It was nothing like the peaceful farm she had grown up on. Thinking about home brought tears to her eyes. One trickled through the grime on her cheek, leaving a clean trail through the filth. She ached to be clean and have some clothing that didn't itch. Her scant bag of possessions was long gone. They had been left in London. She owned nothing but the grey gown she wore. Life was miserable. Now, she was to lose the final remnant of decency.

For all those months, she had fought off every man who threatened to use her. Helena looked over the empty backyard of the government residence. It was desolate and barren. Words from her minister came to mind. "Trust Him." She huffed. How could God help? If only she could spend her time digging in the soil as she had at home, she would be content. She loved gardening and producing food, but worked as a laundry maid here as it was safer than in the government garden. Grief overwhelmed her, and a sob shook her body. She swiped her tears away. As it did so, the door behind her opened. She spun around to see a red-coated soldier in a tricorn hat smiling at her. His face was well known to her.

They gasped simultaneously.

She said, "Crispin, is that really you?"

The stunned lamplighter grinned at her. "It is indeed, Miss Helena."

Helena was stunned. "Why are you here and not in London?"

The soldier chuckled. "I could ask the same about you, miss." Relief overwhelmed him. He had found her and wanted to draw her into his arms.

Helena was about to reply when the cook growled, "Soldier boy, bring the girl in and shut the door. You're letting in the flies." Helena entered and noticed a half-eaten bowl of porridge beside a mug and a plate of toast. Her stomach growled with hunger.

Despite her filth, Crispin took her hand and led her through the warm kitchen and into the corridor beyond. "I have just arrived as part of the new governor's security detail. I'll tell you the full story later, but Mrs Milroy heard what happened and told me to look for you. When I discovered that you had been transported, I followed. They were looking for soldiers to come here, so I volunteered. I came to find you, Helena."

They were standing outside the door, whispering. Helena looked up at the tall soldier. "But why, Crispin? Why follow me?"

He was unable to answer as he heard the call to enter. "Later!" He managed to say, "Trust him, Helena." She nodded and followed him. She didn't know what to expect; the room was dark and dingy. Whitewashed walls would have made it much brighter, but the dark timber gave it an oppressive feel. Sitting at the large desk was a blue-uniform-clad gentleman. She had seen him from a distance, but up close, he was older than she expected. For some reason, she expected to see a man in his thirties, but this man was almost white-haired and obviously in or near his fifties. He had a round face, but his dark eyebrows showed he was of Scottish heritage. She had met a few with such a feature; the Colonial Secretary, David Collins, was one such man. As she stood in front of him, she bobbed a curtsy but remained silent. Over the past year, she had learned to speak only when spoken to. Crispin stood beside her and waited.

The governor watched the pair walk in. Unbeknownst to them, he had been at the door and heard some of their conversation. If she were known to this soldier, whom he had learned to trust over their months of travel, she might not be one of the unruly rabble he abhorred. But where to start the questioning? He swallowed. He was not good at speaking to women. He had never entangled himself with one and had no intention of starting now. "Milroy, you obviously know this female. Can you introduce me?" She gasped.

The soldier's head nodded. "I do indeed, sir. Her name is Miss Helena Rosedale." He gave her a loving look. "Sir, she is the reason I joined up. I came to look for her at my aunt's behest."

John's eyes opened in surprise. His mother's name was Helen, but he wouldn't mention that. Then he noticed the girl had turned her gaze to the soldier, stunned. John planned to question him further when alone. "Miss, what have you to say? Is he just protecting you, or do you really know him?"

Helena gave another servant's bob for being acknowledged. "Sir, I did indeed meet him in London. I know him only as Crispin and did not, until now, realise he was related to the lady I worked for. I was filling in for the lady's sick servant at the Domestic Bureau in London. She fed Crispin every morning, and he came for dinner at night. At the end of that week-long employment, I was offered a new post as a laundry maid. When I arrived there, I found that my job was not in the laundry, but I was supposed to warm the owner's bed. As I had run from a similar position, I fled."

Crispin was horrified. He mumbled softly, "Oh, Helena, I'm so sorry. She would not have sent you there if she had known."

Helena acknowledged his comment with a nod and a smile. "Thank you, Cris."

The governor overheard the soft, affectionate interchange. He said, "Go on."

She took a deep breath and said, "I had no choice but to leave my possessions in my room. I just fled. The man chased me as I ran, and I found myself in the marketplace. I could hear him gaining on me, and I became desperate. Seeing a crowded market, I had hoped to hide amongst the masses and return to the Domestic Bureau to see if Mrs Milroy had another place I could go." Crispin rubbed her back. It was inappropriate, but it felt nice. She sniffed at the memory of her fear. "I wasn't fast enough, and he saw me. I grabbed something from the closest stall and walked off with it. I knew that if I were arrested, he could not touch me. I did not expect to be transported, only arrested. I did not realise I had taken a new woollen coat worth £10. I was given fourteen years, sir."

Crispin uttered another, "Oh, Helena!"

Helena heard but continued her tale. "I was right about being arrested, but the fight for my dignity started anew. I was hauled off to the lock-up and taken to front a magistrate." She shook her head to make the memories flee. "I won't go into what the gaol was like, but men and women are locked up together, and the conditions are vile. The men left me alone as I told them I had the clap. I don't, but it worked! Other women sated their lusts. A few weeks later, I was loaded onto the *Surprize* and brought here." She paused, remembering the conditions on the ship. Her lie worked here, too, until today.

John's compassion was stirred. Very little in his despatches mentioned the privations of privacy for the new female convicts. He had been told that all the new arrivals were whores, and had believed what he read. He should have known better, even though he knew from experience that many were innocent young girls like Aggie Osborne, Connie Waterson, or Bray, as she was now, and others. He presumed that most older women gave their favours willingly. Therefore, separating them from the male convicts or protecting them from the men's attention had not been a high priority. He swallowed in disgust at the neglect of his superiors. He adored his family, including his nieces, and would have fought to protect them. He knew he had to fix this immediately. He said, "Go on, tell me. What was life like on board?"

Helena frowned. How much should she say? She noted only a slight lilt to his speech and figured he had some Scottish connection. She thought she might as well tell him about her Scottish saviours. "On board, there were only twenty-three convict males. However, six of them were known as the Scottish Martyrs. They were being sent here for being Catholics, sir. They have done no crime but their belief in the Roman church. Those Scottish prisoners kept the other men, who included crew and soldiers, away from the unwilling women. There were sixty female convicts, and all of us were under forty. Admittedly, some gave their favours willingly, and they were not stopped, but that protected the rest of us from unwanted attention. Some of the convicts were children of just fourteen or fifteen, and they were abused vilely as a dare." Crispin took her hand and entwined his fingers with hers. He knew he should not have done so, but her story cut him deeply.

She turned to look at him and glanced down at her hand. She did not wish him to be reprimanded but clung to him.

The governor couldn't help but see the affectionate act, but remained silent. "What happened on arrival here? I have not had time to talk with any female convicts and know little about your conditions. Any reports will probably not be accurate anyway. Hold nothing back, please."

Helena thought back to the day of her arrival in the bay. Nodding, she continued. "We watched the new coastline pass through the gun ports. We were offloaded in chains and shackles and then marched up to the female quarters. Overcrowded is an understatement, but at least it was only women." She glanced at her friend. "Crispin will tell you that we first met when I was sleeping in the doorway of the Domestic Bureau. I was cold and hungry, but I was reasonably clean."

The soldier nodded. He thought of finding her as the bells were ringing. "She was indeed, sir." His thumb caressed the back of her hand.

Helena smiled at his confirmation of her acquaintance. "On arrival here, we had one night to settle in and learn what was expected of us. Then, I heard about numerous violations of women doing farm work. When we were assigned the following day, I decided I hadn't come all this way to have that happen to me, so I volunteered to work in the smelliest job I could find. I asked for work at the laundry for the soldiers' barracks and willingly stomped their clothing in stale urine, hence my stench. Few will touch me due to my, um, aroma." She gave a flick of her head proudly and stood tall. "If you heard my words this morning, sir, you will know I still value my chastity. I am a good girl and intend to stay that way as long as I can." Her chin lifted in defiance. Crispin was still holding her hand, and he squeezed her fingers for comfort. She did the same in response. Of all the people in the world, the good-looking lamplighter was the last man she had ever expected to see again, but she was delighted he was here.

John was stunned at what he had just heard. He was amazed that this girl had a champion in one of his own men and that the lad cared for her. The governor was both gutted and flabbergasted at what he heard. He didn't know how to handle the situation. If this female was known to one of his men, then she was a better class of woman. He wondered if there were more innocent ones there like her. "What are conditions like for you now, miss?" He brushed his hand across his nose. She stank. Thankfully, they had left the door open.

Crispin said, "Tell him, Helena. He can't assist if he doesn't know what is happening in this place."

She gazed at her friend in appreciation. She nodded and said, "Very well, sir. The food is regular, if somewhat unvaried, but like everyone else, it is scant. However, it is far better than on the convict ship. Sleeping quarters are also adequate, as since you arrived, we have guards at each door all night. We are not molested as we sleep. Most women would not care, but some of us, the younger ones, are not so inclined. We are housed with hardened streetwalkers, and we have no other option than to put up with their nocturnal activities. Some women willingly let the men inside." She sniffed. "I grew up on a farm, sir. I know the, shall I say, earthy behaviour of animals rutting. That's what I call the joining of these animal-like men who use the willing women. I will not be used so." She released an angry huff.

John was horrified. "These attacks are regular?"

Helena nodded and said, "They were before you came last week, sir. Your added security has protected us from the men's unwanted advances. We can now mostly sleep in peace."

John was horrified that men would force themselves on an unwilling woman. He refused to permit this girl to return to the female quarters. "Helena, would you be happy to work here at the house? I'm sure we could find some work here that would keep you safe."

Her face lit up. "Oh, sir, I would be delighted. I would do anything from being your laundry maid to even tilling that virgin soil in the backyard and tending a new vegetable garden for you."

John put his hands on the desk and stood. "Then that is what you shall do. I was wondering about putting in a garden for ourselves. Phillip's valet, Henry Dodd, oversaw the first one." He turned to address Crispin. "Milroy, find her some new clothes and get the housekeeper to dig out the bath and clean her up." He looked at Helena. "It's about time someone was responsible for keeping you safe. That is now my job. You have at least given me a place to start."

"Sir…" She stopped forgetting she shouldn't speak.

"Go on, speak." The governor saw the girl hesitate.

"Sir, Reverend and Mrs Johnson are a better point to start. They care for us and also for the local Aboriginal people. The reverend has even learned to converse with them through Abaroo. My ship brought news of your appointment, and my friend Connie's husband overheard some men discussing it. She told me you were different, and we would have a chance at a decent life if you were in charge. However, the minister said in a sermon that he knows you. He's a man you can trust to give you an unbiased opinion of what is occurring in this place. The drunken state of the soldiers is a major issue, sir."

John gave a nod of thanks but did not commit to her suggestion. He was about to dismiss them when he thought about her family. "Miss, does your family know where you are?"

She was about to shake her head when Crispin answered. "They do, sir. I was in contact with them after she had been shipped out. I had hoped she had returned home, and I went to find her. When my aunt died, I found Helena's contact details in her paperwork. When I visited the house where my aunt had placed her, I found her gone. I visited her family. After discovering what happened to her, I contacted her parents again and told them I would write when I could." He turned to look at Helena. "My aunt wished to find you, as did I."

"You did that for me, Crispin?" Tears followed. They made more channels through the dirt on her cheeks.

He thumbed them away. A big grin accompanied his nod.

Chapter 3   Clean Again

*F*or the first time since Helena left home a year and a half earlier, she was permitted to bathe and be clean again.

The housekeeper sent in Gillian, the convict household maid, to assist her, and she used the governor's hip bath to wash thoroughly.

She still only had her dirty clothes to put on, but having her hair washed and her body clean was a delight.

On their farm, the family had access to plenty of water, and every Saturday, they all bathed in readiness for church the following day. They swam in the cold creek midweek.

Gillian placed a large towel on the bed and a smaller one for her hair over a chair.

Helena had knelt beside the bath while Gillian washed her locks.

While Helena was washing, Crispin was sent to the Government Store to collect an allocation of convict clothing for her. He had just returned. As Gillian emerged from their room, he handed over the armload of apparel. At least Helena would have some clean garments to put on. She had been wearing the same grey gown since he first met her eighteen months before, and it was now torn and filthy.

He was sure that it could have walked across the room by itself. "Gillian, the governor suggested that she share your quarters. When you are finished here, can you move your things? I have a work detail coming, and they will build a pallet bunk into your room. However, don't tell her yet."

Gillian was delighted. "Okay, sir, but don't worry about my stuff. It's all on my bed. I don't have much, and there is nowhere else to put it but on the floor. I've had black spiders in my things, so now they live on my bed."

In the short time Helena had been bathing, they had chatted about life and what had befallen them both.

Gillian said she was from Kent and had experienced problems similar to Helena's, but didn't elaborate. Gillian bounced into the room and said, "Helena, look what your friend has brought for you."

Helena could not believe what she saw in Gillian's arms. She was now standing in the bath, wrapped in a towel. This was more to soak the stench of urine from her feet than anything else.

After washing her hair while the water was clean, she scrubbed her body with a flannel cloth before she fouled the bath with her feet. She dared not sit in the water as she knew what was washing off her body.

Even after using the flannel, the water was brown. One day, she would love a long, hot soak, but for today, it was enough that she was mostly clean. "Oh, Gillian! New clothes. Where did they come from?"

The maid laughed. "It seems you have an admirer, Helena. Your friend, Private Milroy, collected them for you from Government Stores. We received the same when we landed. Did you not get any?"

Helena shook her head. "No, there was insufficient for everyone, so only those whose apparel was indecent were given new outfits. I missed out."

The two girls hurriedly dressed her, and with her new clothing on, she washed her old garments.

Although the new calico drawers were scratchy, her old linen ones were filthy.

While in prison, her monthly flow had been irregular as food was scarce. Since her arrival here, it had sorted itself out and settled back into a routine. All she had in her possession now were the rags she used to catch the blood flow. Keeping those clean had been burdensome on the ship. At least in the laundry, she had been able to wash them as often as required.

Once dressed, she said, "Oh, Gillian, I feel like a new woman."

The girls giggled. Helena thought of Connie Bray, who worked at the mill. She was the only person who had made an effort to befriend her.

While Helena bathed, Gillian retrieved her hairbrush and washed it in soapy water before using it on Helena's clean hair.

As Helena's clothes soaked, Gillian brushed the knots from her new friend's hair. Having little ones to care for at the orphanage, she knew to start at the bottom and do a few bits at a time.

Helena's hair had been like a birch broom in a fit. She had dragged her fingers through it each morning, but even her brush had been left in her room in London.

By the time the knots were out, her grey dress had been soaking for some time.

Helena rinsed them all in clean water. The grey of the gown was once again visible. It was stained, and the skirt had some small rips. This outfit was the last thing from home, as her mother had made it for her. She would treasure it and keep it for her Sunday best.

Having worked in the laundry for so long, she would work on the marks and try to save the dress.

Hours had passed since her arrival.

The girl who stood before Gillian was hardly recognisable as the filthy wench who had arrived only hours before.

They had no looking-glass, but Helena felt clean all the way through. "Well, am I presentable?" She grinned.

Gillian giggled and nodded. "More than a bit, Helena. The housekeeper and Private Milroy want to see you, so you'd better hurry."

Helena also wanted to see him again, but remained quiet about that.

During the week she worked at the Domestic Bureau, he arrived twice daily and checked that all was well. She presumed he slept through the day because of his work. They had shared mugs of tea and had numerous conversations, but she insisted she keep working as they chatted. His eyes followed her around the room.

She realised she liked him. However, he had made no move for any closer relationship. Not that she would have permitted anything clandestine. She liked him even more because he did not push her beyond where she felt comfortable.

Crispin escorted her if she needed to run messages for Mrs Milroy, but never once did he let on that he was related, let alone that she was his aunt. He always referred to her as Mrs Milroy, even in private conversation.

Helena had unintentionally overheard them chatting a few times, and although always cordial, it was never very personal.

Gillian carried the armload of wet clothing to hang out while the housekeeper interviewed Helena. The young maid was so delighted that she would share her room with a friend that she skipped with joy as she walked outside to the rope laundry line.

The housekeeper was a free settler and the widow of a soldier.

Gillian said she was somewhat of a harridan, but had only met her a few days before.

Mrs Cowdrey was waiting for Helena in the sitting room. The clean girl who entered the room made the housekeeper do a double-take.

The filthy convict was gone, and an almost elegant lady stood before her. Her hair was washed and brushed.

The soft brown curls of her long hair spiralled around her neck. She was breathtakingly lovely, even in convict garb.

Helena noticed her appraisal and immediately gathered her damp locks back and twisted them into a bun. She sank into a graceful curtsy as she dealt with her hair. "I'm sorry, Mrs Cowdrey, but it's still a little damp."

The girl's accent was familiar to her, as the new surgeon from the governor's ship, Doctor Bass, and his friend Matthew Flinders were also from Lincolnshire. Her vowel pronunciation gave her away. They all spoke like they had a mouth full of plums.

She smiled to herself. Rather than be harsh with the girl, her heart softened. "Well, now, lass, the new governor has decided to keep you at the house with us. He's not married and is not used to having women under his feet, so we are to stay well clear of him unless he says otherwise. He does not condone any hanky-panky of any sort. I'm not sure what role he has for you, as Gillian and I manage most of the work in the house. However, he has worded up Private Milroy about that, and that young man awaits you in the back garden. He's a nice young lad, and I believe it's because of him that you have been placed here."

Helena's eyes lit up as she nodded. "I truly can stay? The governor said so, really?"

Mrs Cowdrey nodded. "Apparently so, lassie! You must mind your behaviour, or you will be sent back with the other felons. So no sneaking off with your soldier boy."

Helena flashed a filthy look at her. "I never sneak off with anyone, let alone a man. If he wants me that way, he can have Banns read first and put a ring on my finger. I'm not a loose woman."

Helena again stood a little taller as she spoke. She refused to be belittled or insulted by this woman.

"Good! I like your determination. Keep your nose clean and stay out of trouble." She saw Helena brush her nose. She smiled.

"Did I miss a bit of dirt, ma'am?" The girl's eyes showed confusion.

Mrs Cowdrey smirked and then chuckled loudly. "No, dearie, it means don't meddle in other people's business or get into trouble."

Helena brightened again. "Oh, I never pass on gossip as I don't listen to it." She gave the lady a beaming smile. She glowed with happiness. "Thank you so much for supporting me and giving me this opportunity. I shall do my very best. However, other than with Private Milroy's aunt, I've never done a maid's work indoors, so I will need someone to show me what to do."

Again, Mrs Cowdrey softened her stern persona. "Dear, you will do well. Be quiet, humble and honest and see me if you don't know what to do. There is always work to be done, as I have a list. You will assist Gillian with her chores where you can. However, I will set jobs for you each day. Now off you go and see your soldier boy. He is out the back. Can you find your way there?"

Helena nodded and went to find Crispin.

When she arrived just after dawn, the backyard was devoid of anything but a rope strung between two trees.

Gillian was now hanging her washed clothing after giving it another rinse.

Helena approached Crispin; however, he was not alone, so she did not touch him or speak.

A team of convict men were already tilling the virgin soil and removing the weeds.

Crispin had not heard her arrival and was surprised to see her beside him. "Oh my! Aren't you a sight for sore eyes?" His admiration was evident.

She so wished to hug him and say thank you, but that would not have been appropriate. Instead, she spun around and showed him her new blue serge dress.

She softly said, "How can I ever thank you, Cris? I feel all new."

Crispin smiled. "I'm glad they fit. Mind you, all the convict clothing is one-size-fits-all, even down to the shoes. They do not even have left or right feet."

She knew the sort of peasant shoe he meant. "You need to soak them in hot water, then wear them while wet. They eventually take the shape of your foot."

She watched as the group of six convict men worked. "What are they doing, Cris?"

He wished to take her in his arms and kiss her worries away. "You told the governor that you loved gardening. Well, the colony is very short of food, as you know. We apparently have very few good gardeners, so he has decided that we are to do our bit and have a garden here. Remember, I saw your farm at home, so I know your father had a fabulous garden. These men are tilling the virgin soil and weeding the area. They will eventually put up a fence, but you can take over when the tilling is done. What else do you need?"

Rather than look excited or say anything, Helena walked over to the tilled soil and picked up a half-handful of earth. She spat into it and made a paste. After studying it, she said, "We need lots of vegetable matter mixed into the dirt, or this will just go hard once wet. At home, we have a compost pile, and we let the vegetable matter decompose before adding it to the soil. If we planted something here, the earth would go so hard that the water would not soak in. Soil needs to be light. Papa used to call it friable. That means somewhat crumbly. Is there any old animal dung we can have? Goat, sheep or cow will do. Horse manure has grain still in it, but it will work if nothing else is available."

Crispin looked down at the lovely girl beside him. "You really do know about gardening, don't you? Do I burn the weeds, or will you start a compost heap too?"

She nodded her head. "Yes, please, keep those weeds, but stack them for now. I'll sort that out later. Pile them over near that big rock, please. Where do I get seeds or plants to put in?"

Crispin called one of the other soldiers and instructed that all the weeds be put aside in one pile.

Another soldier took his place as a guard, and Crispin offered his arm to Helena. "Care to come for a walk? I've been told to escort you to talk to Reverend Johnson and his wife. His garden is the most productive in the colony, and Mrs Johnson will have some cuttings and seeds for the governor to use."

Once out of earshot of the house, Helena pumped Crispin for more of his background. "Why did you never tell me Mrs Milroy was your aunt?"

Crispin shrugged with embarrassment. "She told me not to, simple as that. I don't know if she thought you would get your hooks into me, but once I had not mentioned it, then it was easier to ignore the relationship. She never married, so the Mrs was honorific for her work."

He glanced at her to see how she took the information. Noticing a small smile, he continued. "I never called her aunt anyway. She didn't like it. She always thought Mrs Milroy was more formal, even in private. She was Papa's much older sister, and she mothered him, too. He died shortly before I met you, and I only returned to work that week after my illness. It's why I slept so much. She brought me up as Mama died when I was tiny. Papa and I lived with her and worked as lamplighters."

Helena drew in a quick breath. "Oh, I am sorry about your Mama, Crispin."

"Don't be, Helena. I don't miss Mama. I never knew her; she died when I was one. Papa, I miss like crazy, though. When he died, I nearly died myself. We both had a lung complaint, and as my aunt still needed to work, we were left alone. Papa died, and I was too sick to know or care. I felt so guilty that I had lived and he had died. I was only just back on my feet when we met."

He glanced at her to watch her face as he made a confession. "Helena, I found a reason to live again that night we met. I had all but given up hope. Then I found you asleep, and I lost my heart to a sleeping angel. Papa and I had been so close that his loss cut me to the quick."

Helena stopped walking and gazed up at the handsome man she clung to. "Why didn't you say anything, Crispin? I had no idea of any of this."

He shrugged nonchalantly. "I didn't want you to feel sorry for me. I had no money and nowhere to live except with my aunt. I could not even ask to court you as I barely made enough to help pay my way at my aunt's house. Back then, I could not support a wife, let alone a family."

All Helena could say was, "Oh!"

Crispin moved forward again. He knew he couldn't dawdle too much. "Aunt Mildred died only a few weeks after you left us. She knew she was ill, but not how close to death she was. She managed to sell her business before she passed. When we met, she was negotiating a contract, but I didn't know. It was why she let you stay for only one week. As her only relative, I inherited everything, including her tiny flat. It was then that I hunted for you. I met your folks, and by the way, your father permitted me to court you and more if you allow me to. On my return to London, I discovered what had happened to you. One of the girls at your workplace told me what occurred. I tried to get your things, but most had gone. I have your shawl and a brush. I enquired how to get here and found no ships coming this way except Governor Hunter's transport. They would not take passengers, so I sold the flat and purchased a commission. I came as a private on the governor's staff. I plan to stay, Helena. I wish us to be together and make a life here. If not, we will return to England together as soon as you can leave.

That is, if you will have me?"

Helena stopped again. "Are you asking me to marry you or something else, Cris?"

Crispin turned to face her. "I would never demean you to do such a thing, Helena. Of course, I mean marriage. I cannot ask you yet; I must have the governor's permission to court you, but I will, Helena. Know that I will as soon as I can. Once we are at least betrothed, then I can protect you."

Helena was lost for words. All she could do was gaze at him. She managed to say, "But you hardly know me."

Crispin gently moved a lock of hair from her cheek with a hooked finger. "I know enough, Helena. I know I have sailed halfway around the world to be with you. Will you let me court you?"

Helena did not expect her day to include finding a husband. She nodded her reply. "Yes, I suppose so, if permitted, but that's all for now, so we can get to know each other better!"

Here was a man whom she could trust. One who had put his life on hold to seek her out. He reminded her of her father. It was that thought that made her tear up.

Crispin thumbed away the glistening droplet from her eyelashes. "I so want to kiss you, but I dare not. Know that I wish to. I also will not do so unless you give me leave. I respect you too much to manhandle you so roughly."

More tears flowed down Helena's cheeks. She wanted to throw herself into his arms. She dreamed of a man who had cared for her feelings. She had not realised she had already met him.

She should have known because when in London, her heart skipped whenever he visited. However, if she had understood her feelings, her arrest would have crushed her. Here, they would one day be together. "Thank you, Cris. I hope that won't be too far away, for I have never been kissed. You will be the first."

He thumbed away another tear, and it was followed by more.

He sucked in his breath and started walking. "Come, love, before I get carried away. Same with me, Helena; I never found anyone I wanted to kiss. "

Their conversation ceased as they arrived at a small, whitewashed, thatched, wattle and daub cottage surrounded by a lovely garden.

A lady was working in the garden, and she looked up as they approached.

They were introduced upon arrival and again at church.

Crispin greeted her. "Hello, Mrs Johnson. May I introduce my friend, Helena Rosedale? She will be living at Government House and has been asked to arrange a vegetable garden there."

Helena released Crispin's arm and bobbed a curtsy to the minister's wife.

Mrs Johnson had seen the young couple approaching and noted their closeness. She had seen him thumb away her tears and had expected him to kiss her. He had not. She wondered if there was more to this visit. They certainly looked cosy as they approached. If she were a convict, as her garb suggested, it was unusual for her to be happy to be with a red-coated soldier, let alone cling to his arm so possessively.

She did not recognise the pretty girl and knew the governor's ship brought no unattached females.

However, Helena knew this lady well. She was one of the bright lights of the colony. She had never had a reason to converse with her, but she knew she would be welcomed. "Hello, Mrs Johnson. I've not had cause to seek you out before, but I wish to thank you for caring for us. I arrived last year on the *Surprize*."

Mary Johnson frowned and looked hard at the girl, a smile hovering around her lips. Then she gasped, "I know who you are. Helena the…" Mary slapped her hand over her mouth in absolute horror. She never repeated a word like that.

Helena giggled. "Hellcat is the word you are looking for, ma'am. I got that name because I would not let the men near me. I would fight like a cat to be released. On the ship coming out, I spread the word that I had the clap, so I would be left alone. It worked. Out here, I volunteered to work in the laundry, washing in urine as they hated the ammonia smell. I was left alone until this morning. On the way to work, I was accosted at dawn."

Mrs Johnson glanced at the soldier and saw him grinning.

He was biting his lip, trying hard not to laugh. He had not heard of her nickname.

Ignoring his silly smile, the lady asked, "Are you unharmed, dearie?"

Helena nodded. "They chose the wrong place and time. The new governor happened to be at his bedroom window upstairs. He saw their action and heard what occurred. He shouted at his security detail to come and assist me. They did, and long story short, I'm now to work in what is to be a new garden at the back of Government House. Crispin brought me here to see if you can help me with cuttings and seeds for the governor's garden."

Mrs Johnson's eyebrows raised with the familiarity that Helena used for the soldier.

Crispin said, "We knew each other in London. Helena worked for my aunt. I came out here to find her."

He took a half step closer to her possessively. If the minister's wife read anything into that, she would be correct. He returned the lady's fixed gaze with a slight smile.

Mrs Johnson looked away first. Her attention turned to Helena. "My husband is the man you need. He's not here, but I will tell him what you are after. I'm sure he may be able to assist with some seeds and cuttings. You will need to prepare your soil first."

Helena met the lady's penetrating gaze with a smile and a nod.

"Ma'am, I was wondering if you have a compost heap? The soil needs great doses of vegetable matter and aged dung. Being up on the hill, it's solid clay, and I know my Papa used to add loads of such compost to our soil every year to keep it friable."

The lady's eyebrows lifted. "I see you really do know something about gardening. You are correct. The plants will not grow here if the soil is not prepared first. Water is the least of our problems. Also, ensure the garden is fenced, as the beasties here are not just the two-legged thieves. The birds and furry animals will raid what they can. Just when you think you will pick a good crop, you come out the next morning and a half is gone or partially eaten."

The three chattered about plants and what grew well in the local soils for some hours over tea.

Crispin escorted Helena back to the house. He wished to go back on his promise and kiss her, but he dared not.

They would be together most days, and that would have to do until he had permission to marry her. He knew that as a convict, she also needed permission to wed. He presumed it would take time to obtain both permissions. But once they were courting, it would give him some claim on her.

Unable to contain himself, he asked, "Helena, dearest, would you mind if I spoke to the governor and at least asked permission to pay my addresses to you so we can make it official?"

Helena was stunned. "Crispin, although I wish to say yes, I'm not going anywhere. Why the hurry? Courting is sufficient for the moment."

He stopped and turned to her. He didn't care if they were seen. He was uninterested in promotion and would not care if he was sacked. "Why? Because if those convict men know you are mine, they will leave you alone. The incident this morning is proof that they realised you are a maiden. Your words gave you away. I could not believe it when I heard your voice. That was why I was at the door and my breakfast half-eaten. They would take great pleasure in stealing that innocence from us. If you are engaged to a soldier, it would protect you. Plus, the other soldiers would leave you alone, too."

He brushed a lock of hair from her cheek. "Please, Helena, I want you in my life."

She pulled away. "Crispin, I'm not saying no, but can we ask the governor first? He may not agree with you. I don't want to get our hopes up and have nothing come from it. We should be getting back."

She had just seen one of the soldiers walking by, and he was leering at her lustfully.

Crispin noticed him as well. He had not been in the town long enough to know anyone yet. "Yes, let's get back. At least there, you should be safe."

They walked towards the big house through the marketplace and met Helena's friend, Connie Bray.

A few words were exchanged before they parted with a hug.

Connie's mouth hung open in stunned surprise at the handsome couple walking towards to official residence.

Helena looked forward to catching up with her and telling her story.

Chapter 4   Preparing the Soil

On return to Government House, Helena was surprised to see that the area that had been bare ground only this morning was now tilled and shaped into garden beds.

Rather than dig the entire backyard, pathways had been left at one-yard intervals. This would make tending the beds from the paths easier. She noticed a large pile of weeds, and some tools had been left for her use.

There was a sharp spade, a pointed blade trowel, hedge clippers, a garden fork, and a tin watering can.

Helena was delighted. "Oh, Crispin, this is wonderful. I have the bones of a fabulous garden here. Could I get some old manure from the stables? I can dig that in and give everything a deep water. It will be some days until I have any plants, but I cannot put them in until the soil is ready."

She clapped her hands together with glee, almost dancing on the spot. Ignoring the handsome young man beside her, she picked up a garden fork and started attacking the turned sods.

Crispin chuckled at her obvious delight. He said, "Other girls want gems and sparkly baubles; you want a cartload of aged manure!"

She laughed as she nodded. "Yes, can you get me some, or there will be no fresh vegetables for anyone to eat?"

Grinning, Crispin left her alone in the garden to keep breaking the clay sods. He also intended to get her a big hat if they had such things here. The wide brim of that would protect her skin. He discovered that one of the convict men, named Charlie, knew how to make these lightweight hats from the leaves of the local palm fronds.

With no shops that sold hats, they were very popular. Mob caps were all well for the women and suitable for indoor work, but the wide-brim hats were light, comfortable to wear, and very practical.

Before heading down to the barracks, he knocked on the governor's door. The door swung open under his gentle tap, and he saw the empty office.

Mrs Cowdrey saw Crispin and said, "The governor has been called to town. You'll find him at the soldiers' barracks. Is Helena truly staying then?"

Crispin had not realised the housekeeper had approached him. He turned and replied, "I believe so, Mrs Cowdrey. Mrs Johnson will speak to her husband and sort out some plants for us. However, before they can go in, Helena wants a cartload of manure or similar."

The woman nodded her understanding. "Well, then, you had better head off and kill two birds with one stone. His nibs left when you did, so he may well be on his way back. Nathaniel Franklyn is with him today. However, get the girl some work clothes and one of Charlie's palm hats. Her skin will burn if she's out in the sun for long."

Crispin grinned. He fully intended to do all she suggested. Mrs Cowdrey said, "Choof off, laddie, or you won't get it all done. I'll keep my eye on her." She liked this young, handsome soldier. He reminded her of her long-lost husband. It was why she had arranged a cooked breakfast for him this morning.

She usually did not permit the guards to enter the house. Crispin Milroy was the exception.

Her words got him moving. He tipped his hat and exited by the front door. His mind was running twenty to the dozen. He had been relieved of duty for the day to get Helena sorted, and it was like a holiday for him. He wondered which one of his brother soldiers was attending to the governor's security, with Nathaniel who was his secretary. Hopefully, it would be Eric.

Crispin first went to the government stables and directed that the next load of manure be taken to the back of the official residence instead of the community farm.

He knew Helena would also need a load of clean straw, but that could wait. He discovered that this waste product was usually transported to the government gardens and stockpiled, but piles of this rotting stuff were already off to the side of the garden beds.

Crispin had been given a tour of the small town on his arrival. He checked any convict woman he saw, but had not found Helena. Now he knew why.

She was inside the laundry behind the government stables from dawn to dusk.

Little grew as the government garden that Henry Dodd, Governor Phillip's valet, started, was right next to the sea. He'd eventually moved to Rose Hill, where he literally worked himself to death.

Mrs Johnson's garden was further back from the sea and was thriving. She even had roses near her cottage.

He remembered Helena saying you could strike cuttings from these bushes. Maybe Mrs Johnson would permit him to have a cutting.

When Crispin arrived at the barracks, the governor was about to depart. They stopped to chat, and Crispin asked for an appointment. He planned to ask permission to get engaged and hoped the governor would not refuse.

When the governor saw the young private walking towards him, rather than leave for the female quarters, he paused and waited. "How goes all the arrangements, Milroy? Were the Johnsons able to assist?"

Crispin replied, "No, sir, the Reverend was not there, but Mrs Johnson said she would ask him on his return."

They had met some of Helena's friends. "Sir, Connie Bray said to say hello."

John flashed a grin. From his first visit to the colony, he knew Connie and her husband, Nigel, but he hadn't bumped into them yet. He sighed. "The minister will assist. If he knows we can grow more food, he will help with seeds and cuttings. Having been at sea most of my life, gardens are not my thing, but I appreciate good food. I have rarely had fresh vegetables, but I like them when I can get them. Are you after me or something else?"

"A bit of both, sir," Crispin told him of his quest for manure and then asked about an appointment.

John eyed him suspiciously. Before answering, he waved away his other security officer and said quietly, "You really are keen on this girl?"

Crispin nodded. "Yes, sir, I truly did enlist to find her. I had no other way of getting here. I intend to marry her as soon as possible and wish to talk to you about that tonight."

John tilted his head and gazed at the handsome young man. "She is all she says, then? Untouched and fighting to keep herself pure?"

Crispin didn't know and wouldn't until they married. He said, "Of that, I won't be sure until our wedding night, but sir, even if she has been violated, it will not have been willingly. She's a country girl, and when I met her, she had only been in London for a few days. She was as innocent as a lamb, but she is tough. Even more so now."

Another soldier arrived and stood nearby; further private conversation would need to wait.

Crispin didn't know this new man.

Unable to speak privately, John said, "After dinner at seven, in my private sitting room upstairs." He gave a nod to Crispin and walked towards the female barracks.

Crispin arrived at the stables in time for the afternoon cleanup. He was able to redirect the waste cart to the new garden, with instructions for two loads of old manure to be delivered to the official house and for a convict or two to unload it where directed.

He arranged for a few loads of the rotted stuff to be delivered to Helena tomorrow. That done, he needed to visit the Government Stores again.

He returned to the Government Stores for the second time that day. Although he collected her immediate needs that morning, there was still the remainder of her convict clothing allocation to pick up. He had already delivered her dress and undergarments, but stores had not unpacked the new stock of hats, aprons, shoes, stockings or long-sleeved jackets. He had been told to return later. Hopefully, by now, they would be ready for collection. He also had to get one of someone called Charlie's palm hats for her.

Many felons wore these lightweight palm creations.

His arrival at the store was greeted with a cheery hello.

The rotund storekeeper said, "I have yer things ready, sir; I just need yer to sign them out."

Crispin checked what was in the pile and saw that the apron had a significant mark on it. "Are they all like this? This convict lady is to work at Government House for Governor Hunter. Do you expect her to appear in dirty garb like this at the governor's table?"

The man had no idea where the convict was assigned and apologised. He dug under the counter and pulled out another bundle of much better-looking clothing. "Sir, if the young lady is to work there, she will also need a better-quality gown."

He quickly added duplicate items to what he had been given that morning.

Crispin refused nothing. The triple allocation of convict garb could be shared between the two girls. Knowing how little Helena had, Crispin accepted everything. He even took the stained apron. "She can use this one for working outside, but she will need the clean one for indoor work. Sign it out to the governor. He has okayed this already."

He was about to leave when he realised he had forgotten the hats. "I believe they are supposed to be given two mob caps, and I'll also have a palm hat. She'll be working in the new garden."

The man hastened to get the items.

Crispin saw him wipe his brow as he left. He smiled; his large armload of goodies would make Helena one of the better-dressed convicts in the colony. He knew he should not have taken both sets, as it might mean others might miss out, but she had missed out earlier. She deserved this and could share her excess clothing with Gillian, as he discovered she only had spare undergarments.

He had a spring in his step as he returned to work, thinking only of Helena.

He didn't hear the horse approaching or that it drew up beside him. His head was in the clouds. It was one of his fellow soldiers, and the man was annoying, to say the least. However, Eric was the closest thing he had to a friend in this place.

"Hey, Cris, I haven't seen you around all day. What you got there?" He leaned down, pulled the palm hat off the pile, and put it on his head. "Is this a new look for the summer?"

Crispin tried hard to bite his tongue. "No, Eric, it is a convict issue for the governor's new helper."

Eric Bellchambers laughed. "Well, I knew the man was unmarried, but I didn't know he would stoop low enough to take a convict to his bed."

Crispin felt like hauling his friend from his horse and belting him to a pulp. He took three deep breaths and said, "She's to work in his garden, not his bed."

"Likely story," said Eric. "It's no skin off my nose who he sleeps with. Have you found your mystery girl, Bella, yet? You've been mooning around over this female since you left London. I've seen you hanging around the farm watching the women work, so I presume she's one of them."

Crispin did not want him to know he had found her. "No, she isn't. but… um, well…"

Eric laughed. "I bet she's a figment of your imagination. She sounds far too good to be true."

The horse shinnied around.

"Gotta go!" He threw back the hat, wheeled around on his horse and called, "See yer around, Cris." He spurred his horse, and it took off up the road. A dust cloud followed him.

Although Crispin admired the fact that the man could ride, he felt sorry for the poor beast. Although he liked Eric, the animal already had scars where he had been spurred numerous times in the few days since they arrived.

Crispin kept walking up the hill.

Having been caught unawares once, he heard the carriage approach and moved to the side. He expected it to pass; it didn't.

A very familiar voice said, "Hop in, Milroy. I gather you are going home?"

Crispin liked his new boss and didn't know why he had been singled out to work at the official residence.

The kind governor reminded him of his father. "Yes, thank you, sir. Stores have finally unloaded some of the clothing for female convicts. Helena is wearing the last of what was in stock, and there wasn't enough for her full issue. She never received any clothing when she arrived. I know because she was wearing the same grey gown when we met in London; only back then, it was almost new."

The governor looked at the small pile of clothing. "Is that all they get? What's there?"

Crispin laid the bundle on the seat and went through what was there. "This is far more than what the others get, as I also got some stained items for Helena's garden work. Others don't get this much. Plus, I brought her new calico undergarments and a blue drill gown this morning."

The governor frowned. "Really, this is their allocation? What happens if their clothing gets stolen or damaged? Is there no thick coat for warmth?"

Crispin shrugged. "I have no idea, sir. Gillian only has one dress. I believe they are supposed to get two."

John looked at the scant pile and said, "See if you can find out for me, will you? I can't exactly go around asking these sorts of questions, but you've been down to stores twice already. I shall use you as my eyes and ears in the colony. No one knows you yet, and you have already proven yourself trustworthy. You're only a private, so no one will realise you have my ear."

The two men sat looking at the insignificant pile of clothes. Both were deep in thought and did not realise they had pulled up at the house.

A guard opened the door, and as the governor alighted, he said, "Remember, seven sharp, Milroy. Bring an answer, and Helena."

Once he refolded the clothing, Crispin followed him out of the carriage and into the house. He was keen to see Helena but found Gillian first and handed over everything except the stained apron and palm leaf hat. The apron would help make her new gown last longer.

Unable to wait to see her, he immediately carried the two new items to her. He did not call out, but she saw him arrive.

Her face lit up, and her big smile showed he was welcome.

Helena saw he was carrying something. She stabbed the garden fork into the soil and went to him. "Thank you, Crispin. The first load of mulch arrived. I am just digging it in now. The man who brought it said two more loads of well-rotted stuff were coming tomorrow. Is that right?"

Her face was alive with excitement.

Crispin nodded with a frown on his brow. "Is that too much? Should I cancel it?"

She caught his arm. "Oh no, I could use much more, and I was wondering if I could have more of the well-aged stuff from the gardens. Then, next week, I could do with a load of clean straw. I'm pulling out the best of this un-fouled straw and setting it aside for a clean mulch. That will go on top of the garden beds to stop weeds, as it helps retain moisture. Then, I will make holes in the top covering and plant the seedlings in there. It gives the young plants some protection. It's what they are now doing down at the main garden."

Crispin knew nothing about plants. "Why do that?"

Helena explained. "It's hot here, and that protects them. At home, we had to smoke the fruit trees to stop the frost from freezing the buds. That's called smudging. Here, we have the opposite problem. We need to protect the plants from the heat. Last year, many of the crops and plants died in the scorching heat. I also have an idea for that. Mrs Johnson mentioned the birds this morning, and I've been thinking about making some big mesh nets to stop them from gaining access to the garden. One of the things we made on our farm to earn money was making fishing nets. Once the garden is in and planted, I will need a net to cover it so we can lay branches or fronds over the net. That should give some shade as well as keep out the birds. I will need a few spools of coir string or thick thread. If not, I'll ask the Aboriginal women how to make it. Abaroo is the local girl who lives with them; she should know."

Crispin was so out of his depth. "Helena, I have no idea that animals ate our sort of food too. I'm a city boy. I know nothing about this."

She chuckled. "Goats are the worst. They will eat anything, but the big, raucous white cockatoos here are as bad. However, it's the night invaders who are the worst for the fruit. There are two sorts of cute possums and flocks of flying bats that descend on a fruit tree and can strip it bare in one night. I know they have had trouble keeping the animals out of the gardens in town, so I have to work out how to do that here."

She put the apron over her dress as she spoke, but realised her hands were filthy. "This is wonderful, Crispin. How can I ever thank you for all you have done?"

"I have an idea, but I'll wait until we are married." He grinned naughtily. "Re the twine, Helena, Bennelong might be able to help you meet some of the women who will teach you. He went bush as soon as we arrived, but said he would return. He took off soon after landing."

"Bennelong? Who's he?" She had no idea who that person was.

Crispin explained. "He's one of the two natives who went to England with Governor Phillip. We brought him back with us. Governor John knew him from his first visit here. Sadly, his friend who went over with him died over there."

Helena had no idea about this man. "Some Aboriginal women showed us how to harvest the seafood. I don't dare go down alone. But sometimes, a group of us are escorted down to collect shells. The native women also showed us what we could eat."

She brushed the soil from her hands and reached around her back to tie the apron.

He waited until her hands were busy adjusting the ties before he set the palm hat on her head. "I also have this for you. It will keep the sun off your face. Until now, you've been working indoors, but out here, you will get sunburnt."

She had seen others wearing these woven palm leaf hats. "Definitely London fashion!"

She posed with a hand on her hip. "Do I look good?"

Crispin groaned, "Don't ask me that. I want to kiss you anyway, but I won't."

She smiled shyly at that comment. She was looking forward to that day, too. "One day, Crispin, one day! Thank you again, kind sir. It's been hot enough out here to need one today. So, yes, I will wear it. I might see if I can make some string to keep it on."

He was about to leave when he remembered the appointment. "We are to see the governor after dinner tonight at seven."

Unable to resist an endearment of some sort, he took her dirty hands in his and kissed her palms. "Until then, my dear!"

He would have loved to have stripped off his coat and assist her, but he had to find an answer to the governor's question. That meant another trip to Government Stores.

He sighed and left her to the gardening. Here, at least, she was safe. He wondered what other ideas the governor had for him. Somehow, he felt that he may not be in uniform all that often.

As he reached the door, he said, "I'll see you at dinner, Helena."

He had lived his life amongst the rough, tough and poor on the streets in London. He had seen the best and worst of both men and women. It had been his role as a lamplighter employed for so long that the powers that be in London let him transfer into the army, as he was already accepting the King's shilling. A transfer to guard duty from his lamplighter duties was just a signature on a sheet of paper.

After telling the kitchen staff where he was heading, he reluctantly left by the back door and returned to Government Stores.

In the heat of a spring day, he was nearly melting in his red woollen coat.

He had spent so much time wandering up and down the hill that he looked forward to going to bed tonight at the barracks. He could not wait until they were married. He should find out after dinner how soon that could be.

Hours passed far too fast for Helena. Now, she had her fingers in the dirt; she didn't wish to stop.

She forked over the large sods and had broken up the grassy lumps. All the while keeping her eyes open and watching for the insidious black spiders that inhabited these soils. She had not seen any while digging, but two had been found inside the women's tents in the last week. Gillian mentioned she had found two in their room. They were horrible, black, shiny things that, although they moved slowly when threatened, threw themselves back in a menacing way, their fangs dripped with lethal poison.

Helena toiled away until the sun hit the horizon. By then, it was too late to do more.

There would be more manure to dig in tomorrow, and then she could wet the entire garden and let it soak through. She hoped Cris could find some spools of twine.

She was about to go inside when she realised she had better lock away the tools. She had an armload of implements when the governor and Crispin emerged from the kitchen door.

The governor had been busy in town all day and had not had a moment to see what had been done to his backyard. "Oh, my! You have done a lot of work."

Helena was about to bob a curtsy, but realised she would need to drop what she held to do so.

The governor saw her predicament and said, "Don't worry, lass, you'll drop everything. As I told the other staff, once a day will do nicely unless I have visitors."

Helena nodded.

Crispin walked over to grab the rest of the tools, and as he walked past her, he gasped. "Don't move, Helena! Something is crawling on you."

He was about to brush the creature from her skirt when the governor saw what it was and knocked his hand aside.

John shouted at the young man. "No, don't touch it! Milroy, give me your sword."

Crispin hesitated and watched the black creature crawl up her skirt.

John frowned. His eyes had not left Helena's skirt. "Now, man!"

Crispin handed over his lethal weapon, hilt first. "Sir, I'll just brush it off."

In the week since his arrival, he had encountered some swiftly moving spiders, but this one was much smaller. He had stomped on the other ones or just moved them outside. This shiny black one was walking very slowly up her gown.

"No, you won't." John had the sword raised to waist level and moved behind the girl.

He said, "Freeze, Helena; move only when I say." He carefully slid the blade down her skirt and removed the offending creature with a flick. "Now, girl!"

Helena moved like lightning, but it made her drop everything.

Crispin caught her and enfolded her in his arms. They turned to see the governor poke the spider with the sword's tip.

John explained, "When we were here the first time, it didn't take long before we encountered these vile creatures. They are as deadly as they are ugly. We presumed that these fellows caused various deaths in the new settlement, but it was Bennelong who confirmed that they were lethal. We learned quickly not to leave shoes or clothing on the floor as these insidious beasts creep into anything. We were in tents when we landed, so we strung ropes to keep our kit off the ground."

He shivered, not from the cold, but he did not like these nasty beasties. He prodded the spider again, and it sprang back with its front legs, ready to pounce. Glistening drops appeared on its fangs.

Without waiting for it to vanish, John stomped on it and twisted his foot to ensure it was dead. "Nasty thing!"

Helena blanched and sagged against Crispin. "I have kept my eyes open for them all day. I did not see it."

Crispin was horrified. The only good thing was that he now held her in his arms as he had wished to do for some time. He was unaware he was rubbing his hand up and down her back.

Rather than pull away, she snuggled closer.

Crispin said, "Sir, thank you for stopping me from touching it."

John nodded and said to Helena, "You remind me of a convict lass I met when I was here the first time. She was given a patch of land at Parramatta and grew some amazing food. Her name was Annie Gentle. At least that's what she told everyone. She is now the Marchioness of Bowbelle."

He gasped, then grinned. "Oh, I didn't mean to say that. Shh! Ask the Johnsons about her, as she was with them for the first year. She and her husband helped build the church. Richard told me about their secret identity when I returned. She was also an extraordinary gardener."

John was grinning to himself. Helena's hair wasn't as fair or curly as Annie's, but something in her proud stance and the garden setting reminded him of the other lassie.

He knew Annie was friends with Colin and Aggie Osborne, and he often bumped into her at their house in Parramatta. Colin, Aggie and Annie all arrived as convicts in the First Fleet. Colin soon became indispensable as a potter. John still had one of his mugs and the teapot. Colin suggested Nigel as trustworthy and he was installed ass the salt maker and later married Connie Waterson.

Chapter 5   *Setting Things to Rights*

*H*elena was reluctant to draw away from Crispin's arms. She had stayed safely enfolded for as long as she could, but the governor turned and noticed they still held each other. Rather than say anything, he cocked a dark eyebrow, tilted his head, then frowned.

They drew apart, looking embarrassed. Crispin said, "Sorry, sir."

Helena blushed and bent to pick up what she had dropped.

The governor smiled and turned to walk indoors. "Help her store the things, then come inside. You've done enough for today, miss."

John hated eating alone, and his nephew, William and his wife, Eliza, would not be with him tonight as they had found a house for themselves. So, he looked forward to speaking with the young couple after his meal. The girl seemed to be sensible.

After what he had discovered today, he needed an insight into what was happening in the town. He headed to his office as he still had half an hour until dinner was served.

The paperwork took his mind off the needs of what was demanded of him in this new role. Colin and Aggie would be his eyes and ears in Parramatta. He penned them a note in reply to his letter.

Ignoring the hug was not something either could do; both enjoyed it far too much. If they were caught repeating the action, trouble would ensue. The store room was small, and there was no room for them both, so Helena passed the items inside and waited in full view of the kitchen window. She liked Crispin; she liked him a lot, but she was unsure if she would let him break through the well-built barrier of self-preservation. She barely knew him.

After the tools were stowed for safety, he locked the storeroom door, and they walked inside.

Helena asked Crispin, "Did you have any luck getting a spool of twine? I know how to make fish nets, and I thought I would try to make a huge one to cover the garden."

Crispin shook his head. "I didn't see any down at stores, but then again, I wasn't looking; admittedly, I forgot to ask." He shook his head in wonderment at the extraordinary young woman. "What can't you do?"

She shrugged. "If I see a problem, I think about how it would best be solved and then work out a way to try to do that."

He was intrigued. As they walked inside to prepare for dinner, he asked, "But nets? How do you plan to cover the garden?"

She paused and turned to him. "Well, I was hoping you might help me with that, as you had some men dig the yard, you said you might get some to fence the area; if the posts they use for the frames are not trimmed off, I can use those to lift the netting high so you can walk under it. So, about eight to ten feet above ground would be wonderful, but no higher as I can't reach them. I have seen the government gardens and noticed they are also in full sun in summer. The days here are scorching, and the plants shrivel in the ground."

Crispin chuckled. "I would not have a notion of where to start, let alone after one day have it sorted."

They parted company in the hallway, and Helena walked to her room. She had only had time to look inside the small room with a single narrow bed. She was astounded that there was a double bunk. That had not been there when she looked this morning.

Gillian welcomed her and said, "Your man brought you a pile of clothes, but he said we can share the extra garments. Is that all right?" Gillian was hopping from foot to foot with excitement. "I've not had anything new for ever so long."

Helena chuckled. "Of course, Gillian. I'll need the oldest clothes for gardening, and this apron has a big stain on it, so I'll keep that. I have my grey dress for best, and you can have one of the new ones. We will share everything except underclothing if that's okay."

Gillian gave a whirl of glee. "Of course it is! I can't believe I have you here to share with me. I was chosen to work here because I was one of the youngest girls. I have been in Sydney ever so long and still have a few years to serve. I came on the *Boddingtons* a couple of years ago. We arrived in August, and silly me, I thought it would be summer. I froze, as did the rest of us. The seasons are upside down, and getting used to things took me a while."

She chattered as Helena changed into a new brown gown that Crispin had collected for her. She had to see the governor after dinner, but she also needed to get to know her roommate. The girl seemed chatty, so Helena let her talk. She figured she must only be about fifteen or sixteen.

Gillian stood in her calico petticoat and reached for the other new blue drill dress. "Are you sure I can wear this?"

Helena nodded. Surprisingly, her grey dress was dry and clean, but she put on the other gown and apron. She had changed only that morning, and the new apron had kept her reasonably clean. "I'm sure, Gillian, but I'll see if I can get some fabric from somewhere, and I'll make some more."

The girl's eyes grew as big as saucers. "You can sew? Will you teach me?"

Helena frowned. Sewing clothes was something all the girls in her family were taught from knee-high. "Of course I will. We need some fabric and thread. How come you don't know how?"

Gillian shrugged. "I was never taught at the orphanage. I'm a foundling from St Thomas's in London. Well, it isn't really St Thomas's, but Thomas Coram started it, and it was better than living on the streets, so it's what we used to call the Foundling Hospital. I was left on their doorstep as a baby. I was sent to a horrible family for my first place when I turned twelve." She fell silent, and her expression of joy vanished. Her face was awash with grief.

Helena was sure what would follow. She placed a caring hand on her arm. "You don't need to tell me."

Gillian lifted her head, and Helena saw that her eyes were filled with tears.

Gillian shook her head and said, "I want you to know." She sniffed and continued, "I was just a woman, you know, my monthly flow, so I was found a placement from the orphanage. I was told I could not return no matter what, even if I hated the job."

She took a deep breath before she said, "I didn't mind the work as a maid. I was happy for two whole months doing work that I quite liked. But then the twin sons came home from university, and I was vilely used by them both. One held me while the other bounced me, if you know what I mean. It hurt, and I bled all over the coverlet in one of their rooms. The housekeeper came in and caught the second one at it, but she could see the other boy was holding me down."

Gillian stifled a sob. "I was blamed as I was supposed to have tempted them. I was moved to the laundry instead of working indoors. At least I wasn't sacked."

Helena wrapped her arms around her roommate. Her mind was doing the sums. She must only be about seventeen now. "Oh, Gillian, I'm so sorry. I'm here because I ran from a similar situation."

Gillian pushed her away. "It gets worse. I had not had my monthly flow very often, but after the attack, the housekeeper kept her eye on me. She realised I had not used my rags for some months, and then I started being sick at various times throughout the day. They had got me with child, and I was barely out of childhood myself. I was horrified and didn't know what to do. The housekeeper took me aside and asked me all sorts of questions. I didn't know anything about babies, and I was scared stiff. I kept working as long as I could, and then one day, about four months after the attack, I collapsed. I had been hanging out the washing and was found in a bloody mess under the clothesline. I remember feeling stomach pains and then bending over. The next thing I knew, I was waking up in my cot in the servants' quarters, and the housekeeper was beside me. I had lost the baby. I cried with joy, and she gave me a big hug. I had not had one before, and so I cried harder. A hug, I mean."

Helena still had an arm slung around her new friend's shoulders, and she walked to the bunk and sat them down. "Go on, what did she say."

"Oh, she was really nice and all, but about a month later, the boys came back. This time, they forced me into the stables and had their way with me again. I managed to scream, and one of their grooms came, but rather than get help or stop them, the boys encouraged him to do me over, too. I kept screaming. Eventually, his Lordship came to see what the noise was, and apparently, he found me unresponsive with my skirts above my head."

She was gazing at the floor. "I came around in my own cot again. The housekeeper, Mrs Fawcett, was bathing my head, and she had stripped off my clothing. I had not even had a chance to say anything when her ladyship came storming in. She accused me of tempting her sons, but she froze when she saw the state of my face. They had beaten me black and blue, and my lip was split and swollen." She touched her lip. "Rather than continue her tirade, she turned on her heel and stormed out."

Gillian's head shook slowly and turned into Helena's shoulder. She still could not believe what happened in the few days after that. She still had a small scar on her lip from the belting.

Helena knew this could have been her history if she had not run away both times. "That's enough, Gillian; I can guess the rest."

The girl shook her head. Tears spilled from her eyes. "No, you can't; no one can. I still find it hard to believe, but the housekeeper and seven maids asked to see our employers. My abuse was the last straw for them. As I said, I was a child myself. While I was still abed, the female staff demanded an audience with our bosses and exposed the philandering of their sons. His lordship just laughed and said he owned us. Her Ladyship turned and walked out." Gillian was hiccoughing as she spoke.

Helena was distraught about her new friend's situation.

Gillian wiped her tear-stained cheeks with the back of her hand. The sound of her loud sniff echoed around the room. "Rather than achieve anything, we were all sacked on the spot. We were given until the following day to leave. We all left, including some of the footmen, the cook and the butler. The family were left without staff. I could barely stand, so the other maids packed my things. I had no idea that many had all received similar treatment. We had barely managed to get to the bottom of the street when a constable came and demanded to check our bags. I had one small, tattered valise that contained my worldly possessions. I had not packed it but presumed it would only hold my personal things. Unbeknownst to me, all of the maids had packed their uniforms, mine included. We were all arrested for theft and ended up being transported here."

Gillian wiped her tears away on her clean sleeve this time.

"Thankfully, I did not fall with child this time, but oh, Helena, I was a sorry mess. I was only twelve the first time they took to me. Gaol was horrible, but I was too sick to notice for the first months. The men we were locked up with used us as they wished." She blew her nose again. "We were locked in squalor for months, and during that time, many fell ill. Mrs Fawcett died from some illness she contracted before we were moved onto the *Boddingtons*, but the other girls did what they could for me. Again, a few crew members did us over on the way here. Some of the other maids arrived on the convict ship with me, and some were sent to other prisons. I was sick on arrival, and Mrs Johnson took pity on me because I was only fourteen. I was sent to care for Milbah, their little daughter. When we heard the new governor was arriving, I was transferred here for my safety."

Helena drew her a little closer.

Gillian lifted her gaze to Helena's and saw compassion on her face. Another sob escaped her. "Why are men so cruel? Why do they force themselves on us, and then we have to pay the price? The boys got off with no punishment. Mrs Fawcett died because of them. I loved her so much. Connie told me she came on the First Fleet and was one of the women done over when they landed. She doesn't know who Liam's father is."

Helena was gutted. Connie had not told her that. Their evening had started with laughter and joy; now both were tear-stained. Helena said, "I was only seventeen when I left home to find work. When I discovered what my new master had planned for us maids, I applied for a new position with Crispin's aunt in her Domestic Bureau. I was sacked, and that night, I met Crispin. I didn't realise he was related to the lady I worked for. I only found that out today. I didn't even know his last name. I stayed with her for a while, and then she found me another job. I didn't know she was dying and that she had already sold the business. Anyway, I had only been at the new job briefly when my new employer tried to do much the same as what happened to you. I ran and found my way into a marketplace. He was hard on my heels, and I knew what he would do if he caught me. I would be violated, beaten, and possibly mutilated, as he liked to do. I had seen cuts on the faces of some of the other girls I worked with. This sadistic creep liked marking the girls with his knife each time he took them. I refused to become one of his victims, so I stole something in front of the market constable. Being arrested, convicted and sent here was better than my options in London."

Helena retold her saga to the tearful girl; many in the colony had such backgrounds, and the young ones had somehow survived similar abuse. She brushed the hair from her friend's cheek and said, "Gillian, here we have a new future in front of us. We are young and healthy and can have a good life here. Thank God that we are now safe."

Helena had to wash her face and hands, but they knew they were to stay in their room until they were called for dinner.

A gentle tap on the door, a few minutes later, Mrs Cowdrey came to call them to assist Mrs Peach, the cook. "Ready, girls?"

She opened the door to see two tear-stained faces. "I gather you have shared your stories?"

Both girls nodded. She knew the backgrounds of both lassies. She came in and softly closed the door behind her. She could see from their faces that they had been confiding in each other. It was time she let them know she was on their side.

Taking their hands and crouching before them, she said, "Let me just say, not all men are pigs. Some are wonderful, like my beloved Clarence was. If you can find a good man, grab him with both hands and don't let go. Even if you do not love him, your life will be better because he will treat you well. Marriage has many facets, and the physical side is very pleasant if you choose the right husband. He can make your marriage bed far more than just nice."

Her cocked eyebrow made both girls blush.

Helena did not expect to have this conversation with the governor's housekeeper.

Mrs Cowdrey placed a loving hand on the teary girl's cheek. "Gillian, I asked Mrs Johnson if you could come and work here as she had told me of your background. I felt you needed a mother figure, and even though you have been here only a few days, I hope you will come to me if you have any troubles."

Gillian nodded and whispered, "Thank you."

Mrs Cowdrey turned to Helena, "Same goes for you, dearie. I heard what you told the governor, and here you will have a chance in life. You may have already met your match in Private Milroy, but time will tell."

She pushed herself up and said, "Now, the cook needs your help with the dishes, and my knees will not cope with crouching like this. I bend and creak as it is. The governor is nearly finished with his second course, and I believe he wants to see you at seven, dearie?"

Helena nodded. She wanted to hug this dear lady.

The three went to prepare for the evening. They would eat before washing up.

Chapter 6   Paving the Way

*A*s the clock in the hallway started chiming seven, Helena and Crispin were waiting downstairs. The temperature had dropped.

They knew the governor was in his private sitting room upstairs, and they made their way to his exclusive sanctum. Had it really only been this morning that she was attacked? So much had occurred.

As the last chime struck, the Scottish lilted voice called, "Come in and sit in front of the fire with me. This is an informal chat, and it's comfortable in here."

Crispin ushered Helena into the private retiring room of the vice-regal gentleman. "Sir, this is your private area. Are you sure?"

John waved his hand for them to take a seat. "Yes, yes! Sometimes, it's lonely at the top, and as you two will be living here anyway, you had better get used to keeping a lonely man company, so make yourselves comfortable."

He heard Crispin gasp. "Mrs Cowdrey will bring in the tray in a few minutes, and then we can chat about a list of things."

He drained the last of his port from his glass. He should have brought more with him, but he forgot. He only had two more bottles and had no intention of sharing this particular tipple.

Noting they had settled, he asked, "Helena, are you quite recovered from your scares this morning and again this afternoon?"

Helena was unsure of how to address him in such a situation. "Yes, thank you, Your Excellency. To be permitted to get my hands into the soil again is pure joy for me, spiders or not. Plus, it smells a lot better." She smiled.

John chuckled. "Sir will do fine." He saw how nervous the young couple were and wished to say something to make them relax. "When I saw you being accosted this morning, I did not realise such attacks were still a problem. I've been here nearly a week, and I'm still finding my way around the growing settlement. When I was here before, everything was still new."

He smirked. "What's more, I was off exploring for much of my first visit; I do not know the ins and outs of the problems that exist here now. I was not even here when the women were landed. I was off charting our new harbour."

Before anyone could say more, Mrs Cowdrey brought in the tea tray. She poured and then left.

John noticed a glass of brandy under a net covering, and he took it and sat it on the side table next to him. This was his nightcap. He gave her a nod of thanks with a smile.

As she shut the door, John spoke again. "Helena, have you heard about the landing of the female convicts from the First Fleet on the *Lady Penrhyn?*"

Helena nodded. The horrific stories of the pack rapes had indeed been retold to the women in the female barracks. "Do you mean what I heard occur was true, sir? I presumed they were just exaggerated stories. Connie said something."

John shook his head. "If you have heard about the carnal animal behaviour of the men when the women landed, then the stories are true. About a dozen children were conceived that day. However, as I said, I was not here at the time. I was off charting the upper reaches of the harbour. On my return, I had discussions with the doctor on board the *Lady Penrhyn*, Arthur Bowes Smith, who gave me a full report of what had occurred. From what you heard and what he told me, I'm guessing both versions were vastly underrated." A frown crossed his brow.

"I returned to find many of the violated women in the hospital, with Doctors John White and Arthur Bowes Smith tending to them. Connie was one of them. Many poor women had not just been violated but violently beaten into submission to the disgusting torture. Many of us kept a detailed journal of that expedition. However, only a few decided to record that horrific event. I didn't; as for me, it was only hearsay. The doctor certainly did, in detail, and on his return to London, he reported various glaring issues. The Bowbelles, who I mentioned earlier, took over his cause in London when he died. Now, only Naval doctors are permitted to accompany the convict voyages. Many changes have been made because of Arthur Bowes Smith's reports. He was a wonderful man. He died far too young, at only thirty-six. The Admiralty acknowledged he was correct in many things that he reported. The care of the female prisoners was uppermost in his mind. The ineptitude of the unskilled doctors on that voyage was such a glaring problem that Bowes Smith was asked to take over the care of the *Lady Penrhyn* due to the inexperience and illness of Doctor Altree. That young doctor eventually was sent to Norfolk Island with the settlers."

John took a long draw of his tea.

The young couple sat on the edge of their seats and waited.

He continued his story. "Anyway, in my absence, the governor gave the order to unload the female convicts; of the hundred and nine women on board, over ninety landed. Apparently, they were hardly on dry land when the orgy started. The women were attacked after being assisted from the longboats that brought them ashore."

His head shook in disgust at the behaviour of the men. "According to Arthur Phillip, the orgy continued into the evening until a violent storm hit. Only about a dozen of the women remained on board. Annie was luckily one of those. They were either injured or were heading to Norfolk Island."

He took another sip of his tea. "From what I heard, it was far worse than an occasional debauched attack. Men were holding women down as others pleasured themselves and violated them on the foreshore in full sight of the *Lady Penrhyn*. As the surgeon on that vessel, Doctor Bowes Smith should have been with them and planned to come in the last boat. However, it did not return to pick him up, and he was left stranded on his ship."

This time he grunted with disgust. "Therefore, he was unable to assist the poor creatures, so the orgy continued unabated. I'm not sure that the regiment even tried to pause the carnage. Governor Phillip could not halt the activities, but the hand of God did. I'm sorry to use such descriptive terms, but it's apt. I'm telling you, as I need you to know that I understand what the women have endured."

He stared into his tea, deep in thought. "Governor Phillip was so disgusted that the following morning, he gathered the entire settlement, crew, soldiers, and every convict and read them all the riot act. I arrived in time to listen to what he said."

John's hands swept across his brow in disgust at the knowledge of such abuse. "That muster was on February 7th, and while everyone was gathered together. Governor Phillip read the proclamation claiming the land in the name of England."

John chuckled unexpectedly. "We had to do that as the French had not yet left Botany Bay. We only hoisted our flag after we saw them on the morning of the 24th. Had they staked their claim first, I fear what would have occurred had the English ships left the settlement. The French knew we had raised a flag in Botany Bay but were unaware we had not claimed it."

"They walked to our new settlement and boasted that they had a fort set up in Botany Bay after our departure. We feared they would claim the land before us. They were not as kind to the tribal locals as we had been. Had they claimed this incredible land, I dare say most of the Aborigines would have ended up the same as many of the clansmen down there. At least we English tried to work with them."

After another sip, he continued. "Botany Bay Colebee, Bennelong, Arabanoo and others were the first to trade with us. We all would have died but for their assistance. We had grandiose plans to educate and assimilate, to live in peace and harmony with them, but that did not occur. If what the French did in the islands was any sign, they preferred to eradicate their enemy. I heard they massacred over thirty innocent natives in the first week they were in Botany Bay and came here to boast of their actions. I do not know if it was merely a boast. We were disgusted! These were good men we had befriended and traded with. We were shattered that our hard-won negotiations had been put in jeopardy by their actions. They claimed to have been attacked with rocks, but we only saw cockles."

He huffed. "We came to settle, not to kill. This land is big enough to share."

He waved his hand as though to sweep those thoughts aside. "After the atrocious treatment of the women, the men, convicts, crew and soldiers alike, were warned by Governor Phillip about going near the women's tents. Many still risked it and were flogged for the privilege; some were even hanged. Ultimately, we figured the only way to protect the women fully was to permit them to marry. The reverend performed many such services over my first years here." John kept talking about his early years and his first visit.

The young couple sat listening to the man's reminiscences. Both had heard rumours, but they paled compared to what they heard now. They were spellbound by his descriptions and expeditions from his previous visit. More than an hour passed while they listened to him talk about his first journey.

A chink of a china cup being placed in the saucer broke the silence. John pushed the cup away from him and lay back in his seat. "Well, that is all behind us. We must think about the future; however, we must learn from the past to avoid repeating it. Firstly, there is the matter of the two of you. Milroy, do you have anything to say about that?"

Crispin was about to reply when Helena spoke. "Sir, may I answer that? I think I know what Crispin wants, or he would not have come halfway around the world looking for me." Her eyes locked with the young soldier.

Crispin nodded to her with a smile. He knew her hesitation. He knew far more about her than she knew about him. He had met her family and spent a few days with them. He had even asked her father for permission to marry her. She had not even known that Mrs Milroy was his aunt.

John said, "Yes, go on."

Helena did, although nervously. "Sir, I am putting words into Crispin's mouth as he has not actually asked me to marry him. However, we discussed it earlier today. Sir, as much as I like him, I have truly only known him for a week. However, I trust him, and that is not something I do easily. Whatever happens in the future, I would like him to be near me as I feel safe."

John understood what she meant. "You wish to take things slowly?"

She nodded. "Yes, sir, but as Cris made me very aware today as we were walking back from the Johnsons, the women in the colony need protection. If we were to become engaged, it would give me that protection while we truly get to know each other. We discussed having an agreement first, or at least an understanding, but we decided to ask you about that. I believe we both need permission before we even consider an engagement. But, sir, I don't know him very well."

John frowned at her words. "So, you are not rejecting him outright?"

Helena shook her head and said, "Oh no, it's just that he has only just arrived, and well, it will seem very odd to everyone that we became engaged only a week after he got here. That is my only concern for him. I have none for myself." As she said the words, she realised she meant them.

Crispin raised his hand to speak. He felt somewhat foolish, but this conversation involved him. John saw and smiled. "Yes, lad, you may speak. It is your future we are discussing."

Crispin returned his smile. He addressed Helena. "Actually, Helena, none of the soldiers I arrived with will be at all surprised. You see, I told a few of them that I was on the trail of my girl. Word will soon spread that I found you. One of my peers asked me that today, but I didn't answer him."

Helena all but ignored the governor. "You told others about me?"

Crispin nodded. "Yes, but I did not use your real name."

The governor's chuckle echoed around the room. "I tell you what. It will take a few days for the Colonial Secretary, David Collins, to arrange the various permissions for you to wed, which you have, by the way. I am the man who signs off on such things. He will need to draft the two documents for me to sign. However, if I were you, I would not delay the engagement announcement, but if you were wed by Banns, that would be a month away at least. You can always pull out, Helena, should you so desire."

Crispin saw the look of shock on Helena's face. She had not expected permission to be granted immediately. He asked, "Sir, may we have a moment to discuss this, please?"

John nodded. "I'll return in a few minutes." He stood and went to relieve himself. He had more that he wished to say, but the tea had gone straight through him. He said, "Three minutes, and that's all." He left to use the chamberpot in his room.

Crispin waited until the door closed and knelt in front of Helena. "Sweet Helena, I know my heart. It's why I'm here. Your future here is in jeopardy if you are unwed. But I have a proposal; this is another option for you. When we wed, I shall not touch you intimately until you say I can. Even if I never can claim you fully as my wife, only I will ever know. To the outside world, we shall be a happily wed couple."

Helena was stunned. "You would do that for me? You would not force me to… to…"

Crispin pulled back. "Never, Helena, I will never force you; not now, not ever."

He saw a tear trickle down her cheek. This time, it did not leave a channel in the dirt on her beautiful face. He thumbed it away. "Don't get me wrong. I want to hold you, kiss away your fears and make you mine, but I won't. I respect you and love you. Together, we can make a life here. I told you I want to marry you even if I have to keep you at arm's length forever."

He was so close that her blue eyes flicked from one of his chocolate-coloured orbs to the other.

She cupped his cheek and replied with one word. "Yes!"

Crispin's heart leapt. "Yes, we will become engaged, or yes, you will marry me?"

Helena reached out and drew him close. "Yes, to everything, even to being your full wife. But Cris, I will still need time. I have fought for my dignity for so long, it will be hard to relinquish." She caressed his cheek. "Is that okay?"

He nodded, grinning so broadly that she saw he had a tooth chipped on the side.

She leaned closer and kissed him on his lips. The butterfly-like touch ignited a flame in her.

Rather than pull away, she leaned in and slid her arms around his neck.

Crispin deepened the kiss. His senses were reeling. He had no idea that she would agree to his offer. For her to initiate a deeper kiss was beyond his wildest dreams.

Behind them, the well-oiled door opened. Neither realised that the governor had returned until he cleared his throat. They broke apart. He said, "Um, I'm guessing she has agreed to an engagement?"

"Yes, sir." Crispin took his seat and sat very uncomfortably for a while until he regained control of his raging need for her. He was stunned that she had agreed to have a full marriage.

Helena was grinning. She could not stop gazing at Crispin. She found it hard to believe that he was prepared to marry her and still not force himself on her. It was what she had always wanted. He was a man who would cherish and respect her. One who would honour her, just as her father did for her mother. Against all odds, she had found such a man. In reality, he had found her, twice, and travelled halfway around the world to do so.

"Helena, did you hear what the governor asked?" Crispin's voice finally penetrated her thoughts.

She gave her head a microshake to make herself concentrate on the conversation. "No, sorry; I was woolgathering." She tried to focus on the governor, but her mind and eyes kept returning to Crispin.

John took pity on the poor girl. She had just had one hell of a day. "I should not permit this, but go sit next to her lad."

Crispin didn't need to be told twice. He moved to the other settee. He slid his hand into hers.

John said, "Now, do I have your attention?"

The couple both nodded.

Helena moved her hand and interlaced her fingers with his.

John saw and smiled. "Fine, well, we have your situation well in hand. I will get the paperwork sorted out tomorrow. I need you both to listen to me."

They nodded, and he could see they were listening.

John continued, "I told you about what it was like here in 1788 and the first years. Now I'm in charge; I need both of you to work with me. Milroy that means I want you to move in as a resident guard. My nephew

William Kent and the Colonial Secretary, David Collins, who came with the First Fleet, are already pointing out some of the most urgent issues. Still, I have had little time to converse privately with David. I know the Johnsons are also trustworthy, and today, the reverend has filled me in on some of the issues of the previous command. Francis Grose made friends with some of those I now have to rein in. However, these men are strong leaders in the Corps, so I must work with them."

He paused, and his smiling eyes turned to the young, handsome soldier. "This is where you will come in, Milroy. Some of the New South Wales Corps here seem to have forced the hand of Grose, and now the entire colony is at risk of becoming more corrupt than the convicts they are supposed to guard. I need someone in the house I can trust. Quite honestly, I have no idea if there is anything I can do to quell this issue, but to have somewhere and someone to let off steam will be good. Anything I say to William or Collins will be recorded and kept on record, as all our official meetings are. Sometimes, I must voice ideas and run through things with someone as a sounding board."

Crispin frowned, then asked, "Why us, sir?"

John's soft chuckle was followed by, "Why? Because neither of you has come to feather your own nests. James Smith, who accompanied us on the First Fleet, was another such man. He eventually returned to England with me on the Dutch ship *Waakzaamheid* in March 1791, with the Dutch Captain Smit. Crewmen like Thomas Webb came with me. He was a nice chap for a sailor, and he returned here to bring his brother's pay the following year. I only mentioned him as I hoped to meet him again. I heard today that he died a few months ago from a festering wound after a skirmish along the Hawkesbury River. He didn't know the land he was granted had been a traditional hunting ground for the local tribe."

He sighed again. "These skirmishes are becoming far more common, and I am at a loss as to what to do. Bennelong told me soon after we landed that tensions were building. He's gone bush now, so I can't find out more details yet. Anyway, I had many interesting conversations with James Smith in those first three years. He caused many feathers to be ruffled as he had paid for his passage on the First Fleet without Naval permission. Arthur Bowes Smith, no relation, mind you, gave him a good reference, and James found a niche in the infant town as a constable. He was neither convict, crew, nor a soldier. Governor Phillip gave him a token role over the convicts, but in the end, the man returned home with me as he could not settle. He, truly, had come to see what it was like. Therefore, like him, you have no ulterior purpose other than survival. It's for that reason I have chosen you both. Helena, as a soldier's wife, you will be able to walk the fine line between both camps, as you will still be a convict. Milroy, you are a soldier, and as only a private, senior officers often are somewhat loose-tongued in the presence of juniors and servants. I don't need to hear every titbit of gossip, but use your discretion and tell me what I need to know. However, they may clam up around you once they realise you have moved in here with me."

Crispin nodded his understanding. He knew the officers would ignore him if he were in the barracks. Even after marriage, he would still be able to do that.

He was rubbing his thumb on the back of Helena's hand, and she found it delightful but distracting.

Helena didn't know what use she would be. "What sort of things, sir? Will I still be working here when we marry?"

John leaned forward. "For the moment, you are a woman amongst the women. Yes, you will be staying here, but you can mingle in town a little more after next week, once your Banns are read for the first time. However, never go alone. You will need to wait until the convict men are at work, but you have my permission to go to the Government Store if need be, or you can go with Gillian to the market. Do not shun conversations; encourage others to talk. Talk to Connie Bray; she is trustworthy. I know Nigel and her well. Listen to the gossip and tell me about any turmoil you hear about. I need to be made aware of such things if I am to keep the women safe. I wish to keep the peace, and I need to know how to make this colony thrive. Unless the women are prepared to marry and have children, there is little hope for any of us."

As Crispin had earlier, Helena lifted her fingers as she wished to speak. John gave her a nod of permission. Helena said politely, "Sir, I have already heard many women mention they wished to marry; only once they do, there is nowhere for them to live. Currently, we are safe in the women's tents, but once out in the community, problems occur. Even married women are not safe from the lustful gazes of the unwed men. Some of them are also violated; then, fights occur with their husbands. It's not just the convict men but also the soldiers. The minister won't even let Mrs Johnson walk alone. Max Slater accompanies her."

John had already recognised that problem. She was right. He had already thought of the couple's immediate issue. He had checked a room at the back of the house when they were away earlier that day. It was at the opposite end of the house from Gillian's room, near a storage area. It could easily be converted into a bedroom with little trouble. The boxes could be moved to another area.

His reply was, "We have time to sort that, Helena. Focus on the immediate and leave those details to me."

Helena's fingers tentatively rose again.

John said, "Yes, dear. You don't need to do that. Just ask."

Helena had a request that would go against the rules of society. "Sir, will I be expected to give up work once we marry? Having just gotten my fingers back into the dirt, I do not wish to give up the delight of gardening. Spiders excepted! Please, don't make me stop working in the garden."

Crispin noted the tears welling in her eyes and threatening to fall. His heart sank. "Sir, I'm fine with that, but such an edict must come from you."

John nodded. "I had presumed that you would not wish to stop gardening. But in truth, I don't consider gardening such arduous work. The convict men can break any virgin soil areas you wish to expand into, and you will then take over the tending of the gardens. However, we can discuss later the nuances of what you will do after marriage. Here, in this new colony, we set some of our own rules. Women will need to pull their weight as the men do. That means they must continue to produce as much food, clothing and other goods as possible. You have given me much fodder to think over already, and I think I shall address this to the women as a group. I may go down and talk to them in the barracks one night, as they should all be together then. You mentioned the lack of accommodation; I shall attend to that immediately. However, I will also ask the Johnsons for their insight. I will send word to the reverend first thing in the morning, and the three of us will have an interview with him."

He twiddled his fingers while thinking, then said, "It is currently Monday, so we have six days to seek what information until word gets out on Sunday when your Banns are read for the first time. Not many were ever married by Banns when I was here before, so it will cause a stir. Word will spread quickly, and Milroy, aspects of your ability to be invisible will vanish. I have no doubt you will both be somewhat inundated, but it will also open doors for you in the town. I suggest we all turn in now as it's getting late."

The young couple realised the interview was over.

John said, "Off you go, and we'll get things moving tomorrow. Watch yourselves and make sure you do not do anything untoward. You may move in tomorrow, Milroy. Remember, she may be a convict but still a woman and deserves respect. That is not negotiable."

The young couple rose and nodded goodnight.

Crispin nodded his agreement and gave a bow. "Absolutely, sir! I would do nothing to harm her."

They had still not released their hands when Crispin opened the door for her.

John watched them leave and relaxed in his chair. It was not like him to favour a young couple, but they reminded him of his young nieces and nephews. William had been busy settling into their new house today, and John missed his presence.

William insisted on staying near his fellow officers and often refused the privileges a familial relationship with the commanding officer would have given. They had only stayed until this furniture was in their cottage. He intended to enlarge the building they had bought on the foreshore. He was a good lad and had his head screwed on properly. His purchase of Spanish Merino sheep in Cape Town was a case in point. Sadly, half of them had died on that last leg, but those that survived seemed healthy enough.

It had taken only days after their arrival and unloading before Lieutenant Macarthur approached them to purchase the offspring when they were born. After reading Colin's letter, John now felt like stopping that transaction. However, there were currently no lambs to be sold. He knew he had to work closely with Macarthur, so it was best not to start on the wrong footing.

He removed the covering from his nightcap and took a deep sniff. He limited himself to a *wee dram*. He preferred Scotch whisky, but William had opened a bottle of brandy, and it was a good one.

John stared into the dying embers of the unnecessary fire as he sipped his nightcap and thought about how to tackle the problems ahead. He had much to think about, but now, at least, he had a place to start. He had not sought out Richard Johnson before church yesterday for a long conversation but now realised that had been an oversight. He had visited him today only to make an appointment.

Richard was hand-picked for this role as chaplain with a Royal Warrant from the king. He was a man of integrity and faith. John knew he had befriended the local Aboriginals, and they had even given their daughter an Aboriginal name. Milbah was a delightful child and frowned when he said her name incorrectly as Melba. She politely corrected him and then gave him a beaming smile. The impish child had won his heart in an instant.

They had taken in an aboriginal girl who had survived the smallpox epidemic that had decimated the new community. Helena mentioned that this girl now came and went at will. John had given thanks for this lass, as she had rescued them when they were lost during a cross-country expedition shortly before his ill-fated cruise.

John scoffed the remains of his brandy and left the glass on the table beside him. He snuffed the lamp on the sideboard and left the door open as he headed to his bedroom. He half expected the couple to be still cuddling in the hallway before going to bed. However, he found he was once more alone.

Crispin must have departed for the barracks via the kitchen door. He released a long sigh and entered his room.

So much had occurred since he rose at dawn this morning. At least one life would be changed. He hoped Helena was telling the truth.

~

Helena's tilling and digging the dung into the hardened soil was beginning to bring life to the earth. She found and killed a few more spiders.

There was still much to do before the first seedlings could be planted. Helena had a small coopered watering can, and by using this, she could add just enough water to assist in breaking the sods. The large tin one with a shower head would be used once the plants were in and required long drinks.

During the week, Crispin visited the Government Stores twice to look for things for Helena. He found one big spool of twine that the aboriginal women had traded for fresh fish and ordered three more rolls.

~

Towards the end of the week, Reverend Johnson inspected Helena's efforts at garden construction, expecting it to require much correction. Instead, he stood looking in awe and amazement. The compacted soil had been dug over, and four wagon loads of composted stable manure had been worked deep into the beds.

The reverend stood scratching his head and turned to look at the girl beside him. "When the governor mentioned that you needed some seedlings and plants, I wondered how he intended to grow them. I presumed he was going to use coopered half-barrels. I have battled against the soils here and know the work entailed to make it friable. What you have achieved in…" he looked at the teenage girl again before saying, "…in an extraordinarily short time is incredible. If you keep the water up for another week, then I think some of the more sturdy seedlings will have a chance to grow. Planting vegetables is too early, but I will bring you some seeds anyway. What were you hoping to grow?" He didn't expect to hear anything but flowers. He saw an area where she was beginning to weave a net and enquired about that. He noticed that she set up support posts along the new fence structure.

Helena had already made a seed-raising shelf on the protected side of the courtyard. She pointed to that, and they went to inspect the cosy area. She had sourced a few dried cow pats and compost from the government garden. She had mixed that with some freshwater creek sand from the upper reaches of the Tank Stream, and this mix was now ready to plant with seeds.

"Sir, I hoped to germinate some early seedlings and progressively plant over the next months. That means we have regular vegetables rather than a single harvest. Once they have germinated in the manure-rich mix, they should transplant and grow a lot quicker than if they were planted directly in the garden. Hopefully, the grain in the horse manure will also germinate, and I can weed out the seedlings and pot them up for replanting elsewhere."

She looked hopefully at the reverend gentleman. "Perhaps you might want to add them to your crops. If I could get some of the other fallow ground dug over, I could replant a small area of grain for a seed crop rather than harvest it for flour." She frowned; time would tell if that venture would work. Even if this were used for animal food, every ear of grain would be helpful.

~

By Saturday, Helena had planted her first fruit tree. She had found a damp spot in the garden and realised that she could utilise this by putting in a thirsty tree. The governor loved lemons, and these could be used for many sweet and savoury things. This was an area where she could also fence off and use the rocky area for a chicken coop. This would also self-fertilise the tree and keep the weeds away from the roots. She only needed to mention her ideas, and Crispin arranged for fencing, digging or deliveries of manure and straw.

After a hot day of digging, Helena washed her long tresses and stood in the sunshine, bringing in the washing while her hair dried.

The clothesline had now been moved so that it caught more sun. It was out of the way of the garden.

Gillian bounced out the kitchen door and excitedly said, "Helena, thank you so much for doing that. I clean forgot to bring it in as I've been catching up with the ironing. I'm a silly duffer, aren't I?"

The girls carried the basket of washing towards the kitchen door.

Crispin was now in residence. He was now off duty and saw them approach. He held the door open, and as they passed him, he reached out to take the heavy washing from them. He leaned over to give Helena a peck on the lips.

She blushed.

Mrs Cowdrey saw the quick action, cleared her throat, and raised her eyebrows rather than say anything. She shook her head at them, knowing Crispin had initiated the small action.

Crispin blushed. He mouthed, "Sorry!"

The governor walked out of his office as they were entering. He had seen the endearing gesture and his housekeeper's gentle chastisement.

The three young people froze, and each gave a respectful nod as he went to pass them.

"Milroy, Helena, see me at seven again in my sitting room." He didn't wait for a reply but went to the dining room for his evening meal.

The evening passed as the previous ones had.

The staff ate at the table in the kitchen.

The governor's daytime security detail was off-duty. Two sentries always stayed at the house's front door until he retired, and the remainder of the guards slept at the barracks.

Eric had just been seconded to sentry duty as some other soldiers who Crispin recommended were transferred to guarding the women's barracks at night. The front sentries would leave when the house and town settled for the evening.

Crispin was the exception. Since the day after their interview, he slept in a new room. It was small and only had a horsehair mattress, but considering the barracks were either wooden pallet beds or hammocks, he was delighted. He had slept like a log all week and was on cloud nine with how things had turned out so far. He had not seen Eric for a decent conversation since Monday's encounter, and he wondered what his friend would say when Eric heard about their engagement at church tomorrow. He had no idea that he had been noticed while he had been hunting for Helena. Crispin lay on his bed smiling. He would be interested in watching the faces of his peers tomorrow when the Banns were announced. Now, he had half an hour before he had to meet the governor. Hopefully, he would spend a moment or two with Helena before they entered the room. She and Gillian slept towards the other end of the house, directly below the governor's room. He was aware that they were likely to be mobbed after church tomorrow.

At seven o'clock, the pair stood outside the governor's sitting room. Crispin checked; no one was around. He leaned down and gave his lady love another quick kiss. Helena asked, "Do you know what this is about?"

Before Crispin could reply, the governor called for them to enter.

Crispin managed to shrug.

The governor beckoned them in, and they took their seats. He was again enjoying a small glass of port and savoured every last drop of the delicious nectar. He finished the tipple before saying, "Make yourselves comfortable. Helena, I only wish to ask you a few questions, and as Milroy will soon be your husband, I have included him in this conversation. That is, unless you have decided to pull out of the engagement?"

She shook her head. The pair glanced at each other, still none the wiser.

John placed down his glass and relaxed in his chair. "I've been watching your progress on the garden, Helena. You are well taught."

She nodded but didn't answer. Her nerves were making her feel ill.

John smiled at her reluctance to chat with him. It was hard for him to remember that the beautiful and well-mannered girl was a convict. "I wish to ask you about your family."

Helena was stunned. "My family, sir? Why, sir?"

John's fingers were interwoven, and he was tapping his thumbs. "Well, as I said, you are obviously well taught. I figured your father was your teacher?"

Helena nodded again. She was so nervous that her hands shook.

John felt this was like getting blood out of a stone. "Helena, does your father own your farm, or is he a tenant farmer?" He saw her frown.

With a puzzled lift of her brows, she answered. "Sir, my family is poor, as is our farm. Papa can't afford a quality one, and the landlord will not assist us in moving to a better farm. As the family's oldest girl, I offered to leave and get a paying job. It backfired badly, sir. I was not able to send them anything." Although not crying, a tear dribbled down her cheek. The mere thought of what she had hoped to do to assist her family and what she had not been able to achieve made her sad. At least they had one less mouth to feed. She brushed at her cheek. She still had no idea why the governor wished to know. That thought made her look at the grey-haired man; then she turned to Crispin.

Crispin saw her melancholy. "Are you all right, dear?"

She nodded and turned her attention back to the governor.

The man's stance had not moved. His thumbs still bounced against each other, and he gave them a half smile. "Helena, if they were given free passage, do you think the entire family would come here? We need experienced gardeners here in the colony. As they don't own their farm, I gather they will never be in the position to do so?"

Helena shook her head. "Owning land would never even be a possibility, sir. There are far too many children for my folks to save anything.

I have twelve brothers and sisters. My two eldest brothers worked on other farms to make some money, but even that never brought in enough for us all."

John smiled. Good, his proposition may be accepted then. "I gather they are all in reasonable health?" Both nodded. John had forgotten Crispin had met them. "Milroy, would you mind your in-laws living nearby?"

Crispin was stunned at this question. He replied, "No, sir. Not at all! I liked them immensely when I met them. I stayed with them for a few days and saw how hard they all worked. I did what I could to assist, but although I am young and strong, I am a novice at farming. I was amazed that they did not belittle me but were willing to instruct me in jobs I was assisting with."

John was thrilled to hear this. "Milroy, I will address this question to you, as Helena will be somewhat biased." He took a deep breath. "Do you think they would fit in well if we brought them out?"

Helena gasped, but John noticed her gaze was fixed on her fiancé.

The soldier took her hand but turned his eyes to the governor. "Sir, I feel they would be wonderful out here. Mr Rosedale is one of those farmers willing to share his knowledge with anyone interested. He may well be unable to read, but his knowledge is incredible. As Helena's gardening will bear witness, he is not averse to working with girls."

John nodded. He was happy about that. Most men denigrated women. "So, will I write to him and ask if they will come? I will arrange some land for a farm; they will eventually own it outright as a grant. I should ask how many children you said they had?"

Helena swallowed. "I am one of thirteen children, but that was over a year ago; they could have another one by now." She saw Crispin nod. Her brows rose again. "Mama was having another one?"

Crispin grinned and said, "Yes, they had another little girl, Rebecca, a few days before I arrived the second time. I didn't tell you I went back again, but that visit was to ask permission to marry you. Your father gave his blessing and made me stay while your minister wrote a letter, and your papa signed it with his mark. The minister witnessed it." He dug into his coat pocket. He had already shown the letter to Reverend Johnson, but the governor had not seen the document. He held out the parchment.

John took it, briefly perused the screed and noticed the cross instead of the signature at the bottom. "I notice he can't write even his name. If I wrote to the minister, would he read the letter to your parents?"

Helena said, "Yes, sir. Reverend Winchester-Graham is a learned gentleman who likes living in our small village so he can write his books. He is never too busy to attend to the needs of any of his flock. I'm sure he will read the letter to Papa. He attempted to teach all the children to at least write our names, but I only managed to learn my initials. I was more interested in numbers. He taught me to count and do sums." She paused and frowned again. "Sir, it would be amazing if my family could come, but where would they live? Papa is not a builder and would need help constructing something before he could teach anyone how to farm."

John was thrilled. "Leave that problem with me, dear. I gather your home is not too large?"

Helena replied, "No, sir. It's a two-bedroom cottage with a thatched roof. My parents and the youngest babies share one room. The girls are in the other, and the four boys sleep on the floor in the central kitchen."

John sat up in shock. "You only had two rooms for fifteen of you?"

Helena nodded. "Papa's mother, my Gran, lived with us until she died, and we older girls shared with her. Most of us slept on the floor."

John had not shared a room with anyone since his junior years or when he enlisted. He swallowed and said, "Leave the accommodation to me. I shall arrange a land grant in exchange for his expertise. It will be at least eighteen months before they come, if not longer, so I have time to prepare. They may, of course, refuse my offer. It's a big enough upheaval with so many children. I will ensure they have everything they need for the voyage. I will even ask for them to be paid for their expertise so they won't miss out on an income. I don't suppose you know how much the farm brings in a year, would you?"

Helena smiled; she did know, as she was one of the few who could count. The minister had taken the time to teach her. She eventually learned to write her name, but never needed to use it. She said, "The farm made about £12 a year, and after we paid the rent, we were left with about £6 if it was a good season. That is a lot for a small holding."

John looked at this incredible girl. The bottle of port he had been drinking cost that much. They tried to live for a year on that piddling amount.

Crispin said, "How did fifteen people live on that?"

She turned and said, "Sixteen, Cris, remember Gran. We grew or bartered what we didn't have. Clothing was our biggest problem as the fabric was so expensive. We wore a lot of knitted or woven things, as we could make those ourselves. Reverend Winchester-Graham arranged for our village to have a clothing pool at the church hall. The reverend was a member of a missionary group in London, and we would get a large box of old clothing twice a year. We all made do and passed down the items that were still wearable. Fancy ball gowns were cut down into Sunday dresses for the girls. We can all sew."

The two men were in awe of her. John had much to think about. "Thank you both. Now, I think it's time for you to retire. You will be inundated at church tomorrow, but I wanted you to know my thoughts. I hope your family will come, as we need people like them here. Off you both go and don't dawdle too long before parting." John stood as he intended to follow them. "Helena, I will say this: God is using your conviction. Trust Him."

Helena bounced out of her chair. "Sir, I won't ask if I can do this..." She hugged him, then turned on the ball of her foot and left the room.

The two men's mouths were agape at her unexpected action.

It had been so long since John had received a hug that he stood immobilised at the unexpected affection. Aggie Osbourne at Parramatta had been the last to embrace him. He was stunned, but he smiled as he waved them away.

Crispin was about to apologise when he noticed the huge smile on his boss's face. Instead, he bowed and nodded, following Helena out of the room.

She was waiting for him with the intention of saying a long goodnight; however, John caught them in their embrace and shooed them to their respective rooms downstairs.

Chapter 7   Revelations

*T*he governor was correct; the Banns were read at the end of the service. As Reverend Richard Johnson had said, such a thing had not been done since the church was finished. The congregation fell silent, hanging on his every word. When the names of Crispin Milroy and Helena Rosedale were read, the audible gasp was universal.

Sitting in the front row, John could not look around, but from the officer's section, he heard whispers, "He found her then."

Another comment reached his ears. "He's marrying the hellcat? Who would have thought she'd let him near enough to propose?"

Those words were followed by, "I've not seen her this week at work. There's another scrawny wench who is doing the washing. Where do you suppose she's been hiding?"

As John insisted they sit behind him, he beckoned the happy couple to follow his exit when he rose. Mrs Cowdrey motioned for Gillian and Mrs Peach to stay in their seats.

As the three exited their pews and turned to walk up the aisle, an excited murmur and more gasps followed them.

Soon, the church was awash with conversations and suppositions.

Eric's voice carried over the cacophony of noise. "Well, it looks like you chaps have found the reason for Helena Hellcat to have held herself so aloof. For Cris to have chased her halfway around the globe and then propose to her so soon implies that they like each other."

Mrs Cowdrey heard another soldier say, "You knew about this, Eric?"

Eric boasted that he certainly did. "I teased him mercilessly all the way out, but I thought her name was Bella. I saw him earlier this week, and he was evasive about finding her; having said that, now I think of it, he didn't deny it either." Eric knew he needed to apologise to his friend. "I didn't believe him about hunting for her here, but it seems I was wrong."

The soldiers around him overheard his comments. Many were on duty, but they still had to guard the convicts. They juggled guard duty so Eric and his friends could congratulate the couple.

Crispin managed to draw her aside under the shade of a tree. He pulled her into a loose embrace and asked if she was ready to face the multitude of well-wishers.

She replied, "No, so stay beside me, please, Cris. These are the same men who willingly would have had their way with me. I trust none but you." She bravely rested her head against his chest. As the minister and the governor approached, the couple could not kiss.

The four stood together to face the onslaught that was to come.

Mary Johnson was the first to kiss Helena's cheek.

Milbah demanded a hug, and Helena crouched down and warmly embraced the little girl.

As the convicts exited, she saw the two men who had tried to attack her. They were walking stiffly and gave her filthy looks as they passed. Two more were chained to them and hobbled as they walked away in pain.

She stepped closer to Crispin. He slipped his arm around her waist protectively. Many people, including Eric, saw the simple gesture. He waited until many of the convict men had been marched off before approaching. "So she wasn't a figment of your imagination after all?"

She stepped away a little and hooked her arm through her fiancé's.

Crispin laughed and introduced them. "No, Eric, she isn't. Would you stand as a second witness at our nuptials? The governor has offered to be our first one." Crispin's cocked eyebrow showed that he was serious about his enquiry.

Eric was certainly surprised. "You mean that, Cris? I teased you relentlessly, and you are still willing to speak to me?"

Crispin gave a nod. "You did, but you never laid a hand on her, unlike some other fellows who tried to have their way with her."

Eric gave an almost regal bow. "I'd be honoured, my friend. And Miss Helena, you have a good man; I hope he is worthy of you."

Helena had barely spoken to anyone else. However, she replied to Eric, "Sir, it is I who am hardly worthy of such a wonderful man." As she spoke, her hand slipped from Crispin's arm to interlace her fingers with his.

Again, the gesture was witnessed by many and spoke volumes about their feelings for each other.

Crispin should have pulled away, but instead, he drew her closer. This was obviously no marriage of convenience. He had only been in the colony for two weeks and was already engaged. He could not wipe the smile from his lips.

His loving action elicited a longing sigh from Gillian and many female convicts leaving the cross-shaped wooden church.

Richard and John stood to the side, watching how the couple coped.

As the young ones' conversation continued, they overheard the governor and minister chatting. It was a chilly morning, and John shivered.

He said, "Richard, is there some way we can warm the building? The wind howls through the openings, and it's positively frigid in there."

Richard's eyes glinted with delight. He knew the governor's seat was in direct line with an open orifice. Mrs Paterson sat in the pew opposite him. "Well, sir, as a matter of fact, I brought glass for the windows on the First Fleet. However, after I built the church, Major Grose would not release it for me to install the windows. The box of glass I brought from home is sitting in the Government Stores. Once promoted to major, and after he took command, Paterson wouldn't release it either."

John noticed Major William Paterson leave the church. A hooked finger beckoned the major to his side. "Paterson, I believe that you and Grose are responsible for the freezing condition of our Holy building. Therefore, I wish you to oversee the glass installation in the church windows personally. They are to be glazed by Sunday next week." He saluted the man and dismissed him without permitting him to reply.

Major Paterson was not happy. He didn't return the salute before storming off. However, his wife smiled and mouthed her thanks before following in his wake.

Richard waited until the soldier was out of earshot when he said, "For my first sermon, I used a verse from Psalm 116. It was verse 12: '*What shall I render unto the Lord for all that He has done for m*e?' Paterson happened to be sitting close to me, and I saw his face as I read the words out. My first full service was two weeks later. I believe you were here for them both, sir. We met under a canvas covering for our first Holy Communion on February 17th."

John nodded.

Richard's face broke into a smile. His single nod acknowledged John's affirmative response. He continued. "The women had been landed by then." Richard's groan was audible. "After Governor Phillip left, I fought with Major Grose about the church's construction. Instead of getting assistance to build it, Grose removed all but one of my convict servants. Despite the great hunger, even my farm workers were reassigned. A friend and I used his convicts and managed to get it done."

John looked at the reverend in horror. "But Richard, your gardens are the most productive in the colony. How did you cope? Oliver Quilpie?"

Richard shrugged with a nod. "Yes, Oliver, Annie and Max Slater. As you know, I knew Max's family from home. It's why he's always been placed in trusted positions. Mary and I did our best, but that is beside the point. I had been requested in my Royal Warrant to be the moral compass for the new community. Meeting under the trees was all well and good when it was not raining or scorching hot, but it soon became urgent that we have a dedicated church building. The church's cruciform design allows each of the three groups not to have to sit together. Hence, the convicts are in the nave as it's the largest area. They comprise nearly sixty per cent of the population." He released a long sigh. "I paid for it out of my garden produce, a donation from Oliver and my own pocket. According to the king, this building should have been one of the first erected after the most urgent structures." He huffed again. "As you know, that didn't happen." He paused as someone walked by. Once they were gone, he said, "Macarthur out in Parramatta is the man to watch. I gather Colin's letter covered much of what is occurring out there?"

John nodded. "It did. There is no urgency to pay a visit, but I dearly wish to see them again. Thank you for bringing my chair and his screed."

Richard chuckled. "They are well and keeping busy. He did as you suggested and has opened a pottery school. These are held in the mornings, and afternoons are spent educating the same students. Because Aggie is such a brilliant potter, girls can join the school. Aggie teaches them, as the boys won't come if they have to learn with girls. Macarthur and his cronies are not impressed that girls are learning to read."

John's brow creased. "I've already heard of various goings on from Colin in my absence. The missive you gave me from him filled in far more than the official report. Men I did not trust when I was first here have grown too powerful in the intervening years."

As only the immediate group remained, Richard said, "Macarthur, Paterson, my namesake George Johnson, and a few others are thorns in my side. Their wives are not much trouble as they are mostly God-fearing women. More often than not, their men are out at Parramatta or on Norfolk Island. I believe Paterson is leaving on the next vessel due to ill health. None of them like the church or anything it represents. However, I am not here to cause fights; rather, I want to see to the needs of the spiritually poor. I cannot even use the ferry to transport my produce or travel to Parramatta."

John gasped. "Seriously? I shall remedy that immediately."

Richard bowed in thanks.

John knew exactly what he meant by the aggressive nature of the competing prospective farmers. "We were only in the colony a matter of days before Captain Waterhouse and my nephew, William, were all but accosted by Macarthur and your assistant, Marsden. Both were keen to get their hands on any of the lambs from the small flock the two men brought. It was like they were fighting over shiny gold coins, such was the lustful greed in their eyes." John was stunned that Reverend Samuel Marsden was so assertive over a lamb.

Richard agreed. "Don't get me wrong, Marsden is a man of faith, but his actions do not always agree with mine. We do well when working apart." He released another long sigh of exasperation. "I was thinking of asking you if I could permanently base him in Parramatta. We need a full-time presence out there, and I hope he can take over that area. I visit when I can and stay with the Osbornes if I need to remain overnight."

John's eyebrow cocked at the unexpected revelation. Richard was so easy to get on with that for him to have a falling out with his curate could be problematic. "I'll look into it, Richard. Leave it with me. Oh, and consider using the ferry whenever you wish. I shall rescind that order immediately." He watched his friend nod and wander back inside.

John saw that only the young couple and the reverend's family remained on the church grounds. He left that morning's service with a few things added to his to-do list. A house was required for the curate if Marsden were to move to Parramatta. It would need to be constructed soon, but the Johnsons still lived in a wattle and daub shack. They needed to be better housed first. John knew he would also look into funds to repay the reverend for the church that Richard constructed at his own expense. Seventy measly pounds was all it cost. John remembered that it cost a pittance to build the large house and a new pottery workroom for Colin Osbourne for his large pottery barn. Colin had covered the building costs. Surely, the government coffers could afford that. John knew the details as he had been given full disclosure when he accepted this commission.

The military would need to be kept in line, and Macarthur's and others' relationships in the New South Wales Corps would need close monitoring. John rubbed his brow to ease the growing headache that had set in with the approach of some of the undisciplined officers. The man set his nerves on edge. John knew of their dislike of the church and wondered what had caused their animosity. He shrugged off that thought as he turned to the young couple awaiting him. "Come, young ones. We shall return home and have an easy day as there shall be no work today except for food preparation."

With Helena on his arm, Crispin walked closely behind the governor as they returned to the house a few streets away.

John's eyes perused the scenery; once clean and untouched, the Tank Stream stank. The animal dung and faeces that littered the area were disgusting. He had needed to clean his boots from the foul substances more than once, and he was determined to set up public places for people to relieve themselves. The solids could then be used for some purpose. Helena mentioned that this substance could be added to separate compost piles and used in the gardens. He would also look into that. He wondered if Helena would know how long it needed to decompose before use. That topic of conversation between the three would not even be whispered in polite circles.

Helena pointed to where such facilities would be best constructed. "Having one near the women's tent would be wonderful, sir." She also suggested a washing facility for their smalls and private things.

John had sisters, so he understood her extreme embarrassment in this discussion. He agreed that women needed some privacy for their ablutions.

~

By the time Banns had been read three times, the buzz about the union between a soldier and the governor's new gardener had died down.

The transformation of the wild woman into a beautiful and elegant lady made many gasp. None had initially recognised her as the filthy and unapproachable hellcat they knew. A reluctant respect was dragged from them all when they heard about the transformation of the heavy soil. The convicts employed to construct the fence were the source of this topic.

All knew she was still a convict but would now work at the official residence. She was given a modicum of respect as she went about her work.

Helena was no longer fearful of being accosted, but she ensured someone always knew if she was heading to Connie, the Johnsons, Government Stores or the female barracks. However, she rarely went anywhere alone. Crispin was usually by her side.

John wrote to Helena's minister, and the letter would be sent with the next ship returning to England. Once Richard related the saga of the cold church, John rectified the omission of the glass in the windows.

Major Paterson did as ordered and oversaw the project himself. One funny aside from Richard was hearing that Major Grose's wife had been the one to make the first complaint. She personally complained to Richard about the August chill.

Elizabeth Macarthur also accompanied the other women when in town. Since her husband's promotion to oversee the growing area of Parramatta, they had moved into their new dwelling suitable for the area's commanding officer.

Macarthur's large land grant from Grose rankled John. Even as the new governor, John was unable to rescind that order. The land was cleared, and cultivation had started. Although the couple and their children had moved in, Elizabeth returned to Sydney when she could.

Another change that Grose made, John changed. He moved the church times forward again to a much more civilised time of seven o'clock. This is what it had been when he departed just over four years earlier. Grose moved the service to six o'clock in the morning, in all seasons and weathers, and did not require that all attend. Therefore, only about twenty had done so. In the nine months in command, Paterson rescinded nothing. He could have done so much more but did not wish to assert himself.

John reissued Arthur Phillip's order that all convicts cease government work on Sundays to wash and tend to their cleanliness after attending church. At Parramatta, each had their own gardens and could spend the day tending to these unless there was a service on.

~

After a month in command, John felt tension building throughout the settlement. A cut-off conversation here and there or an angry look made him seek out Crispin. "Milroy, I was wondering if you had caught any more whispers of trouble? My secretary, Franklyn, has not mentioned anything to me, which is puzzling. Are there whispers?" He knew Colin could tell him what was happening in Parramatta as he had his ear to the ground out west. Here, Milroy was the only one who mentioned anything.

Crispin also noticed a lack of chatter from his fellow soldiers when he entered a room. Franklyn eyed him with suspicion, and often, Crispin caught a filthy look from the man. He replied, "Nothing, sir! However, I feel they know I am now your eyes and ears. They are clamming up around me. My friend Eric is a little concerned, as he mentioned some clashes between the two sides of the Corps, sir."

John frowned, "How so, lad?"

Crispin swallowed nervously. He replied, "There are many followers of interim acting leaders Majors Grose and Paterson, and then there are those you brought, sir. The two groups are often at a dagger point. Rarely literally, but an occasional skirmish ensues." Crispin paused until John motioned for him to continue. "The barracks has become a boxing ring when we are off duty. I am thankful I have my room here as I am well out of it. But, sir, Eric has come to blows with a few of Grose's followers. He is currently being stitched up by Mrs Cowdrey. I've not had a chance to question him too much. You see, all of them were promised land, and they are furious that your orders have halted the land grants to the Corps, not to mention the convicts will now get some if they work for it. Eric copped a beating last night." Crispin left the kitchen while Mrs Cowdrey treated Eric's bruised face. He would soon be asleep in Crispin's room, as returning to the barracks was unsafe.

John expected as much. "Is it really that bad?"

The soldier moved his weight from foot to foot nervously. "Yes and no, sir! The two groups need firm direction; however, even if you gave it, they would rebel as too many are supporters of the original Corps. They would find something else to complain about. Promising a grant for good behaviour may ease the tension. They would need to earn it rather than get it just for military service. I feel that would go a long way to clipping their wings."

John was stunned. "You think it would work, Milroy?"

Crispin shrugged. "Honestly, sir, I have no idea, but something must be done, and soon. A mutiny may occur if these unruly soldiers' behaviour is not curtailed." Crispin wanted to say something for some time, but he'd not been asked directly. Eric's black eyes and broken fingers today had made him speak up in defence of his friend. He had left him in the kitchen with instructions to use his room to sleep.

John grimaced. He flexed his fingers, then frowned. "The home-brew grog doesn't help. I'm trying to find out who is behind the main trade of this product and have asked Franklyn to try to get to the bottom of it. Most of the time, half of the soldiers seem to be either drunk or recovering from a binge. Many are sourcing the sly grog from somewhere, and all seem flush with funds. I'm stumped about what to do. Many are using the stuff as currency. I trust only a few hand-picked men, and now you know why I want you close."

John turned and looked out his office window. The town spread out before him was absolutely filthy. He released a long, exasperated sigh. "Milroy, I think you are correct. I shall draft a new decree. Grants will be few and far between and need to be earned. In a way, this eases my plans for your future in-laws. Disobedience will void any opportunity to be considered." He turned to look at the young man before him. He had come to admire his determination and knew that he was prepared to literally go to the ends of the earth to prove himself. "Bellchambers said you were looking for a girl called Bella, not Helena. Is this so?"

Crispin nodded with a smile. "Merely a nickname I have for her, sir. I know I sleep talk, and I did not want the others to find out her real name. When I first saw her, the church bells were ringing. It became my code name for her." He gave a cheeky grin and stood at ease, waiting for instruction. He received none, so he remained silent and still.

John nodded and watched his face. The lad received little training as a soldier; then again, many of the Corps had been petty criminals sent out in return for their freedom. The city of London employed this man as a lamplighter, a trusted position. Many such men worked with the Bow Street Runners to arrest felons. He did not doubt that this young lad would have done this but, in all probability, would deny any such involvement. The trained soldiers in the English military were at war. "Move Bellchambers into the small room near you. I will need two guards on hand if this blows up."

John needed to use what he had. He said, "Milroy, I had not considered this potential solution. So I give you my thanks. I shall investigate land that I can allocate." He nodded dismissively and saluted.

As Crispin left the office, he was grinning. Eric would be protected and rewarded. Earlier, they had discussed how to rein in the problems over a mug of tea.

Crispin walked softly down the hall to see if his friend was awake. Thankfully, he was not on duty until tomorrow. Hopefully, he will be well enough by then. Crispin mentioned his idea and saw Eric's eyes glint with delight.

Eric said, "You know, Cris, I think that would work. They are fighting over promises of such a reward. It may not stop all the fights, but it will go a long way to undermining the greed of the others."

~

The wedding occurred following the Sunday service just six weeks after Crispin's arrival.

Mary Johnson loaned Helena her own wedding dress. The lovely light blue gown was beautiful.

Helena had never worn something so fancy and felt honoured to be given such a privilege. The gown had a dropped neckline that showed Helena's well-rounded bust. The full skirt was filled out with four petticoats.

Crispin was in his full uniform with his tricorn hat brushed clean. The governor offered to give her away, and Helena nodded her acceptance in awe of such an honour. There were few places to go for a honeymoon, but the governor had given them two weeks off.

~

In the month since their engagement, Helena came to know the man who would soon be her husband. His respect for her and his protectiveness was enough to realise she trusted him completely. She was now looking forward to him being her husband, including all that entailed. She may not have the white picket fence or the thatched roof cottage dream, but she would have a husband who would cherish and honour her. She was eager for their wedding to occur so they could jointly discover the joys of marriage. His kisses stirred something deep within her that made her want more.

Mary suggested they use a small one-room cottage that had belonged to their friends Oliver and Annie Quilpie while they helped build the church. Annie had served her time, and the pair had returned to England. She was the girl the governor had mentioned earlier, she was now a titled lady. Until recently, the Marsdens had occupied the cottage.

Like Crispin, Oliver came hunting for his lady love. He arrived in the *Kitty*, along with the food he brought for the starving settlement. They married shortly after his arrival, and Richard built the church with Max and Oliver's assistance.

When the Quilpies, or Bowbelles as was their title, returned home a year ago, they gifted Richard their cottage. It was still fully furnished, and up until recently, the Marsdens had lived there.

They had recently moved to a hastily constructed cottage at Parramatta. Samuel Marsden still had occasional duties in Sydney, but most of his work would now be undertaken in the western settlement.

Eric and Gillian stood on either side of the aisle and waited for the governor to bring Helena to Crispin's side.

Crispin had not seen his fiancée earlier in the day and was unaware that Gillian, Mrs Cowdrey and Mary Johnson had dressed her hair in the latest fashion, and it was sprinkled with tiny posies of spring flowers. His jaw dropped open when he saw her. She was stunning. Her face was aglow with happiness, and she would soon be all his.

Only ten people were in the large wooden church to witness the union.

Richard began the words of the wedding ceremony. This was his first proper marriage service in the new church. Most previous unions had been done without the Banns being read. They were, in essence, Special Licence weddings issued by the official leader. Most were convict marriages. A few unions occurred between a member of the Corps and a convict.

Richard knew this couple had faith of sorts but had not had the opportunity to have a long conversation with either of them. Each mentioned this to him but confessed they had not had much opportunity to discuss them privately. From today, they will have two weeks as they dine with them while on their honeymoon. Richard took a deep breath and, with a smile, pronounced them man and wife.

They signed the register: Crispin with an elegant script and Helena with her printed name. The governor and then Eric signed as witnesses.

When Crispin emerged from the church, he did what he had wanted to do for quite some time. He knew now that Helena would not pull away from him, so he drew her into his arms and gave her a long, deep, passionate kiss.

Unbeknownst to him, many from his regiment were watching. They cheered and whistled at them, which drew others, and they were applauded by many. They were a handsome couple.

Amidst the well-wishers were soldiers who had roughed up Eric. Some stood back with their arms folded. They had no idea that the governor had already drafted his plan for reward-based land allocations, but he had only run the draft by Crispin and Eric rather than his scribe, Franklyn. For some reason, the governor only discussed this with the two young guards.

John meandered back to Government House with Eric as his security guard. On days like this, he missed the noise of his childhood. He almost felt jealous of Helena when she mentioned she was part of a large family. His life with his family had been similar to hers. His brothers, William, George, James, and Archie, got along well. As did Sarah Mary, Agnes, Janet, and Margaret. When young, all the children shared big beds to keep warm. Her description of her home had brought it all back to him.

John had no idea when a ship or whaler would come and take the mail and despatches back to England. In the meantime, he kept writing. He missed being able to head off on exploration trips, but roughing it was getting a little beyond him.

He became used to the deck not rocking beneath his feet and being stranded behind a desk pushing paperwork; knowing he had tough decisions to make was decidedly unpleasant. He had yet to take a trip to Parramatta, but that could wait. He had replied to Colin's missive with a long and news screed.

As he approached the house, two men were waiting for him. George Bass and Matthew Flinders had come to relieve his boredom and discuss plans for their adventure later that week.

John's face broke into a beaming grin. He dismissed Eric with a nod and ushered his friends indoors.

Their tiny vessel was so small that John was almost afraid to permit them to journey far from shore. The *Tom Thumb* was so flimsy that only three men could fit into it. They planned to travel south to explore Botany Bay and up the river, then further upstream than the colonists had previously done.

John was jealous but knew that he could not join them. William Martin was the privileged crewman chosen for this expedition. He was George's navy servant. John was keen to share information about their journey and suggested what they should take. Having made similar journeys only eight years before, he knew what they would need. He wondered what the future would bring.

Chapter 8   Back Stabbing Scoundrels

$\mathcal{W}$hile the nuptials were celebrated in Sydney, a small group of men gathered in Parramatta while the governor was occupied.

Murmurs of unhappiness were already afoot, as the gathering men knew the new governor would not bend to their will. They wondered what his first move would be to curtail their money-making activities. They were sure there would be a loophole they had overlooked that would circumvent his efforts to thwart them.

In the four years since Governor Phillip sailed away, they had skilfully manipulated things so their cronies would benefit greatly. This was not only due to vast grants of precious arable land but also to producing grain and, therefore, since Thomas Webb's return, the manufacture of rum.

Due to the shortage of actual coinage, this substance had become the currency of the settlement. Although bartering was still usual, wages and goods were paid with this beverage. This select group of men from the New South Wales Corps were the central figures in this venture.

They brewed liquid gold.

Before Arthur Phillip returned to England, the government controlled all food supplies, convict labour allocation, the military, and land grants.

Civil magistrates existed, which Grose abolished as soon as Phillip departed. In essence, Grose took military control of what Arthur Phillip had founded.

In those intervening four years, Grose and those who followed him undermined not only the king's proclamation but also the religious authority and guidance of Reverend Richard Johnson. Grose flouted his instructions and sided with this group of ne'er-do-well soldiers who were out to line their own pockets.

Once Grose returned to England ill, newly promoted Major Paterson did nothing to rescind the orders when he took control. However, Paterson had tried to rein in the rum.

Thomas Webb, a seaman on the First Fleet, returned to England with

John Hunter to obtain back pay for himself and his brother Robert, who was also a seaman on that fated final cruise of the *Sirius*. When Thomas returned to the colony on the *Bellona* in 1792, just three years before Hunter's arrival, Thomas brought goods-in-kind instead of coinage. Amongst his possessions was a small spirit still.

He and his brother, Robert, were later joined by a third brother, Joseph, and a nephew, James. They set to work distilling some of their local grain into rum.

For the sale of the grain to Government Stores, they would only receive ten shillings per bushel from the commissary. From one bushel of wheat, Robert obtained nearly five quarts of spirit, which he sold or paid in exchange for labour at five and six shillings per quart. This lucrative and entirely legal loophole began a trend.

The small rum still was studied, enlarged and duplicated many times. Although grain was still scarce, the diabolical spiritous liquid was potent and addictive.

Thomas was granted land in Liberty Plains, but he and Robert obtained far better land on the Hawkesbury River, with much more fertile soil. They named their land Webb's Creek.

Thomas became a thorn in the flesh of the Corps as he sided with the reverend and complained against the unfair allocation of goods. The flogging of his very expectant wife for innocently purchasing a pair of stolen shoes for him and her subsequent treatment caused the delivery of a dead child two days later.

Grose was blamed, and Thomas's ire was raised.

This had much to do with Thomas's anger towards this exclusive group of men. Had the original magistrates still been in charge of the law, Catherine Webb would have been held captive for a week and then released, and their child probably would have lived. Her punishment had been vastly unjust, and Thomas had a right to be angry at them. They had abused his kindness and were now profiting from him.

The group now gathered were pleased that Thomas had died earlier that year. He had been caught up in a skirmish with some Indigenous warriors, and a fight ensued over him clearing his new grant at Webb's Creek.

Although they felt slightly sorry for the man, he was a festering sore that was now gone. His brother Robert was much more compliant. He was no farmer but a seaman at heart. They doubted he would stay in the settlement, but for the moment, he was producing the grain they needed to distil their rum.

Robert took over Thomas's farm, and it produced a bounteous crop on the lush, fertile river flat.

With the promise of another good harvest, the group met in the secluded garden to plot and plan their future actions.

Making an effort to keep their voices low, they chatted. "How are we to curtail the intentions of this honourable governor? We all know him as a pious, goody-two-shoes, and I fully expect that he will reinstate the magistrates sooner rather than later."

Another voice answered, "And what do we do about the sale of our booze? Do you think he'll crack down on that too?"

A third indignant voice said, "It seems all my hard work at looking after our own chaps will be undermined by Hunter. I know the man, and he can't be bought. He won't condone our activities or the rum; we'll have to send our stills underground. We should start to do that now." He groaned with frustration.

Not wishing to be left out, a new voice said, "Won't that be dangerous, Frank? I thought we had that all in hand with Nate in charge in town?"

A bevy of "Shhh's" were heard.

"No names are to be used, chaps. We need to keep our heads down and continue as best we can. I heard from our friend in town that Hunter even wishes to permit convicts to get land grants once their terms have expired, but he's not seen any document about that yet."

Gasps of horror circled the group.

The six men each had an empty glass in their hands.

One said, "Damn him! What about us?"

Shoulders shrugged.

No one had an answer.

The first man who had spoken said, "Let's taste this batch. It smelled good when I bottled it." He had actually imbibed freely.

The small two-tone brown and cream ceramic flagon was unstoppered, and amber liquid was poured into each glass.

Each took a sip; some swore, a few gasped, and all ended by agreeing it was a good brew.

Their test was to see if the fiery spirit was strong enough to ignite unheated. It did.

A full glass, drunk neat, would probably kill. This distilled grain would make them a tidy sum if it were not confiscated. Diluted for sale, it would bring in a fortune.

Frank released a long "Ahh!"

The lead man, who was hosting the meeting in his garden, said, "If we can keep Robert Webb onside, then we should have access to enough grain to keep us going for a while. He's still got his still working full-time. If there is not enough for us, we will need to seek grain from some other farmers. That is a problem for the future."

Another added, "Well, I wouldn't like to try to oppose us. Hunter won't know what hit him."

Guffaws and laughs followed. "His hands are tied already."

~

With two delightful weeks ahead of them, Crispin opened the small cottage door for his new bride, then turned, carried her over the threshold, and placed her down carefully. They had walked the short distance from the church to their honeymoon abode.

Mary Johnson invited them for dinner that night, and they willingly accepted, leaving them many hours to enjoy the new delights of marriage. As neither had indulged in this pleasure, both were nervous. The big bed with a feather mattress stood to one side of the room, and it was impossible to miss.

The cooking facilities were a cast iron hob stove. Behind it was an open fireplace that had obviously served as the cooking area. There was a small table, and four chairs were tucked neatly around it. Two lamps sat in the middle of this. There was no wardrobe but a large shelf and a row of brass hooks lined one wall.

As the door shut, Crispin dropped Helena's hand and put his hands on her hips. "Be assured that I love you with all my heart, but having said that, I will still hold to my promise. I will not touch you unless you instigate it. I love you too well ever to force you. You are my beautiful Helena, my Bella. It was by that nickname that I thought of you while I hunted high and low for you."

Helena gave him a micro frown, "Why Bella?" She turned in his arms and placed her hands on his chest. She was as nervous as he was but did not wish to leave his side. Her father's pet name for her was Nella.

Crispin dropped a feather-light kiss on her upturned lips. He slid his hands around her tiny waist and said, "Belle means beautiful, but the bells rang when I first saw you. I stood gazing at you for some time before I woke you. On the way here, no one would realise I was dreaming of you if I called your name while I slept. I schooled myself not to think of you by your name."

Helena had no idea his affection for her was that deep. "You were protecting me even in your dreams?"

He nodded. He wished to sweep her into his arms, carry her to their bed, and consummate their union.

He swallowed nervously. His Adam's apple bobbled as he did so. As this was at eye level with Helena, she realised how he felt. She slid her arms around his neck and drew his head down for a deep kiss.

With no one to visit them and little chance of interruption, Crispin's arms tightened around her. Hopefully, her action would begin a beautiful afternoon for them both.

She pulled away slightly and said, "Husband, mine; I meant it when I said 'Yes' to everything, Crispin. I also mean the marriage bed."

He gasped with delight. "Sure?"

She nodded, continuing, "Oh, don't get me wrong, I'm as scared as heck, but I know you won't intentionally hurt or force me. Mary has told me there would be some pain initially, but if you can stay still for a bit, it will ease quickly. I'm not exactly sure what she means, but… well… I grew up on a farm and know what horses and cows do, so I understand." She flushed scarlet and hid her face in his chest.

Crispin's voice was gravelly with desire. "You're really sure?"

She nodded and lifted her lips for another delightful kiss.

It was not long before the two quickly unclad bodies tumbled onto the coverlet of the bed.

Although they had hours ahead of them, Crispin was nearly exploding with desire. Eric had taken him aside and explained how to pleasure a woman. Crispin was wide-eyed with anticipation. He knew of Eric's carousing ways and was teased mercilessly when he admitted to him on the way out that he had not indulged in such wanton activities.

Eric had actually respected Crispin's abstinence but had not said so until last night. The night before the wedding, the two men had found a quiet spot under a big tree at the back of Government House, and in the dark, Eric gave his friend a detailed lesson on how to ensure Helena would enjoy their union.

Less than half an hour after they entered the cottage, they lay entwined under the blankets.

The first time had been quick but a joy for them both.

Helena's pain had been fleeting.

He realised that her words about being untouched were indeed true.

Crispin discovered that holding a naked nubile female clasped in his arms, one joining would not be enough. He dared not abuse the incredible privilege of using her feminine form to slake his pent-up desires, but when she felt him come to life again, it was she who turned to him.

Much giggling, kissing, and sighs of delight ensued from their bed for the following two weeks.

Mary had given Helena instructions on washing with warm water afterwards, and Eric had told Crispin not to use the carbolic soap to cleanse himself below the waist as she would pay with a rash and great pain. His abstinence from soap below the trouser line would mean she would probably welcome his attention more. That was enough of a reason for Crispin to listen. He had the lye soap in his eyes often enough to know how much it burned.

In a very short time, they became comfortable seeing each other unclothed. Mary had loaned Helena her hip bath, and bathing each other was a delightful activity they enjoyed. By the time their honeymoon was over, the newlyweds were relaxing into their married state. The topic of children had yet to be raised, and neither had even thought that far ahead.

~

On the last day of their two-week break, Helena woke at dawn to the laughter of a kookaburra outside their window. Her dreams were still on her mind, and she turned to look at her husband's sleeping form in the dim light.

She had forgotten about her monthly flow and had meant to get her bundle from Gillian's room to take with her. She realised she was due three days ago, and her flow had not come.

Crispin awoke somewhat chilled to see her sitting with her back to him. "My Bella, is something wrong?"

He slid a hand around her svelte form. Her skin was as smooth as silk and was warm and inviting. He drew her down beside him and into his arms.

Noticing her worried expression, he asked again, "Helena, what's wrong?" He did not expect her to burst into tears and cling to him.

He cradled her tightly. His morning desire faded as she clung to him and wept. He knew she would reveal her distress if he gave her time, so he caressed her hair and held her close.

After a few moments, she said, "I'm scared, Cris, deathly scared." She gave a few more sobs and explained. "I am late for my flow and... and..."

She buried her head on his shoulder again.

She mumbled something that he thought sounded like "child."

He held her until he realised she had said, "With child."

Pushing her away slightly, he gazed into her face. "Did you say you could be having a baby?"

She nodded dejectedly.

Crispin collapsed onto his pillow, taking her with him. "Sweetie, that is wonderful. Why the worry?"

She was now snuggling up to him. "I'm scared, Cris, scared silly. Women die in childbirth, and we've only just got married and... I don't want to die when I've just found you." Her weeping started again.

Crispin had not expected this reaction. They had given conception a more than likely chance to occur over the last two weeks. He realised that their omission in discussing a family was now dire. He presumed she would be as thrilled as he was. He could do nothing but hold her and hope to bring her comfort.

He kissed her forehead as she lay in his arms. "My sweet, we will face this together, but with Mrs Cowdrey and Mary Johnson to assist and a wonderful doctor with Dr Balmain at the hospital, I am sure you will be fine. I love you no matter what. You know that."

She lifted her tear-stained face to his and said, "Even when I'm fat and ugly?" A hint of a smile tipped her lips.

Crispin kissed her. "Especially then, as you will be carrying my baby."

She asked softly, "So you'll be with me when the child comes? I will need you with me, Cris. I am not going to be able to cope without you. I know what Mama went through. I delivered some of hers with Papa's help."

"Of course, I'll be there if you want me to." His stomach crashed through the soles of his feet. He had no desire to be at the birth with her, but he could see that she was scared already, and her condition was only suspected. "Sweet Bella, I suggest that when we rise, we seek out Mary and have a long chat with her about childbirth, babies, and so on."

Her head nodded against his chest. "So you're not upset?"

Crispin moved so that he could look her in the face. "Oh, cripes, no! I'm delighted, absolutely delighted. I never had brothers or sisters, so I've not had much to do with children. I would love to be a father, and you will make a great mum."

Helena's glassy eyes returned his gaze. "You think so? You think we will manage?"

He chuckled. "I have a feeling we will be inundated with offers of assistance. Maybe one of Mary Johnson's students will come and help babysit."

Helena slipped her leg over his and drew him close. His body's automatic response to her action made her give a watery giggle. "I forgot to say good morning, husband mine."

Crispin growled hungrily and flipped her onto her back.

Her arms snaked around his neck, and she drew him down to kiss him. All her earlier fears were gone.

An hour later, they emerged and went to the Johnsons' cottage.

Mary was in the garden and gave them a cheery hello.

Helena had learned to love this dear lady, and in the two weeks they had lived next door to them, they had drawn close. She had no hesitation in bringing up the discussion of children with her.

She only had to mention that she needed to talk, and Mary said, "Let's go inside and have a nice cup of tea, dear. Crispin, this involves you too, so lead the way, lad. Abaroo has the children, so we won't be disturbed. Richard is preparing for tomorrow's service at the church."

~

John Hunter attended divine services and was once again on his way back to Government House. He saw his Colonial Secretary catch his eye, and he beckoned him over.

The newlyweds were due to return tomorrow. He was unsurprised that they came into church late and left early, so they were not inundated with well-wishers or snide innuendos. He found he missed their presence in the house. Helena's humming or whistling as she worked floated through to his office.

London had assigned Captain David Collins to be his Colonial Secretary, and John liked him. David stood waiting for him.

He was thrilled he wouldn't need to return to the oppressive house immediately. John nodded. "Walk with me, David. I don't feel like returning home alone just yet."

David fell into step with his friend. "Governor, I was wondering if you had a moment or two to spare?"

John gave him a micro-frown. "Is this work or pleasure?"

David grimaced. He knew his boss was a stickler for keeping the Sabbath. "Work; sorry, sir, but I want it off the record."

John's eyebrows knitted. "Ahh, then maybe we should return to the house after all. However, it's such a lovely day that we shall sit in my new garden."

The pair chatted about the weather as they walked up the hill to

Government House. They commonly had their heads together over one or more problems in the colony.

Rather than enter by the main door, John skirted the building and opened the back gate into the garden.

Crispin and Eric had installed a bench seat overlooking the tilled garden beds.

A blush of green sprouted through the straw Helena had placed over her planted seeds and seedlings. Turnips, parsnips, beans, and peas were already up, and other vegetables were germinating. John loved watching the new growth appear, and he would regularly be found sitting in the spring sun, drinking his tea while watching Helena water the garden. As a wedding present for her, he had Richard pot a blush pink rose bush in homage to her maiden name. It was awaiting her return. She could plant it where she wished, and he hoped she would like it.

He ushered his friend to take a seat. To break the ice, he asked, "Dare I ask how the children are? I didn't see them in church this morning."

David's brow wrinkled. For the governor to ask about his two illegitimate children was a bit of a backhander. He was not quite sure how much to say.

John noted his hesitation. "I ask with genuine interest, David. We are off duty, and we rarely have time to chat personally. You know I prefer unions to be legalised, but with a living wife in England, you can't do that. You mentioned that you confessed to Maria about Nancy's presence in your life and that you have two children with Nancy. I am interested in their well-being as they exist virtually under my nose."

David sighed. "Oh, sorry! I'm a little on edge as I've had another letter from Maria begging me to return home. She has her family and an ailing mother, and I have my work. However, as to the children and Nancy, they are well, thank you. Sir, I must return to Maria sooner rather than leave it much longer. I have been gone nine years, sir."

David took a breath and blew out his cheeks. His eyes flicked around, checking that no one was within hearing distance. "Sir, this is not about my unusual family structure but something I have heard."

He saw John's eyebrow flick with interest, so he expanded his comment. "Two weeks ago, a small group of the Corps met at a private house in the Parramatta area. I have no idea who was there or what was discussed, but in the years of your absence, these men have been, let's call them, the power pack. I foresee trouble ahead, and forewarned is forearmed."

John's lips pursed. "I have been here, what, six weeks? I'm surprised that the 'you-know-who's' of the colony waited that long to unsheathe their daggers. I have few around me whom I can trust, and David, you are one of them. I have two of my security detail who are not here to feather their nests, so I trust them too, and the Johnsons, of course. In my absence, the clergy couple have been on the end of Grose and Paterson's ire, and I have set out to correct those errors. Hence, the glass is now in the windows of the church." John chuckled. "Did you see Paterson's face when I ordered him to oversee the installation? He was not pleased, although his wife thanked me profusely the following Sunday. She had been complaining to him since the church opened." John's deep chuckle was heard again. His light blue eyes glinted with delight in the spring sunshine. "He's not going to like my idea of permitting the emancipated convict to choose if they wish to return home or get a land grant here and farm. However, I feel most will wish to remain. A decision must be made soon, as many are nearing the end of their sentences."

David grimaced a smile. "In a way, I feel for Paterson, sir, as he was twisted around the fingers of his subordinates. Everything snowballed once he promoted Macarthur to lieutenant, making him the public works inspector at Parramatta. In 1793, the crops all but failed. The Corps nearly mutinied then as Grose and Paterson followed Arthur Phillip's direction of equal rations for all. The Corps objected, and Grose relented and doubled their rations for the Corps but not the convicts. The felons were toiling on the farms while the Corps watched leisurely." He sighed, and John saw his head shake in disgust.

David sighed again, then continued. "As you know, Grose is a staunch military man who could not see beyond the red coats, and he quickly abolished the civilian courts. Seeking someone to oversee the rules, he promoted Captain Foveaux to oversee the justice in the settlements, but Macarthur is at the core."

John had been filled in before about this by Colin, but he had not had a chance to have such a private conversation with David before today. One or other of his security detail had always been within earshot. Although the Colonial Secretary had been invited for meals, the walls were thin, and they couldn't ensure that no one overheard them. John inhaled, then released a long sigh. He said, "Arthur Phillip trusted Grose. He saw him as unassertive, affable, and easy-going. Things were going quite well when Arthur left, and he presumed he could handle taking control." John stretched his neck. His muscles were tight, and his head was beginning to throb. "Grrr, why do people have to be so greedy? Through Helena, I have learned that many of these girls who have been sent here have been treated horrifically. I suppose your lady friend has told you similar stories?"

David nodded, but he didn't elaborate.

John sighed again. "David, you have read my draft announcement. Do you think it will do anything to curtail the issues?" John rubbed his temples. If only he had the answer, the issue would not be solved easily.

David sat staring at his dirty fingernails. He should have cleaned them before church. His dark eyebrows knitted much as John's had a short while ago. Like John, he had no idea how to clean up the town. "It's a start, but quite honestly, sir, I do not believe it will make a great deal of difference. This mercenary group are in for the long haul. They have got their teeth into the land and won't easily release it."

The two men sat in silence for some time. Both were deep in thought.

An idea occurred to David. He said, "Privies, sir. We need more public privies and more cesspits. On the way to church this morning, I saw two women lift their skirts and squat beside the path. The men are worse; they don't even move off the carriageways. Excrement is everywhere, fouling the Tank Stream where the drinking water comes from."

John's eyes darted to David's. "It stinks, doesn't it? I wonder if that is why there are bouts of illness. William Balmain and George Bass are concerned that the water is filthy when the rains flush the streets." He shuddered. "To think that we could be drinking that filthy water horrifies me."

David agreed. "The existing cesspit is adequate only if you are near the gardens. With so many people now in town, duplication of the facilities is needed. If we start doing things for the majority, it will get them onside. The convicts outnumber the military three to one. If you side with the underdog, you may have some sway over the Corps in the long run. Many convicts' terms are drawing to a close, and soon, they will become emancipated. We need a plan for them, sir. In short, you need to butter up the masses."

John smiled. "And so we return to the issue of Land Grants for the hard workers. I think I shall present my ideas sooner rather than later. I will wait until next week, as I feel I may need my security detail at full strength when the announcement is made. I will have Nate Franklyn post a notice. Milroy returns from his honeymoon tomorrow. I gave the lad two weeks off."

David chuckled. "I can't believe his girl was Helena the Hellcat, sir. She fought off every man who came near her. Do you know that her fingernails were cut to a point, and she would scratch, bite, kick, and scream if a man so much as touched her?"

John shook his head. Distraught at what he had witnessed when he had first seen her weeks ago. "I am one of nine children, David. I have sisters, and I would hate to know that lecherous men are accosting them. The first time I saw her, she fought off two convicts trying to drag her into the bushes. She was on her way to work, minding her own business. I was standing at my upstairs bedroom window and saw the entire thing. I had no idea that young Milroy came here looking for her."

He shook his head again. "Did you know she worked for his aunt in London? That's how they met."

"No sir, I heard he came looking for a girl. He had been calling out her name as Bella. Eric told me that Milroy had mentioned his quest *en route*."

John chuckled. "Milroy told me the name change was because he knew he talked in his sleep. He schooled himself to think of her by his nickname for her. I knew he was looking for someone, but didn't know who."

David roared with laughter, "Devious but wise. Other than Eric, few believed that she was real."

John chuckled quietly. "She is. Milroy found her at my kitchen door, but I told you about that. It's why she's now my gardener and knows her stuff. Since Henry Dodd died in 1791, we have no real gardeners other than our reverend gentleman. Oh, I should mention I have invited her family out here and will grant them a farm on condition they teach others to work the land. It's one of the things I wanted to talk to you about. Please find land for them to teach farming. A government farm school of sorts. I'm amazed at how she has conditioned the soil in just a matter of weeks. If you saw the rock-hard, compacted dirt the men dug over on day one, compare it to the sweet-smelling dirt it is now; it's hard to believe it's the same soil. Her father taught her well."

John grinned. "She hasn't seen the finished new fence yet."

David chuckled. "And so, we get back to land again. May I suggest you hold off on an actual grant for her father, but get him working for us for a few years? It will look as though he earned it. Because then we can use convicts to clear the land and prepare the virgin dirt. Maybe you could even build an abode for the family with extra rooms. Once they have proven their worth, sign it over as a reward for services rendered. It will inspire others to do likewise. Paterson allocated more than four thousand acres in the nine months he was in the role. I'm not sure a few more acres will make much difference. Are you serious about also granting land to emancipists?"

"I am, David." John smiled. "But I do like the way you think. Consider it done. However, I would like a farm ready for the Rosedales to start educating others when they arrive. So please, once the land is found, get on with the convict teams clearing it and set about constructing a sizeable abode, as not only do they have a large family, but students will need rooms to stay in. I plan to stay there on my visits as Phillip's old place in Parramatta is ready to fall down. The Rosedales have thirteen children with them at last count."

A thought occurred to him. "David, I am determined to protect the women here even if they don't wish to be. I want you to arrange building married quarter cottages, as I will encourage women to marry the men they are liaising with. I realise you cannot marry the mother of your children, but others are unwed. They would only be small wattle and daub abodes like Johnson's guest cottage, but it gives the couples a huge start compared to life at home."

David grinned. "I love that idea, sir."

They saw the staff returning, and David said, "Sir, I meant what I said about needing to return home soon. I have been absent from Maria for far too long."

John's head swivelled sharply. "Home for how long?"

David shrugged. "Considering everything, she still wants me back."

Their private speech was over for the day as Mrs Peach, Mrs Cowdrey, Gillian, and Eric returned from church. They were now entering the back gate.

Mrs Peach saw them and said, "Stay there, sirs; I shall get Gillian to bring out a tea tray."

John smiled. "I freely admit, sometimes it's nice having staff to pander to my whims. However, I am very unused to having females around me at all. These four seem to stay out of my way, so we cope well enough. I have made a rule that no one is to leave their rooms in their night attire. Even my mother and my numerous sisters did not walk around our house like that."

Chapter 9   New Beginnings, Old Threats

$\mathcal{B}$y the time Crispin and Helena had been married for three months, they had many long talks with Mary Johnson about babies. Helena confirmed she was increasing when she woke one morning and needed to be sick.

Christmas had been and gone, and the summer heat was draining.

Crispin's attentiveness was astounding. Helena had no doubts about her deep feelings for him, and Crispin made sure to tell her every day how much he adored her. If he had to leave for an overnight tour with the governor, the deep kisses he gave her before his departure made him wish it was nighttime and they could return to bed.

Mary had told them they could continue their enjoyable marital activities as they were safe. Helena's need for him would probably increase as her condition progressed. The young couple's astonished faces made her chuckle. Helena discovered Mary was correct and enjoyed such attention as often as Crispin wished. He was everything she could have hoped for in a husband, and she was glad she had fought to keep herself for him. Helena had not visited Parramatta, so she had not met Colin and Aggie Osborne. However, Crispin told her about this lovely couple the governor had befriended on his first visit. Aggie was only a couple of years older than Helena.

On one of Governor Hunter's now regular overnight trips to Parramatta, Helena missed Crispin's absence so much that she snuck into her old top bunk in Gillian's room just down the hall. The girls greeted each other with a hug and climbed into their respective bunks. Rather than sleep, Gillian wished to chat. "Helena, I've been bursting to tell you, but I have not had a moment to do so today. Eric has asked to court me. What do you think?"

Helena yawned. Maybe moving in here was not such a good idea after all. She replied drowsily, "I think it's great, Gillian. He's a good man, and the governor doesn't mind us still working if we are married, so we can convert this room into a double, and you can both stay here."

Gillian realised her friend was tired but chattered on.

Helena interrupted her. Other than Mary Johnson, they had not told anyone about the baby, and she thought now as good a time as any to let her know. "Gill, I might need you to do a bit of the watering over winter if it's needed. I'm not going to be able to get around much." The squeal of delight from the bottom bunk made Helena chuckle.

"You're having a baby? That's wonderful!" Gillian threw back her bedclothes, jumped out, and reached up to hug Helena. "I'm so thrilled, Helena, I truly am. I just didn't want one before I married. I love babies and delivered a few on the ship here."

Helena had, too, and that's what made her so fearful. She knew exactly what was ahead of her and was not looking forward to it. "Thanks, Gill. We're pleased, too, but scared as well. Now I really must get some sleep. Sorry!" The room soon quieted, but alas, Helena lay awake, listening to the sounds of the night. She must have dozed off, but she started awake. Something had fallen, and the noise had disturbed her. She was about to turn over when she heard unfamiliar male voices. She had left the door ajar to let in some air.

A male voice said, "Damn it! She should have been in her room. Where could she have gone?"

Another man replied, "Maybe she went with them to Parramatta?"

Helena slipped off the top bunk and closed their door quietly. She had an idea for their safety. There was no lock on their door, as they had never needed one. She crouched beside Gillian, and with a hand over her mouth, she shook her awake. "Shh, men have broken in, and we need to hide. Make your bed and be quick."

Gillian's head nodded under her hand. The governor ordered a wardrobe to be built in each room, and the large upright wardrobes were delivered two weeks ago. The dark timber cupboard blended into the back corner of the room, making it all but invisible. As both the girls were slim, the narrow wardrobe in Gillian's room would fit them in at a squeeze.

Hastily making their beds, they had just closed the wardrobe as their bedroom door was pushed open. A deep, easily recognisable voice said, "Damn, they are not here either. They must have both gone with the governor. Look, the beds are made. I was gonna make the whore pay for these scars on my back."

Another replied, "I wonder why the governor would take two women with him?"

The guttural laugh of a third said, "Bed warmers, of course. Milroy's pretty woman is just to my taste; it's why I tried for her before. I thought she'd scrub up okay. The other wench has probably been warming the governor's bed for some time. She may even be up in his room now. He must like them young. I would not mind a piece of her, either. Maybe we should check upstairs."

Helena recognised the speaker as one of the two men who had attacked her. The next voice, she also knew well, as he had tried for her the day before the attack.

He replied, "Bellchambers would not like it if someone stepped in on his property. He's asked permission to court the girl, so I don't think it will be the governor's bed she's been warming." This man was the second convict who attacked Helena while the governor watched.

He continued, "I want a bit of the hellcat, too. She owes me for my scars as well."

The first man said, "Well, they ain't here anyway, so let's scarper. Might try the women's quarters and get a bit of relief while the gov is out of town. George is on duty tonight, so he'll let us in. He might even join us. Gotta get some loving from somewhere. Can't hump Helena, so any other skirt will have to do."

The fourth man, who had not spoken much, said, "I can't wait that long. I got a boner already." He uttered a groan. "Gonna palm myself. Been hanging out for tonight." The door banged but didn't catch and swung partially open again. The girls heard footsteps fading away. But had they all gone?

Both girls hardly dared to breathe. If Helena had not been in Gillian's room, both would have been molested. She felt Gillian draw a breath to speak, and Helena placed a hand over her lips again. They remained frozen in their uncomfortable hiding place.

A few moments later, they realised that one of the men remained.

From the noises Helena heard, she realised he was manually relieving himself as he said he would. If they had made a sound, they would have been caught and probably violated. After a grunt and a long sigh of release from pleasuring himself, he finally left. His steps were eventually heard retreating.

The girls remained still. They waited for over an hour, and Gillian was shaking with fear. Finally, they opened the wardrobe door and saw the empty room. Rather than remain inside, they grabbed their shawls, blankets from their bunks, and a pillow, then made straight for Mrs Cowdrey's room. This was off the kitchen at the other end of the house. Mrs Peach was in the adjoining room. They didn't knock but silently pushed open the door. The girls snuck into the housekeeper's room and curled up on the floor on the far side of her bed. They dared not wake her. They would explain in the morning.

~

Dawn came all too soon for the girls. Mrs Cowdrey saw them asleep on her floor, and rather than be cranky, she realised something had happened overnight. For some reason, they had sought refuge in her room. She gently stroked their cheeks to wake them up.

Two pairs of bleary blue eyes opened, and they sat up.

Helena said, "Oh, Mrs Cowdrey, we are so sorry. But we could not stay in our room."

Gillian butted in and said, "At least four men broke in last night, Mrs Cowdrey, and if Helena had not been lonely, we both would have been done over good. She woke me, and we hid in the wardrobe." She spoke, then sobbed as their narrow escape hit home.

Virginia Cowdrey's hair hung down to her waist. Neither girl had ever seen her in a state that was not immaculate. Her night-rail was calico, the same as theirs, but she had added some frills to the hem to lengthen it. She asked, "Do you mean men have broken into the governor's house, and they wanted to violate you both?" The girls nodded.

The lady said, "Well, I never! We must find out how they got in and who they were. I don't suppose you recognised any of their voices."

Helena nodded. "Two were the men who accosted me, and I know they have two close friends. I don't know their names, but I know their faces. One had tried it on with me the day before." The girls were still on the floor, huddled behind the bed. The happenings of the evening could have resulted in a vastly different morning. Thankfully, the governor and his guards would return on the river ferry that afternoon.

Mrs Cowdrey frowned. She stood and grabbed her dressing gown. "Stay here, and I'll make sure the doors are closed. I shall have locks installed later today to ensure this will not happen again."

The girls remained huddled together under their blankets until they heard footsteps approaching. They scrambled up and hid behind the door.

Mrs Cowdrey entered and said, "The back door was ajar, and I placed a chair under the door handle. The guards are at the front door, but we shall ensure this never occurs again." She approached the girls, gathering them in a big hug. "I have checked the house, and it's empty. Go and change, girls. I shall tell Mrs Peach what occurred, but I want you both to stay inside until the governor returns today." The girls nodded willingly. They knew the back gate had no lock, so the garden was not secure.

Virginia Cowdrey released them from her hug and held the door open for them to leave. Her heartbeat was elevated, and when she closed the door, she bent over and took a few deep breaths. Memories of a similar situation flooded over her. Her husband had been away, and she had been unable to fight off the two attackers. That was why she volunteered for this job. She presumed she would be safe here. Only her friend Priscilla Peach knew what had occurred. Their husbands had been killed in a skirmish that week. Virginia was pleased that he had never known what had happened to her. She had been so thankful for that. She realised she was shaking, yet she knew she needed to comfort the girls. She stood up, forced herself to dress, and face the new day with another false smile. Sometimes, she hated men. Her husband had come on the First Fleet trip, and she had joined him later on the *Kitty*. She had met John Hunter before he had returned to London and liked him. Now widowed, she applied to be the housekeeper here. Her offer was willingly accepted by the Colonial Secretary. Her friend was the new cook, and they were reasonably safe there. Priscilla Peach was also a widow. Neither had children. Now dressed, the girls were in the kitchen when she joined them. The four women sat around the table discussing the invasion. Unsure of what to do, they drank tea while the barley porridge cooked. None dared to venture outdoors.

After breakfast, they got on with the chores of the day inside. The hours dragged by until they heard the governor's voice at the front door.

Mrs Cowdrey had not told the guards about the invasion but ensured they remained attentive and in situ. Helena heard Crispin's voice and flew from the kitchen into his arms.

John saw the distress on her face and noticed that Gillian was much the same. Eric held his hand out to her, and she walked straight to him.

John asked, "Mrs Cowdrey, what has occurred? Why are they upset?"

The housekeeper beckoned the three men into the kitchen, away from the soldiers at the front door. On entry, she turned and said, "Sir, we had a break-in last night, and only Helena's quick thinking saved the girls from… well, you can imagine what could have occurred." She filled them in on what had happened. Everyone saw Eric slip his arm around Gillian. She clung to him as Helena was doing to Crispin.

Crispin was horrified. "Sweetheart, how did you know? Why were you in Gill's room and not ours? Are you and our baby safe?"

Helena nodded but shrugged. "I missed you, so I thought I'd return to my old bunk while you were away. I'm glad I did."

John ground his teeth in anger as he listened to the saga. He guessed she was in the family way as she had a glow about her that he had seen often on his mother's face, but he waited until they said something. He was livid that the women were not even safe in his own home, let alone hear that the official residence had been invaded. He looked at the distressed state of the four women. Although Mrs Peach had remained silent, he could tell she was shaken. "Milroy, Bellchambers, your first duty today is to make this house like a fortress. I want door locks and removable long nails in the ground-floor windows. As I know that no locks are available, you must use drop bars to secure the doors. Max Slater is trustworthy; you can ask him."

Crispin had no idea what a drop bar was and looked confused.

John saw his questioning look and explained. "You will need three short lengths of timber, just wider than the doors. The uprights should be about eight inches long and one or two inches thick. Steel uprights would be better if you could source some. These get screwed on the frame side and two on the back of the door. Then, a slab of wood, or a steel bar, slides across these brackets to keep the door closed. The stronger the uprights, the harder it is for someone to break in. Also, get some long bridge spike nails so windows can be locked open or closed. You drill a hole through the window edge into the frame. The hole needs to be larger than the nail, and it can be locked open or closed."

The two soldiers nodded. Although reluctant to leave their ladies, they knew they needed to secure the governor's residence for the occupant's safety. After what they had learned while at Parramatta, the current flimsy timber building out there was unsuitable for anyone's safety; it would fall over if a strong breeze hit it. David Collins suggested that the governor must act immediately. A new Government House was to be built at Parramatta, on the hill above where the soldiers were stationed in the redoubt. They had gone out to survey the site as most of the good farmland was now in this area at Rose Hill. This new house would become the official residence when completed. Plans were put in place for construction, and John had needed to approve some changes.

John was still frowning at the news. He asked, "I don't suppose you know who they were by any chance?" He saw Helena look at Mrs Cowdrey, who gave a micro nod. He saw the girl's distress and decided to question Helena in the presence of her husband. He knew she would reveal everything if he were by her side. "Milroy, come, and I'll show you what I mean about the locks." This was an excuse to get him alone. "Helena, you can come too."

Crispin had no intention of leaving her alone. The pair followed the governor into his office while he waited. He shut the door and waved them to the settee. "Helena, I saw your glance; who were they?"

Helena clung to Crispin's arm with both hands. "It was the same two men who accosted me and two of their mates, sir. I recognised three of their voices." She retold the story of the invasion in full detail, including the man who had stayed behind and nearly caught them. She didn't recognise his voice, so she had no idea who he was. Helena stood to leave, then doubled over and cried out in pain. She grabbed at her stomach and then felt a gush between her legs. She saw bloody fluid pooling at her feet, and then she crumpled. At her cry, Crispin had slipped his arm around her. He caught her mid-fall. At first, he did not notice the blood.

John gave the order. "Milroy, carry her to bed. The baby…" He walked to the door and held it open for them. He led the way, and Crispin followed with his precious cargo. John opened the various doors on the way to their room, then placed a towel on the bed before Crispin lay her down. Hoping Eric would still be there, John rushed to the kitchen after seeing them to their room. Sighing with relief, he said, "Bellchambers, get the doctor on the double. I think she has lost the baby."

A shocked groan of distress circled the room.

No one needed to be told who. Helena had become beloved by them all, and they were thrilled when she confessed their news less than half an hour ago.

John had been delighted as he missed the sound of children. He never had any himself, but his siblings had many. The night's trauma had temporarily been forgotten until the repercussions had been dealt with.

John waited until Eric had left to find Doctor Balmain. Hopefully, he could come immediately.

As Mrs Peach closed the back door behind him, John turned to Gillian and Mrs Cowdrey and said, "Sorry, but you will need to clean up my office. I think she has already lost everything in there."

He had heard a cry of pain come from the Milroy's room as he left their room. And his heart hurt for his young friends. He remembered his flight to Parramatta years ago when he heard Aggie Osborne had lost a baby. They now had four children. John walked to his sitting room upstairs and stayed out of the way. He needed some alone time to pray. He hoped Helena would be all right, but he had seen his mother go through something similar shortly before he enlisted.

Within half an hour, Eric arrived, accompanied by doctors William Balmain and George Bass; they entered through the front door.

John escorted the two doctors to their shared patient. He explained what had occurred the evening before. These were two more men he trusted.

Being medical men, they explained that emotional trauma could cause such a loss to occur. John then returned to his now clean office.

Crispin refused to leave Helena's side, and the two new arrivals, much to their annoyance, permitted him to stay.

There was no easy way to break the news, but at least here, she would be able to be cared for even better than at the filthy hospital. Doctor Bass said bluntly, "I'm sorry, but she has already lost the baby and must stay in bed for a few days." He saw that she had passed the tiny child and the bloody placenta as it lay on the cloth in her bed. He carefully took the mass, wrapped it gently, and placed it to the side. He replaced the bloody towel with a clean one.

Helena realised that this was the most likely outcome of what had occurred.

George Bass left to let the rest of the household know the outcome.

William Balmain remained so that he could talk to them privately.

In a very unprofessional way, the doctor sat on the foot of their bed and explained that she could get up when she wished, but advised a few days of rest. "Crispin, she will be teary and moody. Helena, your body will need to readjust to the loss of the child."

Crispin nodded. He was shattered but tried not to let his emotions show. He needed to remain strong for them both.

The doctor continued. "Helena, Crispin, there is no reason why she won't carry a child to term, but a shock like what she experienced last night is enough to trigger the loss of a baby at this time. This, sadly, is not unusual. A month later, it may not have occurred. Now, what I need to tell you is that marital relations must cease until her bleeding stops. This could be up to six weeks. Her body needs to heal. Also, it may take her a little while to conceive again, so do not worry if this should not occur for some time, but I am sure she will be fine."

Helena sobbed as the finality of their loss hit.

Crispin drew her into his arms.

She said, "You wanted this baby so much, Cris. I'm so sorry." She collapsed onto his chest. Helena's teary face broke him.

William Balmain knew the value of life, and in this place, it was cheap. Many of the convict women had come to him for advice on easy ways to lose a child. He would not give any. He knew some had access to pennyroyal oil, but he refused to use it as it more often killed the mother as well. Life was God-given, and he did all he could to eke out a life for everyone he could.

William squeezed her hand with encouragement. "You will recover, Helena; just give it some time. You won't need sleeping draughts or painkillers as the worst is over. I shall bury the tiny one in your garden so it will always be close to you."

Helena stirred from her husband's arms and said, "Near my rose bush at the top of the back garden, please, sir. Then I will know where it is."

William nodded and collected the bloodied cloth that contained the tiny child. It was barely three inches long, but he would bury it with reverence in the place she suggested. He stood to leave but turned and said, "I believe this child will be awaiting you in Heaven. One day, you will see it fully grown and perfect. I'm not just saying that; I truly believe it, too. It's too small to tell a gender. The other thing is, I feel you should give it a name and talk about it as though it lived. It makes the loss easier to discuss. Do not bottle up your hurts, but talk openly about it with each other. You are both hurting, and you need to share that."

Crispin nodded. He wasn't up for a deep talk right now. He said, "Can we ask you more about this later?" William nodded and took his leave. He had a job to do, and he would complete that before returning to work. Crispin shrugged out of his red coat and unbuckled his sword. He lay down beside Helena and pulled her into his arms. He would not leave her, even if it meant he was booted from his role in the governor's security detail. He cradled his beloved in his arms. He realised he should have removed his boots, but didn't care.

After weeping for some time, Helena finally fell asleep in his arms. Rather than leave her, Crispin closed his eyes and dozed. They had slept in hammocks last night in Parramatta, and he ached in places where he didn't know he could hurt. Now his heart hurt too.

An hour later, the governor peeked into the room and saw them in deep slumber. He left them be. Their tragic loss was caused by his failure to provide adequate safety for the women in his home during his absence. He had never needed night guards before, but from now on, the sentry would be on duty twenty-four hours a day at both back and front doors. He was gutted at their loss. He had come to tell them that Max had added a new bolted bar onto the back door and a lock on the back gate.

~

Helena stayed in bed for a week, during which time she wept and slept a lot. At the end of that week, Crispin walked her out to the garden, and they sat and drank tea while sitting next to the rose bush. They had decided to call the baby Jesse. It could be either a boy or a girl, and it meant 'the Lord exists'.

The four convicts who broke in were captured and each given one hundred lashes, and their convictions were extended to life sentences. Two had scars from their previous attempts on Helena's person. The healed scourge wounds from the previous whipping would be little protection. The one-hundred-lash punishment would need to be delivered in one or two episodes. These four felons were destined to break rocks for the remainder of their lives. They were to be chained up each night.

John refused to give the convicts leniency as they had not given any to the girls. They had broken into the official residence and should be hanged.

Further investigation found that three of the offenders did indeed raid the women's quarters down in the town later that evening. Those three received an extra fifty lashes each.

John was disgusted by their actions, and he asked permission from Crispin to tell the four convicts the outcome of the invasion and the loss of their child.

Crispin's single nod was all he received. He knew men such as these would not care about the loss of a baby. His anger at them knew no bounds.

~

For the remainder of that month, Crispin was put on home duties. Eric and Max had personally installed locks on the doors and windows and ensured all entry points to the vice-regal abode were now secure.

After they visited Parramatta, the news was not unrest, per se, but the Corps' discontent was disturbing, but so far, no word had come about any mutiny.

Colin had no bad news to impart from Parramatta, though he mentioned that their potting business was thriving. He taught others how to pot, read, and write.

Days after their return, John received reports from an expedition that Lieutenant Shortland discovered extensive coal deposits on a northern river while hunting escaped convicts some days north of Sydney Cove. Some fishermen had been stranded in the bay and first reported its discovery. Shortland confirmed that the deposits were vast. Finally, they had coal to use for fuel. Further exploration of the coal river and valley would be needed.

While Crispin was occupied with Helena, John set to work arranging convict teams to extract the coal seam and transport it back to the colony. The new fuel source should be operational by next year.

~

Life fell back into the routine of the previous months, but after eight weeks, Crispin could not settle. He was still hurt about their baby's loss. His anger was beginning to eat away at him. He was angry that he needed to be away from Helena at all. Angry that she could not travel with him when on duty, angry that God let their baby die. He had even once been angry at Helena when she was ready to return to work in the garden. He had never spoken a harsh word to her before, and his flash of temper shocked her. She needed to get him to talk to the reverend.

One afternoon after church, Helena said, "Cris, will you come for a walk with me?" She didn't say where they were going, but he needed to talk to Reverend Johnson. Crispin was becoming bitter and quick-tempered. The loss of their child also hurt her, but she was getting worried about her husband.

Crispin smiled. "Of course, my sweet Bella." He had taken to referring to her by his nickname, which was also worrying. It was as though he was disassociating himself from her as Helena. Even his morning hugs were brief.

Reverend Richard saw them coming. "Welcome, young ones. This is a delightful surprise. Come for tea." He held his gate open for them and led them into his kitchen. Mary was teaching the children and would not be home for at least an hour.

Richard smiled; she was a God-send as a missionary's wife. Now, nearly two hundred children were getting some education. The younger ones were taught on weekdays, but the older children could only learn on Sundays as they had to work. Admittedly, most would be only able to write their names, but it was more than their parents could do. Some who showed more promise were given extra lessons and would soon be proficient readers. Exemption from work was the enticement for them to come and learn. Crispin had asked for a slate and was teaching Helena in private. Most of these children were born in the colony, so they did not have to do convict work.

Richard said, "Let me make a pot of tea to help pass the time of day."

Rather than let him do this, Helena soon had a tea tray on the table while the men broke the ice of the conversation.

After a few minutes, Richard broached the subject. "How are you both coping with the loss of your little one?"

Crispin gave him a look that could have fired daggers at him. He almost exploded. "How the blooming heck do you think we are coping, sir? We lost a child because I wasn't there to look after her!" He pushed his chair back so fast that it tipped over backwards. Rather than storm out, he walked to the window. He gripped the bench that stood between him and freedom.

Richard smiled. Crispin's violent reaction to his simple question broke through much palaver. "Anger is sometimes good, Crispin. Even our Lord showed flashes of anger, but it was justified. He directed it to those who were desecrating the temple. He overturned the tables of the money changers who were stealing from the people and tainting God's Holy place. Is your anger such as this?" Richard leaned over and picked up the chair.

Crispin shook his head. He did not turn around. His eyes were filled with tears, and his heart was filled with wrath and rage, but there was nothing physical to lash out at, so he rocked back and forth on the bench.

Richard asked him no more personal questions. "I will tell you something; all you need to do is listen. I tell you this because I know what it is to lose a child. Our first son was stillborn a few months after we arrived, so I do know exactly how you are feeling. Will you listen? Can you do that?"

Both young people nodded. Neither had known about their loss.

Richard took a long draw of his tea and started his story. "A long time ago, God made everything good. Everything was in balance. He made a beautiful garden containing so many wonderful food trees. Everything they wanted grew in profusion, and they could eat their fill: the birds and animals He made for companionship. God made Adam and then Eve, and they lived in this perfect place where they needed nothing. However, there were two special trees in the middle, and God gave them just one rule. Only one single easy-to-keep rule. Think of the trees as red for forbidden and green for free to eat from. The red one was the Tree of Knowledge, and the green one was the Tree of Eternal Life. I'm sure you know the story, but I will tell you anyway."

Helena shook her head, but Crispin nodded, but he made no attempt to sit down. However, he turned and leaned against the bench, his arms folded defensively.

Richard continued. "Well, God told them not to eat the fruit of the red tree. Remember, this was the Tree of Knowledge. They could eat anything and go everywhere. With just one rule, what do you think they did?"

Helena was listening wide-eyed. "Nooo, did they eat from this tree?"

Richard nodded. "Eve did after being tempted by Satan, and then she gave some to Adam."

Helena wiped away a tear. She gazed at Crispin, overwhelmed by her adoration of him. She thought, "Did Eve feel like this for Adam?"

Richard paused and had another drink of tea. He continued his story. "Once they had eaten the fruit, they realised that they were naked. They clothed themselves with leaves and hid from God when He called for them."

Helena gasped. "God talked to them? Really?"

Richard nodded. "Yes, the story is at the beginning of the Bible in Genesis. Sin manifests in many forms from that day until now and into the future. Back then, after they covered themselves with leaves and tried to hide from God, He knew they had eaten the forbidden fruit and cast them out of that perfect garden. He banned them from entering their sanctuary again, but God promised that one day, He would provide a way to once again find a way back into His presence. God knew their every action back then as much as He does now. He knew what they had done. They tried to hide, like we do, but there is nowhere on earth we can do that. It's like a child playing hide and seek by standing behind a curtain, and you can still see their feet."

Helena gave a small giggle.

Crispin relaxed his folded arms a little. He was listening.

Richard noted his stance but chose to ignore him. "That one action means we were cut off from easy access to God. However, there was more that happened because of their sin that day. Yes, they were cast out of that perfect garden, but the world became out of balance. It was no longer the perfect place God had created. From that day onward, they had to toil and fight for food. As they had not eaten from the Tree of Life, but had eaten from the other tree, sin entered the world, children and people died, sickness happened, earthquakes, fires, floods, droughts and other calamities began to occur. Sin is the second most powerful force in the world. However, God's love is the greatest. Remember that."

In his peripheral vision Richard saw Crispin wipe away a tear.

Helena reached out for her husband, but he shook his head. He refolded his arms again, but his body had relaxed.

Richard noticed Crispin's stance was no longer as rigid as it had been, so he once again continued. "Before that day, none of this happened. Flooding rain, storms, earthquakes, volcanoes, all are part of the Fall."

He glanced up and saw Crispin listening intently. His head had lifted a little, and then he unfolded his arms. Richard kept his story going. "People spent the next few thousand years trying to find a way to access a closer relationship with God. Over time, many people followed idols, and some even sacrificed their children to wooden and metal gods. They fell victim to vices like alcohol, greed, and lust. They murdered to take what they wanted. Mankind went from bad to worse. As time passed, it worsened. Some say all this occurred about four thousand years ago, but God's time is not our time, so we don't know how long it was. In a way, that is irrelevant, but it was far too long to be separated from His awesome presence. In those years, God sent us prophets and wise preachers to start a relationship with Him. He gave Moses the Ten Commandments and the law that, even to this day, we are striving to live up to. Read Exodus chapter 20 for yourselves. It's all in there." He drained the mug before he spoke again. "That's when we get to Jesus. He is God's Son, yet He is God as well. He is the door to Eternal Life, the pathway God promised Adam and Eve in the garden long ago. I suppose you could say Jesus is the green tree's fruit, but He is so much more than that."

Helena refilled his mug.

Richard continued after giving a nod of thanks. "But even today, we are dealing with the consequences of that fateful decision. We get sick and die; we lose children; we cope with fire, famine, and illness. None of these sins are God's will for us. All of it is the consequence of that first sin, which caused us to fall. Remember, God made people and the world perfect. Our sins have built a wall between Him and us, but none of it is a punishment from God, but a consequence of that sin."

Crispin interjected, "None?"

Richard shook his head. "No, none, Crispin! It is all the result of the Fall. The Kent's have just lost their baby boy. So, if you need to chat, they, too, know grief. The lad was named John Hunter Kent after the governor. They also did nothing wrong. But death happens to us all at some stage."

Crispin moved and took his seat next to Helena again. He remained silent, but he was still listening.

Richard waited until he settled. "God did not desert us, though. That is why I'm here in this Antipodean place. It's why the governor is here. God has called us to serve. I have come to tell this exact story to all who will listen. It's what my sole purpose is. The gardening is incidental as we need food. You see, God sent His Son to save us; that is, everyone, not just Mary and me. He is, I said before, the unlocked door back to God's presence. Jesus died, took away our sins and gave us a pathway to follow. He does not force himself through that door or remove the consequence of our sin. He stands and keeps knocking. Waiting for us to invite Him in. We are freely forgiven if we ask for it. Many here won't care at all about what happens to them. They will continue to lie, cheat, rape, pillage, and get drunk. They care for nothing but themselves. Self is all that they are interested in."

The two heads nodded.

Crispin reached out and cupped Helena's hand in his own. He whispered, "I'm sorry."

Helena leaned her head against his arm. He knew from her loving action that he was forgiven for his anger.

Richard knew there was more that needed to be voiced. Yes, they both came to church, but then again, everyone was required to attend the weekly services if possible. But had they grasped the point of what it was all about? It seemed to him that they were hearing the absolute truth for the first time. "Crispin, God wants us to be happy, whole, and above all, His. He promises us joy but not happiness. He promises us a place with Him in heaven but not freedom from pain. However, He will never force us to accept what He has freely offered to give us. He gave Adam and Eve free will back then, and He never took that away from us, but they made a bad choice. He gives us all free will, and like Adam and Eve, we can respond 'No' to Him, but that's not what He wants. That choice is the same one He gave to Adam and Eve. Remember, they only had one decision: to eat from the Tree of Knowledge or not. If they had chosen to obey and eat from the other tree, we would already have had Eternal Life, and there would have been no death, hunger, sickness, earthquakes, wars, greed, or anything else. But that is not what happened."

Crispin had one nagging question. "So our Jesse's death is not a punishment from God for anything we did?"

Richard smiled. He was relieved that Crispin understood. "I can say with absolute confidence that it is not, Crispin. Of that, I am completely certain. It is a consequence of mankind's sin. Jesus took our sins when He died, and by the time He rose again, the doorway to God was open for any of us who believe and follow Him. That is what you must do now. We don't like what happened and certainly cannot change it for others. But we must believe God knows and has a plan for us."

Crispin still needed more. He explained, "I wish to hit out at everything, sir. I even lost my temper with Helena the other day. I don't like this hate and anger that's eating at me." He was holding her hand and thumbed the back of it lovingly.

Richard saw the penitence in the young man. "Cris, you know your problem, and it's not like you to be that way. It was not your fault that you were not there to protect Helena. It was not your fault that sinful men broke into the house, nor is it your fault the baby died. A spider crawling on her could have caused that to occur. Ask yourself if there was anything you could have done to stop it, and you will realise there was nothing. Had you been there that night, the shock of a break-in may still have made this occur. They may have even stabbed you. You must believe me when I say that. Bad things happen to good people, but I will say something that will be hard to swallow. You must trust God that He will make things right. Somehow, some way, He will get the glory from all this. It's up to you two that He does. But more importantly, you both must forgive the men who broke in."

Crispin's brown eyes swam with unshed tears. He tried to blink them away, and he swallowed nervously, but he felt his anger evaporating. He was still hurt, but he realised there was nothing that he could have done differently. He nodded reluctantly, but he was determined to sort himself out. "Forgiveness is hard, sir. I don't know if I can."

Richard reached out and lovingly patted their joined hands. "Nothing worthwhile is easy. Your love for Helena made you chase her halfway around the world. That was not easy, Cris. Trust that God will give you the grace to release that anger. It will take time, but work on it. The governor has dealt with the felons and their crime. Remember, they must stand before God for the ultimate judgement. God will judge them justly."

Neither of the young folk spoke.

Helena shuffled closer and rested her cheek against her husband's shoulder. She clung to his hand.

Richard rose, pushed the kettle back onto the fire, and turned back to the couple. "It won't happen overnight, but don't give up on God because He will never give up on you. You both must give yourself time to heal emotionally." He turned to make more tea, then brought the pot to the table.

Richard turned the conversation to gardening to lighten the mood, knowing their earlier talk was just the beginning of what needed to be heard. As they parted, he said, "Speak to John Hunter, Cris. He is willing to answer your questions. He often tells me when he's at a low ebb, 'Christ is enough'. He is right. When God feels far away, it's you who has moved. Remember that. No matter how far you walk from God's pathway, He is only one step away when you turn back to Him."

Chapter 10 Building Plans

*I*t took another ten months before Helena confirmed that she was increasing again.

She didn't tell Crispin this time until her second flow was late.

She drew him out to the bench seat in the flourishing garden. Her pink rose, Jesse's rose, had its first flower.

Rather than say anything, she pushed him to sit down and then placed his hand on her stomach.

His eyes bored into hers. "Are we having another child?"

Helena nodded. "I think so." She dared not say much, as the builders were frequently nearby.

They were building a verandah on the front of the Georgian house, but the building supplies were stacked next to the fence.

The governor had instructed that no builders were to trample over any of the gardens.

The new netting over the backyard was still loosely strewn with palm and tree fern fronds, which provided shade during the summer heat. Therefore, the bench seat was protected from the visibility of the men working on the house's roof, but not from the kitchen window.

Mrs Peach had seen the young couple walk to their favourite seat. She often saw them drinking a mug of tea while enjoying the beauty of the lush garden.

Today, Helena made Crispin sit while she stood in front of him.

Mrs Peach didn't mean to watch them, but she was preparing the freshly picked vegetables that Helena had grown, and she kept glancing up at them while she worked. Her eyes fell to the bowl she was filling when she heard a shout of joy.

She saw Crispin jump up and cry with delight. He grabbed her around her waist and spun her around.

Mrs Peach dropped the knife and said, "Virginia, come here!"

Mrs Cowdrey, who had been sitting at the table doing her bookwork, walked to the kitchen window. "Oh, wonderful! I was beginning to wonder if she would ever fall with child again. I presume that is what she told him?"

Priscilla Peach nodded. "I saw her put his hand on her stomach, so I'm guessing you are right there, dear friend. We'll need to act surprised when they tell us, though."

The two older ladies were delighted. They had become close to the young couple.

Mrs Cowdrey said, "We really should not be spying on them, Priscilla, but this is wonderful news."

Her friend nodded, and she returned to peeling the turnips.

The pair intended to go back to work.

The vegetables were forgotten as the ladies watched the couple kissing. Both missed their husbands and sighed.

Mrs Cowdrey smiled as she left the kitchen. She had started knitting a blanket for the first baby; she would finish it for this one. She had lost a child at about the same stage herself, and she had never conceived again. She had hoped that the same would not happen to Helena and Crispin.

She did a skip of joy as she walked back to her room to put her bookwork away.

Helena had proven her worth with the garden, and the overhead net had provided respite from the scorching summer heat for everyone. It even cooled the breeze that came into the kitchen door.

A weighted cheesecloth curtain to keep the flies out meant they could keep the back door open during the day.

Over the summer, they had all sat outside in the garden, enjoying the cool shade. Now, their dining table regularly featured a variety of vegetables they had not had for many years.

Richard Johnson had come good on his promise to supply seeds, corms, and bulbs. Their garden now grew cabbages, onions, peas, beans, broad beans, potatoes, pumpkins, squash, turnips, Brussels sprouts, corn, beets, and carrots.

Richard had recently presented Helena with a small asparagus crown and a rhubarb head, and the first stick of each was ready to be served to the governor for his meal tonight.

They had three apple trees outside the fence line and various citrus trees growing. Richard had given John a Seville orange tree for his birthday.

Helena had also germinated some parsley seeds and added a large herb bed.

The entire backyard was stuffed full of edible foodstuffs. The pretty rose was the only flowering plant that was not entirely edible. However, Mrs Peach used some precious sugar and preserved some rose petals by dipping them in egg white and sugar and letting them dry. She also made some rose hip tea, added petals to a jar of light honey, and then used the rose hips to make a cordial and cough mixture.

Mrs Cowdrey purchased a small honeycomb and used the beeswax and rose hips to make a soothing ointment and a lovely rose-scented hand cream for them to share, so even the flowering rose was useful.

Helena had found some yellow daisy-like plants with a tart chemical that kept unwanted bugs away. They had the same smell as the marigolds at home. She had these yellow flowering plants dotted through the garden beds.

The reverend asked her about the incorporation of weed plants. Helena explained that marigolds grew along the edge of each garden bed at home.

Her garden had been so productive that she had let some healthier plants go to seed. Although Helena had sourced some onion seeds, she did not have enough. This vegetable was so useful that she intended to plant more next season. She let two plants mature and now has many seeds in storage for the garden next year.

Even storing seeds were problematic, as she usually stored the seeds in paper envelopes. However, she had no paper, so she had to make some with household rubbish from the governor's office.

She used discarded household paper mixed with pulped fibrous matter and lint from the laundry.

Helena showed the other ladies how to make paper with a frame stretched with cheesecloth. At home, they sold the paper at the markets. She also used dried petals from weed flowers to make decorative cards. She dried the weed petals in the bread oven and folded them into the pulp. This created a rough paper that worked well for holding the seeds.

The variety of things Helena made astounded the household.

At John's suggestion, Crispin went to the Government Stores for a bolt of stained cheesecloth. He had purchased some bolts in Cape Town in 1789 and used them as insect protection when the current residence was first built.

Mrs Peach returned from the market one morning to find Eric and Crispin nailing new screens of this fabric to the kitchen windows. She constantly struggled to keep flies off the food, and seeing a few maggots on a roast joint made her complain in anger at the flying critters. This loose-weave cloth would let in air but not bugs. The old fabric coverings had long since perished. The door covering had undoubtedly helped, but they still flew in through the torn window screens.

It had taken Helena six months to make the full-size net for the fenced backyard.

Once the netting was installed, the birds mostly stayed away. The vegetables were loving the cooler protection, and her soil preparation was now proving that her efforts had paid off.

Others copied her and shaded their gardens during the summer heat.

The governor even suggested that the town garden follow suit. Like her, they used the giant tree fern fronds, which were light and had no prickles. The dead fronds provided a diffused light that helped the gardens survive in the harsh summer environment.

In winter, most of the fronds were removed, letting in the light while dissuading the larger destructive cockatoos and fruit bats from destroying their food.

Governor Hunter acted on ideas from earlier discussions and promised land grants for good and honest labour.

Even the soldiers saw the benefit in this, though it riled the greedy members of the Corps. That group wanted everything for themselves and didn't want to share their wealth. Now, every hard worker could qualify for a grant.

John also instigated another idea he hoped may work. He allocated ten liquor licences for public houses throughout the colony. This would permit people to source their drinks legally. The fees were to be put towards funding an orphanage. One licensed inn was not far from the government abode and military Redoubt in Parramatta. However, it was also close to John Macarthur's home.

John smiled as he signed his name to that document. He chuckled as he was undercutting the opposition.

Newly arrived, Richard Dore, was making his objections felt about where he directed the fees. He had arrived with orders from London.

In Sydney, building crews were constructing a row of housing for nurses and hospital workers.

New cottages were built on another street for couples who wished to marry. These cottages had a small plot of ground for their own use, but the convicts still needed to work the government farms or whatever else they were assigned. With married quarters now available, more couples would wed, eventually resulting in more children needing education. Each needed infrastructure to fulfil their needs, such as hospitals, schools, and more food.

Each ship that left the shores for England carried a few emancipated convicts home, though surprisingly, many did not wish to leave. One vessel returned to England with over fifty women whose terms had expired.

John wondered at the wisdom of letting so many women depart, but that was the edict from England.

John's quest for alternate fuel came to fruition. The coal to the north was now being extracted and used in town.

James Underwood was now transporting this commodity to town from the Hunter Valley. The Coal River, as it was first named, became the Hunter River, and the valley was named after John. He chuckled but was thrilled at Shortland's suggestion. His explorer had not asked permission, but John was chuffed. Finally, things were turning around. Supplying coal would ease the burden of felling trees.

Eric and Gillian were still courting.

Gillian had just turned eighteen, but Eric had yet to propose. Due to her young age, they were in no hurry.

Mrs Cowdrey smiled as she thought about the happiness of her two charges. A few minutes later, she frowned. She realised Gillian and Eric should have returned from the market half an hour ago and wondered where they were.

At that moment, she heard the sound of raised voices coming from the front door.

The governor was in his office catching up on his paperwork, and the house was usually quiet while he worked. However, a banging door was followed by the beseeching cry of her name from Eric, "Mrs Cowdrey, please, come quickly!"

She did. Not knowing what had occurred, she ran to assist.

Gillian was in Eric's arms, and from what she could see of the girl, she was pale and wan. She was obviously in great distress, filthy, and she stank.

John came to his office door, and the two sentry guards were unsure how to assist the young man with a foul-smelling, dishevelled woman in his arms. Globs of stinking ooze dropped from her gown as they passed.

Eric nodded at the governor. He said, "Sorry, sir!"

Then, Eric saw Mrs Cowdrey's approach and explained, "She was set upon at the markets and pushed face-first into the filth. Three women attacked her, and one stomped on her before I could reach her side. She has injured her leg and possibly broken her ankle."

The poor girl stank from the effluent from the street. Her clean blue gown was unrecognisable, and her face was covered in disgusting brown ooze.

Mrs Cowdrey said, "Follow me, Eric, and I shall clean her up."

Before he followed her, Eric asked the governor if the doctor could be summoned.

John nodded and despatched one of the external sentries with a flick of his wrist.

Eric walked to Gillian's room but was unwilling to relinquish his precious bundle.

Mrs Cowdrey placed a sheet on her bed so she would not dirty the covers.

Eric gently lay her down and knelt beside her, taking her hand in his. "Sweetheart, I'm so sorry. I should have been beside you and kept you safe."

Gillian had not said a word since he picked her up. She didn't now, but a tear that made a clean channel down her filthy cheek broke him.

He fell to his knees and said, "Oh, my love. I'm so sorry."

She gazed at him and merely said, "Thank you for rescuing me, Eric."

Mrs Cowdrey tried to shoo him out, but he refused to leave her side. For the first time since they had known her, she raised her voice to them: "Eric Bellchambers, you are not staying while I strip her and clean her up. You are not even engaged to her and should not be in the room."

Eric shot the housekeeper a filthy look. "Well, that's why I wasn't by her side."

He rummaged in his pocket and pulled out a leather pouch. "My darling Gillian, I now have a ring and hope you'll accept my troth and agree to become my wife. You see, I've fallen hopelessly in love with you and want you beside me forever."

He held out the small ring. He had no idea what the blue stone set in the gold band was, but it matched the colour of her sky-blue eyes. He had bought it from a sailor who had come from India on a trading voyage. The sailor claimed it was a sapphire from Ceylon, and he hoped it was true. The sailor's goods were always lovely, and Eric had to wait until the man returned from his merchant trip with his new selection of rings.

Gillian gasped. "You choose now to propose? I am covered from head to toe in poop, and you tell me you love me now?" She giggled. "If you love me looking like this, then goodness knows what you will be like when I'm clean."

Eric grinned almost wickedly. "So, is that a yes?"

Gillian nodded. "Yes, that's a yes! Of course, I will marry you. But keep the ring until I'm cleaned up." A glob of gluey muck slid from her cheek.

Mrs Cowdrey stood still, watching them both. "Well, fiancé or not, you are not remaining while I change and wash her or inspect her ankle. The doctor will be here soon and cannot see her like this."

Eric could not wipe the smile from his lips. "Oh, all right, Mrs C. I shall go and report to the governor."

Mrs Cowdrey eventually shooed him out with a goodhearted laugh. She proceeded to remove the maid's filthy gown. She used the clean back of the dress to wipe off the mire from Gillian's face and then produced a wet flannel to wash off the remainder of the fouled mud.

When the doctor arrived, she had just finished buttoning a clean gown onto the woe-begotten but grinning girl.

Doctor Balmain came in to see his patient.

Gillian was in pain while the housekeeper worked, but even through her agony, she smiled with an occasional grimace when she moved.

Mrs Cowdrey stayed with her while the man inspected a few cuts on her arms.

He doused these with strong rum to cleanse them and then dabbed on some eucalyptus oil. He then turned to her injured ankle.

After humming and ha'aring while prodding and poking the injured appendage, he said, "I'm reasonably sure it's not broken, but I will strap it anyway. However, there may be a hairline fracture, so I would like you to stay off it as much as possible. Use a stick to walk for a few weeks when you need to get up, and no heavy loads for at least a month."

Gillian had not wept as he prodded her foot, but he bumped it as he stood up. Her cry of pain brought Eric to her side. He had been loitering outside and had overheard the diagnosis.

The doctor's brows lifted when he saw the dirt on the usually immaculately dressed soldier.

His look of amazement made Mrs Cowdrey smile. She saw Eric ignore the man and kneel beside his fiancée. He was now dirtier than his beloved.

Eric went directly to her side and kissed her forehead. He took her hand and slipped on the ring. "Sweetheart, my love, I do so wish I could take your pain."

William Balmain looked on in shock.

Mrs Cowdrey explained. "They are newly engaged, sir. We have not yet announced it."

The doctor nodded at the explanation but was still frowning. He said, "Bellchambers, your uniform is a disgrace, and what's more, it is… um… Well, in short, you stink!"

Eric nodded but did not relinquish his position. "I do, sir, and it was into this mire that the women at the market pushed my betrothed. I shall remedy the state of my coat as soon as I can, but I wished to see how Gillian was."

Mrs Cowdrey tapped him on the shoulder. "Pass it over, lad; I shall sponge off what I can, then hang it out to dry and brush off the rest. The governor is not going out again today, so I doubt you will need it."

Eric unbuttoned his red jacket, shrugged off the tight-fitting apparel and white leather sashes, and handed them to the housekeeper. Miraculously, his white trousers remained unmarked by the mire. Now in shirtsleeves, he leaned over and kissed his new fiancée quickly.

Mrs Cowdrey saw and said, "Decorum, Eric!"

The newly engaged couple couldn't care. Both were grinning. This was far from their first kiss, but neither would admit to that.

A new figure reappeared on the scene and entered the room.

John saw Eric's state of undress but realised why when he saw who held his coat. He ignored the doctor and said, "I gather by their grins that he's finally proposed?"

Gillian and Mrs Cowdrey both nodded.

John chuckled. "You took long enough, lad. I wondered if you would ever get around to it."

Eric stood and said, "I was waiting for her ring to arrive, sir. I collected it this morning as this was happening. It was why I was not at her side." He had not dropped Gillian's hand as he turned. "I am guilty of abandoning her for a minute or two, sir." He looked crestfallen.

"You were off duty, lad. It was not your fault." John looked around the room. "Double bunks will not suit a married couple, so I suppose we shall need to work on the furniture in this room sometime in the coming month. I need her there so you will need tome in."

Forgetting the doctor was still there, Eric nearly choked. "We have to wait for the full month, sir? I was hoping…" He left the rest unvoiced, and his mouth snapped shut.

John's gaze fixed on him. "Is there any reason why you need not to call Banns? I know you have been courting for nearly a year; is there a requirement for haste?"

Both shook their heads in unison and said, "No, sir."

Eric reiterated his comment. "No, there is no reason except that if we are married, I have the authority to defend her. Plus, she has had enough abuse in her life for me to add to that. I only waited as I wished her to turn eighteen before I proposed."

John looked at his housekeeper and then turned back to Eric. "She's injured, Bellchambers; the doctor said she is to stay off her foot for a month. The aisle at church is too long for her to hobble down without a walking stick."

Mrs Cowdrey shrugged and nodded. She had no answers and no say in their relationship anyway.

John said, "Ask the reverend and see what he says. I suppose you could always marry here. It will take some time for me to complete the paperwork for both of you, as the Colonial Secretary is currently in Parramatta."

Gillian struggled to sit up. "Sir, we'll wait if you wish. Honestly, there is no reason for us to need to wed quickly. I've waited this long; a few weeks won't matter."

John smiled at her. "Don't worry, I believe you, Gillian. I would have Bellchambers' neck if he had stepped out of line like that. It's not in his nature to hurt you, dear."

Eric gave a sigh of relief, but a grimace and frown swept across his brow. He murmured, "She's still so young."

John heard and chuckled. "I'll sort the permissions for you both, Eric. As soon as the paperwork is done, you can marry. In the meantime, I will arrange for the room to be converted, so ensure everything is stowed away before the workmen come. Milroy can assist with the move."

John looked around, surprised that Crispin was not nearby. "Where is he?"

Mrs Cowdrey gave him a look that made him beckon her out of the room. Once in the corridor, he asked again, but softly so those inside could not hear. "Ma'am, is there something I should know?"

She nodded and was about to answer when the Milroys entered.

The dreamy looks on their faces lifted John's eyebrows, and he said, "Well, don't you two look like peaches and cream?"

An explanation followed a broad grin from Crispin. "Sir, Helena has just informed me we are having another child in six months or so. To say we are delighted is an understatement."

John was thrilled, too, but contained his congratulations by letting them know that Eric and Gillian had their own news. "Go and see her, Helena; she is in her room. Milroy, come with me and bring Bellchambers with you if you can prise him from her side."

John didn't wait but turned and walked off. He knew the doctor was still within earshot, and although he liked him, he didn't live with them. This young couple had become his quasi-family.

After finding his friend, Crispin glanced at Gillian, who was still on her bed. He beckoned Eric and saw him drop a kiss on her upturned lips.

The action in itself was not unusual, but to have it occur in front of the doctor and housekeeper shocked Crispin. Then he realised what Eric's news was. He had finally bitten the bullet and proposed. He said, "Eric, come, we are needed."

Crispin turned and followed the governor's path.

Eric reluctantly left his beloved's side and caught up to Crispin. They shared their news and congratulated each other on their way to their boss's office. Eric was only in his shirtsleeves and, therefore, out of uniform, but he had little choice.

John was sitting at his desk, surrounded by a massive sheaf of paperwork. He had just taken his seat when they entered. He gave an exasperated sigh and said, "Just be thankful you two are soldiers and not the governor. This mostly concerns the new coal on the Hunter River to our north. I'm sending convict gangs up there to extract the black gold."

Standing at attention, neither answered, but both silently agreed. They were glad he had finally approved the new name for the river and valley.

John continued. "I gather you have had time to share your news."

Both nodded.

John smiled, "At ease. You may speak, you know!" He sat back in his chair. "Milroy, while the verandah builders are here, get them to convert the bunks in Gillian's room into a larger bed. Bellchambers, as she will be incapacitated for a while, move her into Kent's old room upstairs until her room is finished. I'm not expecting any visitors, and it's still close enough to the housekeeper and cook. If I get a visitor, they must stay at Kent's place."

Eric gasped. "Upstairs, sir?"

Ignoring his outburst, John paused and had a thought. "No better still, there is a spare larger room next to the Milroys' quarters. That will leave the smaller bunk room for any new staff we choose to get, so fix up that room instead. We have all but emptied the storeroom now anyway. Get the workers to construct a new bed and move the stored items into the bunk room."

Eric was stunned. "But, sir, the guest room upstairs is luxurious. She's your convict maid and won't need to move up next to you if we do up the room near Cris."

John looked up in surprise. "Bellchambers, she is a person made in God's image, as are we. She has had a rough time, and no one will know but us. Should we have anyone come, we can move her out quite quickly. Carry her up there and store the remaining things from the store room in the bunk room. The conversion should only take a few days if that is the case. However, you can't go to the honeymoon cottage next to the Johnsons as it is again occupied by the Marsdens. I propose you have a few days in the guest room once you are wed while Milroy and I head to Parramatta as I need to see Colin and Aggie. You can marry here in the house rather than take her down to the church unless you wish to specifically marry there."

Eric and Crispin looked at each other with concern.

Crispin explained, "Eric, Helena said Gillian wanted to marry in the church. If there are just us, I could carry her down the aisle, and you can carry her out again."

Eric nodded. "I know, but I think she would hate that even more. We will wait, as she's not going anywhere for a while anyway. Yes, I wish to be married to her, but I will not rush her."

John suggested, "Ask her after the doctor leaves. As you say, you're not in any hurry." He turned to Crispin. "Now I believe congratulations are in order, Milroy?" Crispin nodded, followed by an embarrassed smile.

John grinned and continued, "So I presume much of the garden will be fallow in winter. If necessary, I can get one of the convict women to come and till the soil and do the weeding. After last year's incident, I will not permit any men on the property without an armed guard beside the ladies. Thankfully, the garden is now fenced and secure."

Both soldiers were relieved.

Crispin had been worried he would bring in a man to take over. "The baby is due sometime in spring, so from mid-winter, she will need some help planting next year's food in the garden. She should be fine until then. Pottering around will not harm her, and she does love it."

John said, "I have one more thing I'd like to tell you all. Today, I set into action the plan to replace the house at Parramatta. It's being built on the site on the hill we chose earlier. However, the foundations laid before will now be for the staff quarters out the back, and a new Georgian-style house will be moved further forward. The residence will have an upstairs, like this place. I hope to have a cellar, but that depends on whether they can dig through the sandstone foundation. It may need to be a small underground larder. Phillip's dwelling near the Redoubt is about to fall."

Crispin grinned and said, "Well, I can't say I'll be sorry to move from there, sir. In winter, the winds howl through the cracks, and the walls are hot to touch in summer. Colin's place is much nicer, even if we had to share with the children."

Eric agreed but dared not seem unappreciative. He was surprised at Crispin's relaxed familiarity with the governor. He also liked staying with the potter.

Doctor Balmain arrived at the door, and after John saluted dismissal, the two soldiers exited. They went to find their women and discuss wedding plans.

Eric hoped they would be married by the end of the week, but he would leave that decision to Gillian.

John stood when the doctor entered. "William, please take a seat. I have a matter to discuss with you, and as this is not an official meeting, it will not be recorded unless you wish it to be."

The doctor was so stunned at being called by his Christian name that he almost fell into the chair. "Yes, sir! I mean, no, if that is your wish." He had no idea what this was about. Rather than guess, he sat and waited with bated breath.

John took his seat and reclined in his chair. "I find it very difficult to have private meetings with people that are essentially off the record. I will cut to the chase and say I wish to appoint you to the position of Civil Magistrate."

William was flabbergasted. Was this a pay increase, as he had requested? "Sir, I am honoured that you would consider me for such a role." He swallowed nervously.

John nodded and continued. "I know this is not the pay increase you have petitioned for, but the role will bring that in time as it will be paid per case. With David Collins gone, I need a man I can trust in that position. I miss his counsel sorely. I need a trustworthy person to take over, and I know you know the situation out west in Parramatta."

He saw William nod.

John continued, "Well, I think things will come to a head soon. I believe you will be an active and spirited magistrate who will deal with the injustices honourably. You will be paid per case so that it will be worth your while."

William was speechless. "Sir, this is a great honour."

He swallowed again. It was a two-edged sword. It would mean he had the authority to usurp the military and quash their power. A brief smile flashed across his face.

John saw and said, "Is that an agreement?"

William wished he were standing so he could bow his acceptance. However, seated, he asked a few pertinent questions: "Before I accept, sir, I must ask about your wishes in asserting your power. How far do I need to push them?"

John hoped for an outright "Yes." However, he said, "William, you will stick to the boundaries of the law. What the law is in England is the law here. Whoever breaks it must face the consequences, regardless of their status. I must warn you that I have permitted John Baughan to build a grain treadmill. This will set the cat among the pigeons, so to speak, and I imagine that there will be repercussions. All persons in the colony should, no, must, obey the universal rules. Any, and I mean anyone, who breaks them for whatever reason will be dealt with. That goes for the military and convicts, emancipated or free. Do you understand? If a white man kills a native, they get the same punishment as killing a white person."

William grinned and said, "Oh yes, sir, I understand and fully agree. In that case, I will accept it with pleasure. I shall strive to serve you to be the best magistrate of my ability."

John smiled. "Then, I will formally invite you to take the role at our next official meeting. Hesitate a little if you wish, but accept the job. I know this is not what you wanted, but things being as they are, a pay rise for the same work is impossible. There are other medics in the colony to assist you, not to mention George Bass when he's here. The new role will mean extra payment; therefore, you will need to train some new helpers for the hospital. Arndell is now at Parramatta with John Irvine, so that is one less trip you must make. I believe D'Arcy Wentworth has returned from Norfolk Island and can now fill in at the hospital when required."

William agreed, "Yes, sir. I worked with him when on Norfolk Island, and I like to think of him as conscientious because of his kindness to humanity. I believe he has a familial connection with an earl back in old mother England, but he does not hold himself above the common man. In short, sir, I like him. Women adore his blue eyes." He chuckled.

John was thrilled, "Then you will be happy to work with him?"

William acquiesced. "I will, sir. And thank you for the honour." He stood, bowed, and left.

While the meeting occurred, Eric visited Government Stores and had just returned with a walking stick for Gillian to use. When presenting it to her, he said, "My darling sweet, if you can walk on a stick, we can marry all the quicker."

Her head shook.

~

Ten days later, on the morning of the wedding, Helena woke from her slumber and needed to use the chamber pot to vomit in. Rather than be upset, she giggled. "Crispin, now it's real. We are certainly having another child. I hope I'm not as ill with this one as I was last time."

Crispin had discovered how a mug of hot sweet tea settled her stomach. He pulled on his nightshirt, wrapped his dressing gown around him and headed into the kitchen.

Mrs Peach was already there and had the kettle on the hob stove. She greeted Crispin with a cheery grin. "Sick is she this morning?"

Her cheery welcome made the future father smile. "Yes, Mrs Peach, I have come for a mug of tea for her, please." He was hardly awake himself as it was just dawn. They had stayed up too long last night enjoying themselves pleasurably. As they currently had the wing of the house to themselves, they made the most of it. Soon, they would have near neighbours, and both couples would need to keep their conjugal noises down. He had to scrub up for the wedding as he was to walk the bride down the aisle.

The morning progressed much as usual, but Helena had to dress Gillian's hair, and then the governor's carriage would take them to the church. Crispin and the governor would sign as witnesses to the marriage, and then the entire group, Mrs Peach and Mrs Cowdrey included, would return to Government House, where Mrs Peach had a roast dinner cooking. John surprised his cook by purchasing a fresh cut of hogget from his nephew. They were having a wedding dinner together at the main dining table. The Johnsons, their two children and all the government household were to eat in the official dining room with him. John was beginning to feel as though he was once again part of a large family. Sadly, William and his wife were in Parramatta overseeing the building of the new house. His mind turned to the coming baby. He hoped and prayed that Helena would carry this child to term. Since they lost Jesse, his faith had blossomed. Crispin often joined the governor for a prayer and a chat before work each day. Once Eric moved in, that may need to stop.

Gillian hobbled down the church aisle on Crispin's arm and married her beloved Eric. She absolutely refused to be carried into the church by either man or use the walking stick. She said, "Eric, I shall walk to your side, or we shall wait until I can." However, she leaned heavily on Crispin's arm.

After the ceremony, Gillian changed back into her Sunday best gown for the meal, fearing that she would ruin the borrowed wedding finery.

Eric was as good as his promise to the governor and had not sought Gillian out for illicit kisses or other rendezvous. He would move into the house today.

On arrival at the house, as they were married, he took the opportunity to assist her in changing. Her clothing was still in the luxurious guest room upstairs, and he carried her up the staircase.

With half an hour until they needed to be at the meal, Gillian all but dragged him into their room to consummate their union.

Eric was aware that she had been violated when young and had every intention of not instigating matters. He had no idea that she would all but tear his clothing off and bed him less than an hour after their marriage.

When they finally arrived at the table, both were relaxed and happy.

Crispin saw his friend blush and gave him a kick under the table.

Eric bit his bottom lip, winked, and grinned. Then his eyes dropped to the delicious meal that had just been set before him.

He later confessed to Crispin that he had not sought other women to satisfy his desires since meeting Gillian. Hence, he had been as keen as Gillian to satisfy her desires. Both were pleased their lives had turned out so well.

After the governor proposed a toast to the bride and groom and their forthcoming union, the happy couple smirked when he said those words. They were already united.

All enjoyed the luncheon, and memories of the mouthwatering feast were the main topic of conversation for the remainder of the afternoon. Fresh meat of any sort was a festive treat.

Helena's homegrown vegetables were delicious. Mrs Peach had baked potatoes, pumpkin, and some red beets, but there were also turnips, parsnips, and Brussels sprouts drenched in garlic butter. The vegetables were cooked in the dripping from the roast, and blackened with juices and crispy from the fat. Then, the gravy of the joint was thickened and served as a sauce, flavoured with mint and rosemary. Garlic was a luxury that they had rarely enjoyed up until this harvest. This grew well in Helena's garden, and although harvested and left to dry, some crowns were left to go to seed. Helena also picked baby broad beans and cooked them with a garlic butter sauce. None had eaten them this way, and surprisingly, they were delicious. Governor Phillip's French chef, Bernard de Mailiez, taught the previous maid, Angela, to make spicy sauces and cook with garlic, and she had taught her friends. She had taken over the kitchen at the official residence after his death in August of 1788. Angela married shortly before John Hunter's arrival, hence his need for a cook.

John celebrated the dual good news by cracking open one of his precious bottles of wine and sharing the delicious tipple with his household.

Chapter 11 And Baby Makes...
September 1797

The winter months passed with no further significant incidents.

The private grain mill was a thorn in the side of the rebellious New South Wales Corps group, primarily based in Parramatta.

Whispers of its destruction reached town. John's steward, Nathaniel Franklyn, seemed edgy when John Macarthur's name was mentioned.

Although the governor liked his steward, he lived down at the barracks with the other soldiers and did not see him often unless it was to sort out his correspondence. John had only glowing reports about him, as his men spoke highly when his name was mentioned.

~

Two years after returning to Sydney, life in the infant colony progressed smoothly. The water source was clean again; new public facilities were constructed and were kept clean by some of the worst offenders. It became one of the worst jobs a convict could be assigned. The absolute worst was digging coal.

Only months after seeing the governor, William Balmain and his partner Ann Dawson welcomed the birth of their second daughter, Jane.

Helena was now five months into her confinement, and her tummy had begun to show.

Crispin was beside himself with excitement as he could now feel the child move. He grinned no matter where he went or what he had to do.

John remarked on this and suggested that he take her for a long walk each day after duty. He remembered that his mother used to do this as birth approached.

As spring drew near, there was news that another baby would be joining the household.

Gillian was glowing and almost bouncing off the walls with delight. For her to be carrying Eric's child made her blossom. Her cheeks glowed with both health and happiness. She breezed through the early months with hardly a blink of morning sickness.

The two expectant couples were often seen on long walks around the harbour-side town. Both prayed that their babies would be healthy. These two children would hopefully be the first of what would become a large family for each couple.

However, Eric fell silent.

Life had been so busy for all four that Crispin did not ask Eric about his family until shortly before Helena delivered their child.

The innocent question made Eric's fists ball, and he blanched, glared at his friend, got up and left the room without answering.

In the years these men had known each other, there had been no mention of family. Eric knew Crispin was alone, but something had always come up, and their conversations had never touched on Eric's reasons for being here or about his past. Today was no different.

Gillian waited until he was out of earshot before saying, "Never ask him, Crispin; he will not answer. I know something occurred, but not what."

Crispin pursed his lips. How come it had taken him so long to realise that that side of Eric was an enigma? He was joyous on the outside and a black hole on the inside.

After breakfast the following morning, Crispin found Eric in the garden, punching the trunk of a large black pine tree at the back of Government House. He had seen Eric with bruised or bleeding fists before but had presumed he had been in another fight at the barracks. He knew how often those skirmishes occurred, and none dared report them to their commanding officer.

Rather than say anything, Crispin leaned against the fence, watching his best friend take out his anger on the inert tree.

Eric punched with all his might in uncontrolled anger. Only when he started kicking at the trunk did Crispin move and draw attention to himself.

Eric froze mid-kick. He groaned, spun around and sank onto the ground until he leaned against the trunk. "Bloody questions!" His head dropped to his knees.

Crispin was shocked when he heard him sob. He knew they were not going anywhere today, so he sat beside his friend. The pair remained in silence for some minutes. Crispin had no idea what to say, but being beside him seemed enough. He saw Eric's knuckles were bleeding, and one finger was at an odd angle.

Eric ignored them and the associated pain. A muffled voice said, "How am I supposed to be a good father when I have no idea how to be one? If I follow my old man's example, Gillian will be dead the week the baby is born." He lifted his head, and Crispin saw that his face was tear-stained. "I'm scared, Cris! I'm so bloody scared that I feel like running away to sea."

Crispin was stunned. How had he hidden his feelings for so long?

Why had he never realised the depth of his friend's anguish?

Eric continued, "I'm only alive today because my gran took me from him. I had to go back to him when I was six after she died. I think my father was involved with that, too, because I have vague memories of seeing Gran on the floor covered in blood and him dragging me away, then men in uniforms questioning him." Eric shrugged, then shivered.

Crispin realised that he was reliving some traumatic event. He remained quiet.

Eric's voice dropped. "I became his punching bag, and Dar used me… he used me… well, let's just say it was for his relief. Mama was dead by then; he said she had jumped from the top window, but I don't believe she did it alone. After two years of his vile abuse, I ran away when I was eight and signed on with the navy as a cabin boy."

Crispin had no idea what to say.

Silence reigned for a long pause before he said, "I can't tell Gillian. She doesn't need to know that I'm damaged goods, Cris. Every time the topic of family comes up, I freeze, and then it all explodes afresh."

He finally noticed his dislocated finger and grabbed it with his other hand, and, after taking a deep breath, he reset it. A groan of agony was followed by a sigh of relief.

Crispin felt waves of guilt wash over him. "Cor, Eric, why didn't you say anything?"

Eric shrugged before he continued and said, "I knew you had seen my knuckles before, but you never said anything, but presumed it was from fights in the barracks. Some were, but not all."

Crispin nodded.

Eric continued, "With your babe due in the next week or so, I knew it was time to tell you. Cris, I'm petrified that I'll do the same to my kiddies and possibly even yours. You've got to keep me away from them."

Crispin put his hand out, intending to put it on Eric's hand, but moved to his shoulder instead, lest he hurt him. He was at a loss for what to say; he prayed that God would give him the right words. His faith had grown substantially since his talk with the minister nearly a year ago. The words that came out were unexpected. "Eric, tell me about your mama and your gran. Were they violent and abusive, too?"

Eric looked horrified. "Oh, cor, no, Cris! They were loving and gentle. I felt safe around them, and they only sent me to my room if I did something wrong, which was not often because I was a good kid."

Crispin continued his attempt at talking some sense into his friend. "And what about the drink? When you get drunk, are you a violent drunk, or do you just go to sleep?"

Eric looked abashed. "I go to sleep," he replied quietly and somewhat apologetically.

Crispin wasn't finished. "Fine! And when you volunteer on Sundays at Mrs Johnson's school, do you lay into the kids with your fists when they misbehave? No, you don't. You pick them up and cuddle them until they stop crying, but you don't touch them in any other way."

Eric objected by saying, "But they aren't my children."

Crispin replied, "No, they aren't, and all the more reason to get angry with them. Then why do you think you'll be like him when you spent most of your early years with your loving mum and gran instead of a violent father? You have never hurt anyone but yourself in the years I've known you. I certainly have given you enough reason for a belting or two, but you never lifted a finger or fist to me or anyone else but Franklyn."

Eric looked at his friend, stunned. His head shook. He said, "I'd never hit you, Cris; never in a million years would I do that."

Crispin took up that idea, "Then what the blooming heck makes you think you would abuse the woman you love, let alone your own child or mine for that matter?"

Eric shrugged again. "Because my Dar did? But I don't want to be like him."

Crispin then thought about the day in the market. "Eric, the day you proposed, did you lash out at the three women who pushed Gillian?"

Eric's head shook again. He kept his eyes fixed on his friend.

"Then darn it, Eric, there's not a violent bone in your damned body. You're not going to be like that man who fathered you, but loving like your mother and gran."

"Sure?" Eric's face showed hope.

Crispin said, "As sure as eggs are eggs, Eric. I'll be there, and if you do feel such anger, come find me. You will never hurt the little ones, my friend. You are a good man; I know that for a fact."

Eric nodded, then shrugged. Tears still streamed down his cheeks.

"Now, don't you think this poor tree deserves water, not blood?" Crispin asked with a chuckle.

Eric was now a little embarrassed. He wiped away his tears. He had opened his deepest hurts to someone and felt vulnerable. He thought he might as well tell him the rest. "Thanks, mate! Do you know I've never dared have a friend before you, Cris? I was never game to get close to anyone, but you never gave me an option. I tried to push you away by being rude and crude, but you just ignored that and drew closer, like asking me to witness your wedding. That took my breath away. That is why I teased you about searching for your Bella. I waited for you to strike me back. You walked away. You never got angry, not once. For once, I felt safe around someone. I began to seek you out, and soon, I actually felt comfortable around you. Then, after my fight with Franklyn, you recommended me for protective duty for the governor with you. He laid off picking on me after that." His eyes were watering again. "Keep your eye on me, Cris, and kick me up the nether end if you see me going off track."

Crispin nodded. "Let's go and get your hands sorted. I've never seen them so bad."

"Yesterday's questions wouldn't let me go. I lost control today, my friend." Eric glanced down at his bloodied appendages. "Gill will worry."

As Crispin carefully pulled his friend to his feet by his wrists, he said, "Tell her, Eric, she's been through enough abuse to understand exactly how you feel. Her attackers may have even done something similar to her. She will probably know better than I do how to help you. Do not shut her out."

He slung his arm along Eric's shoulder, and they returned to the house.

As they walked, Crispin had one more thing to say. "Eric, you must forgive your father. Until you do, this will haunt you. You heard the reverend talk about that in church two weeks ago. Forgiveness will cleanse your life. Trust me, I know! I had to forgive those four fellows who made us lose Jesse." He expected Eric to lash out at him verbally, but he didn't.

Eric nodded and said, "Okay, Cris. Can we find some time tonight to pray together? It has taken ages before the reverend's words began to seep in. It's actually why I started volunteering at the school. I could listen without being obvious."

Crispin chuckled. He knew that feeling. He loved the governor talking about his strong faith. He opened the back gate and ushered his friend into the garden. "I'll be there whenever you wish, Eric. It's what friends do." He locked the gate, and they walked inside. He had followed the minister's advice and had long talks with the governor about their faith.

Upstairs, John returned to his bedroom for a book and watched the two young men sitting under the tree just beyond the backyard. He had arrived just as he saw Eric punch the tree for the last time. He watched the conversation and saw Eric nod a few times before they stood and returned to the house. From his lengthy discussions with Crispin, he had seen his faith blossom. He wondered what that was all about and hoped one or other of them would tell him. In the meantime, he would pray for Eric. These two young men were like surrogate sons. Thankfully, his nephew, William, liked them a lot.

~

As the time approached for the birth of Helena and Crispin's child, sickness hit the Balmain household.

When Helena went into labour, the doctor was called to assist the midwife with the delivery. D'Arcy Wentworth arrived instead of William Balmain.

D'Arcy brought the news that William's daughter Ann was at death's door, and their baby, Jane, was being kept well away from her.

The family was in isolation in case she was contagious.

Helena travailed all day in heavy labour, and by the time she presented Crispin with a son, news arrived that little Ann Dawson Balmain had died. The bittersweet news muted the joy that would be otherwise experienced with the birth of a child.

The Milroys' little boy was perfect and released a lusty cry when held aloft. After the couple was left alone with their son, Helena asked Crispin what he would name him.

Crispin was cradling the tiny red, wrinkly babe and looked up at his beautiful wife. "He is our precious little red pebble, my sweet. How about Jasper Linus?"

Helena's face lit up. "Perfect, Cris! Jasper will fit in with Jesse's name, too. But can we add your name as well?"

Crispin nodded.

Jasper thrived, and Gillian watched Helena deal with the small child's needs.

At first, the two men were fearful to hold him, but not so John. Like Helena and Gillian, he remembered how to handle a tiny baby. As a gift, John had purchased a locally made wicker basket for his crib. Having occasionally found the shiny black spiders in the ground floor rooms, the basket sat on the top of the drawers out of harm's way.

When Jasper was about two weeks old, John heard him howling while Helena was outside, sitting peacefully in the garden. Rather than let the baby cry himself hoarse, he went and tended to him. Realising the child was wet, he flicked his eyes around the small room, collected a clean flannel napkin, and soon changed the infant.

The lad's flannel gown was clean, and as the day was warm, John tucked the now linen-swathed baby into his arm and went to find his parents. He had been permitted cuddles, but this was the first time since he was a lad that he had changed a baby by himself. He was astounded that he even remembered how to do it and avoid the golden shower that boys released.

Being one of nine children, it was a job that he had done frequently as a boy. As he walked, he found he was gently bouncing the baby.

The baby stopped whimpering and started to seek food with his tiny lips. Rather than call out for Helena, John poked his little finger in his mouth and went to find her.

She was seated in the back garden, looking at the sprouting vegetables. His exit with the child in his arms brought the young mother to his side.

"Oh, sir, I am so sorry that he disturbed you. I did not think you would hear him from your office. I thought he was asleep." Helena reached out for the child, but John refused to pass him over.

He said, "He is such a dear little chap, Helena. He has Crispin's dark hair but your nose. I'm not sure if he has dark blue or brown eyes as he hasn't opened them for more than a second."

Helena replied, "Thank you, sir. His eyes are so dark that I could not see the black dots in the middle. I think his hair will go light as he has my pale eyelashes."

The baby's eyes were flickering open and closed in the spring sun. John put his hand up to shade the child from the harsh rays.

The baby opened his eyelids, and John realised what she meant. The baby had such dark eyes that it was hard to see his pupils. He said, "They are very dark brown, like Crispin's."

John did not wish to relinquish his precious bundle to the mother. So delaying, he said, "Never fear if you wish me to keep my eye on him. I am from a large family and know babies well. However, it's been a long time since I changed one. There is a wet flannel in your room. I was not sure what to do with it."

Helena flushed with embarrassment. "Sir, you did not need to do that."

John grinned. "No, I didn't, but I enjoyed it. I love children and am somewhat saddened that I never married and had my own. I was at sea for most of my life, which is not a life that one can force on a wife. David Collins left his wife on the other side of the world and then took up with another woman here. I would not have done that, so I never wed. I adore all my nephews and nieces, and it's why William and Eliza Kent are here. William's mother, Mary, is my sister. They have filled that need for me. I have been in the navy for most of my life and shall be until I die."

He gazed lovingly at the child in his arms. "Before this posting, I spent little time ashore. The few years I was here, the first time, I was rarely in town. I was off exploring and doing mapping and surveys. I went on expeditions and all ranges of adventures, and I don't regret any of it. I am severely jealous of Bass and Flinders and their exciting jaunts, but I am anchored here. Having your little ones will be like my grandchildren, and I will love them as such."

Helena smiled. "Feel free to cuddle him whenever you wish, sir."

With a long sigh, John handed the child to his mother. Having relinquished the tiny baby, John had no reason to continue chatting with his young convict gardener. Crispin and Eric had been sent to Government Stores for a range of items needed at the house.

John stayed long enough for the roving sentry to pass by the back garden. There were four sentries on duty these days. Two were stationed at the front door, one at the side gate and one on circulating patrol. With a nod to Helena, John returned to his office.

Helena watched his departing figure. The man had aged so much in the short time they had been with him. He could not share the stresses of the job with anyone. Helena knew enough about the infighting of the colony to know that the Corps, who were also farming, were a bone of contention for the governor.

Since the burning of John Baughan's mill in February of that year, Helena knew from Eric and Crispin just how volatile the colony had become.

The governor had a small windmill constructed on Flagstaff Hill, and Connie and Nigel Bray now ran it for government use. He made regular inspections of the mill, but more often to see Connie and to stand at the big window overlooking the harbour. She made oatcakes like his mother and he adored their two little girls. The mill residence was somewhere he could go for peace and respite. Occasionally Helena accompanied him, but more often than not, only Crispin went with him.

The tensions in the colony were a powder keg waiting for the spark to ignite the fuse.

There were two strong forces in the colony, but only one had the official authority of the king. A New South Wales Corps member even challenged Doctor Balmain to a duel. With his recent loss, the doctor didn't need that. Helena knew that with all the stresses of illness and the death of his daughter to cope with, his magistrates' duty had also increased. Helena planned to visit Doctor Balmain's wife when she felt she could leave Jasper with Gillian. It would not be appropriate to take the baby with her.

The governor considered charging the members of the Corps involved in the case of John Baughan's burned mill. The colony was on a razor's edge, with all involved leaders except the governor playing various roles in town. Captain John Macarthur represented the militia, and Doctor Balmain stood for the king. The governor was unable to intervene. He had to let justice prevail.

The court case became a test of strength between the two sides. Ultimately, Doctor Balmain backed down, as there were no witnesses. Officially, he recorded the situation as "shamefully malevolent interference in the affairs of the Corps". He had no other option, as there was no evidence of who had lit the fire. However, the Corps had been put on notice. No one was beyond the law. Letting the matter slide did not help things settle.

The Corps' power grew as rum production increased. The Corps was all but distilling money. With so little cash in the colony, rum became the official currency. Unlike coinage, they made more grog when they ran out of rum. The regiment's name was now colloquially known as the Rum Corps.

The four ladies from the government residence were only willing to leave their safe compound if escorted by at least one armed soldier, be that husband or a guard.

In the years John had been there, only a little power had been wrested back from the Corps, so they still wielded control. Free-ranging convicts were also a problem. The licensed drinking holes had done little to halt the alcohol issue, but they were a start. The licensed Freemasons Arms in Parramatta was a very popular watering hole. Its presence so close to the Rum Corps headquarters and John Macarthur's home brought a smile to John's lips.

~

By the time Gillian and Eric's daughter, Caris, arrived in January 1798, the household began to feel the tensions in the town. What was occurring behind the scenes worried everyone.

Crispin reported much of what was occurring in Parramatta to

Helena, and the rumours were beginning to be alarming. Rather than being called into the sitting room for further meetings, John frequently joined his staff in the garden for an after-dinner mug of tea. The informality of the setting made these evenings a delight. The netting overhead offered a cool place for the informal gathering at the end of the summer days. The rooms were stifling.

Mrs Peach and Mrs Cowdrey had been reluctant to join the four young ones, but the heat inside the kitchen had been overwhelming. After the dishes were done, the kitchen's suffocating atmosphere drove them all outside. The household residents drank tea in the lovely arbour overlooking Helena's garden. She had found some marigold seeds, and they were planted along the edges of the rows. Crispin and Eric added an extra bench seat to the rose arbour, and the seven adults enjoyed their evening tea or tipple out there.

John spoke about the uneasy situation between sentry circuits, timing his comments when the guard was out of earshot. He knew that even his cook knew the Corps' animosity was undermining his authority.

While sitting and staring intensely into his tepid tea, John said, "In the years I have been here, I have never actually thanked any of you for your loyal support. I have the Johnsons, the doctors, and one or two others whom I can rely on, but I trust you six literally with my life. Mrs Peach, you could easily poison me. Mrs Cowdrey, you could leave doors unlocked and let in felons or, worse, my enemies. You four young ones are my sanity. Your two small imps give me a reason to fight to make this hellhole a better place to live. They are the future of this settlement."

He looked at the six astounded faces and continued. "I counted the other day and realised there are only thirty-one people I can count on to support me and the work I am attempting to do. I miss David, but since I sacked his replacement a few weeks ago, the new chap, Dore, is doing quite well, but I'll revise that in a few months. That number is less than one-third of those in authority in this place. It's sad that so few of them are loyal to the crown. Seventeen officials here in Sydney are from the Rum Corps and loyal to themselves. They are responsible for the convict allocations and numerous other roles, including the mail and despatch bag. They tweak the rules for their own rewards. I came here expecting the military to uphold the law, yet they are the ones flouting it. However, as you all know, I found that Major Grose had suspended civil law."

He sighed. "After David left, I promoted William Balmain, so his hands are full. Macarthur and others misused their allocation of convicts to assist in cultivating this raw land. I wrote to London that, and I quote, "scarcely anything short of the full power of the governor would be considered by this person as sufficient for conducting the duties of his office." Macarthur wants power, full power. Far from the two convicts each, Macarthur has over one hundred allocated under his name. Initially, I saw that as a good thing. Governor Phillip only permitted two convicts per allotment as instructed, but as we have so many of them to place, it eases the housing of the felons. Not many farms have as many as Macarthur has, but I must placate him."

The group sat listening to his musings. They all knew that they had become his trusted ears.

There were long pauses in his reverie as the guard passed close behind them.

John took a long draw of his tea, this time draining his cup. He held out his cup for a refill, and Mrs Peach obliged.

The hot, sweet brew had become more potent, but it had cooled slightly, and he took another long drink.

The guard was again out of earshot.

Staring into the tea leaves, John said, "Although older, Foveaux now seems to be in Macarthur's pockets. I presumed that Grose and George Johnson would have kept things under control, but they are mere puppets to the ringleader. I have since learned that Paterson tried to rein them in and failed. From what I have observed, they are out to line their pockets at the expense of everyone else. None are happy with less than one hundred per cent of the profits. I feel they will each come to blows at some stage with Macarthur. I think it's an unhappy partnership. In my last despatch from London, word has reached England that the situation here is unsettled."

He checked the two guards were not within earshot before he said softly, "I confess, I feel my despatches are being opened before I read them, but I have no proof."

Eric and Crispin gasped. Crispin was unable to remain silent any longer. "Sir, is that not treason? How dare they read official reports?"

John gave an uncharacteristic shrug. "I only have suspicions, Cris."

None of his other listeners dared interrupt his reverie. Each would support him to the hilt, but there was little any could do but be his earpieces.

John again tossed back some of his second cup of tepid tea. "When I landed, I expected this place to be as Arthur Phillip had wanted. He had planned a beautiful town to be called Albion. I left a year or so before him, and the settlement was beginning to find its feet but still looked nothing like his dream town. To arrive back four years later and find the place changed out of all recognition for the worse and filthy to boot was a shock. I am accustomed to strict discipline on my quarterdecks, and instead, I find the place in a filthy, near mutinous state. I confess that if London does not act and permit more severe chastisement for the Corps, they will mutiny. Until then, my hands are tied."

He drained the last drop out of his second empty mug. "You will wonder why I'm telling you all this."

Six heads nodded. John sighed. "I received a letter from London that I am to rein in the military, and therefore, I need to warn you that things for us all in this house may become very dangerous. I do not expect an actual rebellion, but I do foresee that one will occur if these disorderly soldiers are not curtailed. Quite honestly, I'm not sure I'm the man for the job. Mayhap they should have installed Gidley King as Phillip's successor after all."

John's musings paused again while he sat thinking of what he could do to defuse the growing unrest. As he did so, the patrolling soldier again passed the back fence near where they sat.

Once he was gone, John continued, "I am strongly tempted to send these leaders home to England under arrest for disobedience; however, should I attempt to do so, I believe it will precipitate said mutiny. Macarthur, in particular, now wields so much power that he has almost made the colony unviable. He is manipulative, and I don't trust him."

Crispin felt he needed to say something. "Sir, we all have seen what you are dealing with here. On arrival, you were lied to and deceived maliciously. It is unfair that you take the blame for their greed and lies."

John looked at the young man. "I wish I had one hundred more like you and Eric. However, you are correct that on my arrival, I was most shamefully deceived by those on whom I had every reason to depend for assistance, information, and advice. I knew these men and had served with them. Yes, they had egos, but I did not realise that those egos had grown to the detriment of all others. Some, like Doctor John White, were extraordinary gentlemen. I was saddened that he left shortly before I arrived. He deserves a knighthood for the work he did here. Others were simple seamen, like Thomas Webb; he was also a man maligned, though I'm not sure about his brother. I think Robert Webb is selling much of his grain to the distilleries as he should produce much more than he sells to stores. When Thomas returned five years ago, he brought out a small still for his and his brother's use. I believe his alcohol-making apparatus was duplicated and enlarged and is partially responsible for the problems we have today. I suspect Robert is involved, but there is no evidence. I admit that if Thomas had not brought his alcohol still, some industrious crooks probably would have made bathtub gin, so I can't blame the Webb brothers. Hence my desire to rein in the distribution."

Eric said, "Sir, you know you can count on us for support."

The others all agreed. The songs of the evening insects started.

John smiled in the fading light. He could still see their faces, but the evening was beginning to cool. "Thank you all. I need that, Cris. I fully expect that London will receive letters complaining about my governorship. I know who they will come from, but there is little I can do but work my hardest here. I ask that from today forward, you four ladies will go nowhere without being accompanied by two armed soldiers. It will be hard, but that is my rule. In reality, it is what I have come out here to tell you. If I have received mail from London, then they will have to. I do not know what their missives will say. I do not even know if all that was addressed to me was delivered. As the military is in charge of both incoming and outgoing mail, I am unsure if my despatches are being read before posting, let alone being sent at all. I do not know if my communications with the admiralty are kept private. Before it leaves our shore, everything must go through the Rum Corps's hands. The despatch box is not locked until it goes on the ship, and I have little chance of making or seeing great change during my tenure. I have already started a list of things that could be done to make this place a thriving success that I hope it will become one day. With your support and those few I can trust, I will endeavour to implement some of these things."

As he finished speaking, he stood. "Now, dear friends, let us go inside. The cicadas are drowning out our conversation. I'm sure the cool air is not good for the babies' lungs." He sighed. "I must remember, Christ is enough. I can't do this without Him."

Without waiting for a reply, he turned and left the beautiful garden, and the others followed him inside.

Chapter 12 The New Arrivals
Early 1798

*H*elena tried hard not to think about her family and whether they would come. She had heard nothing more about the invitation, but she had not expected to unless her reverend at home wrote back. She realised she may be expecting again and had not told Crispin lest she be wrong.

Easter came and went, and more transport ships arrived, bringing more convicts, many of whom were in a bedraggled and distraught state.

The governor was having a dickens of a time trying to work out where to put all these unexpected arrivals. Every barracks or tent was overfilled, and prisoners were doubling up in beds as it was. It was unhealthy, and as usual, these vessels rarely arrived with adequate supplies.

John had no warning of a ship's approach until a flag was hoisted up a pole. Then, everyone would scurry around, making room for the new convicts.

John had visited Nigel and Connie at the mill earlier that morning. While at their residence delivering some good news, word arrived that sails were seen. By the time he departed, the flag on the headland was up, signalling to the town to prepare for its arrival.

This ship was no different from the arrival of any other vessel; it could even just be a ship from the coal deposits in the Hunter Valley. No one knew what this vessel contained. It may have been a whaler or even some other foreign boat.

As usual, the governor was swamped with paperwork. He spent one day a week ploughing through the piles that accumulated on his desk.

To prevent unnecessary pauses in his work, he set up a system where a soldier reported to him as soon as a new sail was spotted.

~

Mrs Cowdrey had just brought in a tea tray when there was a knock at the front door. She opened it to a very good-looking, fair-haired but unfamiliar young soldier. She had never seen this lad's face before. She was surprised as she thought she had met most of the young men in the Corps in the years she had been in the town.

He introduced himself, and she realised that Ensign Thistlethwaite had brought the news of another vessel turning into the harbour. He then requested to see the governor.

She let the young man in and knocked on the governor's office door.

John called, "Enter." Then, he looked up to see an unfamiliar soldier standing at his door. Considering this young man was in his own regimental uniform, this skinny chap was unknown to him.

The soldier introduced himself; he said, "Good morning, Your Excellency. I am Ensign Jonas Thistlethwaite, and I have just come ashore from the *Barwell*, sir. I have been asked to relay messages to you personally and inform you that your invited guests are on board. As well as a shipload of other useful people. The convicts on this craft are well-skilled ones, sir." He bowed and took a step backwards toward the open door.

John's head jerked upwards. "Do you mean the Rosedales are here?"

The soldier's head nodded. "Yes, sir! I came ahead in the longboat, but they are yet to disembark. The *Barwell* is currently being towed from Watson's Bay as the wind dropped as we entered the harbour. Captain Cameron asked me to bring you news of our arrival."

He turned to check that the housekeeper had gone. Without asking, he turned and closed the door.

John watched but remained silent. He was intrigued by the young soldier's audacity, but his hand dropped to the loaded pistol under his desk.

Once shut, the soldier unbuttoned his jacket and pulled out a bundle of letters. "Sir, these are mostly from the Admiralty in London. I was charged to deliver them personally and ensure they did not go through the usual channels."

He handed the bundle over and then stood at attention again.

This unusual form of delivery meant that at least one of his letters had reached London.

John relaxed, undid the string holding them together, and flicked through the mail. Some were from Head Office in London, and some were personal. John grinned. News from home was always good. He lifted his head and replied, "Thank you, ensign. Your efforts will be well rewarded. Are you planning on staying, or are you heading back to London?"

The young man nervously replied, "Staying, hopefully, sir. If I can be of use."

John nodded and then asked something that had just occurred to him. "Why you, young man? What made the Admiralty entrust these to you?"

The ensign said, "My uncle is Lord Phillimont, sir. I'm a fourth son, so I enlisted." He paused and then asked if he could speak freely.

John waved for him to proceed and reclined in his chair to listen.

The young man continued. "Uncle Charles offered me a full

commission as a major, but I'm only twenty and wish to earn my way up, not buy it. I'm sick of getting things because of my birthright, and I'm determined to do something useful, sir. I have no experience commanding men, so I thought to learn on my way up. I'm not averse to hard work; this way, I have a purpose."

He swallowed and dropped his voice. "Uncle Charles received your missive and an official report via David Collins, who delivered it to him personally. None of your previous missives were as um... pressing. That caused much discussion and division in London. The powers that be at home seem to side with a certain captain and major here, but Uncle Charles knows both well; plus, he knows of your reputation and your faith, sir. He decided to ensure you received your mail untainted, so I was charged with carrying his letter. The official despatch box carries a token official letter that gives nothing away."

John's bushy brows lifted in surprise.

Jonas grinned somewhat mischievously. "It's well sealed, but it also has a hair in the wax. If it's steamed off and resealed, I shall know it's been opened, sir. So if I may be here when you open it, I shall check the seal."

John was intrigued but sighed with relief. His report found someone who believed him. He subtly nodded but felt like cheering.

Jonas then added, "And sir, I have funds aplenty, so I have not come to line my pockets but more to escape the giggling misses who seek a title. I'd be happy with a simple but adorable farm girl."

John knew Charles Phillimont and also his brother-in-law, the Earl of Brightwell. He asked, "I'm guessing you are William Thistlethwaite's youngest son?" He knew the earl well enough to call him by name.

Jonas nodded with a grin. "Father sends his greeting to you, sir. Being underage, he only permitted me to come as he knew you were here."

He dug into a different pocket and handed over a document giving John legal authority over him until he turned twenty-one. "I hope you don't mind, but Father said you were to stand in *loco parentis* for me, should it be required."

Jonas had initially no intention of using this until a certain smile regularly appeared in his dreams.

John was intrigued, as he knew William was a man of standing and used his position as an earl to the advantage of many. The three had studied Latin together at university. He liked both men and considered them as friends.

He would keep this knowledge of the lad's background quiet for the boy's sake. However, he realised that this young man could be someone who could be trusted. He needed every eye and ear he could find. In the meantime, Helena's family had arrived. He would make no decisions about the lad yet. "Thistlethwaite, thank you for delivering these and the welcome news about our new farming instructors and skilled convicts. I feel more conversations will ensue, especially about this last document."

John grinned at the lad as he tucked the letters and documents in his pocket. "...but for the moment, let us go."

Jonas chuckled as John moved to stand. "I wasn't going to hand it over, sir, but I'm hoping it may be needed."

John cocked his eyebrow again and said, "We'll see about that later. In the meantime, I would like to inform my staff to arrange for a large contingent of visitors. May I ask how many are in the family group?"

Jonas replied. "There are the parents, and I believe there are thirteen children. The youngest was only born a few weeks ago."

He grinned again and added, "Sir, if I may be so bold to add, they were no trouble for such a large group. The Bowmans, Smiths, and McDougalls, the other families on board, all have children; we could hear their voices from the decks below. The Rosedales refused to sleep in the cabins but used them as secure storage. They slept with us in steerage and barely made a peep. I made friends with their eldest children."

Jonas sighed, remembering how noisy the upstairs cabins were. "The Rosedale family chose hammocks and pallet beds with us rather than the luxury you offered. Sir, may I again be so bold to say that Linus Rosedale is a good man, as are his sons. The children are well-behaved, except the little ones played up when we hit a huge storm off the tip of Van Diemen's land. I willingly admit that even I was fearful for our lives in that horrendous storm. Mrs Rosedale is a lovely lady who is graceful enough to appear at the royal court. I also befriended a man looking for his sister. William Waterson believes his sister Connie is here somewhere."

John was thrilled. "Yes, she is, but we'll also discuss her later." He had seen Connie only this morning. "Connie is Helena's friend. It's wonderful to hear Helena's family have arrived. She is married to one of my personal guards. If Linus is half the farmer she is, their passage will be well worth it."

The young man's brows raised. He was relaxed and used to being with men of authority. He asked, "The girl who came as a convict is here?"

John smiled. "The very same. Do you have a problem with that?"

Jonas shook his head. "Oh, not at all, sir! I take people at face value. It's just that it fits with what Uncle Charles said of you. Mary said..." He stopped, blushed and grinned unashamedly. He didn't finish his comment but added, "Uncle Charles and Father said you studied Latin at University with them and planned to enter the church of Scotland before the call of the sea won out."

John nodded, "All true, laddie." He then moved from behind his desk towards the soldier. "Come, lad, and you can deliver the good news to Helena yourself. She will be in the garden, and you can see for yourself what an excellent worker she is."

They moved through the house as they spoke. "Her papa taught her well, and as you know, he has come at my invitation to teach others. Being a large family, they had no prospects in England, so I thought I could use them here and reward them with a farm. Here, they will become land owners if willing to toil and teach."

As he spoke, he led the way towards the garden. Once outside his office, John asked with a cheeky smile, "I gather Mary is one of Helena's sisters."

Jonas nodded but remained silent with an embarrassed grin plastered on his face.

Mrs Peach nodded a welcome to the young soldier and overheard the last of the conversation. She was thrilled that Helena's family had arrived. She knew the family were to bunk down at Government House until the governor could take them to the farm he had arranged.

She waited until the men left the kitchen and called her friend. "Virginia, they have arrived. I must drain some pickled pork and have a large roast dinner."

Virginia Cowdrey entered the kitchen as the governor departed. She said, "I was wondering if that was the news the lad brought."

Her mug of tea sat on the table, and she drained its contents quickly. "Priscilla, is there any chance you can help me with the last three beds? Gillian is asleep after being up all night with the baby. I think the little one is teething. Eric has her at the moment as the governor was in his office today."

Mrs Peach wiped her hands on her apron and followed her friend out of the kitchen.

By the time they heard the squeal of delight from Helena, they had finished making the first bed and were on to the second. With only the main guest room to do, they hastened to prepare the last room. The parents would be in this room unless they had a baby. If so, the four sons must share the upstairs guest room. Although the bed was large, two may need to sleep on the floor, but according to Helena, that's what they did at home. Here, there would be pillows and blankets for warmth.

Jonas met Crispin and liked him instantly.

The carriage was called to collect the family. Eric would stay at the house while Crispin went to meet the ship with Jonas and the governor.

In the time elapsed since Jonas arrived, the *Barwell* had been towed around to Sydney Cove, and a gangplank now rested on the side.

John took the carriage to the dock with Crispin and Jonas so the Rosedales could transport the youngest children to the house. It was only a short walk, but the Rosedales would likely have hand luggage.

A trail of children and families was slow in negotiating the rickety ramp. Jonas shook his head when John cocked an eyebrow. The new families had over thirty children, most belonging to the Rosedales. However, the paying passengers alighted first, and the Bowman, Smith, and McDougall families stood on the dock. Their noisy children clung to their parents.

John turned towards the ship. More children waited quietly with some adults. A young man stood near the Rosedales on the ship.

William Waterson's eyes scanned the docks, wondering if he would recognise his sister should she be nearby.

John knew at a glance who this man was.

Crispin saw the Rosedale children waiting patiently on the deck with their parents. Each of the younger ones was cradled in the arms of an older sibling. They were well-behaved and quiet, unlike the noisy cabin-class families.

John waited out of sight of the paying passengers who had already alighted. As soon as they left the area to go to the government barracks for new arrivals, he emerged from the office of the attending processing officer. He needed to inspect the convicts on board and see their state, but he also wished to meet the new family.

As he exited the office, William Balmain arrived from onboard after giving the all-clear to disembark. They walked to the waiting vessel together. William returned to the hospital while John was followed by Crispin. They boarded the ship via the long, bouncing gangplank and he was followed by Crispin and Jonas.

Once on board, John spoke to the young man Jonas described so well and pointed him to the windmill on the hill. He would follow up with Waterson and Connie later.

Crispin was on personal guard duty, so he was in his full red and white regimental uniform, which the Rosedales had not seen before. He greeted his in-laws and introduced them to the governor. As they were unsure what would happen, they remained on deck until receiving instructions.

The governor greeted them and then pointed to the carriage. He and Captain Cameron chatted about the convicts' welfare.

After Crispin hugged his new family, he suggested they start loading the children in the coach. He had written to tell Linus when they were married. So that would be no surprise for Helena's family.

He said, "Helena awaits you, and the carriage will take you there. Your luggage will follow later on a wagon."

Each family member carried a small bag of personal items. From the tiniest toddler to the elder sons, all pulled their weight.

The procession of bodies started as Crispin turned to follow the governor, but was waved by John to stay on deck.

The two older sons were already directing the unloading of their possessions from the hold.

By the time he reemerged, the cases from the cabins were beginning to be packed onto the wagon. A large flat vehicle from the government stable had arrived, and Linus gave directions on what was needed immediately. The wagon slowly filled with the items from the two cabins and the large crates in the hold.

Crispin saw all sorts of unusual bundles being placed on the vehicle. There were only seven luggage cases, but there were numerous crates of gardening tools and even a single furrow plough.

As the carriage drove off, he thought he would have given anything to have been there when Helena saw them. He ducked below to ensure the governor was safe.

These two-hundred and ninety felons were men. Many were ill from scurvy, but they would heal quickly. Men were easier to place, but their health depended on where they went.

John was delighted.

Jonas told them that the majority of these convicts were carpenters, farmers, or had building skills; if so, that would be very beneficial.

When the *Britannia* arrived last year, the condition of the poor convicts on board was dire. Doctor Balmain's first case as a magistrate was this case. He found the captain of the ship callous and brutal. She had embarked with one hundred and forty-four male and forty-four female prisoners; ten male convicts and one female died *en route*. The upshot was that Captain Thomas Dennott was found guilty and never permitted to carry convicts again.

On previous visits, Crispin attended the governor when inspecting those poor wretches and dreaded what he would find every time he descended into the bowels of a ship.

This time, he was pleasantly surprised. Considering how long they had been confined, these men were in reasonably good condition. Their journey had taken two hundred and sixty days, yet they were well and seemingly content.

While inspecting the human cargo, Crispin was surprised that the men all seemed older than he was. At twenty-eight, he felt his life was only starting. Even the troublesome John Macarthur was a year younger than he was. He didn't feel old, but he now had a young son. At eight months old, Jasper was already heaving himself up to stand. He was a beefy child and full of energy. He endeared himself to the governor as he quickly learned that this man gave good hugs. John Hunter became a grandfather figure to his son. John had been found rocking the boy to sleep more than once.

Crispin chuckled; sometimes, it was hard to forget that his boss was the governor. He was more like a loving uncle.

Since Eric's marriage, the governor often privately called his personal guards by their Christian names. Crispin smiled at the informality. He knew the position at the top of a penal settlement left the gentle man with no close friends.

Thankfully, the governor had family a few streets away, but they were frequently busy with their own children. William's wife, Eliza Kent, stood in as first lady if required, but that didn't occur often.

The tour below deck, which included inspecting the new arrivals of convicts and steerage-class free settlers, did not take long.

John signed off on William Balmain's health check with the ship's medic. The convicts would be brought ashore later that week as soon as they had accommodation for them.

By the time John returned to the deck, the carriage had gone. He left the soldiers to process all the convicts, and they returned to Government House.

Jonas was to remain with the ship for the moment.

John had barely exited the deck when he said, "Milroy, we won't await the carriage; we'll walk home and meet your family in a more private setting." The pair did not dawdle and soon entered the official residence through the front door.

When the family arrived, Helena fell into her mother's arms. Due to the welcomes, they had no time to catch up on their news, but Agnes saw that her daughter was well and happy. To her, that was all she needed to know.

Helena was bouncing between her older brothers. "Gerry, Jem, I can't believe you are here."

On return to the house, the ordinarily quiet residence was a hive of activity and joyous laughter.

John was delighted but a little hesitant to join in the reunion.

Crispin saw his hesitation and said, "Sir, may I introduce you properly?"

John nodded and was surprised to find he was slightly nervous. Had he done the right thing by asking them here and hosting them at his house? He followed the young soldier to the source of most of the noise. He was not surprised to discover that the entire household was out in the back garden. Rather than stop the children from staying off the garden beds, most were tending to the weeds that had shot up or were watering the plants. All were laughing and working as they chattered.

John released a long sigh. He hoped for this: a family who knew what they were doing. Watching their activities showed that all the children knew how to work the soil.

Crispin called to his father-in-law.

Linus Rosedale placed his mug of sweet black tea on the plank bench. He held his hand out to his wife and two eldest sons, and they came at his call.

The four and Helena made their way through the garden beds to the governor's side.

Helena's face lit up like the sun. It had been years since she had seen her family. To now leave her son in her sister's care and know he would be safe was wonderful. Crispin made the official introductions.

Unbeknownst to John, Helena's eldest brothers were identical twins and were young clones of their father. Gerald and Jeramy were twenty-three. Neither had formed attachments in England, so they were content to start a new life in New South Wales with the possibility of owning land one day. If the governor wanted farmers, then that is what they would do. They had resigned from their jobs and joined the family on a new adventure. Like Helena, all loved the soil and the production of food.

As soon as they met, Mrs Peach and Mrs Cowdrey loved Agnes

Rosedale. She was a graceful lady who adored her daughter. Rather than ask where they were sleeping, she asked how to assist the ladies.

Considering she had a tiny babe with her, they were shocked she was even up and walking.

Her youngest child was a four-week-old baby and hung on her back in a sling. The child had arrived early and failed to thrive, so Agnes kept her eye on her.

By the time the children followed their mother inside, the youngest children were being cared for by three of their older siblings.

The two younger brothers were scouring the nearby bush for some sticks for the fireplaces. This was more to be outside and run around than needing to find wood. There were few sticks there anyway, as other residents had well-cleared the area. They removed a few pine branches from the big tree outside the garden. They eyed it off and hoped they would be permitted to climb it. It was prickly but certainly climbable. With their excess energy burned off, they returned to the house somewhat quieter. As they entered the kitchen, they washed their hands and, without being asked, picked up the vegetable knives and started preparing the vegetables for dinner that night.

Mrs Peach was delighted and rewarded them with the end crusts of a loaf dripping with rich gravy from the large pickled pork roast.

The boys grinned, thanked her and devoured their treats. At eight and nine, they were at the unfillable age.

They attacked the bowl of dirty potatoes and, once peeled, carefully scrubbed off the thin skin of the turnips rather than peeling them. Each was cut into an even size and placed under a damp covering. Before leaving, they asked if anything else needed to be done.

Mrs Peach had already cut up a freshly peeled and seeded giant pumpkin and had it sitting under another dampened tea towel. She waved them away, astounded that the two lads needed no instruction on their chore. Helena usually did the vegetables, but she had been busy with the family. Gillian was now feeding her grizzly baby in the privacy of their room, and she would appear once the little girl was in bed.

Mrs Cowdrey expected the house to be chaotic. It was just the opposite. Mary and Phoebe, aged eighteen and sixteen, had taken charge of all the young girls, including their newest sibling, Samantha, and Jasper.

Helena had hardly needed to tend to him at all. He was on solids and usually sat in a high chair while they ate. He had Crispin's big brown eyes and Helena's light brown hair.

At five o'clock, Mrs Cowdrey received a summons from the governor. He usually ate alone in the large official dining room, and she expected him to wish to do the same. As he did not have the Kents coming tonight, she expected to be informed that all the children would be kept out of his way and silent, not that she had needed to tell them to shush even once.

The governor beckoned her in and motioned for her to close the door.

He stood as she entered, which was unusual. "Mrs Cowdrey, as the house will be full of Rosedales for a while, I request that, unless I have an official function or guest, we all eat together in the dining room. Would this be difficult or awkward for you? William and the family are away for a while."

Mrs Cowdrey's mouth opened and closed. She finally found her voice. "Sir, the little children will mess it up, though."

She could think of no real reason for the children to eat separately. The floor was timber and just as easily cleaned as the unpolished timber kitchen floor. She was more and more impressed with this family. Earlier that morning, she had managed to get Gillian to do the washing and hang it out, but she had forgotten to bring it in. Some of the children had brought it in and folded it, and the older ones ironed the items that needed pressing.

John smiled at her surprise. "So it's doable?"

She nodded. "Yes, sir. If that is what you wish."

John frowned and then asked, "It is. I presume Helena knew how to use her cutlery properly when she arrived? She certainly does now."

Again, his housekeeper replied, "Yes, sir. She had no problems at all."

John said, "Good, she can only have learned that at home. I need to get to know this family, and that means I need to be seen treating them as guests. Linus Rosedale is a free settler and will be vital to teaching others to garden properly. I will take him to meet the reverend tomorrow, and they can talk gardening until nightfall if they wish. The twins, Gerry and Jem, are keen to assist so they can tag along. Dining together will hopefully help them settle in. From what I have seen, you have lots of helpers. By all, I mean you both, too."

Mrs Cowdrey nodded. "Yes, sir, I shall arrange it." She curtsied and left to sort the evening's arrangements.

As she closed the door, she gasped. They were all to eat at the governor's big table. A slow smile crept to her eyes.

John reclined in his office chair and grinned. This group reminded him of his own family. For some reason, he had no doubts they would have good table manners. He was amazed that sixteen new people were in the house, and he hardly heard a whisper. Unlike his home in Scotland, there were no squabbles all afternoon. The two newborns were tended to as soon as they whimpered. He noticed Eric had been relieved of his daughter by Mary, and she had the knack for silencing the fretful babe.

John saw precisely what his new young soldier, Jonas, saw in this capable girl. Although very different in looks from Helena, she was equally as nice.

John chuckled at the astonished look on his housekeeper's face. He was looking forward to getting to know Linus. The man was younger than he was, but he was worldly-wise in a way John was not. John's years at sea meant he viewed his world through a narrow lens. People were not titles or rank; they were God's creations. John looked forward to this dinner and many more to follow.

The meal went smoothly. The children behaved beautifully, and when the older girls asked to be excused, they took the younger children to bed.

Soon, the house was quiet, as all the little ones were asleep.

On returning to the kitchen, Mrs Peach thought she would have all the cleaning up to do. However, she found all the baking dishes already soaking. The teenage girls had their arms in the sink and were doing the plates and cutlery. They were hardly making a sound and working efficiently. They had found the box of linen tea towels under the sink, and the clean dinnerware was being neatly stacked on the kitchen table. She stood at the door with her mouth open.

Mrs Cowdrey came to assist and found the work almost completed. She tapped her friend and said, "Well, my dear, I suggest we leave this to the capable help and put on the kettle for everyone. The governor wants us to join them for tea."

She carried the tray to the dining room. They had agreed to have their tea there while sitting around the table.

The ladies left when their cups were empty.

Soon, only the older family members, including the governor, Helena, and Crispin, remained at the table. Helena poured another cup of the strong, sweet tea. "Mama, we drink tea here as Papa has it: hot, sweet, and black." She poured each of them a mug full and sat listening to the conversation.

New mugs had recently arrived from John's potter friend, Colin Osborne. On his last visit, he complained that the official house only had tiny teacups. Arthur Phillip had taken his gift home. Two dozen new globular mugs arrived earlier that week from Colin. John had his special one from his first visit. It had a ship etched on it. He had been given a pair, but one smashed on the journey here. All admired the new crockery. These held a decent amount of tea and fitted in cupped hands beautifully.

Crispin sat grinning. He didn't care that he had no idea what they were talking about when discussing farming methods. He had sat enjoying a meal at the governor's table with his extended family. His life had changed so much from the streets of London. The night he found a beautiful girl asleep on his aunt's step changed his entire life. He loved it and her more daily. Who knew what more would happen? He was happy, and that was unexpected.

John saw Crispin's grin and knew that the young man was content. As everyone had their tea, John said, "Right, now I suggest we get down to tin-tacks. Mr Rosedale, I am going to throw formality away. We are to be on first-name terms. Linus, I will presume that you know a lot about farming. Here, we have heavily caked clay soil that's never been tilled. It is hard to work and in poor condition. Helena will tell you that. I had a group of convicts break the soil for her gardens here, but it still took weeks before she could plant anything into it."

Linus said, "I've not worked virgin soil before, sir. However, I looked at what my girl had done, and the dirt looks healthy now, so there is potential. The ground in England has been farmed for thousands of years, but it is how you tend it to ensure it stays productive." He gave his daughter a nod and said, "Nella said there are worms throughout the entire garden now."

John looked at Helena and asked, "Worms are good?" He looked surprised.

Helena nodded. "They are, sir. They keep the soil healthy." She didn't explain more, as the governor didn't need to know. "None were there when it was first dug over, only nasty black spiders."

The boys and Linus discussed how they could teach others about farming.

Helena warned them about the dangers of snakes and spiders.

John reclined with his arms folded, listening to the discussion around him. Helena told her father how she had tempered the soil and that the minister supplied her with seeds and seedlings. She enthusiastically outlined what she had achieved since planting her first tree.

After a short time, John interrupted. "That is all well and good, but Linus, Agnes, and boys I must tell you what I have arranged about a farm. I have had the land cleared and dug over. It's partially fenced. A house is built and is ready for you. I plan that this farm will be worked for the government, with eighty per cent of the crops returned to Government Stores. That leaves twenty per cent for your pocket. It doesn't sound like much, but as a government-owned farm, all your food and clothing allocations will also be included while it's under my authority."

Linus looked at his wife. That was a better deal than he had hoped.

John saw them both smile. He added, "That is just the beginning; once you have worked the farm for a few years, I plan to sign it over to you as yours to keep. I mentioned this in my letter." He explained the situation about the Corps, and farms for a reward. Linus caught on quickly and grinned. John continued. "Your farm is about one hundred and twenty acres, of which about seventy acres is already cleared and ploughed. I have left the final fifty acres natural so you can see what you will be battling against. I saw a single furrow plough on the wagon a short time ago, and I'm hoping you may have brought some stock to pull it?"

Linus nodded with a grin. "I brought two working bullocks, one half-grown bull calf, a dozen unrelated cows ready to calf, as I mated them shortly before leaving. We can milk them soon; I also have four dogs. I hope you don't mind, but I'd like to release them soon. They need to run off some energy."

Helena gasped and interrupted, "Papa, did you bring Kelly?"

John's brows shot up. Linus nodded absentmindedly in answer to his daughter's question. Agnes saw John's interest and explained softly, "Kelly is Helena's English Springer Spaniel. She was the runt of a litter on the squire's farm. Our three other dogs are an unusual assortment of mongrels.

However, even though all four are pets, they are also working dogs. They are all good at rounding up stock."

Turning to his daughter, Linus grinned. "I did, my dear. I thought you would throw something at me if I left her at home."

John had also had a springer spaniel when he was a lad, and he adored the breed. This stay was getting better and better. He commented. "I love dogs. When I was here the first time, I had greyhounds. The kangaroos killed them. The roos look cuddly, but do not let the children or dogs near them."

His words made Linus smile. "I'm so glad you like them, sir, for I think you may end up with Kelly living here. She belongs to Helena."

John's face lit up this time. "Does she dig, Helena? Would she destroy the garden?"

Helena shook her head. "No, sir, she'll be fine in there, but she will help keep the birds away. However, she loves to accompany a rider, so you may end up with a shadow if you wish to take her anywhere. She's a good guard dog."

John was thrilled. His springer also loved a good run. "I'd be honoured, Helena. Now, back to the farm. Linus, it's twenty or so miles west of here, so you won't see your grandson often."

Agnes gave a resigned sigh. "Then I'll cuddle him as much as possible while here." She chuckled. "Sir, did I say I loved babies?"

John said, "No need to, ma'am. Like my mother, you have many children. I am one of nine, so I love them too. Jasper has a special place in my heart. I miss our lively household from home."

After much chatter about what the farm was like, Linus thought he had better tell the governor what else he had brought with him. "Sir, we discussed the plough and stock, but the cabins you supplied are filled with seedlings and my stock of grain and seeds."

Helena nearly choked. "You brought your own seed grain and the entire seed library?"

Her father nodded. "Well, I wasn't going to give them away now, was I, miss? The letter said you needed someone to start a farm from scratch; well, you can't grow things without the seeds." He shrugged and grinned.

Helena giggled, then said, "Sir, you have no idea what a monster you have created. Papa has one of the largest seed libraries in England. I'm talking about cases and cases of stored seeds. It's how I knew how to collect and store our seed."

John was thrilled. "Seriously? You and the reverend are really going to be good friends. You didn't, by any chance, bring any rhubarb crowns, did you? I am partial to that and have not had much since leaving England. Reverend Richard gave us a tiny one that has produced one edible stem so far."

Linus grinned and nodded. "I brought a box of them. They are in soil and ready to plant out. They were just shooting when I checked them last week. I'm guessing there are about fifty small crowns."

John's eyes lit up with delight. He loved rhubarb. "I would have been pleased with two crowns. Can Helena have a few, please?"

Linus had taken stock of the governor. "Sir, I think I can spare a few crowns for my daughter. That is a fair swap along with some asparagus for you, considering you have offered me over a hundred acres of farmland." Linus could not wait until John saw what else he had brought for the colony's use. One cabin in the ship was lined with waterproof canvas and looked like an exotic greenhouse. He had instructed the boys to leave emptying that until they had somewhere safe to store it. The tiny porthole in the cabin supplied the required light to grow the plants. He had covered the rhubarb for most of the trip and only uncovered it eight weeks ago to stimulate growth. The plants were tricked into a long, dormant winter. He had chosen to sleep below deck with more room than squash into the small cabins. Knowing that he needed to be ready to get to work, he had already started germinating some of the plants that took a little longer to grow. The other cabin contained his seed library and some large fruit trees. Linus sat grinning at the man he hoped would become a good friend. He liked him.

Chapter 13 The Farm

$\mathcal{A}$fter staying for a week at the official residence in Sydney, a trip was planned to see the new farm. However, first, the diplomatic box finally arrived on the governor's desk and needed John's attention. He had been dealing with the issue of two attempted mutinies on the *Barwell* on the voyage out and had been kept busy with the associated paperwork and keeping the peace between all parties. He immediately realised the official box had been tampered with as the wax seal was off the box latch.

He called Jonas up from the barracks to see the state of the brass box and enclosed leather pouch.

As expected, the documents inside had been rifled.

Jonas inspected the official letter from his uncle and saw that although sealed, the hair was missing from the wax seal. This could only mean that someone had remelted the wax. His uncle's seal was different.

He checked the impression and saw that it was now illegible. As he stamped the ring in the red wax himself, he ensured it was perfect but at a slight angle. The seal was now straight.

The hair Jonas mentioned had not been noticed by the persons who had illegally read the letter. There was a trace of it, shrivelled and burned but thoroughly embedded in the wax seal that had been reheated and resealed.

Who would have done this? Dore? One of his friends?

Jonas and John's eyes met.

A slow smile crossed both faces. "So, you were correct, Jonas. This shows that my correspondence is being intercepted. I need to be more diligent in sending certain official documents. I think I shall repeat your example, send dummy letters via the official despatch box, and ensure the captains carry a more comprehensive duplicate. I shall also repeat the hair trick. I presume your Uncle Charles knows of this?"

Jonas nodded as he grinned. "Yes, sir, he certainly does. It was his idea. He also suggested as to how we can achieve said secrecy. I shall write to my uncle and include a parcel of some botany specimens for Sir Joseph

Banks. He is a friend of my father and yours. Your letter can be enclosed with that. No one will be any the wiser as to the contents of the bulky package. On the journey out, I made no secret of my identity or Sir Joseph's request for me to send specimens."

With the local conspiracy exposed, the pair knew that all official instructions were under threat.

Jonas's delivery brought news that London had heard of the discontent from the Corps.

John wondered what he had done to rile the free settlers except to do as ordered by London. He would continue to strive to clean the place up and develop the farmland. He had not even followed those orders to the letter as he was told to remove all but two convicts from each allocation. Knowing how hard the virgin soil was to break, he had not complied with that directive. Convicts were needed to till the soil and tend the farms. He would allocate more where required.

The Rosedale's animals were carefully unloaded. The livestock was herded into the government stock yard close to the barracks, where the cows were to give birth. The four dogs were the first to be ushered down the ramp. They were taken directly to the house and released into the backyard.

Kelly bounced and barked when she saw Helena. She was soon standing on her hind legs and hugging her lost mistress.

Helena had not told her family she was expecting another child, but Kelly sniffed at her stomach and whined. Helena had seen her do this each time her mother was increasing.

As her mother sat beside her at the time, Agnes realised that her daughter was expecting again. "Does your husband know yet, dear?"

Helena shook her head. "No, we lost our first child at three months along, so I won't tell him until I'm sure. Jesse is buried under this rose bush; hence, this is our happy place. I felt a little ill this morning, so I will tell him soon. I must be about eight weeks along, maybe a bit more."

Agnes smiled. She already loved the warmth of this new place, and they were nearly in winter. Today would have been a hot day for them at home.

Helena said, "Mama, it gets hot in summer here, and by hot, I mean you will feel like you are melting. The days often end with a huge storm late in the evening, and we get an explosion of thunder, lightning, and the heaviest rain you could imagine. But, do you know what...?"

Agnes shook her head.

Helena finished her comment with, "Mama, I love it here. I love the life and the climate, and of course, I have Crispin and Jasper."

Agnes patted her daughter's hand. "It's enough for me that we will all be here together, love. Your father is a good man and gave me the final choice of whether we were to come. I would have sailed all the way around the world to be near you, not just halfway."

Agnes drew Helena into her arms for a hug.

A week after the family's arrival, the governor loaded Linus, the twins, Eric and Crispin and their overnight bags into his carriage. The six men were to view the cleared farmland for the first time.

John, Crispin, and Eric had seen the land when it was first chosen. They planned to stay overnight in the official residence, so the outside guard was doubled to protect the household in their absence.

Nathaniel Franklyn, his steward and secretary, had chosen the regular guards from the daily duty roster, but John had made little effort to befriend any of them until now. However, knowing they would be making this trip and leaving the women alone, the governor inspected the new batch of soldiers to choose new guards himself.

The regiment replacements who had arrived on the *Barwell* were untainted by the Corps. Plus, Linus told him who to trust. Linus stood out of sight of the troops and gave a nod or a shake as John inspected each man.

One man, Ensign Bond, was not amongst the assembly but under arrest.

One of the letters that Jonas had brought with him gave John a brief outline of a few of the new soldiers. Bond was accused of mutiny *en route*.

Nathaniel Franklyn recommended four soldiers as trustworthy.

John knew differently. He had been advised to stay clear of the four men Jonas had already told him about. John was puzzled at Franklyn's choices, but said nothing.

Charles sent unofficial information that John would never have received if it had been sent through the official despatches.

With his mail being intercepted, this information would have been vetted and destroyed, and those men befriended by the power-hungry military here. As John did his inspection, he had each man announce their name.

Jonas was first chosen, and his three friends were selected. New sentry quarters had been constructed near the back of the Sydney house near the laundry. These guards were to use this new are along with four other rotating sentries.

The large room had beds with horsehair mattresses, and the governor had installed a hob stove in the centre of the room. They ate in the kitchen but were permitted to make tea in their room.

Jonas loved the rough life and relished his new role. Even standing on guard duty was not arduous, although somewhat dull.

The guards alternated the circulating sentry duty under the verandah, so they all got to have a regular walk. They each had fleecy leather gloves and a warm cape when on duty. They were permitted to chat and did not need to stand at attention unless someone approached or the governor exited.

Shifts were only four hours long, and Mrs Cowdrey brought them hot tea and cake after two hours.

Jonas also found that the Rosedale boys would come and chat with them to while away the tedious hours. However, soon, the family would move to their new farm. Jonas hoped to be transferred to Parramatta to be at hand for them.

With the men away, Jonas was installed in the boy's room upstairs to be available if required. He had not shared a bed before and had been surprised at how warm two small boys made his bedding.

On board the *Barwell*, he had befriended Gerry and Jem to get closer to their sister, Mary. She was only about a year younger than he was, and she was beautiful. Her shy glances made his heart pound in a very unexpected way. She never stepped out of line by encouraging him, but her sidelong, shy smiles had succeeded in breaking through where the primped and preened titled society misses in London had failed.

As an earl's son, he had been chased since birth. However, he had seen through the shallowness of society very early in his life. His parents had refused to arrange a marriage for him, and for that, he was pleased. He wanted to stand on his own two feet and could do that here. He was thrilled to be chosen as the internal guard for the family he had grown to admire.

As the son of a peer, he should be looking for someone from his own class to marry. Well, that might not happen. His father had given his permission to marry for love. No one was from his class here, and he was darned if he was going to stay single all his life, and he had no wish to return home for more than a visit.

He grinned as he lay in the soft feather bed with a sleeping child to each side of him. He would do what he could to woo Mary with the aim of marriage. He hoped she felt the same.

These lads would then be his brothers. Unlike London, they had come to know each other quite well on the over eight-month voyage out here. He had nearly a year before he could marry without permission. He hoped that he would receive approval from Linus to marry her. He had already given John the signed document from his father assigning *loco parentis* to the governor.

Jonas closed his eyes for the night with that happy thought in mind.

~

The carriage arrived at the farm just after noon. The building was completed two months ago and sat empty. The grass had been scythed regularly, forming a green and lush lawn at the front. All but one of the trees had been cleared around the house, but the bushland still stood tall at the rear of the property. The trees had only been under-scrubbed and dead wooded, so they were not in danger of falling on the shingle-roofed house, but John knew of bushfires that tore through the area and would suggest clearing them back further.

As they alighted, the group took in the view before them. John had not been out here since the house was finished, and he liked what he saw.

Linus was stunned. "Sir, is this really for us? The house is immense and also delightful. We have never had an outdoor area on a house before."

The eight-foot-wide pillared verandah circled three sides of the commodious structure.

Linus was in awe of their new home.

John noted that one large gum tree overhanging the verandah would need to be felled. He was surprised it had been left standing so close to a building. He mentioned their propensity to drop big limbs.

Linus nodded and gave a smile. "Sir, if the inside is half as good as the outside, then a mere three years of work is not enough to pay you for this."

John chuckled. "We'll see, Linus; you have no idea what we need you to do yet."

He led the way indoors. The twelve-foot high ceiling made the spacious rooms feel even larger.

They wandered down the long internal corridor while poking their heads into each room. Some were furnished with basic things; others were empty. The master bedroom contained a large double bed, a chest of drawers and a tall wardrobe. A wicker cot stood on the far side of the room.

Other rooms had stacks of horsehair mattresses on the floors. Some were obviously in the process of being made.

It took some time before all six people made it into the kitchen. There was a new range stove with internal cooking facilities, similar to Mrs Peach's at Government House.

Agnes was intrigued with the contraption in Sydney, as she was used to cooking over an open fire. Mrs Peach was teaching her to use it and how to regulate temperatures.

Linus grinned at his good fortune but said, "Sir, this is a mansion far beyond our wildest dreams. We do not deserve such luxury."

John did not reply this time. He had planned this house to accommodate the whole family. If they keep having children, they may need to enclose the verandah and build more rooms.

The tour took them through the back door and into the vast space that would one day become a vegetable and herb garden.

John said, "Linus, we have huge fires through here. I suggest cutting those trees back and having a wide fire break before you do much to the garden. I will allocate a convict team to assist you in clearing the area, and they will also show you how to remove the stumps. This is some of the virgin bushland in this area. The front paddock was low scrub, but the timber should keep you in firewood for some years."

Linus nodded and walked towards the trees.

John called out to him to watch for snakes. He watched Linus halt and slowly cross the ankle-high grass area to check the timber.

The farm and the house were thoroughly investigated.

The boys pulled out a mattock and spade from under the seats in the carriage and dug a few holes in the backyard to check the soil.

Linus checked these on his return and did the same as Helena had done. He spat in the dirt and checked the clay content.

The three knowledgeable heads poured over the ground and stood discussing the sun and the angle of the planned home vegetable garden. They had already discussed the opposite seasons.

Crispin and Eric stayed with the governor. Both were on guard; although this was an easy chore, this area was close to some of the Corps' farms. No attacks had occurred, but both had their muskets loaded and ready should they be required.

Gerry was the first to return to the three uniformed men. "Sir, is there any chance of a barn or storeroom? If not, may we build one? We can keep the seeds on the verandah or a back bedroom for now, but a dark storeroom would be safer, with a lock if possible. Knowing the need for these out here, the temptation would be great should they be left out in the open; plus, they could spoil."

John asked, "How can seed spoil?"

Gerry said, "If it were to get wet, they sprout and become useless. The seeds must be harvested from mature plants, and the viable grains or seeds are then stored in a dry, dark place. Only the back bedroom is dark enough."

John nodded. "Ahh, right, I'll get on to that then. So, a stable-cum-barn with a lockable storeroom that has no windows. I presume shelving would be required in there? And a stone floor to stop the rodents."

Gerry nodded. "If possible, sir, that would be wonderful."

John was dying to know if they liked the house. He waited for Linus to return before asking. "Linus, do you think farming this ground is possible?"

Linus was still deep in thought and replied seriously, "It's doable, sir."

John probed again, "And the house is adequate?"

Crispin and Linus's eyes met. Knowing they lived in a one-hundred-year-old two-bedroom thatched cottage, this place was a palace. With a sly smile, Linus said, "I think we can manage here, sir. We could fit..." he mused, "...um, another ten children in here."

He noticed John's astonished face and laughed. "Just kidding, sir! This is an amazing house, sir. It's so vast that we won't know what to do with ourselves. Agnes will have her hands full in that huge kitchen; it's just as well the girls will help her."

John chuckled. He wondered how long the older girls would stay. "Don't forget you will have four convicts to assist. Two girls will be inside helpers, and there will be two men once the initial ploughing is done. I suggest the new barn have a sleeping quarter section for the men and others working and learning here. With so many daughters, you won't want the males staying in the house. The small back room on the verandah is for the servants."

Linus frowned. "Oh, sir, I'm not keen on having convicts work for me."

John said, "Linus, I was hoping you could take some of the youngest to protect them. Some girls are only fourteen, and the boys are not much older. They are like Gillian was when she arrived."

Linus frowned, "If I must have any, certainly send us the young ones, as they will need safe places to stay. My Agnes will teach them, and they can then find husbands like my Helena did and live a happy life. If you do that, then I'll take them. If one could read, maybe she could teach our children some lessons. Maybe we could all learn. We never had the opportunity." He gave a firm nod towards Crispin. "I'll ensure they become fine fellows like my girl Nella's man over there. One of your chaps from the ship has eyes for our Mary. I will need to watch them. Though, I'll not let Ensign Bond near any of my girls. You must watch that fellow; he and his friends are trouble."

Crispin heard the compliment and found himself blushing.

Eric almost choked, laughing.

Crispin said, "Ditch the cackling, Eric; you also married a convict. We've both softened with the love of good women."

Eric's grin showed he was not upset at all. Since Crispin's long talk, he had become a different person. His laughter often rang out nowadays. He was his infant daughter's caring and adoring father, often tending to her needs before Gillian could respond. This was the first time either father had been away from their children overnight, and neither was keen on leaving their wives. They may have baulked at going if Agnes and the family had not been with them. After Jonas had been asked to sleep indoors, they agreed that their families would be safe.

John knew that the four men who broke in were still on the road gangs but were chained up each night in cells in Parramatta. They would spend the rest of their lives breaking rocks. However, they were not the only lustful men in the colony.

John was considering sending those particular miscreants to the new coal mine.

Women were in such short supply that men would fight over them. The arrival of a family with ten daughters, some of marriageable age, was a great danger.

In consequence, John doubled the outside guards in his absence.

Eric leaned over to Crispin and said, "Hey Cris, have you ever considered living in a place like this and learning to farm?"

Crispin wondered if his face showed his love of this sort of life. He adored the Rosedale family and would be delighted if they knew he would give his eyeteeth to be part of the close-knit family circle. Crispin knew he had waited too long to give a negative reply. His long sigh was followed by, "I'd love it, Eric, and so would Helena. But the governor has given us so much already, and I am honour bound to stay with him."

Unbeknownst to them, having checked the house again, John and Linus walked up behind them as they eyed off the ploughed fields in front of the house.

John noticed that there were no locks on any of the doors of the new home. He would remedy that. He moved to stand beside Crispin and said, "I won't be here forever, lads. I'd like to see you both settled somewhere before my term ends. From the letters Thistlethwaite brought, there are disquieting murmurs already in London. I do not expect the Corps to go down quietly; hence, I will do what I can to teach those convicts interested in farming to be self-sufficient."

After a lengthy discussion with Linus, he suggested they concentrate on growing consumables instead of competing with them and growing grain. These would include potatoes, peas, beans, and other root crops.

John explained to Linus. "An exclusive group is causing trouble to those growing grain to sell and not to distil, but if your farm concentrates on the fresh food and fresh corn, I don't think they would worry much."

Eric looked at his boss with a frown. "Sir, we will not leave you unprotected. That is our priority at the moment."

Crispin said, "I won't say that Helena and I have not discussed it because we have, but as Eric said, we will not leave your side, sir."

John chortled. "Ahh, but what if I moved out here? The new Government House in Parramatta is half-built. Until it is finished, I will claim a room here on the farm as I do not trust that shoddy structure in Parramatta. I know it will keel over one day. I can't stay with Colin any more as I have filled their guest rooms with more convict girls. It's why we have not been recently. I intend to come regularly to oversee the foundation of the new farm school. It's another reason I had this house built so large, for I have decided to call this place a Government Agricultural Farm School. If I became a regular visitor, then that would give Linus prestige. Plus, I might learn something about the needs of the farmers and free settlers."

Both soldiers gasped. Crispin said, "Sir, as much as I would like to say that would be great, this is but one idea in the grand scheme of things. You are far too valuable to the colony to worry about us and our family. Our women know this and would not wish it any other way. We all love our lives in Sydney with you."

Eric was nodding as Crispin spoke.

John was thankful both refused to leave him. He said, "Fine, but we might be able to work it both ways. You are each entitled to a land grant under Governor Phillip's edict. I agree with that, and giving you both a farm would not be unreasonable. But for goodness sake, do not compete with the Corps. They will do to you what they did to poor John Baughan. They destroyed him and his farm."

John surveyed the cleared land in front of him. He took a long, deep breath. When he released it, he said, "I can breathe here, lads. I still love the sea, but this is good too. I think regular visits here would be good for my soul. I will still need to work, but here I can relax. I can't do that in town any more. With Dore as my Colonial Secretary, I will need a sanctuary he can't breach. These days he even finds me when I visit the Brays at the mill or the Osbornes in Parramatta." He shuddered and groaned.

~

In town, the household was busy sorting the luggage and equipment the family brought.

As Jonas was the inside security, he felt that helping the family where required was part of his duty. Helping Mary, in particular, was noticed.

When the carriage of men returned to Sydney the following day, Helena sought out her father and drew him into the garden with a mug of tea. She mentioned the young soldier's partiality to her sister. "Papa, have you noticed Jonas Thistlethwaite, or are you choosing to ignore the situation?"

Linus grinned. "I'm not blind, love, and you would need to be if you missed the lad drooling after our Mary. He was like that on the ship out. However, he's a bit above our touch. Lass, he's a toff from the second highest tier, you know, and as such, I don't think he would consider a permanent attachment with our farming family, do you?"

Helena giggled. "Papa here is not there. You would be surprised at what goes on. You should say something to him, or he may inadvertently compromise her."

Linus sighed. "I suppose I must; however, that is not a job I relish."

He glanced at Helena, then said, "Nella, I gather things went badly for you in London. You did not let us know about the situation; even if you had, the reverend may not have chosen for us to know." He swallowed nervously. "Did someone… I mean, were you…?" He couldn't ask what he wished to know.

Thankfully, Helena knew what he meant. "No, Papa, I was not molested that way, but two men tried. I quickly received the nickname Helena the Hellcat because I fought all the men off. I spread the rumour I had the clap, and they left me alone on the ship. I met Crispin in London, and he followed me out here. He will vouch that I was not violated, so fear not."

Linus released a long sigh. "Thank the good Lord for that!" They had finished their tea, and he slid his arm around his eldest daughter's shoulders and drew her close. "I missed you like crazy, you know, Nella."

His cheek rested on her head, the loving gesture wiping away the years of separation.

Helena rested her head on her father's chest. She was pleased they were now reunited, but life would move on. She was already married, and Helena expected Mary to follow, regardless of what her father thought. She liked Jonas, and so did Crispin.

As the *Barwell* brought in a few other free families, the governor had his hands full finding somewhere to bunk them down until they could settle.

William Waterson found Connie and moved in with the Brays at the mill.

Others needed land allocated to them.

However, there were other issues.

There had been two attempted mutinies on the vessel. Thanks to the Rosedales and Jonas, John knew who the perpetrators were. An ensign in a hammock near Jonas was overheard plotting with eight fellow soldiers. Ensign George Bond was arrested on the voyage and was still awaiting John's attention.

John realised he should have attended to this before visiting the farm but needed a short break before dealing out the required summary justice. On his return from Parramatta, John summoned Jonas, and they were closeted in his office for over an hour.

After this meeting, John Murray, William Hallam, Gregory Belloe, James Nevil, Patrick Welch, John Brown, John Broadbent, and Ensign Bayley were arrested and charged.

John planned that these soldiers would all join the other convicts in irons. The nine men were livid, as were some of their officers. These men arrived as part of the New South Wales Corps under John's authority. He intended to deal with them in such a way that silenced the Corps in the colony. However, he knew they must have a fair trial. A court was arranged for August, and the nine were to stand trial with George Bond as their ringleader.

While the case was assembled, John was busy sorting the new settlers and arranging appropriate work for the new convicts. For once, they had been sent some with usable skills. These included bricklayers, stonemasons, carpenters, brick-makers, and burners to make both lime and charcoal. The group also included labourers who removed earth, gravel, and mud and formed sloping embankments for levee banks. All were skills needed in the colony, but still, there were no other convict farmers.

John had yet to interview the Scottish Bowman, McDougall and Smith families. He suspected they were not skilled farmers as claimed, but had yet to confirm that.

He was correct. They had been sent to construct a corn mill in Parramatta. Building such a mill could be the spark to ignite a coup. Thank goodness he had the foresight to bring out the Rosedales. John's head shook. Why had the Admiralty sent such persons when he specifically wanted gardeners and farmers?

John Bowman had potential and struck up a friendship with Linus on the voyage out. He was a carpenter and an experienced mill builder. With the land allocation, this man was willing to learn to grow other crops. He would become one of Linus's first students and qualify for an allocation and a land grant.

The governor quickly moved these two families to the large house just out of Parramatta. Knowing they had to share the home until Bowman's grants were finalised, the two groups were told not to spread out too much once at the farm as others may join them.

They had become used to being confined to a small area on the ship, so the children shared two rooms. This meant that others could come for visits without juggling beds.

By the time the new barn and stables were finished, the McDougalls had joined the expanded Rosedale household. The three families toiled until the back paddocks were cleared and the stumps burned.

Linus showed them how to cross-cut the stumps and burn them without digging them out. A slow burn over the cold months would not need to be watched overnight.

While behind the house was being cleared, Linus re-ploughed the front field and sowed his first crops. He had brought various seed stocks and segmented the field into barley, corn, oats, and vegetables. He also planted test patches of various grains.

These crops would be for family use and not be sent to market. However, the harvest would supply seed for the new farms. The house was packed to the rafters, with nearly thirty people over eighteen in the house. The numerous children were each allocated chores. These included jobs like making beds, laundry, milking the eclectic herd, collecting the eggs, or, if old enough, assisting on the farm. Firewood and kindling needed to be collected daily, and this was a job all enjoyed.

A small structure was erected near the back door to store cut logs and kindling.

~

By the time the first shoots were poking up their heads, the Bowmans heard they were being given a one-hundred-acre land grant out on the Hawkesbury River not far from Robert Webb. They were delighted; this area was lightly wooded, requiring little clearing.

Linus visited the new grant with the governor and John Bowman. While the two Johns wandered the area, Linus stood looking at the hilly area. He noticed a row of fallen trees behind him and realised it was flood debris.

On the return of the two men, Linus pointed this out. "Bowman, when you build here. Make sure that the house is well above the flood level. Move higher if you see old signs of water covering the area. I would even elevate the house on stilts just in case."

He pointed to the row of trees behind them and the difference in the tree line of the scrub further up the hill. "See how the growth changes. I'm guessing that this river has some mighty floods. So stay well clear of the water. Look, on the other side of the river, you can easily identify a similar change in vegetation." Linus pointed to the bushland at eye level on the valley's far side. The vegetation had been scoured away only a few years earlier. There was sparse growth over there at a much lower level.

Linus went on to explain. "Bowman, the benefit is that the flat areas will be very fertile and have access to water. You will get good crops in most seasons; however, you will probably lose one in ten years through a flood. Ensure you factor that into your farm figures, and you should survive."

The governor was astounded. He had seen lower evidence of the floods but had not realised that they rose so high. Once Linus pointed out the signs, they were apparent. He would suggest, if not require, that all homes be built above this level.

Linus pointed to a line of trees on the river's edge and said, "I suggest that you leave those trees and even plant more to act as both a windbreak and flood protection from the fast-moving water when it comes. Do not try to plough all the land, but leave a buffer for grazing. Fence the fields vertically so the animals can move from the river."

With the land survey done, the Bowmans arranged a large tent and eventually moved to their new farm. The McDougalls chose land closer to Linus. Their grant was only a few miles away, near *Bella Vista* farm that Macarthur purchased from Foveaux. They visited often, and the Rosedales and McDougalls assisted each other when required. The third family were the Smiths. John Smith had some farming experience and was allocated an abandoned farm near the McDougalls. The land he chose was not ideal, and he would have difficulty keeping water up to any crops. Linus gave him various suggestions on maintaining moisture in the soil and protecting against evaporation by mulching his fields well.

By the end of September, Government House was once again quiet. The immediate needs of the four families were met. Mary would have loved to have stayed, but Linus put his foot down. She would accompany her parents to Parramatta.

Chapter 14 Holy Smoke
Spring 1798

On the last day in September, the household at the vice-regal residence was up and ready to attend church. The small children delayed their departure from home, and eventually, the governor, who was waiting in the carriage, called for Gillian and Helena to travel with their husbands to the service. Usually, they would walk while the three men went in the carriage.

Much to John's regret, Jonas volunteered to be absorbed back into the Corps. However, he dug for information and passed on any undercurrents. As an ensign, he could still move through the Corps somewhat incognito. He moved to Parramatta and found a unique and trustworthy way of sending messages.

Two letters addressed to Helena arrived, and the writing was so atrocious that they were almost illegible. She chuckled when she realised the missive was from Jonas for the governor. No one was any the wiser, thinking it was a letter from her all but illiterate family.

The wax seal was not stamped but embedded with a gum leaf and fingerprint. Like hair, this could not be easily reheated with a candle.

With a potential colony-wide intrigue now unveiled, John needed to discuss his findings with Richard Johnson. Running late as he was, he decided he would invite the Johnsons for tea after church.

Thankfully, the partially chanted Eucharist was now at seven o'clock in the morning rather than dawn. As the day warmed, the many bodies heated the cool air in the church.

The building seated nearly five hundred people and was packed to the rafters. More people lined the back walls and sides.

The convicts filled the nave with the bulk of the soldiers seated in one transept and the free settlers in the other with the officers.

The unique design of this wattle and daub building suited its purposes and kept the vying groups apart.

The thatched roof insulated the building somewhat from the harsh climate outside. Since the glass installation in the windows shortly after John's arrival, the building was much more comfortable, not that one ever looked for comfort in a house of God.

Today, all the windows were propped open to catch any breeze.

The service concluded at half past eight, and on exiting, John congratulated Richard on a good and challenging sermon. "Reverend, are you both free for tea, let's say, in an hour or whenever you can make it?"

Richard glanced at his wife, and she nodded acceptance. "Yes, sir, we are. We should be finished here by about ten."

John smiled. He knew the forthcoming conversation would interest the gentleman.

Richard had come to greatly respect the learnéd man who was now governor and knew that, although his style of worship was not one he would have chosen for himself, coming from the Church of Scotland, it met the town's needs. Roman Catholics and Jews were part of his congregation. All were part of God's people.

At ten o'clock, the security guards saw the Johnsons approaching. They had been told to permit them entry as soon as they arrived.

Mrs Cowdrey opened the door and ushered the couple into the sitting room. She took the children and Abaroo out to Helena in the garden. Abaroo lived with the Johnsons for over a year when smallpox claimed her family in 1789. She stayed with them long enough to learn English before returning to her tribe. However, she still made regular visits. She had not been with the family this morning, so she was surprised to see the lass.

Abaroo would come for a few weeks and then disappear again for months.

Mary Johnson had a deep affection for the unfortunate, scarred girl and adopted her. The two Johnson children, Milbah and Henry, known as Harry, adored her.

Eight-year-old Milbah also adored Jasper, and she entertained the delightful toddler, while six-year-old Harry helped weed the garden, having been taught by his father to watch out for spiders of any kind.

Crispin and Eric stood guard outside the governor's door while Gillian helped prepare the meal in the kitchen.

Caris was now nine months old and crawled everywhere. However, as she was in a growth spurt, she was currently asleep in their room, which was rare as she was often in tears, as was Gillian.

The two guards had a quiet conversation as they stood watch.

The thick timber door soundproofed their chat. "Cris, have you thought more about the governor's offer of a farm? Gill and I have thought of nothing else. We can't imagine having a place of our own."

Crispin nodded. "Too right we have. Helena is itching to go and join her family, but she knows I won't leave the governor. After the news that his despatches are being intercepted, our first duty is to him."

Eric frowned. "But sir said he would see us with some land anyway. Are you going to accept it if he offers?"

Crispin's grin answered his question. "I'm not an idiot, Eric; of course I will. But I won't leave until he does. It can lie fallow, or Linus can use our land for his farming class and prepare it for us as part of the school. Gerry and Jem have already agreed to oversee it for us."

Eric's face lit up. "You've asked them already?"

Crispin nodded. He didn't answer as the door swung open.

The governor stood there and said, "Come in, lads; we need to chat. There have been developments."

Crispin and Eric glanced at each other and entered.

John waved them to a settee near where the Johnsons were seated. He was frowning, which he rarely did.

He walked towards his window and looked out. His hands were tapping as he clasped them behind his back. "When I say there have been developments, Richard has told me that he has already heard of stirrings of discontent, and he wrote to London some months ago voicing his support of my government. Therefore, I'm guessing that his letter was one of the reasons for the subterfuge from Jonas and his uncle, Lord Phillimont. I wondered why they made such an effort when I had heard nothing. David's despatches didn't say very much, but the two together, with my impassioned pleas, were obviously enough to make Admiralty House listen. David may have been interviewed and given more information than he could put in writing."

The soldiers were both stunned. They had heard nothing, but that was not surprising, as they were now ensconced at Government House. Jonas was right to remain with the Corps. Not knowing what to say, they remained quiet. John returned to his desk.

Richard piped up and explained. Scanning his gaze across all three men, he said, "Good sirs, being in Holy Orders, I am privy to things I cannot pass on: confessions and the like. However, other means of reporting such murmurings to sources who will listen and have not been sworn to secrecy exist. A word or two in the right ear in London will be far more beneficial than stirring up trouble here. There is enough of that as it is."

He looked directly at John. "Sir, since you saw to refund me the full £67 12s 11½d for the cost of the church, I felt it right that I return the favour by writing to support your upright leadership. Within a week or two of your arrival, I heard the first murmurings of discontent by those responsible. Sir, you are known to be good, upright, and incorruptible. I know of at least one anonymous letter sent to England claiming the opposite. The writer, sadly, must remain unnamed, but suffice it to say his letter went on the same ship as mine. I cannot even tell you to whom both letters were addressed, but I was pleased to hear of Jonas Thistlethwaite's arrival. You are right in trusting him, sir. But besides those here, be careful of all newcomers except Jonas and those he trusts."

Mary subtly dug her husband in the ribs.

Richard shook his head. He knew much more, but he would not break his vows of the confessional. In his few words, he had said much.

He released a long and frustrated sigh. How could he tell John that his aide-de-camp was one to keep at arm's length as well as his personal secretary? An idea occurred to him. He brightened and said, "Sir, keep your friends close and your enemies even closer. Some close ones need to be at arm's length. Except these fine gentlemen and Jonas."

John was stunned. He reclined in his comfortable chair his hands arched together and fingers tapping against each other.

The furrowed brow showed he was deep in thought. Did he mean Franklyn? He already didn't trust Dore. Surely not, nor the female staff. Richard had exempted the men.

The giant clock ticking outside the room was the only sound heard.

John's brow cleared, and he looked up and said, "I feel we must prepare for a long, drawn-out battle. They clearly intend to get rid of me somehow. I admit I could have done things better, but I arrived to find everything in great disarray. However, I have not, nor will I, fall victim to the rampant cajoling and bribery in the Corps. Many are now too drunk to even report for duty, and they are willing to succumb to any offer of alcohol. The freed convicts are no better, and I am more than willing to let many of them return home. London can deal with them there."

His listeners remained silent.

John's brow furrowed again. "The Corps turns a blind eye to what the poor women endure, and occasionally, they partake in the abuse as well. According to Helena, some of the guards are among the perpetrators." His quick intake of breath and immediate exhale displayed his frustration with the men under his authority. "I trust few here. Reverend. To be precise, there are less than thirty of you; since David left, I have lost one confidante. None of you can be on duty all the time."

His eyes met Crispin's. "You were a Godsend, lad. You too, Eric; I heard rumours of Crispin's quest on the voyage here from Bennelong, believe it or not. It took some time before I figured out if you were serious, but it was the reason I gave you as much free time as I did that first week after my arrival. I didn't know who you were looking for, but realised you weren't here to line your pockets."

Crispin nodded his thanks but did not interrupt.

John continued, "I had heard about the reputation of some of the women soon after my landing. One, in particular, had an interesting nickname of Helena the Hellcat. The name alone makes a lesser man than you quake in fear. For her to be the person who, in a roundabout way, is now responsible for the light at the end of our farming tunnel is delightful."

Mary chuckled, her eyes twinkling as she met Crispin's amused gaze.

John turned his attention to Eric. "And you, my boy, have changed since your marriage. I won't say Gillian has affected you that way, but the anger that I saw deep within you, but well hidden, seems to have gone. Dare I say, your soul seems lighter and may I suggest you are now at peace?" The cocked eyebrow in a silent question elicited a nod.

Eric smiled as he spoke. "Yes, sir, one day I shall explain if you wish, but Cris set me right on that score. He taught me to trust the good Lord, and I did! No, I do. Wholeheartedly, I do now."

Richard grinned and met John's eye.

Both leaders had a strong faith and prayed together often. Eric had come to him for a long, heartfelt conversation following Crispin's talk.

Over the previous year, Eric and the vicar met a few times and discussed the lad's anger issues. The young soldier rarely lost his temper now. He had never raised a hand to his wife, daughter, or any other children, and Richard doubted he ever would.

However, that anger was not gone. Richard was sure it would resurface quickly if anyone dared to threaten his loved ones. The boy had grown into a loving husband.

The Johnsons were invited to stay for luncheon, but declined as Mary had Sunday School at one o'clock.

Eric assisted them when he was off duty, but apologised for not being available today. Nearly two hundred of the colony's children attended the classes where they learned to read and write.

Connie's brother, Wil, was teaching the older children alongside Mary. Lessons were conducted with slates and chalk, and they used the church building as their classroom. They had cleaned out the storeroom next door to provide the older children with more comprehensive lessons.

As they took their leave, John dismissed his two guards.

After the Rosedales left, John refused to return to dining alone. When there was just the household present, all joined him in the formal dining room. Evenings were once again enjoyable and filled the loneliness John had previously experienced. He adored the children's chuckles and chatter. He loved how Jasper called him "Guddonor." He encouraged the little boy to interrupt when the tea tray came in.

Soon, it became a ritual between the two, although the name changed to "Captain John."

The outside guards rotated duties, and most returned to the barracks for meals.

Crispin and Eric followed the governor wherever he went. The guards' muskets were always loaded and ready to fire. Thankfully, there were no further break-ins at the governor's residence or attempts on his life.

Hopefully, the peace would last.

The heat was sapping, and the weather showed no break.

Drought!

If only it would rain.

~

On Monday evening, the seven adults and two children had just finished dinner but were enjoying conversation around the table.

Having not left the dining room, they were interrupted by hammering on the front door. Hastily leaving the table, the three men went to see what had occurred.

Rather than anyone coming, one of the guards had banged on the locked front portal. "Sir, Your Excellency, open up!"

The guard's voice was frantic. He could see smoke billowing from the back of the thatched roof of the church, and from their elevated vantage point, he could see an assemblage of people begin to run towards the building. With a timber frame and thatched roof, the structure was unlikely to be saved.

Crispin opened the door, and Eric stood in front of the governor to protect him if necessary. Both were armed with their muskets, which, thankfully, were not needed.

The guard, Jonas's friend, Travis, beckoned the three men outside and pointed to the church.

Although the sun had just set, the glow of the flame was easily visible, as the light of the evening had not faded.

A plume of black smoke billowed up from the church, which was enough to realise the danger was not to the official residence.

The other guards had come to the front to see what the ruckus was about and stood gawking.

Within seconds, John was bellowing orders. "Eric, stay here and guard the women, as you are a better shot than Cris. Bolt the back door and stand alert."

He sent two of the four guards to the barracks. "You two assemble all the help you can, and you two go and see if the vicar needs any help emptying the church of what he can save."

Once they were gone, John turned to Crispin. "Cris, I'm going down and want you to shadow me. This could be a ploy, so I need you to remain close. Bring the loaded pistols, too."

Crispin nodded. "Absolutely, sir!"

In the minutes since his orders had been issued, hundreds more people were flocking to the smoking building.

As John and Crispin walked down the hill to the church, they saw that many had gathered, attempting to toss buckets of seawater on the stricken building.

The thatched roof was now aflame, and a line of people were still passing things out from the sanctuary end of the church.

The vestry door was open, and a snake line of people carried items from the vestry at the opposite end of the building to the fire.

By the time John and Crispin arrived, they could see a growing pile of items.

The large Bible came first, followed by silver candlesticks, pillows, altar linings, liturgical linens, prayerbooks, and Richard's black-and-white robes. His cassock, surplus, and preaching stole were lying in a pile on the grass.

Nigel Bray and Connie's brother, Wil, were two of the men ducking in and out of the building.

Others soon joined Richard in emptying the vestry. They made numerous trips into the burning building.

John picked up the Bible and held it for safety. This was one irreplaceable item.

Connie Bray came to his side, and they watched over the growing pile of things as the church was emptied.

Crispin saw the pile of church registers and collected them. He would not leave the governor unprotected, no matter how much he wanted to assist. He gathered the bundle of robes and church linens, which would all need cleaning.

The cacophony of shouting was overwhelming, but there was little anyone could do to fight the fire.

Crispin saw Mary Johnson appear in tears. Because of the noise, he nudged the governor and said, "Sir, Mrs Johnson is here."

They moved towards the weeping woman, who clung to her two children.

John hoped Richard wasn't still inside. As they reached Mary's side, they saw Richard step out of the vestry with a box in his hands.

As Richard stepped away from the vestry door, carrying the last candlesticks and a box, the far transept roof caved in. He placed the candlesticks on a pile of rescued items, then noticed Mary waiting. He walked over to her side.

Mary Johnson's scream was deafening to those next to her.

Others on the other side of the building joined in.

Leaving the frightened children with John and Crispin, Mary ran towards Richard and all but fell onto his chest.

He wrapped one arm around her.

The clergy couple stood gazing at the inferno of their hand-built church.

Sparks were carried on the wind as the roof-thatch sizzled above them.

The wattle and daub walls ignited, and the timber frame uprights worked like a thousand candle wicks. The thatch roof was already gone, and the daubed walls were beginning to crumble.

Richard drew Mary back toward their children. As they walked, he still had one box under his arm.

John waited until his friend arrived and released Harry's hand.

The frightened child tried to run to his mother.

John peered at what his friend carried. "Richard, other than these munchkins and this..." he lifted the Bible momentarily, "...what is so important that you would risk your life to retrieve?"

Richard's soot-covered face met John's gaze. "This!"

He opened the lid of the metal box to reveal an assortment of documents. "These are all from the First Fleet voyage and soon after. I kept them under lock and key in the vestry as I thought they would be safer."

Mary gently chastised him, saying, "Oh, Richard, really!"

John replied tersely. "Nothing is worth your life, my friend."

The reverend shrugged and said, "John, these are all my personal documents, journals, and writings since I embarked from London. My diarised journal was written whilst on the *Golden Grove, en route* to this place, and my musings about everything from theological observations to my ministering of Father José de Mesa from the *Malaspina's* Spanish expedition. This is, in reality, my life here in the written word."

He turned to Mary. "Sorry, love, but I wanted to get them out. I knew the fire had started at the nave door, so I had time."

Another crash behind them made them all turn. The walls of the nave collapsed in on themselves.

The burning building illuminated the entire town, sending sparks high into the night air. The gentle breeze carried the smoke out to sea.

As they watched, a cry came from the other side of the church.

The next-door storeroom was also now alight. It had just been cleaned out to use as a classroom.

A wagon full of shale slabs stood off to one side. Wil Waterson planned to use these as chalkboards.

More people ran to fight the fire there. A few buckets of sand dealt with the smouldering thatch.

Milbah still clung to Crispin until she saw Abaroo appear from the darkness. Moments later, the two frightened children sought refuge in the scarred black girl's arms.

Although Abaroo no longer lived with the family, she came when she saw the glow of the fire. Now in her twenties, the girl must have a life and possibly a family somewhere, but no one knew where. Wherever it was, it must be close at hand as she reappeared whenever most needed. Abaroo took the children back to the cottage and put them to bed.

At John's command, everyone had given up fighting the church flames. The fire was too ferocious to quench with buckets of seawater or sand. He commanded that they douse the surrounding cottage roofs to stop them from catching alight.

By midnight, only a smouldering shell remained. The residential cottages, thankfully, were untouched as they were some distance from the church, but their place of worship was a complete disaster. Nothing usable remained of the cross-shaped edifice. However, Richard and his helpers saved many of the irreplaceable things.

With Mary still firmly under his arm, Richard stood looking at the ruined shell of his church and quoted quietly. "*Wherein ye greatly rejoice, though now for a season, if need be, ye are in heaviness through manifold temptations. That the trial of your faith, being much more precious than of gold that perisheth, though it be tried with fire, might be found unto praise and honour and glory at the appearing of Jesus Christ.*"

Crispin had not long read those words and did not understand them. "Sir, is that from the book of Peter? What do the words mean?"

Richard nodded. "1 Peter 1 verses six and seven." He released a long sigh. "My heart is heavy, as it took many years to construct a building for our divine worship, and now it's gone, so I am saddened. Mayhap, we are being purified by fire. Therefore, tonight, I identify with those words most sincerely."

The small group nodded in agreement.

John asked, "Do you have any idea how it started? Did you leave the candles burning?"

Richard gave a grunt of disapproval. "Not likely, sir! It started outside the main entry door. There were no candles in use there and no rubbish either. No, sir, this was deliberately lit. I saw a small group of convicts running away as I ran to get the sand buckets, but even by then, the fire had reached the thatching, and I knew it was useless. Hence, I rescued the items in the vestry. Thanks to Wil Waterson, we cleared the nave to install the chalkboards tomorrow. Everything but the hymn books and pillows were in the vestry."

Richard nodded his thanks towards Connie, Nigel and Wil as they moved away.

At Richard's words, John and Crispin gasped in unison.

John swore. Something he rarely did. He apologised to Mary and said, "So, it was arson? Do you know the identity of the felons?"

Richard shrugged. "It doesn't matter if I do. The church is gone, and once again, I need to start from scratch."

John verbally pushed his friend. "Do you know why, then?"

Again, Richard shrugged. "I can only guess it's in reaction to everyone being forced to attend divine worship again. The malcontents did not like that order. We live in a penal colony, John. Take your pick as to who set the fire."

Mary felt him draw her closer. She knew her husband was despondent, and he had reason to be so.

Leaving the burned-out shell of the church, they walked around the building in time to see the roof of the storeroom fall in. The almighty crash sent sparks spiralling into the air. The outer walls collapsed in on themselves like dominoes.

They held their breaths to see if the other thatch roofs nearby would catch on fire.

Thankfully, nothing did, and the other buildings were safe.

Realising that the saved items were at risk, John motioned for Crispin to follow him.

While Richard and Mary stood watching the buildings burn, the men vanished unnoticed around the side of the burning shell of the church.

John ordered the soldiers at hand to carry the saved items to Government House.

Richard reappeared beside him with a similar fear of the rescued items being pilfered.

John said quietly, "I'll take charge of this stuff, Richard, until we arrange services elsewhere."

Richard nodded disconcertingly. He was too tired to worry; he nodded his approval and left John and Crispin to their work.

Each man still held an armload of items. Richard returned to Mary while John, Crispin and a bevy of soldiers returned to the official residence, each with an armload of saved items. These could sit in the downstairs room next to Mrs Cowdrey until they decided what to do next.

As they walked, John realised another church would be required immediately. It was the only building in the town that could seat five hundred people.

When John and Crispin arrived home, it was well after midnight.

Five hours had passed in the blink of an eye.

John wondered if Richard would tell him who the convicts were or if he would take that responsibility on his own shoulders. That was a problem for daybreak.

For now, he had to arrange out a crew to remove the debris and start to plan a new church. He also needed to find a temporary structure to use until the church was replaced.

As he unbuttoned his ash-covered clothing, a thought occurred to him. A large stone grain storehouse had recently been completed at Nigel's instigation, and although not ideal, the structure's top floor was unused.

John washed the soot from his face and then crawled into bed. A final thought appeared to him as he drew up the sheets. Thankfully, the library of four thousand two hundred books they had brought on the *Golden Grove* was now housed in a purpose-built building. That had been completed not long ago, so they were safe! There was so much needed, and the church's rebuild was one more thing required.

Before he slept, John decided that the new church would be made from brick or stone so this could not happen again. He would set up teams to help Jim Bloodsworth increase the volume of bricks for the new buildings. As he was falling asleep, he realised that the bricks made in the colony were not strong enough for a substantial building like a church. His final thought that night was that the new building would need to be made of stone and constructed on a different site.

Tiredness overwhelmed him. He closed his eyes and knew no more.

~

A cock crowed before dawn, and John groaned as he rolled over. He couldn't even see the clock face, so it was still night, but what time? He waited; his travelling clock struck four. He groaned again and snuggled under the blankets. Sometimes, he did not wish to get up and run the colony. He could hear his mother's voice in his mind, telling him he needed to rise to do his work. He smiled at that memory. Only when in his comfortable bed could he fully relax. The nightmares of his shipwreck had been washed away by convict and soldier issues. Although tired, he closed his eyes, but sleep avoided him, so he put his mind to work. He rolled onto his back and thought about the buildings in town. Before John left the first time, Nigel suggested they build a new grain storehouse. John had, and it was huge. It had two floors; the lower floor could be used for its original purpose, but the upper floor needed windows. It could be used as a church for services and also for a school. Smiling, he finally slept.

Daylight arrived all too soon. The cackling of the kookaburras outside his bedroom window and the noisy calls of the cockatoos woke him with a jump. Blowing out his cheeks as he resigned himself to start a new day, he still did not rise. His thoughts returned to the felons who had started the fire. He was sure Richard would not tell him who the culprits were. A notice in the Government Gazette might loosen some tongues if there was enough enticement.

John threw back his blankets and slid out of bed. He pulled on his dressing gown. On such a morning, he had first seen Helena on her way to work, and much had occurred since that day. He padded to his window and gazed out at the approaching dawn. Rather than stand there and pray as he often did as the dawn broke, he had another idea.

The first light set off the remainder of the dawn chorus of bird song. He returned to his bed, slid his feet into his slippers, and quietly padded to his office downstairs.

Eric or Gillian was tending to their daughter, but otherwise, the house was quiet.

He struck the tinderbox and lit a candle. While the idea was fresh in his mind, he picked up his quill and wrote the words that had come to him earlier. *"Whereas some worthless and infamous person did on Monday last between the hours of seven and eight in the evening wilfully and maliciously set fire to the Church and Schoolhouse by which it was completely consumed. And wheels the discovery of characters or extremely dangerous to the Colony as large, as well as to its inhabitants individually, is of the utmost importance.*

Notice is hereby given that if any person will come forward and give such information as shall serve to convict so horrid a character before a Court of Criminal Judicature, they shall receive a reward of £30. And if the informer shall happen to be a convict, such convict, in addition to the reward, shall receive a full and absolute emancipation and be recommended to the master of any ship in which he or she may desire to leave the Colony.

JN. HUNTER"

John had just finished writing when he heard the clock tower strike six. He couldn't hear it from his room since it was on the other side of the house. It had chimed the half-hour upon his arrival. The house would soon be stirring. Once he completed his declaration, he reclined in his chair, deep in thought. The large storehouse was located at the corner of High Street and Jamison Street, and it would certainly suffice for holding divine services. He would need to build a Communion Table and arrange some seating and windows. The convicts could sit on the floor. He thought about the convicts who had burned down the church. The arsonists would be shocked to find that not a single service would be missed. They wouldn't set fire to this building as it was made of stone, with the colony's grain stored on the lower floor. The felons would go hungry if they burned this.

His rule that everyone must be dressed before leaving their rooms also applied to him. Somewhat guiltily, he returned to his room and dressed for what he anticipated would be an exhausting day.

He ate his breakfast alone, contemplating the day's needs. Meeting the Colonial Secretary would be the first requirement. However, first, he sent Eric to escort the reverend up to the office.

By mid-morning, Richard Johnson had been and gone.

The poor man was exhausted, as he only had a few hours of rest due to the fire. The day was far from over. At least the minister knew where services would be held for the immediate future. Of course, his friend refused to say whom he suspected and who the culprits were.

After his friend left, John sent one of the outside guards to summon the Colonial Secretary. Since David Collins returned to his wife in England, he was trying to accustom himself to Richard Dore.

Something about him riled John. This man had been all but forced upon him as a replacement. He missed David greatly.

John had already had a run-in with Dore as the man had the audacity to add a paragraph to a letter to London extolling his own virtues. John was livid and put him on warning. He probably would not have minded if it were true, but it was not. To make matters worse, that had been the month before Dore had officially been given the role.

John wished to sack him after only three months. Dore was a magistrate with William Balmain and others; therefore, John saw him far too often for his liking.

He waited impatiently for what was a necessary appointment. The man was the only fully trained lawman in the colony, and he was now the Associate Judge Advocate.

Chapter 15 Land Claims

October/November 1798

$\mathcal{R}$ichard Dore appeared with a ledger under his arm. He also had a notebook to record their conversations, but John knew this ledger to be the land grants book. His breezy greeting attempted to set the tone of the morning. "Top of the morning, sir."

John felt like harrumphing but grimaced a smile in return. He saluted the man but greeted him only by acknowledging him with his name. "Dore!" Then, he waved the Colonial Secretary to take a seat. He did not like this man's cock-sure attitude, nor did he particularly like working with him. However, for the moment, he had little choice.

Crispin stood on guard outside the open door.

Dore laid the hefty tome on the desk, flipped up the tails of his coat, and seated himself. Realising what the summons was about, he had a suggestion for the governor. "Ahh, yes, well, I have a few ideas about a new church, sir."

One of John's eyebrows cocked, intrigued at the unsolicited comment. "And they are?" This man was infuriating. He was used to David coming out and saying what he wanted done; this man waffled. John just wished he would say what he meant without faffing around. It's what he loved about Linus, no beating around the bush.

Rather than answer immediately, Dore flipped open the ledger. Inside the front cover was a town map divided into allotments, and each plot was numbered in David's neat script. John had seen this map numerous times.

Dore explained the blatantly obvious allocations. "This is the Sydney Cove land allocation map, sir. I know you realise that, but I thought that as we need to rebuild the church, there are few options available other than the present situation. If I may be so bold, one space is glaringly obvious."

John peered at the map. Both David Collins' and Dore's writing was legible and easily readable. Each allocated block had a name or number, and a key was at the bottom. Near his own residence, there was one large block that stood all but vacant.

John's eyes alighted on it, and tapping the square, he asked, "What's that area? It is much closer to my house but looks large enough to construct a sizeable church. I was thinking of a building about 150 feet by 50 feet. We need to be able to fit everyone inside comfortably."

Dore grinned. "I thought you would ask about that one. Sir, it's where the clock tower is, but there is ample land for the church to adjoin it. The tower could even be incorporated with the building, and then we can continue to use the crenellated top of the clock tower for patrols as we currently do. As you know, the tower was completed in January this year and has a firm base. So I do think this could work." Dore held his breath as to what to say next. He was on tenterhooks and nervous, as he could tell his boss was in a foul mood.

John's brows furrowed. After a few moments, he said, "Stone or brick? I had thought of a new site, but incorporating it with the tower is a grand idea. A church bell could easily be added either on top or in the void of the tower."

Dore smiled. Talking of building materials meant his idea had been accepted. "I'll leave that to you, sir."

John gave him a curt nod. With the land found for the new church, John folded the map, pulled the hefty tome onto his lap, and flicked through the pages. He knew that the Parramatta and western land allocations were further over in the book. Dore shifted uncomfortably in his straight-backed chair. John found what he was looking for and noted that D'Arcy Wentworth had a five-hundred-acre grant at Toongabbie. There were lots of smaller holdings out that way yet to be allocated, and he saw a cluster of smaller blocks nearby that had been surveyed but not yet distributed. A slow smile spread across his lips. "Are there any grant promises for this area?"

Dore looked at the area that John was pointing at. "No sir, no one wishes to go that far out yet. D'Arcy Wentworth's land is still being cleared, but the smaller plots have not been popular. However, these are fertile soil with a creek and permanent water. Hence the smaller sizes." Dore rechecked the map before asking, "Do you have an idea for them?"

John nodded. "Ahh, well, yes, I do. I have promised a grant to each of my three trusted internal guards. Each can have a forty-acre grant, so mark them down for Milroy, Bellchambers, and Thistlethwaite. But that one-hundred-acre lot, allocate it to Rosedale's twins. They can work it together and subdivide it later. They will use it to teach ploughing as the Rosedale farm is already ploughed." He looked and saw a few more small lots, yet unallocated. He would keep them in mind. He said, "The family will not receive a salary for teaching farming; the farm will be their recompense. Linus Rosedale's one-hundred-and-twenty-acre farm can then be left to his younger sons. These ones are close to the Government Pig Farm at Rooty Hill, and there is accommodation there for trainee farmers. Oh, and keep those small farms around them unallocated for the moment."

Dore frowned. He had met Helena's family and also liked what he saw. He was not always keen on the governor's friends; however, this farmer seemed to favour no side. He knew the governor intended to utilise the knowledge of this family, and having seen the rear garden here, Mrs Milroy undoubtedly knew how to garden. The allocation of these farms to the older sons was not out of line as, in essence, this was bartering land for knowledge. But who were the other blocks for? "Consider it done, sir. I shall write a note to ensure I allocate the correct blocks."

John watched as he scratched a note on a sheet of rough homemade paper, rather than his notepad and recorded the lot numbers. He pointed to the three surrounding lots and tapped the map, saying, "Keep those free as well."

Dore nodded. "Certainly, sir. I shall get these documents drawn up for you to sign."

John nodded. If Foveaux would milk the system and claim the vast four-hundred-acre plot he called *Bella Vista*, which Macarthur purchased from him, those who deserved it should also get good blocks. Macarthur had been granted *Elizabeth Farm*. John was merely balancing the allocations. He had no idea if Dore was in Macarthur's pocket or if the man just had an irritating ego. Whichever it was, Dore's one dishonest action ensured that John did not trust him. If this man would add unauthorised paragraphs to an official letter to London and presume he would not be found out, he was not a man John wished to have in a position of authority. However, he was stuck with him. No, he certainly did not trust or like this man. He was determined to watch him like a hawk and question his actions. All this was going through his mind as he gazed at the tome on his lap. Satisfied with his actions, he closed the book with a snap and handed the leather-bound ledger back to his secretary. Job done! John looked at the smug man sitting opposite his desk. The satisfied look on Dore's face riled him. He gave him a curt dismissal. Without another word, he dropped his eyes to some work sitting on his desk and flicked his hand for him to go. Dore knew he was dismissed. Crispin ushered him to the door and closed it with a snap.

John didn't look up until Dore left. He then pushed away from his desk and released a long sigh. He was glad Dore was gone. He walked to the window and watched the man's hobbling departure. He smiled to himself. He was fully aware that Dore had gout and hated walking anywhere. He knew he should have called the carriage for him, but he refused to pander to the man's ego. A mischievous smile spread across John's face. He spun on the ball of his foot and walked out of his door, calling for his security detail as he left his office. "Cris, Eric, don your jackets, lads. I need your company." No reply was forthcoming. Frowning, he went in search of them.

The men were in the kitchen having their morning mugs of tea. Rather than waiting for them to come to him, John followed the sounds of jovial conversation and joined them in the kitchen. "Button up your jackets, lads. Dore has gone. We're off to pace out the new church; then, over luncheon, I have a surprise for you all. Noon meal together in the dining room, please, Mrs Peach; I'll explain why then."

Eric had not heard the secretary arrive, or he would have been at the governor's door. The two soldiers jumped to their feet as the governor entered. Crispin looked tired, and John knew he'd had little sleep.

John saw that Eric was about to call for the carriage to be brought around. He stopped him, saying, "We're walking, Eric, so don't bother with the carriage." He saw his housekeeper sewing, and she had a tape measure on the table. "Mrs Cowdrey, may we borrow your tape measure, please?" She nodded and handed it over. Two pairs of eyebrows shot up, but they moved to follow their boss.

With the children soon to be mobile, a gun rack had been built above the internal door. The men grabbed their muskets from the wall rack and followed John to the front door. The three uniform-clad men walked past the sentries. When they were out of earshot, John said, "We're only going as far as the clock tower. I want to measure the area, but it should be big enough for a one-hundred-and-fifty-foot-long building. In the meantime, we will hold services on the top floor of the new grain store. We'll need some form of seating for half the building, and the convicts can sit on the floor for the time being. I saw Richard Johnson this morning, and he's thrilled."

An hour had passed by the time they measured the block of land. Then, they walked down to the burned-out church to inform the minister of their decision. Richard was soot-covered and exhausted. John greeted his friend. "God works in mysterious ways, Richard!" Ensuring no one else was listening, he said, "Dear friend, your new permanent church will be built incorporating the clock tower."

John gave the measurements and saw the delight on Richard's face.

Richard's eyes lit up. "Sir, until this moment, I have been disheartened. However, having a permanent stone building would be a delight. And as to your earlier suggestion of services on the top floor of the storehouse, this is wonderful. I have six days to prepare the area, and we will have a service ready for seven o'clock on Sunday morning." A grin spread across his blackened face. "I have ideas about seating, but I need help with this, sir."

John nodded. "Let me know what you need, and I will get on to it."

With the hint of a smile on his lips, Richard gave his thanks and watched the three leave. He lifted his eyes heavenward and mouthed his thanks.

The men were home just before noon and had spent the gentle walk up the hill discussing the new church.

John had not mentioned the farms to either of the men, as he wished to tell them when everyone was together. He felt a little guilty that Mrs Peach and Mrs Cowdrey would not get any land, but he knew neither was interested in farming or remarrying. Both had asked to remain at Government House for the time being. He planned to give them a bonus of similar value when he left.

When they arrived home, lunch was ready to be served. It was a simple meal of creamy pumpkin soup with fresh bread and butter.

John waited until everyone was seated before he gave thanks. He surprised them by adding some unexpected words. "Dearest Lord, thank you for surrounding me with faithful friends who look after my health and well-being." He heard astonished gasps, but no one spoke. After saying grace, he opened his eyes and saw all the gazes fixed on him. "We'll eat while it's hot, then I shall explain." He looked at those around him and realised they were friends. Something changed in his attitude toward them. Contentment.

The meal progressed with the discussion circling about the fire.

John was served first, so he finished first. He placed his spoon on his empty plate and watched as the others at the table finished eating.

When all bowls were empty, he said, "After the happenings of the past twenty-four hours, I again realised just how blessed I am at having trustworthy people around me. I won't go into what has occurred, but suffice it to say that it has made me value your presence even more than usual. In consequence, I have allocated four farms. There is a forty-acre one each for Cris and Eric and the same for Jonas. Helena, your twin brothers will get a one hundred acre one that they are to use to teach from. All are virgin land. These farms are out near Rooty Hill at a place called Toongabbie and close to the barn accommodation on the Government Farm."

Crispin and Eric were stunned. The governor mentioned that this may be possible, but they had no idea he acted on it already. To be granted so much land was incredible. Both soldiers' jaws dropped, and neither knew what to say. They glanced at each other. Both shrugged.

John saw and smiled. "There is a condition, though, lads. Yes, these farms will be yours, and they each have the same permanent creek running through them, so access to water will be easy. However, Helena's brothers will need to oversee the four farms for the moment, and they will incorporate the clearing of it into the farm school. This includes clearing by convict students and the preparation of the land to till it, as I will not release you two from your security roles until I leave. I need you both. Only after I leave will you be able to live on your new properties. I do not know when that will be, but with the goings-on in town, you may find that is sooner rather than later."

Everyone hoped that would not be the case. Mrs. Cowdrey said, "Oh, sir, I do hope that will not be for many years yet."

John shrugged uncharacteristically. His eyes showed his concern. First, he told the two senior ladies they would not miss out. He looked around at the people sitting with him, then, as he had not told them about his discovery of Dore's dishonesty, proceeded to do so.

Crispin nearly spluttered with disgust at the man's actions. "Sir, how dare any person make additions to an official document? Is this not some form of treason?"

John shook his head. "No, for in this case, it was pure ego on his behalf. Dore's paragraph was grandiosing himself. I'm not sure that's even a word. He used terminology that looked as though it was at my dictation. Be assured I have set London right. But, for now, I am stuck working with him as a magistrate. Cris, as I delegate more to Franklyn, I may even use your writing skills to scribe the more important letters. If you are unavailable, I may even write my own." A murmur of shock and surprise circled the table.

Crispin said, "I am available when you wish, sir."

Each of the others voiced their approval of the governor. John harrumphed and crossed his arms. "Fine, fine! I appreciate your support, but now, let's return to the farms." He turned to Helena and said, "Since Gerry and Jem will also be working with your father, you will need a convict team to clear the land and build dwellings. These initial structures will only be barns for the housing of the farm students, not your homes. Later, I will use convict teams to learn how to construct houses." He paused, looked around the table, and smiled. Clearing his throat, he resumed. "So your two homes will be used to teach these new convicts how to build such structures in our harsh environment. Jonas will need to build his own. Most convicts will have never seen a verandah before we added the one on the front of this house, let alone know how to construct one. These skills must be taught on actual structures." John saw everyone nodding in agreement. He added, "However, this means that once they are finalised, you will each inherit a finished, unfurnished dwelling and cleared land. You will each need to furnish your homes."

~

A fortnight after the church fire, another blaze consumed the medical residences and hospital storeroom. That fire burned nearly as far as the boathouse. The lack of rain and intense heat did not assist, as the dry conditions made all the parched buildings tinder dry. John presumed that these fires were deliberate, but no one stepped forward even though his decree of £30 reward had been widely circulated throughout the community.

Early in November, John was in his office when he overheard two voices talking outside his window. He stood out of sight and listened.

Crispin saw his door open and was about to speak when John silenced him. He beckoned him to his side, and the pair stood listening in horror at what they heard. One name mentioned made John gasp. His steward and personal secretary, Nathaniel Franklyn, was named the rum trade's main instigator. Richard had tried to warn him. If this was the case, it was no wonder that the rum sales had soared rather than been reined in. Having heard enough, John swivelled and motioned for Crispin to follow him into the kitchen. In a few words, Crispin filled in Eric without naming names. Mrs Cowdrey had the tea tray ready, and rather than waiting for it to be taken into his office, the three men poured a mug of tea each and exited via the back door into the garden. Even on the late spring day, the shade under the covered netting brought some relief. Remaining silent for some time, each took a deep drink of the strong brew.

John finally spoke. "I'm blooming-well stunned, lads! I trusted him. Am I so blind that I can't see what's before me?"

Both soldiers had reason not to like the man, but neither realised that Nate was the leading man named in the rum trade. Nate Franklyn had completely pulled the wool over all their eyes. This meant he was also in league with the Corps and the illegal grain trade. Crispin agreed that the governor was far too trusting but did not feel it was his place to say as much.

It seemed John did not require an answer. He continued, "First Dore, now Franklyn, how many more will back-stab me?" He took another swig of his tea. He wished it was laced with something potent.

Crispin waited for what was coming.

John said, "Cris, Eric, will you help me draft a letter to the Home Secretary when we go inside? The Duke of Portland must believe me this time. I have already written numerous times about the state of things, and this letter includes a bit about the torching of the church and the nurses' quarters, but this is almost the last straw. On top of this never-ending drought, we are now desperately short of blankets and clothing since the fire at the medical quarters." He released a long sigh. "It's spring; it should not be this hot or dry. I hope the duke finally sends us the equipment we need."

John hardly realised that he called both men by their names most of the time now. He did this quite often, but usually when they were alone. His head dropped despondently, and he stared into the mug of tea.

After some time, John said, "Cris, we're going to Rosedales' farm. I need to get away for a bit and think about this. I will talk over with Linus about how best to deal with Franklyn. However, before we leave, I will challenge the man and ask him directly if what we overheard is true. I want you both there to hear his reply." John's heart hurt. Betrayal was horrid.

Crispin's eyes met Eric's gaze. He knew that Nathaniel Franklyn had been the man who had beaten Eric so severely. That beating was responsible for the situation that led to Eric being offered the guard position. Eric still carried scars from that interaction. However, that fight had not been over rum but over Gillian. Crispin knew that Eric didn't like or trust Nate. If either of them had heard any rumour that contained information, they would have reported it to the governor. Crispin was sure Eric would have given him any names of traitors if he knew them.

At two that afternoon, Crispin and Eric stood at attention outside John's office with their loaded, bayoneted muskets at their sides. They waited until Nathaniel was ushered into the house by Richard Dore, then followed them in. The two trusted soldiers blocked the only exit with their bayoneted muskets crossed. They also stood as witnesses to what would pass in the room.

John initially ignored the entrance of the four men. When he lifted his head from the letter he was writing, his face was contorted with rage. He was seething with anger.

The governor's furious face wiped the smile from Richard Dore's lips.

John gazed directly at the two men but did not invite them to sit.

Dore drew a breath to speak.

John said, "Silence! You've done enough harm. Speak only when you are asked."

The man snapped his mouth shut and stood a little more upright. Anger was now visible on his face. No one spoke to him like that.

John slowly drew himself out of the chair and turned his attention to his steward.

Neither man had ever seen the governor anything but calm.

Today, his angry voice reverberated around the timber-lined room. "Nathaniel Franklyn, I thought I could trust you. I thought you were carrying out my orders and attempting to right the wrongs of this corrupt town. However, today, it has come to my attention that you are behind the growth and distribution of the local rum trade. It is through your hands that illicit brew transactions occur. All this was your responsibility to quash, and you failed in your job. Franklyn, you failed me dismally, and you failed your king. You are a disgrace. What do you have to say for yourself?"

Nathaniel Franklyn flushed but remained silent. His head shook slowly, and his eyes bored into John's. His boss was livid and barely controlling his temper. His only response was an angry silence.

Dore gasped but did not look at Franklyn. Instead, he swung around and gave Crispin and Eric a challenging look.

Dore's actions showed John that he knew something as well. John said, "Don't look at them, Dore; they know nothing. My information came from the loose lips of two of your own soldiers. And by your reaction, you have just confirmed my suspicions that you know what is going on and refused to make any report to me either. You, a London-appointed, trained lawyer. Your accusing gaze at my guards confirms my supposition." John was furious at both men standing before him. "Have you heard the saying, 'Loose lips sink ships?' Well, in this case, it's sunk both your jobs. I'm here to clean up the filthy settlement, and I turned to both of you for assistance. Dore, you are an educated man with a law degree. You should have known better."

Dore didn't reply, but he gave a slight shrug.

John had no doubts that Dore kept a lot of information from him. Since he had caught him out in his own lies, he didn't trust him with anything. John muttered, "So much for upholding the law!" He left his desk and walked to the window. His heavy footfalls echoed around the timber room. The outside guards had changed.

John paced the floor behind them. He gave his two inside guards a smile and a wink before saying to his once-trusted scribe, "I shall think about what I will do to you for a few days, but for now, you are dismissed. I shall make my own investigations. You shall be tried in London for your crime. I know many will talk for a handful of money. Franklyn, you are relieved from all duties and confined to barracks until further notice.

Dismissed. Dore, don't you leave town."

Franklyn flung him a filthy look, swung around and pushed Crispin and Eric out of the way to exit the room.

Eric was sorely tempted to trip him as he left but refrained.

John waved Dore away by saying, "Get out of my sight. I have nothing to say to you. It seems I can trust even fewer than I thought in this hellhole."

Dore, too, turned and left the office without uttering a single word. If he didn't like the governor before, he hated him now.

Eric and Crispin followed them out and ensured they returned to the barracks. Their bayonets remained trained on them until they left the immediate vicinity.

The two external soldiers on the afternoon shift had changed from those loose-lipped ones on duty earlier that day. The two current guards, Travis Garvin and Arnold Kerr, arrived on the *Barwell* with Jonas. At Jonas's suggestion, they had been added to the security roster and placed on duty that afternoon. So far, they have helped report information about the goings-on in town. They were promoted to the governor's security detail on Jonas's recommendation. Crispin told them to ensure the departing guests did not return. Both young men nodded.

With the front door closed behind them, John said, "I am going to have some time in prayer before I work out where to start our search for more information. Prepare for a few days of legwork before we leave. Franklyn couldn't have been in this alone, and I want to know who he was working with. He will merely be one link in the corrupt chain. He may well have been selling the grog, but he's not intelligent enough to be behind the entire operation."

Crispin was worried for his boss. "Sir, with this exposed, I feel you will be even more in danger should you tarry in areas where these felons dwell. May I beg that you not be tempted to go anywhere unescorted? Travis and Arnold should be moved into the small guardroom at the back and replace Franklyn's men." Although built, it had not been used often.

John nodded. "This could well set the cat amongst the pigeons, Cris. I am well aware that this could be the match striking the tinderbox. However, it could also be the thread that will give me the way to unravel the entire scheme. So, yes, I will stay close to you both whenever we leave the house and also ensure the house is well-locked up at all times. I may even recall Jonas for a while. He won't like that as he can see Mary every week out there."

The remaining hours of the day were quiet. The evening passed with the children settling early, and the house fell silent as all turned in.

John could not sleep and knew that even with his hours of prayer earlier in the day, his heart was seriously disquieted. How could he have forgone his life of discipline at sea to attempt to rule this corrupt colony? After some time, he finally retired for the night. Tomorrow, he and the lads would start investigating the depth of corruption. He wondered how many of his so-called trusted regimental men were involved. Were there even twenty he could trust?

After a restless night, the next two days were tiring.

The three men and Richard Johnson questioned as many likely people around the foreshore as possible. Richard suggested a few people to speak to first. While helpful, no new information was uncovered. The only ones to talk freely to the governor were those with licences to sell spiritous liquors, and they couldn't say enough against those who undersold them. However, they provided no worthwhile information and gave no names except Franklyn's. All coughed up his name.

Four days after the accusations were made, John decided to bring Nathaniel Franklyn in for further questioning and sent word for him to attend an interview that afternoon. The man refused to answer questions. He stood mute and looked almost ill. John dismissed him.

~

On the morning of November 11th, six weeks after the fire that destroyed the church, they were walking past the clock tower towards the house when the sound of a gunshot echoed through the valley.

Shots were rare as there was little ammunition in the colony.

Crispin and Eric closed ranks around the governor and hastened him to the official house. Travis and Arnold ushered the governor inside, and Eric slid the drop lock bar on the door behind them. Then, they checked the kitchen door. Crispin asked the governor to wait in his office while they investigated. John complied but knelt in prayer while they searched.

It took an hour to find the source of the shot, but Nathaniel Franklyn's body was found in the scrub just beyond the big black pine tree outside the back garden of the official residence. A recently fired flintlock pistol was in Nate's hand. His suicide inferred he was guilty as charged. For his death to be so close to the official residence was in itself telling. Did Franklyn lay his death at the governor's door?

John was waiting for his men to return with news. Rather than wait in his office, which had front windows, he sat at the kitchen table, which was more secure. Jasper sat on his lap and fell asleep.

When Crispin returned, he informed the governor of what had happened. He looked into his boss's eyes and saw great sadness.

John was shattered but knew that Franklyn would have been hanged. With glazed eyes, he said, "Cris, how did I get it so wrong?" Horror registered on his face, and his lips were grey. Handing the sleeping child to his father, he stood, turned on his heel, and returned to his office. He needed to be alone and pray.

Crispin could only watch as his boss's shoulders slumped as he walked away. They heard the office door shut firmly.

Chapter 16 Drought and a Dance
December 1798

*A*s no rain had come to germinate the crops by December, rations were reduced again. Far too much of the grain was being converted into spirits, and John could not stop it. Stock in the storehouse dwindled.

Nigel complained that he needed more grain to mill into flour to stave off hunger for the people. Meanwhile, more alcohol was arriving by ship, and drunkenness was rife. The colony needed food, not rum.

Franklyn's demise had done little to stop the trade, as someone else had obviously stepped into his shoes. John didn't know who that was, and no one was prepared to blow the whistle on the new middleman.

With Christmas nearly upon them and the Government House in Parramatta still not completed, John decided to move the entire household staff to Rosedale's farm for Christmas week. He had letters to write and reports to do but could work at Rosedale's house more peacefully than in town.

He looked forward to seeing the Osbornes while out west. Their latest arrival, Crispin Colin, was born in October. John had been so busy in town that trips west were rare. Colin's letters came regularly.

Linus and the boys were steadily preparing their farm, and John wished to see their progress. Unlike the other farms, they did not stop work on the land over the summer, but it was done in the early mornings.

During the heat of the days, the children were learning to read and write. One of the convicts assigned to them was a young, literate girl. Part of her duties was to educate the Rosedale children.

Linus had piled up some of the thinner felled trees with plans to fence the land into smaller plots. Rather than burn them as other farmers did, he made fencing out of the logs and mulched the leaves. These thin logs were split when green and laid aside to use as fence rails. The thicker logs were chopped into eight-foot lengths and set aside to be used as uprights. Longer straight logs were set aside for future buildings. They were to be slab-sawn and then dried.

Part of the farm school included a wagon and a pair of workhorses. Linus inquired and discovered that various farmhouses had heaps of manure they had discarded. Their new wagon made daily rounds of several barns and stables to collect the fouled straw and manure. Instead of digging this into the soil, a large compost heap was created to allow it to decompose. After several months, the once-steaming pile of rotting vegetable matter was ready to mix into the dirt. Over the summer, the bullocks were put to work with the single furrow plough, following the horses and wagons. The four boys shovelled the aged compost from the horse-drawn wagon while Linus drove the plough pulled by the bullocks. Gradually, the soil transformed.

Linus and his four sons had their hands full, tilling the hard dirt. The soil responded to their efforts and improved. They had never worked with such dry and desolate ground, and doing this in the middle of a drought was even more challenging.

The heat was almost soul-destroying. Eventually, they worked from the pre-dawn light to eleven. The animals worked until they flagged, then rested for a few hours. Late afternoon, they ploughed again until dark. On many hot days over the summer, only the morning was productive. The farm was not all that suffered.

Work did not cease when Samantha became sick.

The Rosedales baby never thrived, and the heat gave no respite. Tiny Samantha grew weaker. Agnes tended to her ailing child. The tiny girl seemed to have lost her will to live in the heat.

Crispin mentioned Samantha's sickness to his boss, and John sent the young couple to assist wherever possible. The young couple was permitted to spend a week with her family.

Little Samantha died the day after they arrived. They were able to grieve as a family.

In England, Agnes had lost a baby between the twins and Helena. This child was born on the voyage out and had never thrived. Although Agnes was hurting, she knew she had other children who needed her.

Agnes tried to put on a brave face. All the family rallied around her and gave her time to grieve. Agnes turned to Linus, who had taken the day off work, and they walked to the waterhole at the back of the property. There, they sat and prayed. They needed strength to get through this tragic loss. Through grief, they drew even closer together.

The Milroy's daughter, Jillian Judith, had been born ten days earlier. Like Jasper, she was fit and healthy. Although they had planned to call her JJ, Judy seemed to be what the other children called her.

Jonas was called to Sydney from his placement at Parramatta and took over Crispin's guard duty while occupying their room. Therefore, the unexpected break for Crispin and Helena was a bittersweet event.

The governor's retinue still planned to join the family for the Christmas break.

The death of the Rosedale's youngest child made settling in this new land even harsher.

~

A week after the Milroys arrived at the farm, the carriages carrying John, Eric's family, the two older ladies, and Jonas came from Parramatta.

Eric and Jonas were tooling the reins of the two carriages.

The official household planned to stay the ten days until New Year's Eve and help wherever possible. Part of the reason John had come was so that he could investigate rumours of growing tension between the English and the Irish settlers and convicts. He had asked Crispin to sound out a few of the local farmers. The report he sent back made John throw back his head and roar with laughter.

The dispute, far from being about grain, alcohol or anything significant, was between three Englishmen and one poor Irishman, and it was over some women. Rather than being an all-out pitched battle at five in the morning as he had been told, it was a minor squabble and not one to concern the governor. The second incident was supposedly a mass gathering on a Sunday morning. However, it was nothing more than religious squabbles after Irish people had gathered for a church service.

John should have realised they were petty, as Dore's name was signed on both reports. Since discovering the added paragraph, John had thrice chastised the man over other issues. The main problem was that he had taken it upon himself to dish out punishments rather than sit in court with his other magistrates. Dore was getting just too cock-sure of himself; he counted himself above the law. John needed to rein him in.

The arrival of the two carriages at the farm was met with great joy.

Mrs Peach and Mrs Cowdrey were to have what they called a 'working holiday.' They would take over the cooking for the multitude and give the poor grieving Agnes some respite. They were not worried about the extra work as the household girls always ably assisted.

A delighted Jonas was to stay on the farm for the duration. The official household was drawn into the loving arms of the large family group. Mary greeted Jonas warmly and hoped he would get a chance to speak to her father this week about officially courting her. He had whispered his intent to ensure she would welcome his advances. Her shy nod made Jonas whoop with delight.

Christmas gifts were what people could find in nature. They could be a special rock, feather, or leaf, but each was to hold meaning.

John had brought a few boxes of vegetables from their garden to everyone. He had sent a barrel of pickled pork out with Crispin's family to ensure there was plenty of food for them all.

With nearly thirty people to feed, food production took up much time and energy. Most of the second carriage was filled with food for their stay. Knowing the farm was still unproductive, John refused to drain the family's resources since they were already on rations, just like he was.

Linus suggested that the governor bring some civilian clothing; if he had something he could swim in, he should include that.

John had no such attire but brought clothes he could relax in. He usually lived in his blue woollen commander's uniform coat and had little need for other clothing. He swam well, as his father had taught him when he was young. He knew the farm had a creek but didn't know of any waterholes.

Years earlier, Bennelong had shown him a waterhole some distance from here. They had walked for some time from Parramatta to reach it. For the governor's swimming attire, Eric had obtained a set of convict ration trousers and a linen shirt from stores for his boss. He signed them out under his own name.

John chuckled when handed the garb. He looked forward to using them.

The day after the official party arrived, Linus took the governor aside and asked if he would care for a walk. John was dressed in his new clothing, such as it was. It was so hot that he did not even wear a coat, nor did Linus.

John nodded his assent. The heat was sapping, so he hoped it was just a short distance away. They walked out the back door and towards the bushland.

Linus said, "Sir, we are meeting someone who you already know. However, I ask, do you trust me?"

John frowned and nodded in the affirmative. He knew there was a waterhole nearby.

Linus smiled and said. "When you placed us here, you asked us to clear the back seventy acres of land. We did one acre immediately at the back of the house for fire safety reasons, but we will not clear any more."

John looked puzzled. Linus explained. "I know Bennelong returned with you nearly four years ago. Well, his tribe are nomadic. However, I found an area that is virtually all but untouched land they have left. Oh, sir, it is so beautiful I cannot bring myself to destroy it. If I may be so bold, I would like to give them a place to live safely. This is their permanent waterhole, and although they will still move around to find food, they can have a safe place to return to and camp. We have cleared out some of the excess rock and fallen trees. He is here now and would like to talk to you. This area is delightfully cool, and we use it for respite on a hot day."

John's face lit up with delight. Was this the waterhole Ben had taken him to years earlier? He liked the Aboriginal man and was sorry he had fallen foul of the drink. He asked, "Ben is safe? Truly?"

As they walked along a well-worn track through the coolness of the scrubby bush, John began to hear laughter.

Soon, they came upon an opening with a large, expansive waterhole.

Smooth-sloping rocks bounded this area on one side, and a plethora of wet, black children were frolicking in a fabulous cool waterhole.

John exclaimed. "Oh, Linus, this is a bit of paradise lost."

The area was cool and shady. It was twice the size of the pool he had seen before.

Linus released a sigh of relief. "It is, sir, and I wish to keep it this way."

Bennelong and a group of other adults were relaxing on the rocky shelf, watching the children play.

As they approached, Linus called to them. Some women made as though to flee, but the exodus halted at Bennelong's word; one woman stayed hidden behind a large rock.

John was welcomed with a big smile, and Bennelong patted the rock beside him. "Hey, Captain John, you come. You make me welcome in your home; let me do the same in mine."

John and Linus joined him in the shade. The area was delightful.

After weeks of scorching heat, John relaxed. His linen shirtsleeves were cooler than his woollen coat. He saw Linus roll up his sleeves and followed suit.

The children's sleek black bodies continued to frolic in the water, and at Bennelong's call, a couple of them came over to him.

One very small boy threw himself into the black man's arms. Bennelong did not introduce the tiny lad, but John wondered if he was one of his children.

John was aware that Ben had lost a daughter but also knew his friend to be a virile young man with a healthy appetite for Western food, alcohol, and women. He liked the alcohol a little too much.

Bennelong called over four women who were about the same age. He introduced them as his sisters. Beneláng, Munanguri, Wurrgan and Warreweer each giggled as they presented themselves to the two white men.

All the women had been in the water. Their curly hair was wet, and their near-naked bodies glistened with water beads. "One more sister, Captain John, but Carangarang is not here today."

Bennelong waved them away. "Sir, Linus, good man. He let us stay here, safe. I want you to know where Bennelong stay, and that here we have no bad drink."

He shook his head and made a funny sound with his lips and cheeks. "That evil brew does bad things to my head, Captain John, and Linus says you battle with men making bad brews."

John nodded. "I do, Ben. I have a big fight with them as they make a strong drink that makes many people silly."

Bennelong's eyes followed the lovely shape of a girl who had finally emerged from behind a rock. He beckoned her, but she shook her head, but waved. Bennelong smiled at her reluctance. He said, "My *duba,* Boorong."

They all gasped when they saw her, as they knew her well. They now knew where Abaroo lived, but they had no idea she was Bennelong's third wife. They knew she had two names and had reverted to using Boorong after she left the Johnsons' place.

John was stunned to find she was part of this tribe. Being naked, she did not wish to embarrass the white men. He was delighted to see her again. He did not push her to come closer but waved in return.

He turned his attention to the man and child beside him. "Bennelong, I'm having a few days here because those bad men won't listen to me. I may do some plant collection while I'm here, and I would be delighted if you and your people could show me some of your medicine plants. Sir Joseph wants as much as I can send him." He was thrilled that the tribe had found a safe place to live and access to clean, fresh water.

John watched as Bennelong released the small boy. John added, "I am trying to stop the brewing of grog, Ben. But the greedy men turn our food grain into bad drink, and we are going hungry. Also, I have made new laws about your people being killed. Same rule for black and white. Same punishment if anyone dies."

Bennelong growled angrily, saying, "Them plenty bad men, Captain John. One man, won't say who, but he gives with one hand and then takes away with the other. We pick fruit from our lilli pilli trees, and then he tells us not to come for tucker again. Them farmers cut down lots of our food trees, and now we go hungry too." He made a guttural sound in anger. "I learned something in London, Captain John; you have a saying: the enemy of my enemy is my friend. I like that because you are my friend and that bad man will cause you trouble. You watch this bad man big time, and we will watch out for you, boss."

Ben pulled John up, and they swam before returning.

They arranged for John to join them each morning and learn some of the plants used for various medicinal purposes and record more of their language.

John learned a lot on the journey back from London. His *Dharug* dictionary was now quite lengthy. John had a special set of secateurs and a leather pouch to store the collected specimens. The week ahead would be wonderful. It was just what John needed to relax: a mini adventure holiday. Something he had done frequently on his first visit, but since his return, his duties had precluded any exploration trips.

Bennelong made a simple suggestion. "Eh, Captain John, you teach Linus to read like you taught me?"

John grinned, "Deal, Ben!"

~

Christmas came and went, and days passed far too quickly for John. He spent a lot of time with the tribe but always had one of his soldiers with him. They, too, were in casual clothing rather than uniforms, but they carried their guns. It was too hot to plant anything, so John did as Bennelong suggested.

John and Linus spent days together learning the basics of reading.

Crispin and Eric also spent time with Bennelong on the voyage out and knew their boss was safe with him. However, accidents happen; therefore, one of the three security guards accompanied the governor with the excuse of assisting him in carrying his equipment.

Mary usually accompanied them when it was Jonas's turn for guard duty. Today, Jonas sent her away with John, Ben, and Eric.

Jonas approached Linus, who reluctantly permitted the lad to court her. Knowing that the boy was the fourth son of a peer and his older siblings had a bevy of sons, the lad had been well bumped down the succession for the title. However, there was always a possibility that a catastrophe could occur, and they would need to return to England. Jonas remained behind to assure Linus that he had no intention of leaving the country unless that happened, but even that was unlikely as his brothers had sons. He would do his duty in England if necessary, but he planned to embed himself into this family. His father wrote often, and Jonas told him of his intention to marry a farm girl. He had expected an explosion from the earl, but he received a letter of congratulations and his blessing. Awaiting a reply was why Jonas delayed speaking to Linus. It had come, and the earl's permission was given.

The explorers were returning from a day spent collecting plant samples when a bloodcurdling scream shattered the silence. Even the cicadas fell quiet.

John motioned for Eric to leave them and investigate the sound. Running ahead, he found Helena's sister, Phoebe, frozen to the spot.

Phoebe shouted. "Stay away, Eric, but stomp on the ground as hard as possible."

Eric had heard about doing this to scare away a snake but had not tried it himself. "Okay, but I don't know if it will work."

He stomped on the ground as hard as he could, and the thing he thought was a stick in front of her flattened itself and slithered off. "Was that a brown snake?"

Phoebe nodded. She could still see it and dared not move. Another minute, and it vanished into the dead grass. "Cor, Eric, your timing was perfect. I was coming to find you to ask if you could come and help Cris and Papa."

By the time he reached her side, John and Mary had caught up. Mary realised how close her sister had come to being bitten and enfolded her in loving arms.

John expected tears from Phoebe, but they didn't come.

The four stood talking until they heard a call of "Freeze, boss" from behind them.

None had seen or heard Bennelong approaching, but they realised one of the tribe was at hand when a spear sped past them and landed about six feet beyond John.

The snake had returned and slithered towards him as he shuffled his feet where he stood. Bennelong's spear hit its target. He collected his weapon with the snake neatly impaled on the end of the lethal shaft. "Him good tucker, boss; tastes like your chicken." Bennelong slid the snake off the spear and hanged the dead eight-foot creature around his neck. Rather than recoil from the evil beast, all four wished to feel it.

Eric asked, "Is it slimy, Ben?"

The black curly head shook. "Nah, 'Ric! Smooth, like skin. You feel." He held out the tail for the group to touch. It was silky but not wet or slimy.

The section near the head where it had been speared was dripping a thick red ooze. Bennelong held it a little away from him.

The group walked towards the house with Bennelong, who entertained them as they walked.

Linus greeted their return with a wave. Both eyebrows lifted when he saw what hung around Bennelong's neck. "Is that a snake, Ben?"

The pearly white teeth shone in the afternoon sunlight. A missing front tooth spoiled the perfection of his smile. "It is, boss, I come to tell you to clear around the house. These fellas bite bad, and you die."

Bennelong put the snake and the spear on the verandah. "Missy here knows what to do and told 'Ric to stomp big-time. They don't like... um." He shook himself, starting at his head down to his feet.

John knew what he meant. "Vibrations, Bennelong?"

The curly head nodded in agreement. "That good word, Captain John. It makes me... um, like this," he repeated the exaggerated shudder. His descriptive action made them all chuckle. "Missy, *butt butt* is it good now?" He put his big hand on his heart.

John had spent some time with him and knew the words *butt butt* meant heartbeat. He translated the word for her.

Phoebe smiled and nodded. "Yes, thank you, Ben, but I did have a mighty fright."

Bennelong beckoned an unseen child to the verandah.

The cherubic, dimpled, dark-skinned girl came at his call and collected the dead snake. "I come tell you *yurangai* come in tonight. You plenty people feed we bring *yurangai* and show you how to cook."

The growing group stared at Bennelong, confusion etched on their faces. Even Linus was unsure of that word. Ben chuckled, tucked his hands under his arms to mimic wings, and said, "Quack, quack."

With everyone realising he meant the wild ducks, they laughed again.

He continued with his explanation. "You need a big fire and plenty hot stones and coals. We *darunga* for you all tonight. Tell Dreamtime story by *darunga*."

This time, John frowned. This was another word he had not heard before. Ben saw his confusion and acted out part of his dance. "You *darunga* this way, boss John." He grabbed Phoebe's hand and executed a perfect bow, then took her hand so that he mimicked the minuet dance. His movements were smooth, and besides the fact that he was wearing few clothes, he could have graced a London ballroom floor.

Phoebe chuckled. "You dance well, Bennelong."

The man's face lit up. "Dance, that's what *darunga* means. We have a *corroboree* tonight. You see!"

John and Linus were delighted. John said, "The tribe will do a full dance for us tonight. Really? I have heard about how you can make animals come to life with your dance, but I have yet to see this."

Bennelong grinned. "You see tonight, Captain John. We bring many *yurangai* for everyone. So you eat good tonight. *Yurangai* land at dusk. We come liddle-bit after that. Tonight, you eat big!" Without waiting for a reply, Bennelong collected his spear and was gone before they had time to discuss the evening's activities further.

During the extended family group's stay at the farm, the barn was lined with daub, and internal walls were added so that the loft now had divided sections for sleeping. Assistance was required to elevate a set of new steps into the loft. The staircase was heavy and needed every hand available to move it into position. It would have been better to have built it *in situ*, but they did not realise how heavy it would be. Even John held a rope around a supporting post in the loft to prevent it from falling.

The older girls did their part by handing up tools. With access to the loft now in place, the family prepared for the nighttime *corroboree*.

Gerry scythed an area in the backyard, and they rolled over some logs for seating for the women. Five chairs were brought outside for John, Linus, Agnes, Mrs Cowdrey, and Mrs Peach; everyone else would sit where they could. The younger boys, Nick and Tris, collected kindling for the fire, and by nightfall, the stage was set for the dinner and the performance of a lifetime.

Rather than leave all the food for the tribe to bring, Mrs Peach and the younger girls had been cooking up a storm. Knowing they had to return soon to Sydney, Priscilla Peach had cooked cakes, biscuits, and a dozen loaves of bread with some of the flour they had brought. With a long sigh, she realised that much would be consumed tonight. However, there was still plenty for everyone. They could replace most of it tomorrow. Priscilla loved roast duck but wondered how they would cook enough for everyone in such a short time. If all the tribe members came, there would be more than forty adults and many children. Agnes and the older girls dug out every eating utensil and all the plates they owned.

Mrs Cowdrey and the girls peeled and cored a half-bucket of apples that were beginning to shrivel. The heat had ripened them, and they were no longer crunchy. They made a huge apple cobbler in a large baking tray. This delicious treat would be served with a dollop of cream, and there was ample for everyone.

The evening cicadas sang their deafening but merry chorus as the sun sank. The noise was so loud that it hurt the ears of the listeners. With all the chores done, the youngest children were fed and put to bed for a nap. As the family emerged from indoors, thirty tribal members appeared from the gloom. Each carried something to contribute to the feast. Many women carried strange clay balls; one man had a dead wallaby thrown over his shoulder.

Bennelong carried his snake, and another man had a large goanna. Boorong arrived for the dance dressed in her calico gown. She waved to Helena.

Within a few minutes, the native *dubas* had taken over the fire and spread the coals. The round balls turned out to be clay-encased ducks, and the snake, goanna, and wallaby were placed directly into raked-out the fire. The snake and lizard were near the edge, and the wallaby was sitting in the middle with its legs elevated. It was turned regularly to burn off the fur.

Many occupants from the two households found their stomachs roiling when presented with live witchetty grubs wiggling in a wooden *coolamon* bowl. Most refused the tasty morsels. The children shared one large one but surreptitiously spat it out.

With the food now cooking, the preparation for the dance began. Smaller timber *coolamon* bowls held clay paint, and the colours were daubed onto the dancers' faces and chests. Soon, the *corroboree* began.

The first sound was an eerie, ungodly roar from behind the barn. As the noise drew closer, Bennelong appeared with Bungaree and Goomberri, other men from the tribe. All were swinging something that made this spine-chilling noise.

John was surprised to see Bungaree with the group and waved to him. Bungaree and Matthew Flinders had just returned from Norfolk Island. John then realised that Bungaree's wife, Cora Gooseberry, was overseeing the cooking.

As the sound faded away, some women jumped up and started to dance. Some acted out a hunt for emu and kangaroo, and others followed, mimicking different animals.

After Bennelong's dance, he sat near John and described what each performance meant. Linus strained to listen. Each dance that followed left the watchers spellbound. There was no doubt about which animals were retold in the presentation as the actors were so lifelike. Even the tribe's children joined in and almost became the animals they portrayed. With Bennelong, Bungaree, and Goomberri performing the final dance of the evening, the corroboree drew to a close.

The farm occupants witnessed something few other white men or women would ever be privileged to see, and they were awestruck. The portrayal of the natural world and the hunt was vivid. Ben explained that the bull roarer was only played for special ceremonies and always by men. The performance was so enthralling that they could barely move. Agnes and Helena noticed the tribe's ladies were removing the baked ducks and dead animals from the fire. A few younger women tended to the balls and turned the food throughout the performance.

An hour had passed in the blink of an eye, and the meal was now ready.

Soon, the bustling of many hands and feet laid out the unusual banquet along the verandah's edge.

The clay balls were carefully broken open, and they saw that un-plucked ducks had been whole when encased in wet clay. The feathers were embedded in the now-baked clay, and the ducks inside were perfectly cooked. All the juices were collected in the casing and consumed by the waiting children.

Each person ate their fill of the sumptuous repast.

The Rosedale and Hunter households hesitated about trying the goanna, snake, and kangaroo, but each swallowed their pride and tasted the unusual foods. The snake did indeed taste somewhat like chicken, and the roo meat was rich and somewhat like venison. All had eaten the tails before, as well as possums. The goanna was an acquired taste, so the oily, tough, chicken-like meat and the remainder of the live witchetty grubs were willingly left to the tribe to consume. The ducks and roo, however, were delicious. The loaves of sliced bread supplied by the household were buttered and soon vanished, as did the large tray of roasted potatoes.

Once the main course was finished, Mrs Peach and Mrs Cowdrey brought out the dessert. The apple cobbler was more like a sticky, sweet cake. This was a treat even for the family, let alone a group of people who had never tasted such sweet food besides bush honey. Therefore, the cake-like dessert was cut into squares and served with a large dollop of whipped cream on each cube. All the children scraped the huge baking dish until it was clean. Small black and white hands grabbed for the last crumbs.

With tummies full, the evening soon drew to a close.

There had been much laughter, and each had learned much about the other group. Two of the children had minor burns, and they reacted similarly. Both mothers, one black and one white, tended to their crying infants.

Bennelong had watched on intrigued. "Look, Captain John. You see we same-same under black skin. You hurt, we hurt. You cry, we cry. Same-same, you see?"

John nodded. "I do see, Bennelong. I have known that for a long time. I want to learn from you, as I have been doing these last few days. You learned from us and even travelled to England to meet King George the Third. You learned that although we are very different over many, many things, there are things the same. We get sick, as do you. When Yemmerrawanne died in England, I saw his death saddened you. I saw your grief at being far from home and knew I had to bring you back here. I wanted to bring his body back, but I was not permitted to do so. I do understand, but many others don't. Don't judge us all by a few bad folk. I'm sure you have some bad folk in some tribes nearby?"

Bennelong nodded. "Plenty bad ones, Captain John, but I stay clear of them big-time. Bungaree, he see many new things travelling with your friend, Flinders. You right. I miss Yemerrawanne. He was a good man, and me glad to have him with me in your land. I am sad when my friend died. He never come home now to his people!" Bennelong shook his head sadly. "I learn plenty when I meet King George. Got new clothes then, but not comfortable for me. Still got blue coat same as yours. You kept safe for me." Bennelong's white teeth were again visible when he grinned. "Do you know, Captain John, you look liddy-bit like the big King George: hair, face, and clothes." He threw his head back and laughed. "Meybe, I call you King John, eh?"

John and Linus chuckled. John said, "No, Captain John will do nicely, Bennelong. I prefer that to even the title of governor. I love the sea."

As the three men had been speaking, they had not realised that the area was now all but devoid of people.

Bennelong stood to leave. "Boss Linus, tomorrow, we come, cut all grass down real low as fire comes soon. You clear away everything from the house and keep snakes away, too. One week, maybe two, until fire comes. Big rains come after that. You watch ants; they tell you. You safe here on the hill, but other houses wash away." His curly head shook with sadness. "Some do not listen to us, and they wash away bad. People die." He motioned with his hands that the houses would float downriver. "You good to us fella, so we come to help tomorrow and keep house and family safe." He turned and was gone from sight before Linus could agree. His dark skin absorbed him into the blackness of the night. The household quickly settled and was soon asleep.

~

At dawn the following morning, approaching voices woke the family.

Someone banged on the kitchen door and called, "Come, boss Linus; we got work to do while cool." Bennelong and friends had come to work.

Linus and Agnes were awake and enjoying a morning cuddle when they were rudely interrupted. Rather than attend to their unexpected visitor, he called, "I'm coming, Ben. I won't be long." Linus groaned as Agnes giggled.

The family members rose quickly, grabbed a slice of bread and bush honey that Ben had supplied, and began working.

In the cool morning, the household workers cleared the knee-high grasses from a wide circle around the residence.

By noon, the work was done. The heat was nearly at its zenith, and Bennelong suggested that most of the family come to the waterhole for a dip.

Knowing how cool it was at this delightful grotto, there was a mass exodus towards the pool. The women had shed most of their excess underclothing weeks ago. They wore their drawers but little else under their calico or drill gowns. Petticoats lay or hung unworn in their rooms. All intended to immerse themselves in the water.

Mrs Peach and Mrs Cowdrey had planned to stay and prepare a meal, but Agnes finally persuaded them to accompany her. She knew a private spot where the men couldn't see them.

Agnes also wished to take them to a tea tree swamp where women bathed. She had seen both ladies scratching their hair. The water here looked stagnant, but whatever was in the brown swamp killed lice on their bodies. Boorong had taken her soon after arrival. For the first time in years, the women were critter-free. Men were not permitted in this area, and the women could almost strip off and bathe virtually naked.

By two o'clock, a trail of cooled bodies returned to the house. On arrival back mid-afternoon, they were surprised to see John's security guard, Arnold Kerr, who they had left in town, sitting in the shade on the verandah.

Arnold jumped to attention as the bedraggled group approached and buttoned his woollen coat. He hardly recognised his commanding officer, who was relaxed and laughing. The big man wore shirtsleeves, and his convict-issue clothing was dripping wet. Arnold heard his boss's booming voice and an accompanying volley of guffaws as the returning group rounded the barn and storeroom. He'd had time to look around the farm and liked what he saw.

John noticed Arnold first. "Hello, Kerr. Is something the matter? Has the town finally rioted, and they need me to pour oil on the troubled water?" John was relaxed after his long break. He had not been so at peace since he had been home shortly before sailing five years earlier.

Arnold Kerr stood at attention, perspiration dribbling down his face. The woollen uniform was stifling, and the heat radiating from the dry soil was unbearable. He nodded and was about to answer when everything seemed to start swaying. He crumpled where he stood.

Phoebe's anguished cry of "Arnie!" was followed by an impassioned, "Catch him, Cris!" Her flight to his side made her father gaze in surprise. How had he missed this budding romance? Crispin and Eric were close enough to catch him, and Phoebe took possession of his gun. The men lay him down, removed his coat and stripped off his boots and sword.

Linus sent Jem for a bucket of water from their well. Phoebe hovered as close as she dared, wishing to be at his side and assist him. Her words revealed her deep feelings for the young soldier.

The sick man was soon rousing. The remains of his uniform were now saturated as Jem all but doused the man with the entire bucket of water. However, he was feeling much better. Arnold struggled to sit up and was ashamed to realise he had collapsed.

John was sitting in a chair nearby, watching his guard. Arnold began his apology by saying, "I'm so sorry, sir." He saw Phoebe standing off to the side, looking somewhat stricken. He hoped he would get a chance to speak to her. John waved to him to stay resting. "It's at least over one hundred degrees in the shade, laddie, and I don't see a horse, so I presumed you walked from town?"

Arnold nodded carefully. His head hurt. "I did, sir. The Corps would not permit me to use the mare." He felt ill and lightheaded.

His boss said quietly, "I'm surprised you even made the effort to come." It was not New Year yet; would this mean their stay needed to be cut short? He sighed.

Arnold said, "I brought news, sir."

Mrs Peach arrived with a jug of cool drink and some honey. "Drink up, Arnold. You have heat stroke. You need to drink all of this now." The pitcher held two pints of sweet apple-flavoured punch with a hint of salt. Drinking it was easy. By his third glass, he was feeling better. "Sir, I came to bring you some mail that I thought you should have sooner rather than later." He reached for his coat and dug into the deep inside pocket. He extracted three letters and handed them over.

John took them, and as he did so, he sighed and said, "Ah, well, I had a nice break. I dare say my time here needed to draw to a close."

During their week at the farm, various despatches arrived, and John replied to each. One of the three soldiers accompanying the governor had taken them to Parramatta. Jonas had sent his friend a note saying he was permitted to court Mary, and the way was now clear for Arnold to approach their father. Linus was a stickler for the unwritten rule that the younger daughters could not marry until the older ones were safely wed. Jonas mentioned he hoped their marriage would be as soon as he could arrange quarters or, better still, a house.

Arnold saw the look of sadness that appeared on Phoebe's face. However, she had not moved from her spot further along the verandah. In the searing heat, everyone's wet clothing was almost dry. As John moved along the expansive deck to read the screeds, Phoebe took his place. She refilled his glass and asked, "Mr Kerr, are you feeling a little better now?"

Arnold had made his feelings known on the voyage, but she had not turned sixteen until shortly before landing. "Miss Phoebe, I was hoping to ask your father if I could write to you or if we could court."

Arnold waited for her answer. Phoebe softly replied, "I'd like that, Mr Kerr. I'd like that very much." She blushed prettily but did not leave his side until he saw her father approach.

Linus came to see how the patient was, and Phoebe left them together. After their brief talk on the verandah, Arnold asked Linus for permission to court Phoebe. After another lengthy discussion, Linus discovered the lad was from a farm in Derbyshire and had no plans to return home. Permission was granted. Linus shook his hand and stood to leave the still woozy soldier but turned and said, "Arnold, if you lay one hand of violence upon my girl, you won't know what hit you. My children have never known such physical injury, and I have no wish to hear of any in the future. Understand? And no heavy drinking either."

Arnold nodded willingly. "Of course, sir. I would never do that."

Linus smiled and said, "Good! A man who does is not a real man."

Arnold was surprised when Phoebe once again returned to his side. This time, she bravely took his hand.

Within the hour, the household was a flurry of activity. The holiday was indeed at an end, and everyone was packing to return to Sydney. However, Phoebe stuck to the side of her new beau. He officially asked to court her, and she accepted with delight. While still holding her hand, he stroked it with his thumb. When everyone was inside, he boldly kissed her palm.

The pair was all but oblivious to the activity surrounding them.

Mary and Jonas managed to exit the building together and carry some containers to the barn. It was some minutes before they returned to the house. When they did, both were flushed.

Arnold was jealous but remained quiet. He had yet to kiss Phoebe.

The following morning, bags were loaded into the three carriages that waited in the courtyard. The horses were rounded up and backed into the shafts. Jonas and Arnold each had to say farewell to their girlfriends. Both girls decided they wanted a kiss. The two new couples delayed exiting the house until everyone else was outside. Mary and Phoebe used the time wisely, and their dual purpose was achieved. Two stunned soldiers received an inexperienced but certainly welcome kiss from their new girlfriends. However, the girls were firmly enclosed in strong arms and fervently kissed in return.

With a smile, a chuckle, and a blush from both ladies, both couples left the homestead grinning. Each man turned to kiss their respective lady's hand, and then they climbed up onto the luggage carriage driver's seat.

Crispin and Eric led the way with the two passenger coaches, and Jonas brought up the rear with all the luggage and empty food baskets in the rear coach. The Rosedale family lined up on the verandah, watching the group depart. Linus slid his arm along Agnes's shoulder. "Come, love, we'll visit her."

Agnes reached for Linus's hand, and the grieving parents visited their daughter's grave together. They had buried her under a gum tree, and the grave was covered in gum blossoms from where the cockatoos had been feeding above them. A tiny twig of blossom had landed on the white cross. After a hug and more tears, they returned to the house refreshed.

Their summer sojourn was over, and life in the heat had to continue. Thankfully, they had planted little that they could not hand-water. The rhubarb and asparagus were doing well. Like Helena's garden, they were planted in a fenced vegetable garden with a net covering the area. The shade protected the valuable plants from the intense sun's rays, and their deep well gave ample water for the stock, house, and plants.

After Ben showed the tribe the well, they were given free access to it.

Agnes now had the house to herself. Over the last few days, with the many people comforting her, she found that her grief, although still raw, had eased somewhat. Little Samantha was at peace; everyone knew she would be in Heaven with Jesus. One day, they would see her grown up and perfect.

Until the rains came, lessons would be in abeyance. Keeping the plants and stock alive was a full-time job. Agnes quickly learned that the women of Bennelong's tribe called themselves *dubas*, and they promised that they would be happy to trade food with them. Mrs Peach had left them masses of cooked food, yet if the family could occasionally have a duck or wallaby tail meal, that would be wonderful. The tribe liked flour, and the children adored the apple cobbler. Agnes had invited some of the *dubas* in for cooking lessons. Many came and Boorong translated for them.

With the carriages gone, Linus called his two daughters and questioned them about their soldier boys. By the time the girls left their father in the sitting room and sought out their mother, the youngest children had already stripped the beds and started the laundry.

Chapter 17 A Firm Foundation
The End of 1798

With their expedited return to town, there was little fanfare on the journey. They dropped Jonas off at the Redoubt in Parramatta, and the inexperienced driver Crispin, Eric, and Arnold drove the carriages to the official residence in Sydney. The guards on duty took the reins while the passengers alighted. Arnold would drive one to the stables while Crispin and Eric remained with the governor.

The following day was New Year's Eve, and a pile of mail awaited John's return. He hated paperwork and had delighted in a week-long break doing some specimen collecting. He had jotted some notes to add to the manuscript he was writing about the progress of the settlement. He had already published his first book before his return from this tour of duty and planned that this document would also make it into print one day. That would need to wait until he returned to England.

He sighed and opened more letters. One letter made John roar so angrily that Crispin and Eric burst into his room, thinking he was being attacked.

Rather than upset them, he explained the latest deceptive action of the man who could angrily stir the governor without lifting a finger. Since discovering Franklyn's betrayal, John only used first names for his internal guards, even in public.

John was pacing his office and reading as he did so. "Cris, can you believe Dore is now making judgements alone all the time rather than sitting on a magistrates' bench? He was permitted to do this once over a minor situation earlier this year as no one else was available. That was before I knew what the man was like. I forbade him to do this again. He ignores Balmain's pleas to consult him."

Neither Crispin nor Eric understood the ramifications of this accusation, but the governor's anger inferred that it was dire. John waved his hand to dismiss the men and sat at his desk to reply to this letter.

By dinnertime, John had a big grin plastered on his lips. There were no visitors, so the staff joined him in the formal dining room. After they seated themselves, John smiled at each one. His eyes twinkled with delight.

Crispin asked somewhat tentatively, "Did you deal with the issue, sir?"

John nodded. Once everyone was comfortable, John replied with words that surprised everyone: "I sacked him as my secretary, Cris! Another letter contained news that London had never appointed him as Colonial Secretary. Dore lied. He was only to be a magistrate, nothing more. However, he must hold that role for the moment."

Without waiting for a reply from anyone, John gave thanks to the Lord for the meal, tucked his serviette into his collar and sipped his soup.

A murmur of conversation followed the declaration.

All wondered how the annoying man would retort.

The soup was followed by cold pickled pork and fresh salad.

They chatted while they ate.

While they had been out at Rosedale's farm, a convict girl living with Connie Bray had been instructed to water the garden. She had done well, and many vegetables were ready to eat.

The family tried hard to settle, but the heat made the children miserable. They had no waterhole to swim in, and there was still no rain.

By Caris's first birthday, Gillian told Helena she was expecting again. Everyone welcomed the news of another child. Eric was delighted. He adored fatherhood, and he delighted in his adorable daughter.

The highlight of January for John was the visit of John's friends, Bass and Flinders. They brought the news that they had followed John's supposition and discovered a passage between the mainland and the island known as Van Diemen's Land. He knew they were back because he had seen Bungaree.

When George Bass told him of the discovery, John smiled, knowing that it was up to him to name the body of water. "George, it is my honour to name it after you. I think Bass Straight is an admirable name."

The astonishment on his face made up for the disappointment of what was occurring in the town. George's face broke into a beaming smile. "Sir, thank you. This is a great honour."

John looked up from the chart and said in a thick lilt, "*Nee bad*, laddie. "Tis *braw*." He was thrilled his hunch had been confirmed. On the journey out in 1795, he had watched the waves as they drew close to the land. There seemed to be no backwash on the rolling seas. If they had hit any landmass, this would have occurred. The young Lincolnshire man looked puzzled. The double-negative comment sounded like a put-down.

John chuckled and explained. "George, that means that it's not bad, which, coming from me, is the height of excellence."

George sighed with relief. "Oh, sir, you had me worried for a bit there. Matthew and I have all sorts of ideas for future trips. I want to extol the virtues of the Derwent River. It is an amazing area. Bungaree is brilliant. I would take him anywhere. Oh, sir, I wish you could have been with us."

"As do I, laddie! As do I." John spent hours with the two young men. He was jealous that he could not go adventuring with them. He said, "After the wonderful Christmas I spent out at Rosedales' farm, I managed to collect a goodly amount of new plant specimens. I also met with Bennelong again, and he gave me instructions about some medicinal uses of such plants. The knowledge they have is astonishing. Bungaree is a jovial chap, so I suggested you take him along. He was there with Ben, so I knew you were back."

~

January faded into February with more fuss and noises from Richard Dore. Barely a day passed without some complaint from some of his brother magistrates or another person making an official complaint about the man.

John wrote extensively to the Home Secretary, the Duke of Portland, and he wondered how to ensure the letter reached London without being intercepted when Jonas offered to include his missive with a letter to his Uncle. He had arrived in town to see if he could purchase a ring for Mary, and he had brought some letters from the farm to Helena and Arnold.

The weather was still dry, and even the wax candles melted in their sconces. The tallow candles melted much more quickly, but the wax ones usually survived the heat; not so this week.

Helena kept the hip bath full of water so the children could cool down; however, even that was warm.

At midnight on February 11th, John was awoken by screaming and cries of "Fire" from outside. Jumping out of bed, he dragged on his dressing gown and looked out of his window. He could see a glow, but the angle of his window precluded a good view. He met Crispin outside his office and explained he thought the gaol was on fire.

Crispin had been up with Judy when he heard the first call of "Fire." He carried the child to check where the blaze was and noticed it came from near the prison. "Sir, I will wake Helena and go and find where it is."

The voices and continued calls from outside soon awoke most of the household. Eric emerged from his room in a nightshirt. Even the two older ladies exited their room in a state of *dishabille*.

John was surprised when he saw them. He had no idea that Mrs Cowdrey's hair was so long. Mrs Peach, he only glimpsed as she hurried into the kitchen. No doubt she had gone to put the kettle on the hob. "I don't know the problem, but I suggest we all dress and prepare for whatever catastrophe has occurred."

Soon, only the children were asleep. Crispin returned with the news that the gaol was well alight, but somehow, they had managed to get the twenty incarcerated prisoners out of the cells. They had minor burns but should all survive.

Eric and Crispin decided it was safe to escort the governor to view the destruction. After telling the outside guard to remain vigilant, the three uniform-clad men walked the few blocks to the remains of the gaol.

Like the previous two fires of the church and nurses' quarters, this thatched wattle and daub building was consumed quickly.

The following day was spent investigating the start of the fire. Again, it had been deliberately lit, but no one could determine why.

To top off a bad week, news arrived from Parramatta that the official residence that Governor Phillip had erected had finally collapsed.

Colin wrote with much more detail than the official despatch.

John disliked staying at the unsafe building and had stayed with Linus on recent trips. He was aware it was unsafe, so he ordered the furniture to be stored. The new house he was having built on the hilltop was nearly complete. Within the next few months, it would be worthy of an official residence. He would then have the Sydney residence re-shingled.

Once they moved, he would transfer the ownership of the farm to Linus.

The heat was sapping everyone's energy, and tempers were fraying. Squabbles occurred frequently, and soldiers were called to break them up. The drinking water tasted horrible and slimy, so John ordered it to be boiled before consumption where possible.

February was even hotter than the preceding months, and fights broke out often amongst many groups.

A few nights after the gaol fire, the newly arrived missionary staying in Johnson's guest cottage was attacked, and the man was set upon severely.

Three Irish convicts who were responsible were arrested and taken away for later prosecution and flogging. The men were instantly identifiable as they had all blackened their faces. If they hadn't, they may well have escaped notice.

~

The dry weather lasted until the first week of March.

John was tearing his hair out over the wilful disobedience of Richard Dore. He may have been sacked as Colonial Secretary, but the man still held the London-appointed position as a magistrate.

It was as though the man intentionally thwarted John's official instructions at every possibility. In one situation, he had ordered seven hundred lashes for one man known to be innocent of a crime.

John mentioned the injustice to Crispin, who was equally upset. After hearing the man's plea for mercy, John issued a writ of clemency.

This action prompted Dore to write a curt letter demanding an explanation of why his authority was usurped.

John delighted in explaining that he could and would grant clemency or mercy where and when he wished in his role as governor. He was prepared to do so for every unjust metering out of punishment.

He replied to Dore in the same curt vein as the magistrate's abrupt letter, then added, "If it is good enough for Jesus to take our sins for us, and we are all guilty, then in my role as the Governor of New South Wales, it is my right to give a pardon where I see fit. It is what our good Lord did."

Dore's reply brought a volley of letters all containing vitriol in a cascade of unanswerable missives.

John ignored most of them and consigned them to his bin.

This was just one of the many situations in which John was battling nearly everything.

The rum production had not lessened, drunkenness was rife, and the dry heat was never-ending.

John and his household prayed for rain each time they met for a meal, but God withheld the thirst-quenching fluid.

~

The sound of the first rain on the shingle roof above his head made John lie in bed with a smile on his lips. However, the droplets turned into sheets of rain, and the rain to torrents. Bennelong had been correct. This rain was heavy, far heavier than usual. Ben had shown him the tall ant-tubes, then pointed to the screeching black cockatoos who endorsed the approaching deluge. John listened and issued orders to prepare for floods. Not all obeyed.

Over the next few days, news trickled in about the farms along the Hawkesbury River that were not faring well. The rains out west had been heavier. One report that landed on John's desk described flooded buildings and people stranded on rooftops. Andrew Thompson, an emancipated convict who became a policeman in Toongabbie in 1793, did what he could to save as many as possible. Many survived because of his actions. John was determined to ensure he was rewarded.

John wondered how the Bowmans were faring and hoped they had built high enough. He knew the Reiby's farmhouse was out of flood reach, but Robert Webb's land was low-lying. Linus had thankfully warned the Bowmans to build high on the hillside. He knew he should have checked if they had, but you can't force people to do what they don't wish to do. Hopefully, they had listened to Linus. He knew they were still living on Government Stores, so they had no harvest that year due to soil preparation and drought.

~

Two letters arrived at Government House three days after the rains started.

The Bowmans wrote and reported that all was well. Thanks to Linus's instruction, they were all safe. The house was built well out of flood level, and they had installed vertical field boundaries so that the stock could quickly move out of the flood waters. The stock only had to walk up the hill to the house, which they had done. None had been lost.

Linus's convict girl wrote the other letter. He had dictated it, giving a complete account of the farm and the rains.

Crispin read the screed aloud over luncheon.

"*Bennelong has brought the tribe to the house, and they are currently camped on our verandah. He warned us where to build the storeroom for my seed barn soon after we arrived here. He told us that this area was above the flood waters. I'm guessing he may have suggested where to build our wonderful home; if so, thank you for listening to him.*

Our wide verandahs give them protection that they otherwise would not have. Ben explained that they used to have access to a series of caves, but they were out of reach due to flooding and clearing. The smaller ones are not large enough for them all.

Sir, I do feel for these people. We have taken their land without asking, and when some less fortunate than our group retaliate, it always seems to be their fault. This is not so. They are a kind and loving people, but I know troublemakers are in all groups.

Sir, did you know that the violation of their women is almost commonplace? Because of their lack of clothing, the convicts and some settlers feel that they are enticing them and make themselves free with the wives and daughters of these dear people; even the little girls are not exempted.

Sir, you tell me that the King ordered us to befriend them; I find this is easy to do. They are prepared to trade food, and we have plenty to share with them. Ben has even offered some help from the tribe when harvest comes as a swap for some of the various crops. I heartily agreed as they have kept us supplied with fresh meat. However, I have drawn the line to eating more goanna or those white witchetty grubs. They are vile!"

LINUS

Linus signed in capitals with his own hand, and it looked like a thumbnail dipped in tar.

When Crispin passed the letter to John, he saw that his friend's writing had improved.

That last comment brought a chuckle from everyone listening. All had been persuaded to taste both so-called delicacies and thought some of the bush foods disgusting. The rest of the letter was family news for Helena and the children's doings.

John left the gathering and returned to his office with much to consider. The letter made him think hard. He knew of the violations of the native women, but he was unable to be everywhere at once. The men in the colony abused and violated the convict women as much, but he couldn't flog them all.

Although he had insisted in a few prosecutions when he had hard evidence, most of the time, his hands were tied. He occasionally heard about the death of a native, but he had not thought of the continued abuse these people suffered. The deaths were punished, the same as any murder would be. The women especially were vilely treated, and consequently, there were few Indigenous people left in the area.

Most of the *Eora* clan had gone. The loss of one man or even one woman threatened the survival of the tribe. John had all but stayed with them for a week, and over the many months on board the *HMS Reliance* with Bennelong, he now saw them as people of different skin colour, just as Bennelong pointed out. They were friends.

John set out to write an edict that better protected the area's Indigenous people. He told Bennelong he enforced equal punishment for anyone who killed another, regardless of colour. He wished he could do more, but once again, the greed of the grain growers and those with livestock was causing most of the trouble.

Deaths occurred, and no one reported them.

With his lips pursed in frustration, he returned to his desk to tackle the paperwork.

~

Easter came and went with more complaints about Dore.

Eric and Gillian's second daughter arrived safely. Ellen was unlike her sister and slept well from the time she was born.

As winter set in, the foundations of the new church were finished, but there had been little progress on the walls going up. The circular clock tower was to be incorporated into the west end of the church.

One habit formed by accident was the interruption of morning tea each day John worked from home.

A tap on his door was followed by a small smock-clad boy sneaking into his office. This always brought a smile to John's lips, and he put his quill down and closed his ink pot.

Jasper had become the forerunner of his tea tray.

The three-year-old lad knew no bounds of authority and would tug at his blue coat and demand a hug.

John loved it when the child came for Grandfather time. He willingly complied and would be found with the boy's arms wrapped around his neck when the tea tray was brought in. The child's innocent hug was almost soul-cleansing. He looked forward to this interruption each day.

The pair would move to the settee and share a biscuit.

Jasper was given a very milky tea while John drank his strong, black brew.

The child's chatter was a balm to his soul. His innocuous conversation gave John a break from the stresses of the constant fights within the colony.

At the end of the tea break, Mrs Cowdrey would remove both the child and the tray.

Having spent half an hour in innocent chatter, John could return to his paperwork somewhat refreshed.

When this first occurred, Jasper's disappearance caused an uproar.

Helena had been feeding Judy, and Jasper had been playing nearby. When she looked up, the child was gone.

She and Crispin had found their son in the governor's arms. The child had found a yellow and white cockatoo's feather and had gifted his prize to John. He had fallen asleep on John's shoulder with his arms wound around the debonair gentleman's neck.

~

By June, the cold winds had brought the colony the most horrific conditions. A three-day storm damaged the new windmill base, and then a wind bullet severely damaged the clock tower.

Nigel and Connie's small mill on Flagstaff Hill escaped significant damage.

John had been at the church when Liam Bray brought news of rain. They had returned home quickly. He didn't expect it to be more than another short, sharp shower, but Jasper had alerted him to the approaching violence of the storm.

Only an hour after seeing Liam, Jasper burst into his office, shouting, "Captain John, Captain John, the sky has gone green. Come look, quick."

Jasper took his hand and dragged him out to the back garden.

Helena, Crispin, and Eric were trying to protect the vegetable garden with various covers, rags and the old fern fronds.

With one glimpse at the sky, John sent the child into the kitchen to Gillian. He helped protect much of the garden from the forthcoming hail.

The group spread the last of the canvas sheets when the pea-sized hail started.

As the first tiny lumps of ice fell, they made it indoors.

They stood in the kitchen, watching the storm drop a white sheet of walnut-sized hail over the town. Some large ice balls were fist-sized.

The household gathered in the kitchen and watched as the storm enveloped the town.

It looked like a winter wonderland; only everyone realised there would be a lot of damage.

Within a few hours, the town was strewn with debris, and there were numerous minor injuries reported.

Over the following three days, gusting winds and torrential rain fell.

On the afternoon of June 4th, the weather cleared enough for the clean-up to begin.

The clock was removed from the partially fallen tower and placed in storage.

The storm did a lot of damage throughout the entire colony, and convict gangs were set to work clearing away the debris. The partially built new windmill had been severely damaged, and other partially built superstructures in town were now in peril. Trees were down, and the hail punctured thatched roofs all over town. Shacks had collapsed, and the Tank Stream had flooded and washed away whatever had blown into it.

Days after the first storm had finally passed, many animals were found dead, impaled on logs or wedged up high in trees. Many fresh kills were collected for food, but others were already rotting.

Linus sent word they were fine.

~

The town had just been cleaned after that storm when another one descended, wreaking havoc on already damaged buildings.

The walnut-sized hail of the first storm was small compared to what arrived with this supercell.

This storm also lasted a few days and completed the destruction of the previously damaged buildings with a mighty tornado that tore through the centre of the town.

The second storm was far more destructive than the first one. It flattened the damaged windmill.

The gale-force wind also caved in the side of the clock tower, rendering it completely unusable. Thankfully, the clock itself was saved.

The church was little more than a few rows above the foundations, but now, as there was no tower to brace it, the entire structure would need to be redesigned.

Once the skies cleared, the convicts again cleaned the town of debris.

The second storm brought about the news of a drowning. A man had attempted to cross a creek in the middle of the downpour and was carried away by the fast-running water.

John awaited news from the outlying areas and hoped that no one had died.

After the second storm passed, Thomas Reiby eventually sent word to John that the Bowmans', Webbs, and their neighbours' farms were all safe. There had been no reports of injuries in their area after the second storm, but no word had been heard from the Rosedales.

Having not heard from Linus, Arnold was sent to see if the family and tribe survived. He set off on a horse and carried letters from the governor and Helena to her family. He took the twenty-mile trip as fast as he could.

When he reached the house, his steed was nearly ready to drop. However, he had a feeling something was wrong, so he had pushed the mare.

Nick was on the verandah, and he took the reins of his horse and filled him in about where everyone was. "Arnie, Mary and Phoebe are missing. Mama and I are the only ones here. Everyone is out looking for them. I twisted my ankle yesterday, so I'm grounded with Mama."

Arnold swore. "How long have they been gone, Nicky?"

The injured boy said breathlessly, "The girls went out as soon as the storm left yesterday because two of the little children from the tribe ran off as soon as the rain stopped because their dog had headed bush during the storm, and no one has seen any of them since." His long explanation had nearly left him winded. "The children have been missing since before dawn yesterday. The girls went out yesterday mid-morning to look for them. They didn't come back last night."

Arnold ruffled his hair as he walked indoors to see Agnes.

A hobbling Nick led the tired horse to the barn.

Arnold had come to know his future in-laws well, as he and Jonas had spent their days off on the farm for the last six months.

He greeted a very worried Agnes. "Hello, Mrs R. Tell me how I can help."

Agnes turned as he entered, and he noticed she was crying. She said, "Oh, Arnold, you're a sight for sore eyes. Do you know where our girls might be?"

She swallowed a sob but couldn't contain her grief. Tears streamed down her cheeks.

Arnold adored this gracious woman. She was a mother figure to him. He held out his arms, and Agnes walked into them, grateful for a comfort. A thought occurred after a few moments of respite from the turmoil raging in him. "Mrs R, has anyone checked the upper rock ledge cave? Phoebe took me up there the last time I was here. She said some of the children had shown her their special place."

Agnes pulled away from his arms. She was stunned. "There's a cave? No one mentioned anything about that. Can you find it again?"

Arnold nodded. "I'm pretty sure I know which way we went. Have all the tribe gone?"

Agnes shook her head but then nodded. While wiping away her tears, she said, "Everyone is out looking for the four of them. But they are all looking along the water, not up higher. I hope they have not drowned."

Arnold thought they would not have had anything to drink if they were stuck up on the cliff. "Do you have a flagon or some water I can take?"

Agnes's face lit up. "I have something better. I made some canvas bags and lined them with wax. They are quite watertight and are much easier to carry." As she spoke, she filled up a water carrier. "Arnie, go and put on some of Jem's work clothing and leave your uniform here."

Arnold left immediately and walked to the boys' room. Since the four boys shared one room, he would wear whatever clothes he could find that fitted.

When he returned, Agnes handed him the bulging water bag and another food satchel. "I hope you find them, lad. When the others return, I'll send them all up the hill. Give them a call as you go. The searchers will return for tea tonight. Arnie, if you find them, call *cooee*, as Linus taught you. They'll know they have been found by replying twice and come to assist."

Arnold nodded and headed up the path toward the rock face Phoebe had taken him to only a few weeks ago. They should not have gone alone, but her parents trusted him not to do anything inappropriate to their daughter. He hadn't.

One of the tribes' children had shown Phoebe this cave only the week before.

He walked for over an hour, retracing their footsteps. It had not taken that long when they visited, but the storm had knocked over many trees, and the path was no longer easy to follow.

As he walked higher, he occasionally called out the girls' names.

He finally reached the rocky outcrop and was horrified to see that there had been a significant rockfall. His heart plummeted. Had they been underneath it? Were they trapped? He called Phoebe's name and heard a muffled reply.

He climbed higher and finally rounded the top of the outcrop to see that the large rock that had overhung the entrance to the cave had indeed fallen and blocked the exit.

He called again; this time, the reply came from inside the depths of the now-buried cave entrance. "Phoebe, are you alone, or is Mary there too?"

Phoebe replied, "Arnie, the two lost children and their dog are here with Mary and me. We are all uninjured but so thirsty."

Arnold was thrilled that ed he had brought water. "I have water and some food with me. I'll see if I can dig away some of the smaller side rocks, but I want you all to stay at the back of the cave. Before I do, I'll call the others to help. They are all searching along the creek."

He walked to the edge of the overhang and called out a long *"Coooeee"* as Linus had taught him.

The word echoed down the valley and along the creek. Hopefully, someone would hear and come to assist.

Having shouted a few times, he finally received a *cooee cooee* in reply.

Returning to the rockfall, he checked the stability of the cliff. Having walked around the collapse, he realised there was only one safe place to set to work.

This area was covered with smaller rocks that should not bring down larger slabs.

The enormous overhanging ledge had collapsed and covered the entrance. It had brought down an avalanche of smaller boulders. He carefully rolled one large rock away and discovered a tumble of smaller rocks behind it.

He set to work clearing these. Soon, Phoebe could reach out her arm and grasp his hand. The hole was not yet big enough to pass through the water bag, so he kept digging.

The food pouch was smaller, so it fitted through the hole only a few minutes later.

He was still pulling away rocks when he heard footsteps behind him.

Bennelong and Goomberri stood with their mouths open.

Bennelong was the first to speak. "How you find this place, Arnie? This special cave for sacred women's business."

Arnold said, "Phoebe showed me the last time I came. She didn't know it was a sacred place. I'm sorry, Ben. We wouldn't have come if we had known."

Bennelong shook his head. "That okay, Arnie, not bad for you fella, but blackfella like us. Blackfella men are not allowed inside. Well, it's all gone now anyway."

Goomberri remained silent but started digging in the area Arnold had been working on. After another fifteen minutes of shifting the fallen rocks, more of the tribe and most of the family arrived.

Jonas was kneeling, and Mary poked out her hand this time. He said, "Mary, are you really uninjured?"

Mary was borderline crying with relief. "I am Jonas, but we're so thirsty."

With a squeeze of her hand, he said, "Give us a few minutes, love, and we'll pass in the water."

Arnold took his place, and Phoebe came to the opening. "Phoebe, I just want you to know I love you."

She chuckled. Her reply was, "I love you too, Arnie." Her answer was soft enough for only him to hear.

Arnold was overwhelmed by how he felt. He had torn his nails to the quick dragging at the rocks to reach her. "Marry me, Phoebe. Please, will you marry me?"

Phoebe giggled, "You ask me now? When I can't throw myself into your arms and give you a smacking big kiss. Get me out safely, and I'll show you just what I mean."

"So, that's a yes?" His heart was pounding in anticipation.

She replied, "Yes, that is a yes if Papa agrees."

Moments later, Linus and the two oldest boys arrived.

With the arrival of many more hands, another large rock was shifted, and the water bag was passed in. Linus brought a second bag that had been refilled and passed up from below.

After half an hour, the six men managed to clear away a few more large boulders from the mouth of the cave. With the rolling of one big rock, the hole was now large enough for the two small children and dog to wriggle out.

As they were hauled clear, the two young imps squealed with delight at their adventure. They had a few cuts and scrapes, but nothing that a hug and kiss from their mothers would not heal.

The missing dog followed them out. He was filthy but unharmed.

The remainder of the tribe was waiting lower down the rock promontory.

Goomberri took each child down as they were extracted and then told the bulk of the group to return to Agnes and tell her the girls were found and safe. He noted that Tris had already gone.

After some questioning, Goomberri told Linus that Agnes would already know the girls were found uninjured.

They had about four hours before sunset to extract the two girls. The six men digging were exhausted but constantly worked to enlarge the hole. A few times, they wondered if the next rock would fill in the hole again. Some smaller cave-ins did occur, but these made the digging easier.

Now and then, they would pause and let the two courting men have a few words with their girlfriends. Arnold was ready to toss every rock off the cliff.

An hour before sunset, the exhausted men tied a rope around one last big flat rock, which would provide an exit.

Jonas made both girls move well away from the hole as they tugged out what they hoped would be the last blockage.

On the count of three, the six men pulled, and the enormous boulder moved slowly. As it didn't cause any further instability, they continued to shift it away. Inch by inch, the rock revealed a large opening.

It took them half an hour to move the offending boulder far enough away for the girls to fit through.

Mary insisted that Phoebe, being smaller, be pulled out first. Next, she passed out the empty water and food bags before putting both of her arms out to be eased through the gap. Being larger than Phoebe, it was a very tight fit. Her hips were wedged in the hole, and she had to twist them to wiggle through. Her gown ripped as Jonas and Gerry helped her out, but she didn't care.

Arnold stood with his arm around Phoebe. Realising there would be little room on the platform, he escorted her off the promontory.

Mary was finally out, and Jonas could not resist, but he pulled her into his arms, and he didn't care that her face was filthy. He kissed her. He lifted his head and said, "Marry me, Mary. I've been so afraid I had lost you, and I never want to go through that ever again."

Linus cleared his throat as he watched the couple embracing.

Without releasing Mary, Jonas said, "Sir, I would like your permission to marry Mary. Can we have a private talk later?"

Linus was chuckling. "If you want her while looking so bedraggled, you must really love her, laddie."

Jonas grinned. "I do, sir, a lot." He dropped another kiss on the lips of his beloved.

Linus chuckled again. "Permission granted, but we'll still meet later."

Jem untied the rope from around the last rock and rolled it up.

Once done, the group carefully descended from where the cave had once been.

As they reached the waiting women of the tribe, Linus saw Phoebe enfolded in Arnold's arms, being thoroughly kissed and enjoying every moment of it. "Laddie, release her, please. There is a time and place for these things, but you are not yet betrothed."

Arnold dropped one arm, but the other remained around her shoulders. "Um, actually, sir, I was wondering if I could see you on return to the house." Although he had already proposed while she was trapped, Phoebe's reply was conditional on her father's approval. She was only just seventeen, and he knew her father would be concerned about her young age. He was nervous about how Linus would reply, but the man's reaction was unexpected.

Linus threw back his head and roared with laughter. "Well, this is not how I expected the search to finish. Mayhap I should lock up a few more of my daughters in caves in future years. You two men can see me while the girls clean themselves up. Three down, only eight more to go."

Chapter 18 Unsigned Betrayal
1799

$\mathcal{A}$s Sydney struggled to rebuild after the June twin storms, the situation with the Corps, the free settlers, and the town's unbalanced official authority grew increasingly tense.

The Osbornes in Parramatta, Rosedales on the outskirts of that town, and the Brays at the mill could avoid most of the unpleasantness. Not so those in the official residence.

A terse letter arrived from London, complaining of the governor's willingness to associate himself with corruption. This was the opposite of the situation, and all in the household knew that.

John was so confused. What had been written to Head Office?

Not knowing what it was about, he put the letter aside.

~

In March, Major Paterson returned with the ship that brought the mail. He seemed healthier than when he departed a couple of years earlier. He came with orders to investigate the officers' trading in spirits. Had the mysterious letter been from him to the Admiralty?

Richard Johnson and his revised plans for the church were a welcome distraction from the palaver John was dealing with daily. He discussed the situation with the minister.

The report of such unwarranted lies disturbed them both.

Richard Dore was banned from John's office as he had been reprimanded so often that John wanted to ignore him.

John was barely controlling his temper while scribing letters to Dore. As the man was still the official Colonial Secretary, John had no choice but to communicate with him. However, he did this by letter rather than in person.

He had received word from London that Dore had been promoted to the head magistrate. This made it impossible for John to dismiss him completely. He growled in anger.

John insisted that Crispin, Eric, or Arnold attend every meeting. They were there to take the meeting minutes and then write an independent report.

John had taken to penning some of his own correspondence is Crispin was not on duty.

He found that having a third party in the room when Dore visited was necessary. Dore quibbled over everything, and John realised that he had even questioned whether John's new scribes recorded his comments correctly.

~

As Spring drew near, so did the date for the double wedding.

The stone church in Parramatta was half-built. It had already been used for other weddings, baptisms, and funerals. When the need for a permanent church was first mentioned years ago, Colin Osbourne joked about naming it after John. As one of the emancipated men who was now a churchwarden on the parish vestry, Colin suggested calling it St John's, and the name stuck but was not yet official.

John was honoured but also embarrassed.

Jasper often sought John out and climbed onto his lap.

John usually told him stories of his life at sea until the child fell asleep in his arms.

On Thursday, Crispin, Helena, and the children left for Parramatta with Mrs Cowdrey. The rest of the household would follow on Friday, November 1st.

Arnold was to stay with Jonas for the night at the barracks, and they would meet them at the church the following morning.

The day boded to be fine.

The two grooms were nervous but excited.

As the family gathered on the grassy area outside the church, they discussed a name for this brick edifice.

Colin came to John's side and reminded him of his promise made shortly before his own wedding.

John was outvoted over naming the church, and the new building would be named in his honour.

As senior minister, Richard Johnson had the final say. He had offered to officiate but remained in town to perform the Sydney service.

St John's Parramatta saw its first double wedding with Reverend Samuel Marsden, the assistant minister officiating. He would unite both couples, and then the family would retire to the farm for the extended celebration.

The wedding went smoothly, and the newlyweds shared a carriage back to the farm.

Everyone else, including John, climbed onto the flat wagon, the governor's carriage, or Jonas's new buggy.

The wedding party lasted two days.

Colin's family had their own vehicle and came each day from their home.

The bunk room at Government House that had originally been Gillian's room would be the Kerrs' once they were married.

The bunks had been converted into a big pallet bed.

Helena was thrilled that one of her sisters would be living with them.

Jonas sold his commission, and this was finalised two days before the wedding. He would move to the farm with Linus. The twins had already started clearing his new land, and he planned to build a two-story home for his lady-love. He was also overseeing the clearing of the other farms.

Over the winter, they had put a small back-burn fire through the cluster of farms to clear off most of the ticks and shrubs.

Arnold and Travis were also allocated forty-acre plots.

Travis was not so keen on the idea of turning to the hard work of farming. However, Arnold's farm completed a square of allotments, and Travis's was on the far side of Jonas's property, adjoining the twins' one-hundred-acre block.

The governor and his entourage intended to take a weekend holiday, and the double nuptials were undoubtedly a good excuse for such a celebration.

John and his two household ladies were always included. He was a grandfather figure to them all; he adored the informality of this family, and they were his sanity. Here, he could forget the tension and the lack of discipline in town. He refused to do any paperwork during this visit, so he relaxed.

After the storm hit Sydney, the priority was to rebuild the damaged buildings rather than complete the church in town. Services were still held upstairs in the store room, and they were adequate.

John had Nigel Bray to thank for encouraging him to double the size of the planned grain store. He had not planned to construct a double-story building, but Nigel mentioned needing larger secure storage to Arthur Phillip. It was underway before he returned. John wondered why it was required, but had long ago learned to listen to God's not-so-subtle prodding. He looked heavenward and thanked the Lord.

Progress on the new church in Sydney was halted until repairs on other essential buildings were finished. The loss of the tower also reduced the church's size. Sadly, some of the church site footings were unsuitable for the structure's length. John was unhappy about that; at least a permanent church was underway. A new tower replaced the old round clock tower, and the church was now firmly attached to the new structure, which would continue to be used as a guard tower for the settlement. Thankfully, the clock had been undamaged by the first storm and, after minor repairs, was now awaiting installation in the new tower.

With the wedding celebrations to look forward to, John could leave his worries behind for a few days and enjoy himself. He adored the way the children had little regard for his rank and would all but attack him for hugs.

These people were his family. He often had two little ones in his arms when walking and more on his lap when sitting.

Each newlywed couple had a room to themselves. The remaining rooms were filled with children, other couples, and two older ladies who shared. Many of the smaller children slept on the floor on shared mattresses.

On the Monday after the wedding, they all said farewell.

John was sad to return, but a pile of paperwork awaited his attention. He had received news that another ship had been sighted off the coast and should dock today. More convicts would need placement, accommodation, food, and rations.

Linus offered to take more young felons.

~

The day after arriving in Sydney, Mrs Cowdrey heard Jasper knocking on the governor's office door.

Usually, he would have been called to enter at his first knock, but today, he had not been permitted in for a hug. He looked puzzled but knew not to enter unless permitted to do so. He realised that he was not to harass the governor. He turned away forlorn and sought his parents and sister in the back garden. Rather than say anything was wrong, he plopped himself on the bench seat and sat sulkily.

Crispin noticed his son's morose mood but knew he needed to finish the task at hand. He and Eric were busy installing the fronds on the net, and they only had four more to poke into the netting.

Once they completed the job, Crispin sat next to his son. "You look as though Kelly ate your cake."

The dog had just come over to the little boy. She was licking his hand.

Jasper stroked the dog's head as its tongue lolled out to one side. The boy's head shook. "Captain John wouldn't let me in today, Papa."

Eric had collected the despatch bag from the *Walker*, which was the most recent arrival, and delivered it to the governor. This ship brought more military personnel, and a swathe of information and mail came from London.

Crispin knew that it would have despatches from the Home Office. He tried explaining to his son that sometimes the governor needed to work and not hug small boys.

Jasper's face showed his despair. "I know Papa, but when he's busy, he still comes to the door and tells me so. Today, he just ignored me. That's not like Captain John, Papa. Something is wrong."

Crispin noticed Mrs Cowdrey at the kitchen door, attempting to beckon him subtly. He tousled his son's hair and said, "I'll go and see if everything is all right. Stay here and help Uncle Eric and look after the little girls."

Jasper nodded and watched his father walk towards the house.

Mrs Cowdrey had gone indoors but waited for Crispin to enter. "Something is wrong, Cris. He's got his head in his hands and didn't even acknowledge me when I brought in the tea tray."

Crispin nodded but didn't reply. Jasper was correct. He said, "I'll go see if he needs anything. Jasper is also worried."

He walked towards the governor's office. As the secretary-cum-scribe, he had permission to enter the office unannounced. He knocked politely on the door, but without waiting for a call to enter, he opened the door.

The governor sat as if frozen. His head was in his hands and as still as a statue.

Crispin wondered if he was dead and walked towards him to see if he was breathing.

John raised his head and met Crispin's anxious gaze. "I'm alive, lad, but read this. It has just been delivered from the latest ship to arrive."

He held out a long letter to the young man, then reclined in his favourite padded leather chair looking worried.

John's cheeks were sallow, and he didn't look well. His skin and lips were grey.

Crispin seated himself in a chair on the opposite side of the desk, having glanced at his boss's face, then at the screed. It obviously held terrible news. He swallowed and started to read with some trepidation.

Less than halfway down the first page, Crispin gasped. "Sir, seriously? Someone sent an anonymous letter to London making an official complaint about you encouraging the illegal trade?"

John nodded. "Keep reading; it gets worse."

Crispin's eyes fell back to the page. He kept reading, flipping over the page, and he released a strangled cry. "Nooooo! They are recalling you?"

John gave him a crooked smile and said, "Lord Portland is not here, so he can't exactly force me onto a ship, can he?"

Hope budded in Crispin. He had learned to adore the quiet man. He had become a replacement father figure. They had many discussions about faith and everlasting life. Since the loss of their first child, this was a topic that had all but obsessed Crispin for many months.

Reverend Johnson had given him a lot of time, but the informal discussions with the governor answered his questions. The minister's explanation of the red and green trees stayed with him. But the question remained: what about their child? Agnes mentioned she believed Samantha to be in Heaven. William Kent said the same about their first son, John, as did the Johnsons. If the babies never had a chance to sin, would they be with God? He knew the governor studied Divinity at university before leaving and returning to the sea and that his faith had never wavered.

John assured Crispin that from what he had read and believed, the children would be awaiting them in fully grown perfection. This thought was the turning point for Crispin to finally release his anger.

In the years since then, their faith had drawn them close. Working with the governor as scribe and secretary forged a bond as close as father and son.

Crispin finished reading the official blast from London and looked up at his boss. "What are you going to do then, sir?"

John shrugged. "Cris, I did not tell you, but I learned about the anonymous letter months ago. Jonas brought the first information. His uncle warned me about that with the mail that arrived in the *Hillsborough*. I replied via Jonas and sent my thanks on the *Hunter* when it sailed. My letters were officially personal, so I didn't send them in the official despatch box but with the ship's captain. I told you about Jonas's trick with the hair in the seal?"

Crispin nodded.

John continued. "Well, I addressed my letters to Jonas's uncle, Lord Charles Phillimont. He's an old friend from my university days, rather than the Home Secretary. One sheet contained my single-page and somewhat abrupt reply to the Duke of Portland's note about the unsigned letter. My words were not subtle. I pressed my innocence and mentioned the other letters I knew they had received and asked them to compare the writing. Reverend Richard told me he had also written to tell them it was a pack of lies and that although he could not confess who the perpetrators were because of the confessional, the accusations were all untruths."

John sighed. He had done his best, but this was a war that he could not win. It was like fighting ghosts. He was fully aware that one day, it would boil over and come to a head. In a way, he was pleased he would not be here when that occurred. This was merely a skirmish, and he had been defeated.

Crispin knew about the plethora of mail containing untruths and outright lies forwarded over the past year. He presumed there would have been many more of a similar vein in the years preceding that. He asked, "Have you thought of an official reply this time, sir? This letter will have been read by the scum here, and they will know about it even if you do not tell them."

John agreed. "Yes, a duplicate screed came in the official despatch box, which had been tampered with, so they will know." He sighed. "I know, Cris, but can you keep this to yourself until I reply? I have about a month until the *Britannia* sails, so I don't need to pen my reply today. Leave it with me, lad."

Crispin knew he was dismissed. He went to leave but turned back again. "Are you all right, sir? Jasper was worried about you, as am I."

John looked up and smiled. "I wasn't, but I think I am now after talking to you."

His light blue eyes were now glassy. This is not how he wished his term to end. "Cris, pray for me as I write my reply. I shall, of course, vehemently deny the accusations again, but this letter is final. I am being recalled; that is not negotiable. However, I shall not leave the colony devoid of leadership again. It was that vacancy that caused this issue in the first place."

Crispin frowned. "Who is Phillip Gidley King, sir? Do you know him well?" The letter mentioned the name of the new man.

John relaxed back in his chair. "I do, actually, Cris. Sit down again, and I'll tell you about my time on Norfolk Island."

The pair made themselves comfortable. "You know about the speed that a gale can blow up here? Norfolk Island is worse. If nothing else, a retelling of my time there will take my mind off this." He tapped the missive on his desk.

Crispin nodded.

John gave a long sigh and then retold the story of that fateful day of the wreck. "Cris, I was captaining the *HMS Sirius,* and we had just finished unloading urgent food supplies for Norfolk Island, and one of those violent squalls blew up. The winds were soon gusting terribly, and to cut a long story short, we managed to unload most of the passengers but not the cargo before the wind became too strong."

Crispin sat listening to the story recounted. He knew the outcome but had not heard all the details before. He knew that John still had the occasional nightmare about the wreck as he heard him call out in his sleep.

John got up and paced the room. He paused and looked out of the window but kept the story going. "I was court-martialled over the loss of my beautiful ship, but I was exonerated, or I would not be here today. As you well know, I still have nightmares of that day, but not as often now."

He ran his hand across his brow. "However, before I was promoted to governor, Phillip Gidley King's name was put forward to replace Arthur Phillip. Admiralty ignored him, and I got the commission. I held dormant orders on my first visit in 1788. Sometimes, I think King may have done a better job. I came to know him well after my shipwreck and during our time on Norfolk Island. I like him, and I hope he will succeed."

He drew a deep breath and turned to his young listener. "Cris, I will not fight this. I have done what I could, but it was not enough. Even though I wish to stay, this settlement needs a stronger hand who will see through the blarney and lies of the rabble Corps. Richard told me to keep my friends close and my enemies closer."

He choked a laugh, then turned again and stood looking out his window at the town below. The new church construction site was visible from his office window, and he could see some work being done there. "My friend, my departure's delay will give you time to build your houses. I presume that you will stay here in the colony with Helena. I also wish to see the Brays at the mill settled, as I have work to do there. They need security, as does your family. We need another small mill; my big one will be years away from completion. Nigel can run both small mills. I intend to see them secure. They can't be embroiled in all this corruption."

Crispin nearly wept. He choked out his words. "Of course, sir. I have not even thought about returning to London. My life is here with Helena and her family. They are now my family too, as I have no one else in England, so, yes, we will stay. However, you are correct. I shall sell out, and we will move to the farm, but not until you leave. We cannot thank you enough for that bountiful security you have arranged for us all."

John remained at the window with his back turned to Crispin. He was watching the new guards come to relieve those at the door. "Cris, I'm thrilled you lads will have Linus to guide you. Jonas had some initial anxiety about marrying and staying here, but having had information from Lord Charles, he had no inheritance prospects in England. He's the youngest of seven children; the three eldest are brothers, and each has sons. I believe he's seventeenth in line to inherit the earldom now. As Lord Jonas, he has money available to him but little else. He even refuses to use his title unless he must. However, Eric and Arnold are like you; no one is pining for them in England. The Rosedales have already absorbed Eric and Gillian into the extended family. You have wonderful support around you, and I'm sure you will settle well. Please keep the Bray and Osborne families under your care. They have no one at all."

Crispin chuckled. "That's a given, sir! Eric and Arnie are like the brothers I never had. Jonas..." Crispin thought about the young soldier. "Jonas, I just adore. He's like a little brother to us all. He was born with a silver spoon in his mouth, but he's as happy to get down and muck out a stable with us or get on the other end of a double-handed saw. He calls them a misery-whip. We all know he's loaded, but he doesn't rub it in our faces. Mary will want for nothing, but Jonas has ensured that our houses will not shame her. Apparently, the cost of our new houses was each the same as a tailored set of evening attire for him at home. We have left the planning of our homes to him. It is one thing he does very well. We are not too proud to look that gift horse in the mouth. Nigel and Colin are older than me, but I trust them."

John knew Jonas had paid for the building supplies, but he ensured that the most experienced crews worked on the various dwellings.

Crispin continued. "Sir, thank you for supplying workers to clear our farms. That was an added bonus and one we will never be able to thank you enough for."

It was Mary who persuaded the three men to accept assistance from Jonas and John. All three single-story houses cost Jonas less than one month's allowance. As the three men were absent from their farms with their sentry duties, they had no choice but to leave everything in Jonas's hands. The Thistlethwaite's double-story house would be ready for them in about a month. Completing the other houses would take at least six months, and then they had to furnish them. The other houses were clones of Linus's home but not as big. Each had two double-sided fireplaces and a wide verandah circling the home. Jonas's house also had a surrounding verandah on the top floor. All had underground cellars as a refuge from the heat.

John turned around slowly. "Cris, in this place, there are very few I trust as much as I trust you. Our wonderful reverend is another such man, Linus, too, of course, and young Jonas and even Eric has his moments. But, lad, you are special; therefore, I have a favour to ask. When I leave, can you write and explain what's happening here? I want to know how Phillip Gidley King and whoever follows him fare. One day, these pesky malcontents must be brought to justice, but I feel they will mutiny before that occurs."

Crispin's eyebrows lifted in surprise. "Of course, sir, but I thought you would want to shake off the dust of this place and get back to the sea."

John shook his head and made a sound almost like a snort. He returned to his desk. He said, "Them, yes; you, Colin, Nigel and the other lads, no!" He walked to his favourite chair and sat down. "I have not told you or anyone else what's been happening, but I feel they will not permit me to appear in front of the Home Office Committee. You see, I don't think Dore is well enough to travel and face any inquisition. All I can say is that the truth will be revealed one day. I hope the colony does not pay with a full-blown mutiny, but it may take that before London listens. I suspect the free settlers I brought in, as well as you chaps, may hold the balance. I doubt you will be strong enough to stop the rot. Many more convicts will soon be fully emancipated as their fourteen-year terms end. You should be safe enough with four ex-soldiers and Linus's boys near you. Bennelong's friendship should also give you somewhere to flee to if necessary. Oh, laddie, take care not to stir the beasts out here. At home, we would call that a *stramash*. I suppose you could translate that as a riot. They will know that you are a friend of mine and will do what they can to destroy you."

Crispin was astounded. "Thank you for caring, sir. If worse comes to worst, we know we can all go home once Helena's term expires."

John sat up straight and pulled his chair into his desk. "Ahh, about that, Cris."

He pulled the drawer of his desk open and extracted two documents. "I drew these up some time ago; here's one for Helena and you, the other is for Eric and Gillian." He handed over the rolled certificate to the outstretched hand.

Crispin wondered what it was until he unfurled it. The document was a Certificate of Freedom, dated from the day of their marriage. "Sir, this is…"

John lifted his hand to stop him from saying more. "I should have given this to you ages ago, but I thought you might leave me if she was free. Quite selfishly, I wished you both to stay. That one is for Gillian, and I also have one for Connie Bray. Arthur Phillip ensured the Osbornes received theirs before he left."

John felt guilty he had held on to these for so long. He intended to give them to each couple as a wedding gift but had reneged from fear of their desertion. He knew he could produce the signed and dated forms, but he should have at least told the husbands that their wives were free. "Sorry, Cris!"

Crispin chuckled. "You need not have worried, sir. I doubt she would have left you even if we had not married. Her conviction meant an entirely new life for her whole family. That includes wealth they never dreamed about. And now two more of her sisters have wonderful husbands, both met through you."

He wondered if he should say more about the care and compassion he received at his boss's hand. He did. "Sir, you mentored and supported me through my anger and grief. You have been with us through the joyous births of our children, and we will miss you greatly when you leave. I can confidently say that you are loved by us all."

He stood to leave, knowing that his boss was now in a much better frame of mind. "I arrived as an ignorant young man in search of a dream. Through you, that dream was realised. However I had no idea that love could be so painful. Through our talks and prayer times you set me straight. I owe you far more than a few years of service. The words, thank you, are vastly insufficient."

John smiled and gave a nod of acknowledgment. He was once again relaxed. Through those times of prayer he had grown close to this young man. "Cris, I shall send a large convict team to finish clearing and ploughing the farms and get cracking on finishing the houses and outbuildings you will require. Call it my gift to you. Next month, I will finalise the transfer of Linus's farm to him, free of any further costs. Then we'll see how long it takes for Gidley King to get here."

Cris felt like yelling in utter frustration at the situation. "I speak for Eric, but we will not leave you until the ship taking you away is out of sight. The new man will need to find his own guards."

John nodded. "Phillip King will probably bring staff from Norfolk Island anyway. I would not worry about his security detail. I shall, however, let him know you fellows are trustworthy, and he can turn to you all for assistance if required." John knew he had to get back to work. "Keep our conversation quiet until I can get things sorted. I want to see Richard Johnson first; then, I'll make plans afterwards. My nephew William Kent will also need to know. I hope they will return with me. If they do, they must move in with me, and Phillip can stay at their house until we leave." Crispin moved to leave, but John said, "Cris, can you see if Richard Johnson is free? Then we'll escape to the mill this afternoon as I need to get out of here."

Crispin nodded, then exited the room. He wondered what he was going to tell the family. He hoped he would not have to keep it to himself for too long. Outside the door, his son was waiting for him. He said, "Hello, my boy. Captain John has a lot of work to do now, but he's fine." Crispin hoisted him up and walked to the garden. Helena greeted him and asked if everything was sorted. He nodded. "Yes, love, but I'll take Jasper with me as I have to run a message to the reverend. Don't do too much in the heat, so take care."

Helena chuckled at her overprotective husband. "I'll be fine, you wonderful man. Jasper, look after Papa, won't you?"

The boy's head bobbled back and forth. Crispin hoisted his son onto his shoulders, and he now sat on his neck high above the ground. Crispin's ears were used as handles. Jasper wore his father's tri-corn hat.

~

John's household moved to the farm for a few days respite. Over Easter luncheon, John told everyone that he was to return to England as he had been recalled. This announcement cut short the festive, celebratory mood at the Rosedale farm. While at the farm, the official residence was moved to Parramatta. He was determined to spend his last months in his new house. It also allowed him to spend time with Colin and Aggie's family. Their son Jonny had grown so much and now had five more siblings.

Only Crispin knew John's entire history. The staff was to keep the news to themselves, but the two older ladies needed to make some hard decisions. The one piece of happy news was Helena's announcement that she thought she was expecting again and was due just after mid-year.

Although the new residence in Parramatta still needed finishing touches, another storm shortly before Christmas damaged the Sydney residence to the point that it was all but uninhabitable. The shingle roof over John's bed sprung a big leak. He moved into the guest room next door. The Sydney house could be refurbished and reroofed before the incoming governor arrived. Once the building was repaired, the carpenters made furnishings for the new governor.

Within weeks, word in the town spread about the governor's imminent departure. With them living closer to their family, the young soldiers could more easily oversee the clearing of the farms and the construction of the new houses. Teams of newly arrived convicts were assigned to clear and dig over the virgin soil. The skilled convicts who had arrived on the *Barwell* with the Rosedales had done well in constructing the new Georgian-style Government House in Parramatta. The new residence sat on a hill overlooking the growing town. It was far more comfortable than the draughty house in Sydney. The thick stone walls added protection from the heat. The small underground larder meant that food could be kept cool. Mrs Peach loved the massive fireplace and bread oven to the side. However, there was no hob.

~

Three days after Christmas, the gaol in Parramatta was deliberately set alight. Unfortunately, twenty people incarcerated there suffered severe burns, and one died. He was the man who instigated Helena's attacks.

The town's Christmas celebrations drew to a close.

From his new office, John could see Colin's house. Students came and went, and convict girls worked in their large vegetable garden. With a sigh, John set about detailing his achievements and doing an itinerary of the stock and food stores in the settlement. Compiling this list entailed many field trips to various farms to assess the crops to go into Government Stores.

With the storms came the rain, and the improved soil on the new farms was ready for their first crops. Linus planted oats, corn, and potatoes rather than wheat or barley. These crops would not worry the illegal brewers as they were used for immediate food consumption. They also had artichokes, onions, parsnips, turnips, swedes, carrots, leeks, celery, cabbage, lettuce, and cauliflower, plus vine crops like beans, broad beans, peas, passionfruit, cucumbers, and pumpkins. Linus also brought sugar beets and he planted a full field of these. All the plants loved the new, improved soil and grew well. The fallen logs were piled and set aside for use later as split rail fences to enclose the new orchard.

More convict vessels arrived, and John had to work out placements for the numerous felons. The existing convict barracks were already overcrowded. Eventually, some convict women unused to hard labour were put to work spinning and weaving on the top floor of Parramatta's newly constructed convict men's quarters. Over one thousand felons arrived in a matter of weeks, and John was tearing his hair out. He sent many to clear farmland around the government plots near Rooty Hill. Tents were the only abodes he had access to.

Chapter 19 Tossed by the Billows
1800

Whook hen the *Speedy* arrived with Phillip Gidley King and his wife, Anna, and daughter in mid-April.

John was surprised that King had a wife and child as he knew Phillip's convict mistress and their children lived on Norfolk Island.

The ship brought another scathing despatch from the Duke of Portland.

This letter itemised the apparent ineptitude of Governor Hunter's leadership. Lord Portland criticised the high cost of spirits, the trading of the officers, and the quantity of convicts assigned to settlers. He then complained that John had intentionally misunderstood and wilfully not complied with the orders from London.

John was aware of his shortcomings, such as trusting the wrong people. Maligning his leadership when the duke did not understand the situation first-hand was a kick in the guts.

Again, Jasper notified his father that Captain John was sad. With only a handful of government farms and no facilities to house the multitude of unexpected convict arrivals, John had little choice but to put the felons where they could find a safe place to sleep and access to food. What did the duke expect him to do with so many prisoners arriving unannounced? Since the Parramatta Gaol no longer existed, he could not lock any up.

Crispin knew the machinations of what was happening far more than anyone else, bar Richard Johnson.

When Cris entered the governor's office, the governor was standing at the window that looked down over the grassy hill towards Colin's house and the pottery school. Some of the front hill was being dug over to plant new gardens.

John acknowledged Crispin's presence by saying, "I'll hand over everything to Phillip Gidley King as soon as possible, Cris. As your crops have been harvested and added to Government Stores, the titles for all your farms are now dated and finalised. Seeing you lads safe and settled is the least I can do. Nigel Bray's new mill is nearly finished, and he's been ramping up flour production for the colony. Send your grain to him for milling."

Crispin waited to see if he would say more. He did.

John stayed at the window but said, "Read the letter on my desk, lad. You'd better sit down to do it, as it will knock your socks off. If the duke knew what we were up against here, he would have a little more respect for what we were battling." He sighed in resignation. "I wish he could come and see the conditions for himself. When I arrived, it was me against the Corps. Now, the Irish convicts and the latest English free settlers are ready to clash. I include the soldiers who have sold out in that group. I think, overall, I shall be glad to go. Give me an angry sea any day! Life tosses rubbish at you any which way, but the sea's billows are more forgiving than this God-forsaken hellhole. I would rather have a violent storm at sea and be rocked to the scuppers than this bickering and constant squabbling. It's so wearing. What is worse, I can put it all down to greed and self-importance from a handful of men, and I don't think the new governor will have an easy time of things here. I should have listened to Richard's advice to keep my enemies close. Mayhap, I should have brought Macarthur into town and assigned him here. I'm sure he's behind most of the discontent."

The Sydney house was still not ready for habitation, so the King family lived with Lieutenant-Colonel Paterson, as he was now, until it was completed. This was far from ideal, as John knew Paterson to be critical of his administration, but he was working towards the same goal; reining in the alcohol.

Another massive influx of convicts preceded the weeks leading up to Phillip Gidley King's arrival. John was overwhelmed, with no idea what to do with these latest felons. Many were well-to-do Irishmen and unused to hard work. He called them political prisoners. He set them to chores as best he could, but he could feel tensions were already rising amongst the growing number of Irishmen and their English guards.

For the first time, John was pleased to be leaving.

Only days after the Kings', the new governor's name was officially announced on April 20th.

The news was met with awkward anticipation. The Corps knew this man to have been at loggerheads with acting governor Grose, and his appointment did not bode well for them. King made it clear he was here to clean things up.

The rebellious group was unsure how easily the new man could be duped or if that was even possible. The supportive ones were sad to see

John leave.

John related the current situation and outlined their problems. He made Crispin sit in on their meetings. The governor-elect listened intently as John listed the issues he was having with Dore, Paterson, Macarthur, and others, ensuring that the new incumbent was fully aware of the mammoth undertaking ahead of him.

John outlined the lack of farm stock and farmers and the scattered government-owned animals on various properties. He also mentioned the exorbitant cost of the most basic necessities. He then showed King the letter from Lord Portland and laughed, saying that the only way he could rein in the spread of alcohol was to raise the cost.

Crispin presented relevant documents to support his words.

Even though ill, Dore was quick to write to King. His first letter arrived within hours of his arrival.

Dore also wrote to John one last request for an Absolute Pardon for his clerk.

John denied the request and only issued a Conditional Pardon, meaning he could not leave the colony.

Phillip King agreed. He also decided that he would not be pushed around. He realised he needed to set a firm stance and stick to it.

Unfortunately for John, King fell ill. So, rather than handing over authority to the new leader, John retained command. This delay gave King the time to observe the colony's residents. He sat in on the numerous court cases involving prosecuting people for illegal distillation of spirits or theft of food. This gave King a sense of what a grave undertaking he was taking on. Word came of a possible Irish rising, and he participated in raids on some Irish households to find hidden pickets and weapons that could be used in a war. Tensions between the two groups were heating up.

By May, King realised that trouble was imminent. He suggested to John that the *Buffalo* be sent to Norfolk Island and return with a detachment of soldiers to reinforce the town's command. That being done, King wondered what else he could do until the current governor departed.

The *Buffalo*, which would carry John home, had an estimated departure date of August, though that now depended on its return from Norfolk Island with the military passengers.

Although John had completed a food and stock muster, the estimated number of people residing in the settlement was just that. He had no real idea who was living where, and records had not been accurately kept before he arrived. King conducted a complete muster of all the colonists and determined the number living on or off Government Stores.

John and Crispin were snowed under with preparing the paperwork for the numerous convicts arriving almost fortnightly. They had barely processed one shipload of convicts when more arrived.

King realised that the governor's role involved loads of paperwork. Norfolk Island was nothing like this. He tried to assist where he could, but his health made him wonder how he would cope long-term.

~

By mid-June, King wrote to John, who was still in Parramatta, acknowledging the extent of his discovery and the deceptions occurring throughout the settlement.

Living in Sydney, King saw that in one month alone, over fifty thousand gallons of alcoholic beverages were imported into the colony, and he acknowledged that John had no way of stopping this. King had the idea that once he took control, he would try to turn some of these beverages away, but he knew he was fighting a losing battle even before he started. With what was being distilled in the settlement, drunkenness and debauchery were widespread. He doubted what he heard could be accurate, but his eyes were well and truly opened. So much so that the farmers out on the Hawkesbury settlements had been so distracted by alcohol that they had forgotten to sow their crops. It was only because of King's visit for the muster that they had stirred into activity.

~

Phillip King had completed his muster by the end of July, and the figures were disturbing. He set about trying to purchase various buildings for the government to use as orphanages and other official places.

The Kents were leaving with John, so the government purchased his large Sydney waterfront house. At Anna King's suggestion, it would be enlarged and repurposed to house orphans as soon as it was vacated.

Mary Johnson was thrilled. She had long wanted to house the waifs.

King realised that John had faced a significant battle as even more convicts arrived unannounced under his watch. John had left him to oversee their placement, and he realised there was nowhere to put them but with private settlers, thus breaking his edict from London with his first official job.

After being given this role, he learned how stupid Lord Portland's rules were. Farms needed workers, and the convicts needed places to go. It was a win for everyone.

Unbeknownst to John, various supporters wrote letters to England, decrying his recall and the injustice of London's lack of support.

Maurice Margarot, one of the Scottish Martyrs who protected Helena *en route*, wrote a long letter fully supporting John's governorship and detailing the difficulties of the corrupt Corps and its leadership.

Richard Johnson wrote numerous times, as did Colin, Nigel, Crispin, Jonas, and also to Linus, who had also mastered the written word well enough to scribe a letter with his own hand.

John did not know of the many epistles winging their way back to London, but he knew he had some supporters in the colony.

The *Friendship* departed only weeks after Phillip King arrived. The letters described just what an uphill battle John had in maintaining order, let alone tightening the reins on the illicit activities of the Corps and some free settlers. Drunkenness was rife, and the prostitution of even the children was pitiful. Getting these young girls off the streets was urgent. Kent's home was perfect, but it could not house them all.

John was determined to address this situation and charged Richard Johnson and Samuel Marsden to work with King to buy or construct buildings to house, feed and clothe these bedraggled children. Many were billeted with families until something more permanent could be found.

King realised that not having a secretary was impeding the governor's work and saw that John was battling to have any effect on the ailing colony. Crispin worked tirelessly, writing and assigning convicts wherever possible.

After checking it, John signed off on his work.

King also sat in on many court cases that Dore and his brother magistrates held. He was horrified by how easily they handed out death sentences and punishments of five hundred lashes or more.

Dore was often more lenient than the other magistrates. Even on Norfolk Island, such extreme penalties were rare. Here, one hundred lashes seemed the usual punishment for minor infractions. He had already drawn up a plan of action for when he took over and realised that this six-month delay had given him time to see the situation for what it really was. Dore looked ill but refused to hand over his power.

King had no intention of riling him.

~

Some months after John announced that he was leaving, he returned to Sydney to ensure the repaired residence was now fit for the incumbent. He checked that the vegetable garden had been adequately cared for, and he left Crispin and Eric to pick some vegetables and lemons to take home.

The back door was not the usual entry point for most visitors, especially at an official residence. The two guards were still in situ at the front door; however, the entry mode was not unusual for this person.

Richard Johnson adored the lovely vegetable garden and was thrilled at how it thrived. He had been overseeing it in the governor's absence.

Richard greeted Crispin and Eric and made his way through the kitchen to John's office door. After knocking and being invited to enter, Richard settled on one of the new chairs somewhat awkwardly. He was gazing at his feet, wondering how to say what he needed to voice.

John was seated at the new desk. He looked at his friend with a wrinkled brow. He was holding something back. "Richard?"

His friend replied in a gush, "John, we're coming with you." He released a long sigh of nervousness.

John jumped to his feet. "You're what?" His eyes flew open in stunned surprise. A slow smile spread across his face, reaching his eyes, where lines of happiness appeared. "Truly?"

Richard nodded. He had been anxious about telling his friend. "John, Mary and I will return with you if you permit us to. We need to leave. Marsden is skilled enough to cope here now, and I'm sure the London

Missionary Society will replace me easily enough, but we're going home. Marsden can do the running around for a while."

John was stunned. "But the church here... Your work... and the orphanages. You were only saying how much there is to do the other day."

Richard nodded. "Oh, there is, but a younger, fitter person now needs to step up, and I feel we're being called home. Despite my pleading, I've not heard from London. It's become too much for me, John. My body never fully recovered from the stresses of those early years and that first major illness. We've been here twelve years, John. I've had enough." Only in the privacy of one of their offices could they call each other by name.

John sat down again with a plop.

Richard rubbed his brow. "After thirteen years, we've had enough. I'm approaching fifty and must settle my family in England before I'm too old. Would you mind if we travelled with you?"

Another slow smile crept across John's lips. "Actually, dear friend, I would be delighted. It will make the trip enjoyable. I may need to call upon you to vouch for the state of the colony and attest to how rife the corruption is here. Phillip King has already caught an eyeful of the Corps's embedded corruption. I do not envy him taking over this position. I don't know if the Duke of Portland will listen to me, but you're a man of the cloth, and he will surely give you some time."

Richard was now grinning. "Assuredly, I will, John. That's a given! Let me say that our Harry was over the moon that we could travel with you. I know he's not little Jasper, but he adores you just the same."

John chuckled. "And I him, Richard! You have made my day. May I let Cris and Eric know? Do you mind if I tell the Brays? I'm heading to the mill next. I have Connie's paperwork."

Richard nodded. "Of course, John, but get them to keep it quiet. I need to let the Marsdens know before they hear it through gossip."

John gave a nod of understanding.

Richard only stayed briefly and exited out the back door again.

John called in Crispin and Eric to inform them of the newest development. Although they were sad to lose such a wonderful man, their families would also leave the town and move westward. Their wives were already making curtains for their new houses and dolling them up so they would be comfortable. At John's suggestion, the four homesteads were built in the corners of their farms and were within sight of each other.

Of the original household staff, only Arnold's friend, Travis, would remain with the new governor. He decided to lease his farm to Jonas with the option of selling it to him in a few years if he didn't want to live there, as he was already contemplating his return to England.

The other two surprise passengers listed on the *Buffalo* were Mrs Peach and Mrs Cowdrey. John gave them a bonus from his private funds. With £50 each, the two ladies planned to move to Kent, buy or hire a small house, and take in boarders. When the women brought him his evening tipple, they asked to chat with him. Both desired to return to England.

John had another idea about their future. He heard that his cousin was now a duchess in Kent and needed trustworthy staff.

John had sold his steadily increasing share of stock, and his nephew and his family completed the passenger list; only William was to be the captain of the *Buffalo*. They were also returning home, and like his uncle, he had sold most of his land and stock but not their main house on their farm or their land.

~

With the preparations for the departure of the *Buffalo* now in full swing, Jonas and Linus had taken to overseeing the various crops and harvests as they were to occur. Life for the extended family would soon be vastly different.

Helena delivered their second son on John's sixty-third birthday, and they named their child John Henry after John and Crispin's father.

Jonas commissioned a shipload of furniture from India, which arrived with a load of food for the colony. Each new house would have a carved, four-post double bed, and Jonas had also purchased one for Linus and Agnes. Each arrived with a huge feather and down mattress securely wrapped in a thick, waterproof, oiled canvas. The wrapping itself was valuable and would be put to good use. When Jonas placed the order, he requested that all items be wrapped in top-quality waterproof coverings.

The shipping agents excelled by waterproofing everything and sending it in solid packing crates that were usable as furniture.

~

The three new single-story homesteads were furnished by the end of August 1800. Jonas's double-story home overlooked the creek but was subtly situated not to overshadow the three smaller dwellings.

Mary and Phoebe were both expecting their first child, and Gillian finally announced that they were due to have a third child some months later. She had a rough time after Caris was born, but Ellen had been a delight. Hopefully, this one would be a boy for Eric.

When Caris was born, Gillian struggled severely with the demands of being a working mother and a miserable baby. The little girl had been a grizzly babe who rarely slept for long, and it was only when they were visiting Agnes for the first Christmas that the experienced mother offered to bathe the child after one exceptionally dirty napkin that had gone everywhere. Agnes had let the little one soak in the hot water, and then she had placed her on her tummy and massaged her back while Gillian watched. For once, the child relaxed. Her little legs had been stiff, held up as though in pain.

Caris cried when they were straightened.

Agnes showed Gillian the method of massage to ease the child's distress. Agnes rubbed her back and pointed out a small lump on the child's spine. "Gill, look at this. Has she always had that?"

Gillian nodded. "Yes, and she doesn't like me touching it. I'm amazed that you can now without her screaming."

Agnes continued the massage, and then Caris coughed while she was rubbing; the lump vanished. Within minutes, the little one was asleep peacefully.

After months of coping with a screaming baby, Gillian and Eric now had a peaceful child. The poor mite had been in pain, and they had not realised.

From the day of the massage, Caris slept and ate and slept again until her parents were worried for a different reason. The little one was soon up and walking, and there was no stopping her. Her blonde curly head was seen toddling everywhere.

Gillian already knew she was expecting another child, and she was exhausted. By the time the baby arrived, Caris would be three, and Ellen would be eighteen months old.

~

The final week before sailing, John visited Linus and Agnes's house. Everyone but Travis was there. He had volunteered to be in Phillip's security detail and, therefore, had to stay with him in town.

John's arrival was an excuse for a final corroboree with Bennelong and the tribe. This would be a fond farewell as they would not meet again.

Bennelong and Goomberri greeted him with the eerie whirring of the bull roarers, which rose and fell in tempo and volume depending on how fast they were spun. The presentation of dance and song that followed was moving. Although October, the open fire in the backyard ensured that all were warm.

Everyone pitched in with the extended family, and visitors packed into the large house.

The five older folks, John, Linus, Agnes, Mrs Cowdrey, and Mrs Peach, sat on a bench. The various young folk intermingled with the tribal group, and all the children played together. All were friends.

John and Linus discussed the changes in their lives when Jasper came up for a hug. Rather than release the big man, he settled in his comfortable arms and promptly went to sleep. John teared up, knowing that this may well be the last time he would ever hold the child. Subconsciously, he was rubbing the boy's back.

Linus turned and looked at his friend's sad face.

Deep in thought, John stared into the dancing flames, but he saw the sidelong glance. He said, "Linus, my compassion was stirred when I first saw Helena. I had little idea what was before me, but I was determined to leave this colony a better place than the filth I had walked into. By the time you arrived, I had been here for two years; believe it or not, it was much cleaner. However, I failed in what I wished to accomplish. I fought a losing battle and feel there will be at least one clash before things settle. The Corps is oppressing the Irish, and I disagree with how they are treated, but the soldiers will not listen to me any more.

The Irish leader is Phillip Cunningham, and he is a worry to me. He is overconfident and not at all fearful about causing trouble. The Irish are forbidden to worship God in their own way, and this will make things boil over soon enough. Three hundred years ago, we all worshipped as Catholics. Admittedly, I do not believe as they do. I follow the faith of Scotland. England even has issues with us, but we jog along peaceably enough, even if they do not recognise our marriages and Scottish traditions."

Linus didn't know about that and asked, "How so, John?"

John chuckled. "Well, in Scotland, we can marry by declaring in front of two witnesses that we are man and wife. On the whole, we are poor folk. Our countrymen are not known to spend a year's wage on a feast to celebrate a union. This is not feasible for the majority of us. Hence, our marriage by declaration rules. In England, Gretna Green is well known for such declaration nuptials, but any town in Scotland would suffice. Here, we are supposed to marry after Banns are read, but even that is hazy. I have heard that even some who marry again here already have a spouse back at home. Such unions are considered voided by distance. I do not think this is legal, but at least the couples are committed to each other. From my talks with Bennelong, marriage in the tribe is much the same. It is often negotiated with a neighbouring clan, but sometimes, a man takes a liking to a girl, and he takes her as his wife. At least in Scotland, they both must be willing, or it's not permitted. Even in England, a girl can be forced to wed someone she dislikes. It has not even been fifty years since this rule was introduced, so as I am over that age, I suppose you could call me illegitimate as my parents married by Scottish law, and I was born before 1753. By the time that rule came in, I was serving on the *Grampus.*"

Linus nodded. "God made the rules, John; mankind distorts them for their own purposes." He chuckled, then said, "I suppose you could say that even Adam and Eve were not married according to English laws."

John roared with laughter, then realised he still had the sleeping child in his arms. "I'm going to miss this, and you, Linus. I will miss the informality of your family and the wonderful people you have in it. And I'm going to miss this little fellow."

John brushed a lock of the boy's straight, brown hair. He adored the little chap. "I have asked Cris to keep me informed about what you are all doing and of any new additions, as well as the state of the settlement. Will you write to me too?"

He was about to say more when Bennelong said, "No more talky now, Captain John. You watch; we do a special *corroboree* for you tonight. You good fella, so we show you dance no white fella has seen before." He grinned. "Captain John, me bring you a gift before you sail away. Two black swans and three emus. You said you wanted to take to London with you for King George and Joseph Banks. You build cages good and strong, and you need to pack plenty of food for birds."

John nodded his thanks. He was delighted. They had discussed which native animals would travel the best, and Bennelong said he would catch some. He wanted to take one of the incredibly unusual water creatures back with him, but could not keep it in freshwater or feed it. Ben had shown him one of the duck-billed, egg-laying, water-lizard-like animals.

The dance started with the bull-roarer calling all to attention.

The presentation was followed by a descriptive dance of the coming of the sailboats. Billowing white flannel napkins were used to show the ships' sails arriving.

Bennelong and Goomberri portrayed their first contact as Bennelong wore his blue naval coat. There was no animosity between the two characters. The tribal children portrayed the hunger and ignorance of the white settlers while the women and some of the younger men bartered for food.

John watched as the story of the last twelve years was acted out before him.

The story of the settlement was revealed in all its glory and gory pain, from the terrible diseases the settlers had brought to the many changes that had taken place.

As he promised Bennelong, John instigated a punishment that any murders, black or white, would be punished alike. Deaths still occurred. He felt he was living through a play of his life. In reality, it was precisely that. John had a knot in his stomach, knowing he should have done so much more to protect these wonderfully kind people. He did what he could in a situation where his hands were virtually tied behind his back.

John's eyes welled with tears for the first time in a very long time. Once he was gone, would these people be safe? Had he left enough land for them to survive? Would the following governors be as kind? Only time will tell. John had done what he could. As he was holding Jasper, he could not wipe away the drips that slid down his cheek. He hoped in the dim light that no one would notice.

Two had. Crispin and Helena kept an eye on their sleeping son. The flickering firelight illuminated the governor's damp cheek. The trail of glistening tears and his glassy eyes lit up like mirrors to his soul.

Helena remained silent, but a squeeze on her shoulder showed Crispin understood his sadness. She was cradled between Crispin's legs, as were other couples. She had their baby in her arms and watched as some of her younger sisters kept their eyes on Judith. She rubbed her head against Crispin's chest lovingly. Their marriage was everything she had dreamed about as a child.

Having sold his commission, Crispin was not in uniform tonight but refused to leave the governor alone until his ship sailed away.

Eric had also sold out but had few other clothes to wear as his funds had been ploughed into the farm and setting up the house. His money from selling out had yet to come through.

Crispin leaned forward and whispered, "I'm going to miss him, you know."

Helena nodded. "Me too! None of this would have happened if he had not saved me that day."

Across the backyard, their eyes met John's.

Helena smiled, as did John.

~

The *Buffalo* was tied at the dock and ready to leave.

Days earlier, John had moved all his possessions from Parramatta, and these had been loaded onto the ship. He officially handed over the colony's management to Phillip Gidley King as the third governor.

John commandeered the vessel, assigning his nephew William Kent to captain it home. William, his wife Eliza and their three children were installed in the oversized captain's cabin.

Eliza acted as First Lady when an official function was held at Government House. Thankfully, these were few and far between. They were pleased to head home.

As the Kents had their own residence, John spent more time with his household staff than his nephew. William's children would go to school in England or get a governess.

John adored the family and was pleased to spend time with them. It made the parting from his adoptive family bearable. Mrs Peach and Mrs Cowdrey had a cabin each and stocked up with books and sewing materials to occupy themselves for the next six months. They had been given a cash bonus, and John had arranged positions for them in Kent with his cousin.

The Johnsons decided to leave their vast library of books in town. The crates of books they brought were the only reading material in the colony. John gave them a donation from his own pocket so they could purchase new books in England. Their two children were sad to farewell Boorong, but they still called her Abaroo. She had her own life to lead. She had appeared the night before they left.

Mary Johnson gave Abaroo a large bundle of things they were not taking with them. She had been going to leave them with Crispin for her, but giving them to her personally was much better. They parted with a big hug. Milbah and Harry would have friends on board with the Kents' children.

John occupied himself by double-checking the food supplies for the stock and the birds, storing all the cargo, and ensuring the passengers were as comfortable as they could make.

As promised, Bennelong arrived a few days earlier with his unique gift. He brought a pair of black swans and three emus. The five birds were secured below decks, and John ensured they were safe. Young Harry Johnson had to be warned to stay well clear of the emus as they had already had to rescue him the day after they arrived. He had been caught trying to enter their cage.

The day prior to sailing, John returned to his old office for the final time and looked around. He found his writing paper had not been packed, and he knew Crispin would write if he had some stationery. Another item caught his eye. Years before, Jasper had gifted him a cockatoo's feather, which sat proudly on his desk. John picked it up and tucked it into his pocket. The packers had left a few other trinkets on the shelves that the lad had given him. These, too, were collected and added to his pockets. A round red pebble of jasper that had been used as his paperweight. He refused to leave this as he had been given it as a birthday gift by Jasper. This red jasper was how he got his name. There was a small chunk of white quartz and a smooth river rock, but there was also a selection of small fossils in shale from a trip to the beach. He gathered his rock collection and stuffed them in his pocket. Each was a treasured memento from one or other of the children or the Rosedale family. A cluster of gum nuts from Judy, a parrot's feather from Caris and a pair of long and twisted gum leaves from Eric and Gillian. Many had been given as Christmas or birthday gifts from the children.

He knew the packers would not have understood the value of such items, but each held many happy memories. With his pockets bulging with his beloved treasures, he turned to leave.

The King family would move in that afternoon. With the open ream of paper in his arms, he wanted to see Helena's garden again before he left. He knew not much would be left as Crispin and Helena harvested everything they could to send with them on the ship. It now sat in the hold, stored in straw.

John was surprised to hear voices outside, and on exiting the kitchen door, he saw the Milroys waiting for him with his namesake.

Helena had her latest child in a sling on her back. Jonny was just a month old. Rather than say anything, Helena came to his side and threw her arms around him.

John passed the paper to Crispin and hugged her tightly.

She had obviously been crying. "I did this once before, sir, and it was the day you saved me. That was a huge thank you back then, and this is another one. If you had not rescued me that day..." She couldn't continue. A sob caught in her throat as she hugged him tighter.

Crispin picked up where she left off. "Sir, if you had not saved her that day, we would not have a wonderful life here now. We are landowners thanks to you, and we have a future here where none of that would ever have happened in England. We would have lived a life of poverty and been lucky to survive."

As he spoke, Jasper tugged at his blue coat. "Up, please, Captain John."

Parting from this lad was nearly John's undoing. As John picked up the small boy, Helena moved to her husband's side. Jasper tucked his head into John's neck and said. "I love you, Captain John, and I will miss you so much."

Jasper's tears trickled down John's neck. He didn't care.

John hugged him tightly and replied, "I will miss you too, my boy. You must look after your family for me. You must write to me and tell me how you are all doing. Can you do that?"

John had a belated birthday gift for the lad. It was an empty journal and a quill from his desk. He was going to leave it for Travis to give to them, but this was better. "I have an early birthday present for you, Jasper, but I must put you down."

Jasper released him and stood waiting.

John dug into his back pocket and pulled out the wrapped gift. A white feather pen was tucked under the string.

After another hug of thanks, Jasper sat in the dirt and carefully unwrapped his gift. He handed the string and paper wrapping to his mother and was overjoyed to see that it was one of John's empty leather-bound journals.

John squatted beside him and told him that when he learned to write, he was to record all his significant findings and thoughts.

The gifts were almost flung at Crispin, and the boy was again cradled in the older man's arms. "I don't want you to leave, Captain John. Don't go!" This time, the child sobbed as though his heart would break.

After a few minutes, John realised he had to leave. "Why don't you all walk down to the ship with me? Cris, this will be your last security duty. And you, young man, I will carry you. Would you like to see me on board the ship?"

Jasper nodded. He refused to release John's hand.

The small group left by the backyard gate, and for the last time, they walked down the hill toward the foreshore.

John gave them a tour of the ship and then said his final farewell. "Pray for me, won't you? You are in my prayers each night, and please ensure you write. I hope the journey home is smooth and the billows of a raging sea do not rock us. When upon life's billows, that's when I turn to God."

Helena nodded and gave him another hug. Then she collected her son and fled lest she weep again.

Crispin was about to leave the ship to follow her when a hand on his shoulder stopped him.

As a father would give his son, John pulled him into his arms in a bear hug. "Take care, laddie. To me, you are the son I never had. Remember, Christ is enough. When He feels far away, turn around. It only takes one step to find Him again."

Crispin hugged him back. He was not far from tears himself.

Half an hour later, the ropes were cast off, and the *Buffalo* was towed out into the middle of the harbour by two longboats. Crispin, Helena and Jasper waited until the ship was out of sight before turning towards the Parramatta ferry.

The three were quiet, all sad but still somewhat excited. Their life as farmers was about to start, and although they knew it would not be smooth sailing, as life on the land was often fraught with many difficulties, Governor John Hunter had paved a road for them that would ease their path. They had much to thank him for; but now, John was gone.

Walking toward the waiting ferry, they saw the carriages and wagons heading towards Government House from Paterson's place. The new incumbent was about to start his term in office. They would do their best to support him, but their lives were now turned in another direction.

Connie and Nigel were up on the hill, waving from there.

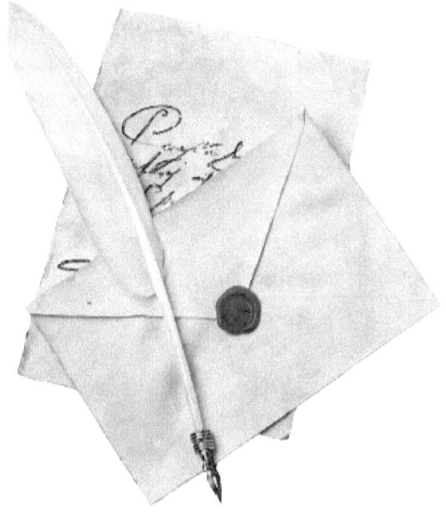

Chapter 20 Letters from Home

Over the years, letters traversed the oceans between the Rosedale, Milroy and Hunter households.

The family would gather when one of John's lengthy screeds arrived, but the reply, Crispin, would read aloud to Helena.

Linus wrote a few times, but the effort took a lot out of him. He usually dictated his epistles to one of his sons-in-law.

> *Leith Vale Farm*
> *Toongabbie*
> *September 1801*

Dear Sir,

Greetings from our farm.

As I write this, I realise that you have been gone for nearly an entire year. We greatly miss you and your outstanding presence.

I hope you are home by now and fully exonerated of all charges.

I am writing this letter with news that the rot has started.

Paterson and Macarthur came to blows this week and fought a duel. The upshot is that Macarthur is to be sent home for trial at the end of the month. What this shall achieve is unknown, but with him gone, hopefully, Phillip King can sweep aside some of the other malcontent Corps. If nothing else, it should break the cycle of disobedience from the Corps.

One titbit of news you may not have heard is that Richard Dore is dead. He died in December 1800, shortly after you left and was bankrupt, owing much money. I had no idea what ailed him, but he's gone!

Phillip has instigated the sale of spirits from here at a fixed price to undermine the alcohol income. He had developed your coal industry and added cotton, hemp, and wool that are now being exported. He is also establishing a whale oil industry.

The emancipated convicts are encouraged to be industrious and inventive by having alternate commodities. With a severe lack of currency, rum has become the most popular form of payment. I'm pleased to say that he has taken your advice and fully supports the emancipated convicts. They are encouraged by being given similar positions of responsibility as free settlers. He has employed four of them as his security detail rather than using the untrustworthy military. Again, this has riled the Corps.

Phillip said emancipists should not be condemned to disgrace forever. His meeting with Colin, Nigel, and Max was encouraging. He listened to their wisdom about the opportunities available to freed convicts. Many do not wish to return home and are keen to work hard to make a new life for themselves and their families. Once released from the bonds worn in shame, most realise that the opportunities here outweigh their lives in England.

Mrs Anna King is a delight. She has overseen the new orphanage that was once your nephew's house. They have erected a picket fence along the waterfront to protect the little girls from falling into the water. I presume one must have come to grief for this to occur. There are still many waifs and stray children living on the street. We will work on that. We are billeting more into emancipated families.

Onto nicer things. Little John Henry, born the month before your departure, walked across the room this week.

He's happy to let his siblings get things for him and grunts until someone responds. His chuckle is infectious, and he delights if he can make someone laugh at his antics.

Phillip has endorsed your trust in Andrew Thompson out at Windsor. While he still holds the position of grain assessor you gave him in 1799, Phillip assigned him constabulary duties for the surrounding district. Andrew's work is so good that he has been granted further allocations. He leases out and assigns new tenants for many of these, encouraging many with no farming skills to forge ahead and make new lives. He is a pleasure to work with. Linus's twins help establish the new farms, and I assist where I can.

Andrew still lives in his big red house, which is high above the flood level in Windsor. He has a new agent who works well with us all. He has also built a large store, which has become the central hub of what will become a new commercial centre for the northwestern riverside lands. I foresee tremendous growth in this area. The soil is fertile, and crops grow well.

Your nephew William's sheep that he gave us has significantly multiplied. Phillip is thrilled to discover that there is enough wool clip to export this year. I had no idea William had kept his farm here. Are he and Eliza planning to return? I thought, like you, he was wedded to the sea.

Macarthur has some sheep, and of course, Marsden purchased some of William's lambs, but their flocks are insignificant compared to what this land could produce. Talking about sheep, Helena and I met Elizabeth Macarthur at church on Sunday, and we chatted about our flocks. She checked that her husband was not around before saying she had ideas about crossing our stud ram over her Barbary ewes. This ram is from William's few surviving sheep from 1795. It is a Spanish Merino, but the Merino ewes are renowned for dropping only one lamb at a time, and many of those die as they are not good mothers. Elizabeth explained that Barbary ewes often have multiple births. We spoke about selective breeding before her husband took her home.

Consequently, since John Macarthur left, I have been working with Elizabeth Macarthur on the sly, as we have *used our Merino ram to cover some of her Barbary sheep. The lambs are healthy and favour the ram in looks. The benefit of this is that the ewes drop multiple lambs and nurse them well.*

We eat the lambs that favour their mothers in looks.

Marsden is keeping his Merino flock pure and can't work out why our lambs thrive, while his die. We have promised not to share the reason.

With Elizabeth's husband now absent, she has time to work on improving the breed. I'm happy with the small flock we have as they keep us in meat and wool.

Sir, a year ago, I would not have known what she meant. Now, I can have an intelligent conversation about the subject.

Helena and I are keen to work with her in whatever way we can.

I must finish as I come to the end of my paper. I look forward to hearing you arrived safely.

Cris and family.

~

By the time Crispin put pen to paper again, it was a year later.

John Macarthur had been gone for over a year, and although the colony was relieved he was absent, the Rum Corps were still active.

> *Leith Vale Farm*
> *Toongabbie*
> *29th August 1802*

Dear Sir,

It was wonderful to receive your letter. I'm glad you are now settled. Happy Birthday from the Antipodes. We never forget your special day.

On reading your report of Reverend Richard Johnson, I find it hard to believe that he has only been given one year's pay for his twelve years of service here. I do understand he is facing some ill health, but not giving him a parish is unbelievable. He gave so much to the foundation of this colony. All I can say is that he will reap his reward in Heaven. The orphanage was his idea, and it is flourishing.

Now, for the family news.

Helena has just risen from the birthing bed after

delivering our second daughter. Jennifer Agnes, was born a week ago. Both mother and daughter are well. It's hard to believe it's been nearly two years since you sailed away.

Everyone else is well and healthy. Eric and Gillian now have four little ones; Jonas and Mary have twin boys, and Arnold and Phoebe have just had their second daughter.

As you can imagine, the place is chaos when we all gather at Linus's farm. Gerry and Jem are engaged to Irish girls (Colleen and Erin, respectively). They arrived last year and were assigned to the Rosedales as maids. The boys are in no hurry to marry as the girls are only sixteen. Though their engagements have given the girls security.

I'm glad you arrived safely, but I was surprised to read that your journey took eight months. I thought the route you were taking would have carried you more swiftly. You mentioned some stormy seas, so I hope you did not get rocked to the scuppers as you feared. When you described the seas you sailed, I understood your term of being tossed by the billows. Your graphic description of that particular movement of the ship nearly made me seasick.

Thank you for the copy of your second printed book. When you mentioned that you had a manuscript you were working on, I did not realise that it focused on the state of corruption in the colony or that it was a tome of over seventy pages. I shall look forward to reading it in detail. I hope it stirs those in charge at the Admiralty to read it.

I am glad that many letters preceded your arrival and that you have been exonerated from all blame about the appalling state of the colony and the false reports that were filed against you. However, I doubt that the Admiralty or whoever makes the decisions will listen to you. Were you able to compare the anonymous letter's handwriting with that of Dore, Macarthur, or Paterson?

If it is any consolation, Phillip King has much the same problem with the same men. (He asked that I call him Phillip). Like you, he has kept allocating convicts to free settlers, if for no other reason than to get them off Government Stores. He has also moved his headquarters to the new Parramatta house to keep his eyes on the goings-on of this area.

Agnes was thrilled to hear that her friends, Priscilla Peach and Virginia Cowdrey, are now living with your cousin.

I had no idea you were distantly related to the Duchess of Gracemere. I saw her once shortly before their engagement when I was lamp-lighting in London. My Papa and I had lamp-lit the street outside Parliament House the week he got sick, and Lady Susanna Bland, as she was then, was alighting from her carriage with her father. As a young man, I thought she was among the most beautiful women I had ever seen... for a blonde. (Helena is reading over my shoulder and asked me about her. I sense a touch of jealousy!)

It's lovely that the ducal couple now have three boys. I'm sure both ladies love living at what I hear is a fantastic crenellated castle in Kent.

Now, for news of the doings in the colony...

Last year, as I previously mentioned, everything came to a head when Macarthur and Paterson finally fell out. I mentioned this before. As you know, Doctor Balmain and Macarthur had many more issues, but after the duel with Paterson, Governor King banished Macarthur to London to be tried.

We do not know how long he will be gone, but things on that front are currently peaceful. He is known to be a manipulator of men. That man's absence is a delight!

Maybe you have seen him there already, but if not, he should be in   London by now. Because of this, we have befriended Elizabeth Macarthur and greatly admire what she is doing to improve the strain of sheep. She has continued to cross William's Spanish merino ram with Barbary ewes and is keeping them on our farm. Most of the second generation resemble the fathers. We purchased one of Marsden's Merino rams so we can diversify the flock. The flock is much more robust. She selectively breeds the best fleeces and sells the ones resembling Barbary sheep for meat. We keep some to eat, and these keep the grass down near the house and away from the breeding stock. The remainder we sell butchered.

I hope John Macarthur stays away long enough for Elizabeth to have perfected the flock before his return. I'm sure he won't even be able to tell the difference.

Reverend Marsden is not pleased as the new crossbreed produces amazingly fine fleece and delicious meat (not that he knows about our breeding experiments as he has only seen our meat sheep). He only knows that our newborn lambs don't die. However, the cross-bred ewes also have multiple lambs, so the flock grows quickly. All Marsden realises is that more lamb, mutton, and hogget meat is available from our farm.

We ensure any Barbary-looking ones are not included in our breeding programme. So far, we have been able to keep the work quiet. Elizabeth wishes she had more land, but the selective breeding stock is hidden on our farms. She dares not move the new flock to her land yet.

Agnes has been teaching some of the newest convict girls how to preserve food, and this includes drying or bottling meat.

Sir, did you note the name of our farm? Because of you, we are all here; we named our place after your hometown. We have much to thank you for; saying it daily will never be enough. Leith Vale Farm *produces many varieties of fruit and vegetables.*

Linus has been an excellent tutor for we three novice lads. Arnold is in his element and knows a lot about mixed farming. Although we each have a field of wheat growing, it is just enough for our use at home. We sell none and, therefore, are not a threat to the Corps. Nigel mills it for us.

Travis has just sold his farm to Jonas and is heading home. I expect that this letter will arrive when he does as he is posting it in England.

I am at the end of my second page, and as writing paper is still scarce, I shall end here and write again soon.

Yours sincerely and with great respect,
Cris, Helena, Jasper, Judy, John, and Jenny

~

Shortly before Easter in 1804, another letter was delivered to the farm. It arrived at an uneasy time for the settlement, as there was a conflict brewing, and the convict girls on the farm had been approached to get involved.

Thankfully, they not only refused but also reported the conversations to the boys.

John still wanted to know what was going on in the colony, and he had heard about the growing Irish unrest from Colin Osborne.

Crispin realised that his mentor wanted to know all the gory details, as he had foretold this clash years earlier and had not been believed.

Crispin revealed everything he knew, including any relevant newspaper clippings about the Irish uprising.

> *Leith Vale Farm*
> *Toongabbie*
> *5th March 1804*

Dear Sir,

I write quickly to inform you that the Irish unrest has finally boiled over. Officials call it the Vinegar Hill of our new land, but the uprising occurred not far from Linus and Agnes's farm at Castle Hill.

All of us are safe and well.

The Irish rose in force, with Phillip Cunningham at the head (just as you predicted. You picked him as a stirrer). He stood against the English forces, and George Johnson reinforced his leadership. They aimed to take over both Parramatta and Sydney and establish Irish rule.

Over a thousand convicts were involved, and it started with three hundred of them breaking out of the convict stockade at dusk. Their catch cry of 'Death or Liberty' could be heard on the verandah at Rosedale's farm.

We wondered if our girls, Colleen and Erin, would leave and join the rabble. Thankfully, they refused. It was because of them that we were able to be prepared. They had been approached earlier that week, and although they were not given details of where or when, we could tell Phillip that something was afoot.

We assembled everyone at Linus's house as it was the easiest to defend, and it had room for us all, if somewhat squashed.

Because we had not been entirely unprepared, troops were gathered, and the rebellion was quickly crushed.

It started with a hut at the Parramatta Government

House being set alight, and that was the sign for the assigned Irish convicts to break free.

Major George Johnson really showed his colours last night, sir. He, trooper Thomas Anlezark and Father Dixon, a Catholic priest, attempted to convince the rebels to surrender.

The rebels refused, but the delay allowed the troops to get in position. A battle ensued where Cunningham was arrested as he retreated.

All hell, apparently, then let loose. Fifteen Irish convicts died immediately, and at least the same number died from wounds received after they fled. The majority either surrendered or were captured.

Phillip trusts his soldiers so little that he has employed five more emancipated convicts as mounted security guards, such as Eric and I were for you.

A week later

I didn't rush to finish my last missive as I knew a trial was on the horizon. The outcome of the rebellion was that Phillip Cunningham and eight others were hung without trial. It's estimated that thirty-nine Irish convicts died during, or as a result of, the uprising, though the exact numbers may never be known. Seven convicts received sentences of between 200 and 500 lashes, while another twenty-three rebels were banished.

Sir, you warned the authorities that this clash would happen, yet no one listened. I fear that a brewing mutiny is not far off. The rum trade here is simply unbelievable.

Nathaniel Franklyn had no chance of standing against them. I don't know if they had something over him, but many have taken his place. No sooner is one man revealed than another assumes the role.

Rum is now the official currency; few can obtain goods without it. It buys more than the scant amount of coinage. Things are dire.

Grog arrives by the shipload and sometimes under the cover of dark.

Thanks to Bennelong's tribe for their assistance, we are nearly self-sufficient.

Eric and Gillian have chosen to focus on dairy cows instead of beef, and they are now producing a significant amount of dairy products. Emily, a girl from Devon, has been assigned to help them, and she knows how to make basic cheese. It's certainly better than what was previously available. But I dare not call it top quality. They now have several young female convicts assigned to them as dairy goods are supplied to the government. They produce butter, cream, and a form of hard cheese. It is quite palatable.

Gillian wants to get some goats, but Eric is resisting.

Again, I have filled my paper. I will use only one sheet, but I have used both sides.

Everyone sends their love.

Jasper asked me to enclose a new feather for you. Not to be outdone, Judy, Jenny, and John found gifts for you. Judy sent the leaf.

Helena and I wish you well and send you our love. That you have in abundance.

Cris + all the family

~

Over the year, every ship brought new letters from John. They carried replies as they sailed home. The latest screed from John brought disturbing news.

Crispin could not write back fast enough when he received news of a third shipwreck with John on board.

It took so long for letters to traverse the world that news was well out of date when it arrived.

Long ago, John had told him of the shipwreck that occurred off Norway when sailing with his father when a boy. The second was at Norfolk Island. To read of a third wreck off the English coast brought many of the family around to read the saga in John's own descriptive words.

Leith Vale Farm
Toongabbie
12th June 1805

Dear Sir,

We have just read your latest screed and are most distressed about your news of the wreck of your latest ship. We were overjoyed to read that you had been given command of the Venerable, *but to lose her in such a disastrous way is heartbreaking.*

I remember the thickness of the fog in London and how I often became disoriented, trying to find my way home on dry land. Sailing in such conditions would be horrific, and it would be even worse at night.

Eric's maid, Emily, tells us Torbay is in Devon near her home. She knows the Paignton Cliff well and said it had wrecked many a ship in just such a fog. Our deepest condolences on the mishap. We are so pleased you were not injured, even though some of your crew could not be rescued. I am glad the Admiralty has acquitted you.

On the plus side, we are pleased to read that the Admiralty finally granted you a pension for the time spent here. I'm pleased that they are finally climbing off their high horses and acknowledging that the situation out here was not of your doing.

I have obtained a copy of Philip King's new book, 'New South Wales General Standing Orders,' and I enclose it with this letter.

You will notice much of what you wanted to occur is now law in this land. His way of restraining the importation of alcohol was to build a brewery here. It has not succeeded as the convicts refused to work it in their own time.

Phillip has imposed a 5% tariff on imported liquors, as you suggested. This has helped, as has the rationing of the amount each man can purchase. However, there is much more to do.

We have had four years of peace as John Macarthur has been in England until he returned last week. Therefore, I expect my following letter will bring news of more turmoil and disturbance that he has stirred up. That man... Grrr! His ego is beyond belief. He has banned Elizabeth's visits to us.

The governor visited last week and informed me that he had been in regular contact with Sir Joseph Banks. I know he's a friend of yours. I mentioned that I was writing to you, and Phillip asked me to send his regards. He also wanted me to pass on a message. His words were, "He was right, you know. This is beyond one man to control. I feel it will explode soon, just as he said it would. The Admiralty should have listened to him." (you)

If that offers any consolation, Phillip is facing the same issues as you, only somewhat magnified. The volume of alcohol landing now is beyond belief.

The mail is closing as the ship is about to leave, so I have no more time to write of family doings.

My previous lengthy letter tells you of the doings of our six imps. I'm sure I wrote to you about the birth of the twins, Julien Eric and Janette Elizabeth, on 11 June last year. Our latest little girl is Helena (Nell), after your Mama and my lady love. However, her full name is Janice Helena. She was born on the twins' first birthday. Sir, I had no idea Helen was your Mama's name until your last letter.

I must away as the ship is due to leave in two days. My screed must be first taken to Sydney.

May God bless you, and again, thank you!
Cris.

~

Crispin collected the mail when at the market. Reading through the swathe of letters, he noticed nothing had arrived from John.

Helena said, "Crispin, I think it's about time you wrote and told Sir about what's happening here. He may not have heard about the new governor."

Crispin chuckled. "I started a letter to him this morning as it's his birthday. I told him all about the new governor. Here, let me read it to you."

Leith Vale Farm
Toongabbie
29th August 1806

Dear Sir,

Happy Birthday, sir. I hope you celebrated the day with your family. I remember the beautiful dinners of roast pickled pork that Mrs Peach used to cook up for you. To celebrate such a festive day without you is... well, we miss you.

As to the news from here...

Governor Phillip Gidley King has gone due to ill health, and we have a new governor. (I groan!)

I do not know if you know this man personally, but his reputation has preceded him. You may have met him through your contact, Sir Joseph Banks. Captain William Bligh is the man's name, and I first remember you telling me of him on the voyage out to Sydney. I know I should not state this, but I freely admit that I am over the fuss rum has caused here. I do not think this man will have any better success than you or Phillip. Honestly, I feel the king himself would fail.

On a brighter note, my darling wife delivered another son this morning. So, sir, we have two imps born on your birthday. His name is Jonas William, after my beloved brother-in-law and your papa. I was keen to reverse the names and break with the 'J' tradition, but the family overruled me. Both mother and child are well.

I think back to the day we married and the trauma of that month. It seems like a lifetime ago. Leaving everything I was familiar with to chase a girl who hardly knew me in the hope that she would marry me was nerve-wracking, to say the least. I had no skills but lamp lighting.

Sir, you took me on spec and changed all our lives.

I was a complete novice and had never even seen the sea, let alone been on it. I freely admit I was petrified of Bennelong when you introduced him onboard in England. He now spends his time between Linus's house, our farms, and a spot near the point where the ferry kisses the bottom as it nears Parramatta. It is now called Kissing Point, which he now calls home.

Ben and Boorong are expecting a child. To say they are excited is an understatement.

Your last letter announced a new appointment for you as the superintendent of ship payments. I'm sure you miss the sea, but at least you are involved in the Navy and interact with the men who serve under you.

Sir, can you pray for the colony?

Before Bligh even arrived, there were more murmurings of rebellion. I feel he's walking into a powder keg of problems.

If you think things were troubled before... Ahh, sir, we are happy to keep our heads down and mind our own business.

My paper is once more full, and I will write again soon.

Take care, sir.

We all send our love.

Cris, Helena and family

Letters kept crisscrossing the oceans and now arrived or departed with each vessel.

Sometimes, a few arrived at once, depending on how much was occurring on each side of the world.

Chapter 21   The Rum Rebellion

*J*t didn't take long for news about a coup in Sydney to spread to Parramatta. The morning ferry brought the information of the *coup d'état* the evening before in Sydney. Crispin heard all about it as he was at the King's Wharf in Parramatta to unload his produce into the Government Store building. However, Jonas visited their home with Mary late on the evening of January 27th, and the Milroys were given a complete description of what had occurred.

Crispin once again put his pen to some very scarce writing paper and informed John about the fulfilment of another of his words. In his excitement, he even forgot to write a greeting.

> *Leith Vale Farm*
> *Toongabbie*
> *30 January 1808*

> *Dear Sir,*
> *It has happened! They are calling the uprising the 'Rum Rebellion'.*
> *On the evening of 26th January, the officers and men of the New South Wales Corps marched to Government House in Sydney in rebellion against Governor William Bligh's attempt to rein in their control. You knew this would explode, and this week, it did.*
> *You warned London, and nobody would listen but Jonas's uncle, who was howled down by his superiors. We are all safe and far away from the strife occurring in Sydney, but the town is in turmoil.*
> *Jonas assures me that Colin and Nigel's families are safe, but I'm sure they will write. Jonas was in town with a load of vegetables from our farms and heard about the coup. He saw the troops gathering and watched what occurred. Sir,*

Macarthur was, of course, central to the explosive situation. Soon after Bligh's arrival, he came into conflict with the troublemaker, who, by the way, has sold out and is now a full-time farmer. I think he and Elizabeth are at odds as they live separately. Issues occurred over Macarthur's land grant of the Cowpastures land where you found the missing cattle. Bligh threatened to remove Macarthur from his prime land.

The animosity continued until Bligh had Macarthur taken to court over an incident involving one of Macarthur's trading ships. The jury of Corps Officers refused to recognise the trial, and Bligh indicated that he intended to charge them with treason.

The Commanding Officer of the NSW Corps, George Johnston, defended his men and claimed that removing them from duties would compromise the safety of the colony. He claimed Bligh needed to be removed from office for everyone's good.

Sir, Bligh is under house arrest, and I have no idea what will happen now. He can't return to office as he has lost charge of the entire situation, and I don't know who will be brave enough to follow him as governor here. Whoever it is, he had better be a Godly man.

George Johnson has taken temporary command.

Two days later

I have just received your latest letter. I send hearty congratulations on your promotion to Rear-Admiral. I know it occurred six months ago, but news takes that long to reach us. I wonder how high you will be elevated when the powers-that-be hear about the disastrous situation over here?

They cannot deny that all you said was true. I remember you remarking, 'The truth will prevail.' I believe it has. Whoever comes, I do so hope that whoever comes next is a man of God. He will need to be, and we shall support him as we did with you. It would be even nicer if he's a Scotsman like you.

I found out more details about the coup on the 26th. In the evening, the men of the New South Wales Corps marched from the parade ground on High Street up Bridge Street to Government House. They marched to the tune of 'British Grenadiers' and were followed by hundreds of spectators. (Jonas at a distance). When they arrived at Government House, the soldiers searched the property before finally locating Governor Bligh, who, according to hearsay, was hiding under his bed. He was found by Sergeant John Sutherland, Corporal Michael Marlborough and Private William Wilford. I have no idea if this is true, but knowing your room was upstairs, I imagine he thought the troops would not dare to invade his personal space. He was wrong! He was arrested and deposed from his position; as I mentioned, George Johnston took control of the colony. I do not remember him being a thorn in our sides, but time has changed the situation. Bligh was very well thought of, out Windsor way, as he supported the farmers out there somewhat forcefully.

Nearly a week has passed since this occurred, and the military presence in Parramatta and our area is strong. I will keep you informed.

Again, everyone sends their love, and Linus asked that I pass on his thanks again. My next letter will contain news about our next child. Helena is due in a few weeks, but the ship carrying this letter will have left by then. I'm sure I wrote last year telling you about Janice's arrival. Would it be possible to send some writing paper as we cannot access any here? I am down to the last few sheets of the part ream you gave me.

Take care, and God Bless!
Cris

The families stayed as far away from politics as possible.

However, the arrival of a new face elicited another long letter from Crispin. He was down to the last sheet of the paper that John had given him when a parcel arrived. John must have realised he would need paper soon and sent it some months earlier as it arrived on the latest ship. The gift from John contained two reams of writing paper, new pens, and powdered ink. Such a luxury was no longer available in the colony.

Crispin planned to share it with his family. He knew that John would wish to know about the arrival of the next new governor.

Leith Vale Farm
Toongabbie
31st December 1809

Dear Sir,

I do so hope you are still well. I am writing to you in Devon, as that is the last address I have for you. I believe that you now own a property in Hackney, London. This is where my Aunt's house was, so I know the area well. Your last letter mentioned that your niece Penelope has taken over your care. I am glad you have family members who care for your well-being. This is of great comfort to us. I'm guessing she is William and Eliza's youngest child. If so, I remember her first steps.

As you can see, I received your generous gift of paper, pens, and ink. I hope you do not mind that I have shared the paper with the family. I will now use some of my gift to tell you about recent happenings.

Sir, our fifth governor, Lachlan Macquarie, arrived this week and will be sworn in tomorrow. He has taken over from Foveaux and Paterson.

Foveaux arrived a few months after the Rebellion on the ship carrying two young men. I tell you of these two lads as I'm sure you would have loved them. When they arrived last year, they moved into the Rosedale Farm. Ben Parker and George Ellis are soon to be family. Both are keen on two of Helena's younger sisters (Kath and Charlotte, respectively). They are a saddler and a tanner and are wonderful chaps. George is the most amazing violinist. This was a skill he hid for a long time. More about them anon.

Anyway, we plan to attend the induction ceremony of the new governor and introduce ourselves if possible. Jonas has arranged this for us. We have been told that Lachlan Macquarie is a soldier through and through, and I hope he has the strength to push the Corps back into their boxes. (I'm heading to Linus and Agnes's place, so I will finish writing this there.)

John Macarthur and George Johnson have already left for England. I hope they will be imprisoned or even impaled on the spikes of Westminster Bridge, for they have caused so much trouble here. Elizabeth Macarthur is much relieved. These men and their friends have decimated much of the tribal hunting grounds, and our dear friends have now moved across the river into lands that are not usually theirs. Bennelong and his tribe had little choice in this. They occasionally come for a visit and always arrive with a gift of some sort for us.

One of the little boys rescued from the cave with Mary and Phoebe is now one of the clan's elders. He is only eighteen but is very mature for his age. He speaks English almost perfectly and can also read and write well. He presented me with a stone axe head that he had made. It is of grey stone, and he said it was made at the crossing at Emu Ford.

I have never been across the river, and, unlike you, I have little desire to explore. My life here vastly differs from my cloistered life in London with my father and aunt. I was fearful enough, leaving everything I knew to follow Helena. Thanks to you, that worked out well. She is still as wonderful as ever, and I still adore her. (No, she is not looking over my shoulder this time.)

Our life in the colony is delightful. The house is full of the sounds of laughter. Helena and our youngest, Jeramy James Rosedale Milroy, born in February 1808, are currently sitting in a rocking chair on our verandah. The two children above him are Jonas and Joanie. They are under the care of our newest maids.

I find it hard to remember those cold and dreary days in London. Here, our life is filled with sunshine and laughter. I never thought I would become a farmer, but I find the peace of this vast brown land soothing to my soul. However, the raucous noise of the cicadas is grating this year. My smooth soldier hands are long gone and are as rough and gnarled as Linus's are. He now spends most of his time tending to the vegetables around the house but is otherwise well.

As you taught me, I rise before the family and start each day in prayer. Helena and I finish each day the same way each evening before we sleep. We read a chapter of the bible every night. The other couples in our cluster do much the same, and all send their love. Sunday after church is spent together, and we always remember you when we gather in prayer.

I will finish this letter in a few days and tell you about the upcoming festivities. Again, I can't thank you enough for our farms and for suggesting that we build within cooee of each other. (I do love that word).

I shall finish this screed after the visit to Sydney. (I will take some paper to Nigel and Connie as we are to stay with them).

No sooner had I penned the last words than a carriage pulled up at the front of the house.

Lachlan came bearing mail from you for Linus and me. Oh, sir, I do enjoy hearing from you. He has already delivered your letters to Nigel and Colin. I do like him!

He demanded that we be on first-name terms as you spoke to him about me. I have yet to meet his wife. I had no idea he brought your gift of writing paper.

Thank you!

A week later

Now, about the installation of our new governor...

We are finally home from an exhausting week in Sydney. Colin and Aggie refused to join the festivities, but Nigel, Connie, Wil, and Deb were there. We stayed with the Brays. Helena's family looked after all the children, so it was like a holiday for us. After all the official palaver, we finally met Lachlan and Elizabeth Macquarie together. We had a long talk with them because it was somewhat rushed when he visited the farm with his security guard, Mark Duffy. He said he would come back and seek more information about the state of things, so I think we shall see quite a bit of this gentleman. Colin and Nigel have also been asked for information.

Sir, Lachlan mentioned that you attended their wedding in Devon. I realise he is from a different part of Scotland, but hearing his lilt reminds me in some way of you. He knows much about this place, so I'm guessing he met with you often before leaving. He just missed Macarthur et al., in Rio De Janeiro, so he knew they were gone before he arrived.

With the colony cleared of the rebel leaders, I hope Lachlan can achieve what you and those following you could not. I offered him my copy of your second book only to find that you had already given him one. I know he is in contact with Governor Phillip, and with all that information, I'm sure he will achieve much. He has already visited the Osbornes to get their view of what is happening in town.

An interesting aside is that the two Elizabeths, Macquarie and Macarthur, are known to each other and are quietly friends. This may well assist the new governor in the absence of the latter's husband. In the four years that John Macarthur was absent after his duel with Paterson, Elizabeth Macarthur and her overseer successfully bred the most fertile sheep with a wonderfully fine crimp fleece. They were even better than our initial experiments with her flock.

When John returned with more Spanish Merinos, he demanded that the line be kept pure. When he left the second time, we sold Elizabeth the bulk of our flock. John was unaware that we had already improved the breed. This, of course, riles Marsden as his sheep are purebred Spanish merinos and do not produce live lambs well. While Marsden's flock may have fifty lambs surviving from one hundred ewes, Elizabeth's flock produces twins or even triplets, and most survive. Therefore, her flock is increasing astoundingly.

I am sure John Macarthur would not be pleased if he knew, but he is no longer here. Elizabeth is now relaxed, and you can see it on her face. She now hardly stops smiling when out in society, which is often. Her hands are rough like Helena's, so we know she is also a hands-on farmer. Unfortunately, her kitchen caught fire, so they built a small cooking area in the adjoining dairy at Elizabeth Farm in town. As we helped her while she was alone last time, she gave Linus some of her flock as a gift. He has never been a stock person, so the improved strain of sheep are now on the twins' farm. With Elizabeth's blessing, they will focus on breeding them for meat (I should have offered ours to them), along with some pigs George Ellis purchased and did not want. Gerry and Jem's hundred-acre block is now mainly for livestock. They grow grain, but it's only for stock food.

Linus taught us how to lay down silage pits as we had a bumper year last season. We have just finished the fifth pit, and each will feed all our farm stock for about a year. They decided to do this rather than sell the excess grain as the situation here was volatile at harvest time. Nigel still mills our grain for flour. The store rooms are full to the brim, so we could not add more.

Bennelong said that after so many years of good rain, the next few may be dry, so we are all preparing madly and stocking up on everything we can.

Usually, the tribe heads to the coast at this time, but their land there is no longer accessible to them. He said they now go across the river and further up the coast. They join a small family group that he called something like the Bouddi people. Apparently, they are a mix of various clans, from Garingai, Dharug, and others. They have some beaches up there with good food and shelter. However, many more have settled in different regions.

The Rosedale twins have left a large area along their creek for the tribes use. Ben's people are free to come and go, and we are willing to trade anything except tobacco and alcohol, which are not permitted on our farms. It may well be why we see little of Ben, as he seems to have hit the bottle again, which is so sad. He still has his blue coat, but it's very tattered. I have offered him other clothing, but he is wedded to that thing.

Now, back to our meeting with our new governor. I may be judging too early, but I like him. Sir, I do believe that Lachlan Macquarie has the ability to turn this place around. One day, it may become the New Albion Governor Phillip wished it to be, but Macquarie has his work cut out for him. With Macarthur gone, at least, that is one thorn he does not need to cope with.

As you can tell from the length of this screed, I appreciate the stationary parcel you sent us. We shared it amongst the family and will value it. Jasper said he also loved his new set of journals, and I enclose his letter for you.

I think he has added a small gift, but I have no idea what it could be. It is hard to believe that he is now eleven. He is a keen geologist, which may be because of his name. That first red pebble I gave you when he was born sparked his interest.

Linus sends his regards; he's ageing quickly. His chest has never fully recovered from his illness last year, but with Tris and Nick's assistance, their farm is prospering.

I will sign off now and look forward to your following newsy letter.

All of our love and appreciation to you.

Cris and Helena ++++++++++

(that's from all the children, incl Jesse)

~

Two years later, in 1811.

Helena found Crispin sitting on the verandah, looking at the sunset. Her rocking chair was some distance away, and she moved it closer and took her husband's hand. "Have you written to Sir yet, Cris? It's been over a month, and Papa would want him to know." Crispin shook his head. Just thinking of the third most influential man in his life not being there still hurt. John Hunter had become his surrogate father, but Linus had been a close third. "I know I must love, but I have been putting it off as once the news is on paper, it makes it final and closes that door in our lives."

"It is final, my beloved. But Papa was suffering with every breath he took. He is now at peace." Helena caressed her husband's calloused hands lovingly. Gone were the smooth soldier-boy hands he had when they married. He now tilled the soil beside her and their children. He had callouses as did all the men in their family. As she had done beside her father, their children now worked beside them. Three convict girls did the inside work, cleaning and cooking, and another young convict girl was a nursemaid for the younger children. Helena toiled just as hard as Crispin. She took his hand and waited until he turned to her. She said, "He needs to know, love."

John's last letter contained the news that his niece Eliza, William's wife, had died. Crispin hated death but knew it was the consequence of the fall that Richard had so aptly described so long ago. Death had taken all his family in England, and he had felt so alone. He had followed Helena because he had no one left to care for. The loss of their first child from miscarriage had eaten away at him for months until he understood the consequences of sin. The baby's loss had not been anything he had done but a repercussion for a fallen world. However, it still hurt. Linus had been the lynchpin of the family, and with his passing, there was a huge void.

Crispin nodded. "I shall write tomorrow, but I shall add the news as an aside rather than make the letter morose."

Helena smiled. "Please, send him my love."

Crispin tried to smile. "I always do, sweetie." While holding hands, they sat back and watched the sun sink over the hills. The light faded quickly, but the evening was surprisingly warm, and they enjoyed a few moments of peace before the evening duties of parenthood for their ten children called them inside.

True to his word, Crispin sat down and wrote to his friend the following day. All other work was put aside so he could concentrate on the wording of this letter.

> *Leith Vale Farm*
> *Toongabbie*
> *26th September 1811*

Dear Sir,

I hope this missive finds you well. I find it hard to believe it is sixteen years since we arrived on these shores. Overall, this letter contains good news, so relax and enjoy reading about what your fellow countryman is doing. First, I want to congratulate you on your promotion to Vice Admiral in July. What an outstanding accolade, and well deserved. (Not that I am biased!).

In the nearly two years since his arrival, Lachlan (as he insists that I call him) has drastically reined in the importation of spirituous liquids. Phillip managed to turn only one ship away. Bligh... well, I won't even try to explain what he tried to do, but suffice to say, he managed to rile all the Corps. But Lachlan ripped the value out of the grog by introducing tariffs.

Knowing that Lachlan could not fight the consumption of the drink, he put an exorbitant tariff on its import and told them they may import what they wished, but they must pay the duty. That's precisely what Lord Portland said NOT to do, but it works. With the grog no longer as profitable, the import of such products has reduced, and the price has skyrocketed, so there is much less drunkenness as the poor cannot afford the luxury of the stupefying beverage. This tariff is being directed to construct a new hospital, which D'Arcy Wentworth will run. The foundations are already in. Then, to improve the roads, Lachlan has made the main thoroughfares toll roads like the ones we have in England. (I no longer think of the motherland as home). One toll gate is as you leave Sydney, and two are on the western and northern roads out of Parramatta.

Mark and Cathy Duffy now oversee the tollgate near the Parramatta cemetery. They arrived with Lachlan. Cathy's son, Josh Callan, will be groomed to run it when he's old enough. Currently, his family is doing this. To explain who they are, Josh's widowed mother, Cathy, married Mark Duffy, one of Lachlan's security detail, on the voyage out to meet her son. Mark and I have become friends as we have a lot in common, for we are both Londoners. Mark, Lachlan, and Colin meet with us for prayer once a week, and having a kindred spirit with strong faith is a delight.

Eric comes to our prayer meetings when he can, but his family ties keep him busy. He had no idea twins ran in his family, and for them to have three sets in four years, and as they have three older little ones, it keeps them on their toes. We thought ten children was enough to cope with, but they now have nine, and Gillian is expecting again already.

Lachlan and Elizabeth have entrenched themselves in your delightful home, although there are moves to extend it. They have no children, but two of their nephews are also in the colony. Both young men are serving in his regiment. They are very busy; during my last visit to Sydney, I found construction sites and substantial building projects everywhere. They are certainly industrious. St Phillip's church is finally completed and looks incredible. I won't say it is beautiful, as it is the most unusual structure I have ever seen. St John's at Parramatta is also finished and is now fully utilised. I know you laid the foundation stone for the new building, as I was there in April 1797. It is where we now worship, and I think of you every time we enter.

Marsden is capable but draws a thick, uncrossable line between convict and free. He rarely acknowledges Helena but gives much time to the rest of our family. This does not worry me as Helena has become fast friends with Elizabeth Macquarie and Josh's mother, Cathy. The three ladies are constant companions, and their laughter often rings over the congregation when we exit after a service. Marsden blames

Helena for the unruly sound, but she shrugs off his disdain with a laugh. She is actually the quietest of the three. That, of course, riles him more. He is not impressed that the Macquaries hobnob with such fallen people as Helena and the twins' wives. I laugh as my Helena is far from that, as you well know.

Sir, the following paragraph is difficult to write. I have held back for a long time as I find it hard to reconcile that he will not appear and give his incredible wisdom. You see, my sad news is that Linus passed away last month. We are so grieved that I have been unable to put pen to paper and tell you. His lungs finally could not cope, and he drew his last breath with Agnes beside him and the vast family surrounding his bed. One of the last things he managed to do was subdivide the farm so that each of his younger sons would inherit a sixty-acre block.

Nick and Tris are both married now, and I find it hard to realise they are grown men, and both their wives have babies on the way. Kath married Ben Parker, the saddler, and plan to move to Castlereagh. He is a saddle-maker with much skill. Charlotte is engaged to George Ellis, who arrived with Ben and Foveaux in 1808. They plan to live on the outskirts of Parramatta but will not marry for a couple of years as they are still too young. Charlotte is impatient but is biding her time learning to decorate George's leather. He is not yet twenty-one, and she is younger still. The other older girls are all either engaged or married to ex-soldiers. Linus approved of all of his daughter's chosen men and wished to see the girls settled before he died, so he permitted them to become engaged.

We are all adjusting to Linus's significant loss with difficulty. He was a vast fountain of knowledge, wisdom, and strength, leaving a great void in our lives. My eyes water as I write this to you. He died knowing that Jesus loved him and forgave his sins; shortly before his death, he said that his angelic helpers had arrived to take him home, so we are to be assured that we will meet again in Heaven.

We all miss him. (Sorry about the inkblot - it hit a tear)!

Back to Lachlan. He has great plans and has renamed streets and cleaned up the main town. High Street in Sydney has been renamed George Street, and the cricket field where the horses are exercised is now known as Hyde Park. The streets in town are now clean, and it is an appealing place to live. Even the stench is minimal. The water flowing down the Tank Stream is once again clean as it had reverted to filth after you left, and the fish returned to the cove. I recently saw a tiny seahorse on the timbers of the main wharf while waiting for the ferry. And for the people, the orphans are being fed and clothed, and he has also arranged education for them. The convicts now have adequate food, clothing, and blankets. He purchased shiploads of fabric from India and arranged for the convict women to make clothing for the Government Stores. Depending on the season, the women are now dressed in a brighter blue drill or warm woollen brown serge gown. Each is also allocated a calico apron, mob caps and undergarments. The men are in black and yellow woollen coats and trousers and wear a white linen shirt with a blue pinstripe. It is easily identifiable as convict garb but is very practical. Overall, they are much better cared for than London allocated and, therefore, much less trouble.

Oh, sir, the change is incredible. When he arrived, I wondered if such a slight and sickly man was strong enough for the work ahead of him. His stature gives the impression of illness as he suffered from a debilitating disease contracted in Egypt. His face is pock-marked from the mercurial treatment he is taking, which shows he is still not well. However, his frail stature belays the man of steel beneath. He is strong, sir. He is, indeed, a man who can fight against the rebels in the military here. His wife, Elizabeth, has incredible ideas of the order of things, and they are a powerful team that is not easily duped.

Although they have won the hearts of many, there are, of course, the nay-sayers. These will grow over the years, but in the meantime, in the absence of Macarthur, they are forging ahead with their plans. The group, who now call themselves 'the exclusives,' remain a thorn in his flesh.

After one of our prayer meetings, Mark, Eric, Lachlan,

his cousin John Campbell, and I started a list of buildings that could benefit the colony. Mrs Macquarie had already compiled a list with plans for proper government barracks in Parramatta, a law building of some sort and various other structures. Phillip King had already suggested a new female convict building, but it was never started. Bligh had no time to do anything as his hands were full with the Corps. The list so far includes a new parliament building in Sydney, the hospital, as I mentioned, new government stables, and a substantial barracks in Sydney that will house not only convicts but also the military. There will be a law office or courtroom in town, various dwellings and numerous other projects. The list grows daily. Mention of a second church in Sydney has been thrown around.

Ahh, sir, I rattle on. Suffice to say, I am impressed that this man will succeed where others, yourself included, fought an impossible fight. Mayhap, things will change again when or if Macarthur returns, but if Lachlan has heard correctly, that is some years away. You may know more about that than we do here.

With my second sheet of paper now filled, I enclose this in Jasper's parcel and send it on its merry way. We still pray for you, sir, and thank you for your assistance in transforming our lives.

I am sending you hugs from all the children and us, too.

Cris, Helena, Jasper, Judy, Jonathan, Jennifer, Julien, Janette, Janice (Nell), Jonas, Joanie, and Jeramy.

Chapter 22 The Sea Billows Roll

*J*ohn's next letter revealed that William Kent had joined his wife in death. Considering how much younger he was than John, Crispin was stunned. He knew John would be sad to have outlived him. He knew he must write a condolence letter to his mentor. He worked out that William would have only been fifty-two at the time of his passing. He had died at sea. John now looked after the youngest child, Penelope. He wrote a short condolence note, then added a longer letter to his post.

Leith Vale Farm
Toongabbie
21st August 1813

Dear Sir,
Happy Birthday again (one week early)! Sir, this greeting comes from us all with our warmest blessings.

I am addressing this to your Judd Street address in Hackney, as I know you have now officially retired.

I was saddened to read of the death at sea of your beloved nephew, William, although I believe it occurred nearly a year ago. I gather he was at sea when this event happened. He was a good man, and I remember many wonderful evenings at your house, laughing over some incident or other. He will be sadly missed.

I have let Lachlan know.

I was thinking about the situations that led to your recall back to England. The entire fiasco over the John

Baughan trial and the dismissal of charges against the perpetrators has been fully exposed. All those in the Corps have now been reprimanded or dismissed. Unfortunately, many remain here. Your actions rightly exonerate you back then.

With The Duke of Portland now dead (I should say, may God rest his soul, but I wish that he rots elsewhere for the pain he caused you.) I believe that The Right Honourable Spencer Perceval (that's a mouthful!) would have been a much more reasonable leader had he not been assassinated.

I was pleased that he was against slavery, hunting, gambling, and adultery, and that would have made him unpopular with the upper echelon of society, and for him not to imbibe in drink, the Empire would have been a better place under his watch. You mentioned Lord Liverpool replaced him. I hope he is also a strong personality and will have the strength to stand firm. Like you, he will have a force against him as the corrupt people in leadership will never leave quietly.

Over here, all is calm since Lachlan came in with his big broom. Many new farms have been granted, but unfortunately, they need to encroach further into the Aboriginal lands. I know this will cause future problems, but we have little choice. I must confess that some grants were given to various members of our family.

Our farms are growing cash crops and supplying the Government Stores at a much lower price than we could get at the markets, but this is a guaranteed price, and as most of it is earmarked for convict consumption, they are not too fussed with the quality. Linus only permitted us to sell the best and preserve the remainder of the crop for ourselves and the tribe. I had no idea how many things you could use corn for. Nigel told me that when the kernels are dried, they make flour and grits; you can dry fry the kernels, and they pop. This is a delicious way to eat them when covered with a bit of butter and salt, and then, of course, you can eat them fresh.

There are so many children in our extended family that we can no longer gather for an indoor meal in any of the houses. It's like feeding an army when we all gather. Eric and

Gillian are the only ones unrelated, but they and their dozen little ones have been absorbed into the fold.

Mark and Cathy Duffy grew up in the Rookery area of St Giles, London, and their descriptions left little to my imagination. Father would never let me work closer than Bethel Green Road, so I avoided it. According to Mark, they did not have street lighting there anyway.

Lachlan has severely blotted his copybook in Marsden's eyes. With the support of William Wilberforce in London, emancipists were reinstated to the roles they held before their conviction. Consequently, some ex-convicts now hold higher positions than Marsden does. Need I say the man is not impressed or happy? Simeon Lord and Andrew Thompson (now dead after flood rescuing many earlier this year) were elevated as Magistrates alongside Marsden. He refused to serve with them. Marsden would pointedly leave a room if they entered. I feel this may be the beginning of another issue that could be blown out of proportion. We shall see! Lachlan has all but castrated the Corps. One of his men, Rudi Greenwood, made a passing comment and the next thing he knew Rudi was in charge of a new small mint. I could not write about this before as it was being kept under wraps. The new coins are to be released in increments from next month.

You may be interested to hear that Gregory Blaxland, William Lawson, and D'Arcy Wentworth's son William crossed the Blue Mountains in May. They went a long way past the first hill and saw good grazing was west of the mountain range. Lachlan is thinking of sending some more explorers to determine how feasible it would be to farm this discovery.

Bennelong told me he knew there were vast plains, but I refused to pass on the information, even to Lachlan. Ben's people had had enough taken from them, and I would not be a party to more killings and displacements from their land. In the end, another member of the Dharug tribe told someone, and the next thing you know, a trip was planned.

The explorers only returned about eight weeks ago, but Lachlan is so desperate for new grazing lands that he's thinking of sending the surveyor, George Evans, over to see how quickly the area can be farmed.

Sir, Bennelong died a few days into the New Year. His wife, Boorong/Abaroo, died shortly before him. Their son, Dickie, came and told us the sad news. I saw Abaroo a few times before her death last year. As you know, she had fully reverted to using Boorong as her name. Was the name given to her after marriage? I dare say we shall never know unless you asked her. The tribe lived on James Squire's farm at Kissing Point when Bennelong died. Squire buried Ben next to Boorong in a place the tribe chose. They are now together for eternity. Unlike most tribal deaths, they were buried, not cremated.

If you see the Johnsons, please tell them she found happiness with Bennelong. Dickie is now ten and is comfortable in both the tribe and in town. Although now called Thomas, he attends school and is quite clever. He drops in occasionally to us, but Agnes sees him often.

Sir, the colony has again been hit by drought. The rains have held off once more, and the land is parched. Bennelong was once again correct. Their people have an astounding ability to read the weather. The feed that didn't shrivel got burned in the numerous grass fires that passed through this year. Even the cold weather over winter gave us little respite from fires. I now know why the tribes used to burn off every winter. It was for safety reasons during dry summers, as well as hunting for food.

The ship Phoenix *sails tomorrow, so I will give this to Captain Parker to deliver to you. With warmest regards.*

Cris and Helena +

~

1815

Over the years, Crispin wrote many more letters with family news, each containing some information he wished to share with John.

John replied in turn and updated him on the numerous nieces' and nephews' activities. Penelope now cared for him rather than the reverse.

Crispin knew he needed to write about the next phase of their farming saga. Telling his friend about selling the original farm John had arranged for Linus would not be easy.

Leith Vale Farm

Toongabbie
January 1815

Dear Sir,

I do hope you are faring well.

I'm so pleased Penelope cares for you so well. She deserved your glowing words. Retirement is never easy, and you have had such an active and exciting life that it must be hard for you to be officially grounded. I said to Helena that this is your last shipwreck! She chuckled and said this would be the hardest for you to accept.

Our family continues to grow. Agnes has moved in with us, as her younger boys, Nick and Tris, have sold the big farm. All the other girls, except Rebecca, are married. I won't go into details as I'm not sure there is enough paper to permit that.

After some trauma, Charlotte finally married her tanner-cum-saddler, and George has a new leatherwork and saddlery shop in the front room of their house between the original farm and Parramatta. Unfortunately, sales are hindered by the tollgate that people must pass before they come for a browse. He will likely need to open a store in town.

After Kath married Ben Parker, they decided to stay with George and Charlotte for the moment, along with many of the older orphan boys. They have taken in these boys to teach them a trade. One lad, Quinn, has even taken George's name.

Quinn and his friends were thrown out of their billeted homes due to their age. They were living on the street until George discovered their plight. Like Colin, George and Ben have taken numerous lads on and are teaching them to run their own businesses. They are good boys and keen to learn. The girls' orphanage in William's old house on the foreshore is bursting at the seams.

I mentioned George's violin. On a still night, the haunting tunes are heard on the evening breezes. No one knew where it came from, but eventually, Ben let the information drop. Oh, he is so clever. He can make his instrument cry.

Lachlan had George play for a concert. You could have heard a pin drop. There was not a dry eye on the hillside. Even Lachlan was seen to swipe a tear or two away.

Sir, tanning is usually a smelly job, but how George manages not to stink is astounding. He told me that dog excrement is used for tanning in England. The children who collect this filth are called 'pure collectors.' On his way here, he found a substitute in Cape Town. George now collects and uses our excess vegetables to make the tanning solution.

With your recommendation of their farming skills, Lachlan has asked the boys, Nick and Tris, to establish the new farms west of the Blue Mountains and become mentors for the new settlers out there. So, although they have sold the big farm here, the money will return to the land.

They have each been granted one thousand acres and allocated a team of hand-picked convicts to fence their land and tend their herds. Both accumulated an assortment of stock over the years, and they now have nearly one thousand head of cattle, sheep, and pigs between them, not to mention horses and work bullocks. Most of the livestock has been on agistment on other farms until their fencing is completed.

This move has provoked much discussion, but it is a good decision.

Only through careful selection could the original farm be sold. Lachlan eventually chose someone himself, and it was done conditionally so that the tribe could keep their waterhole and area safe. No further clearing is to occur.

Sadly, few Aborigines are left in the area now, those who are, remain on Squires Farm at Kissing Point. They rarely go 'walkabout' any more as there is nowhere to go except into the neighbouring tribal area to the north. Their dwellings are far from adequate where they are living, but they prefer that to the cabins at the farm. Jonas built a series of timber huts for them a short walk from the waterhole. They still use them when they come, hence the conditions of the sale. Nick and Tris each have three children now. Like their brothers, they also married two Irish convict girls, Rachel and Bek, assigned to Agnes. Their wives would only go if the other went too. So, they go as a group. Rebecca, the youngest

Rosedale girl, is going with them. She is nineteen now and is going to teach the children. All of the family are now literate. Your influence achieved that goal. Thank you!

With the influx of settlers heading out that way, I have no doubt some young lad will snap her up quickly.

Two very interesting people turned up a few months after I last wrote. The first came on a convict ship in a cargo of women. Helena has taken to checking on the comfort of the female convicts with Elizabeth Macquarie and Cathy Duffy.

This convict was a young woman who was obviously from the gentry. The doctor on board and the captain introduced them to Kate, as she was then known. She had recently given birth to a healthy male child. That drew my Helena to her side immediately. Less than a month later, a man with half a face presented himself to Lachlan in Government House in town.

Lachlan and Elizabeth were in Sydney seeing the doctor and checking her health as she was expecting a child (I mentioned that as young Lachlan was born March 1814 and is well). The man, with two small girls at his side, appeared unannounced at Government House in Sydney. He, too, was obviously gentry, if not more.

Sir, I mean it when I say he has half a face. The other half is melted from a horrific fire that killed his wife's father. The short story is that he came looking for his wife, Katy. Sir, she was the convict woman my beloved Helena noticed with the newborn babe.

Now reunited, this couple is known as Perry and Katy White, but I discovered he holds a title. Sir, Perry is an earl, and he is using his scars to connect with scarred, beaten, battered, and bruised souls, sharing his faith with them. The horrific wounds this man courageously bears resonate with the convicts, allowing them to open up to him in a way that no one else, including the pious Samuel Marsden, can. Katy and Helena are doing the same for the women.

Perry and Mark Duffy have grown close. So, Perry has joined our prayer group. Together, we are making a change for the better for some of the male convicts. Lachlan fully endorses our actions but keeps well out of the work as he knows he would hinder rather than help it.

In the year since Perry White's arrival, our men's group, which by default also includes Jonas, Eric, Arnold and Colin, welcomes other newcomers. We don't see Nigel and Connie much, but they and their family are well. Her brother, Wil, is the headmaster of the school and is also teaching at the orphanage. His wife, Deb and her sister teach with him.

Having brothers in Christ to pray with is like our morning devotions in days gone by. As a consequence, our faith is bolstered by the others. We all meet at Perry's large house, and our families have become friends. We treat them as extended family.

A spin-off is that Lachlan has used our friendship with Ben's tribe to meet them and get to know their needs, and the children often return home. He is learning their language and has already started a school for them. But I feel the one thing he has done wrong is suggesting the Aboriginal children live away from their families to learn. Poor Dicky rarely gets to see his tribe these days. They do not understand that such a way of education is usual in England. Sir, I'm not sure this will work.

As usual, everyone sends their love to you. I will mail this today and look forward to reading about who you have met in London.

With love and great affection.
Cris, Helena, and the children.

~

A new decade.

Years passed, and many more letters shuffled back and forth across the billowing seas.

Letters now took less than a year to receive a reply.

Crispin was stunned to read in one of John's long screeds that William Paterson was dead and his widow, Elizabeth, married Lieutenant-General Francis Grose.

Another missive brought on the next ship informed them that Francis died a month after his marriage to Elizabeth and that he had left £2000 to his son, Reverend Francis Grose, Junior.

Crispin chuckled. Not at Grose's demise, but considering his animosity toward the church, the fact that his son should become a minister made Cris and Helena laugh.

Crispin and Helena had no more children. Ten living imps were enough for them to cope with, and they were all growing quickly. Eric and Gillian had fourteen children, including four sets of twins.

Jasper was twenty-four and still wrote regularly to John. He was engaged to a lass named Jane. John sent £5 for them as a gift. He would one day inherit their farm, as per John's wishes.

John replied to every detailed screed he received.

Crispin often knew of happenings in London before Lachlan did.

The years passed too fast.

~

As time marched on, Crispin noted that John's handwriting was getting increasingly shaky. His regular letters often reminisced about their happy years in Sydney and discovering Crispin's faith. John nurtured him, and his paternal love for him was now stronger than he ever had for his father.

Crispin wrote about the arrival of more men joining their prayer group. The first arrival was Bill Miller, who ran a new upper-class inn in Parramatta. He, too, was a man of learning and faith.

A friend of Perry's arrived the following year. Major Ned Grace, who was just twenty, came in January 1820, accompanying a shipload of convicts. Among them was a convict who caught Ned's attention. Charles Lockley could have been Ned's brother, yet Ned denied any known connection. Once Charles cleaned himself up, they looked remarkably alike.

Ned arranged for Charles to be assigned to Perry. So, the group that now met at Perry's house had representatives from all walks of life in England. From the convict Charles; Perry's children's tutor, Buck; the soldier, Ned; and Perry, the earl in hiding.

Each soon had families, and the group expanded again.

Then, soon after Ned's arrival, Billy and Bryn Williams appeared. They set up a new dairy behind the Government Domain in Parramatta.

John wrote of the monarch's passing on Jan 1820 and gave news of the new king.

Prinny, as he was known by many, took the throne.

Thankfully, John had nothing to do with the royal court.

~

1821

One morning in August, Crispin and Helena were having tea on their verandah when a dust ball moving down the dirt road told them they were about to have visitors.

The small, unmarked black carriage frequently seen going to and from their farm pulled up slightly off to the side.

When the dust settled, the passengers alighted.

Crispin was not surprised to see Perry White, Lachlan, and Lachlan's security guard, Ned Grace, who was in the driver's seat.

Mark Duffy's presence was a surprise. Crispin stood to welcome them. Mark once held the same position as Cris had with John, but he worked with Lachlan. His presence with them was unusual, as he was now running the toll gate. Crispin' heart started racing.

Along the verandah, there was a row of wicker chairs with extra seating for anyone who called. The visitors were warmly greeted and seated in the winter sunshine.

Once seated, Lachlan said, "I come bearing mail, Cris." He dug into his inside coat pocket and pulled out two letters. "This fat one came last week, but I wished to deliver it myself."

At Lachlan's words, fear shot through Crispin. Beads of perspiration appeared on his brow.

Helena noted his concern and reached for his hand.

Crispin' did not want to accept the mail.

Lachlan continued. "It was enclosed in my official despatch box. This fat one came with one for me from John. Nigel and Colin have their screeds, but I did not wait to hear what they contained. I know who it's from, and John's handwriting is now shaky at best. I believe he's about eighty-two now."

Crispin nodded.

Lachlan sighed. He knew what news it contained as he had also received one. "The other only arrived this morning. I gathered your friends and came immediately."

The small envelope Lachlan held was tiny and featured handwriting unfamiliar to Cris. It seemed much more feminine than John's script.

"No!" Crispin shook his head and pushed his chair backwards, stood, and moved away. He did not wish to read either letter. His eyes filled with tears. He did not want to take either missive. He held his hand up to ward off the bad news he knew it contained. "No, please, no!"

He took a few steps away. He knew what it would say. John was dead. He knew it, but he didn't want to read the words. His face contorted in anguish as his head shook in disbelief.

Lachlan waited. His heart bled for this man. He gave him time.

Crispin bit his top lip, then nibbled his lower one. Eventually, he took the fat letter.

He sank into his chair reluctantly, broke the seal on John's epistle and spread the page.

It contained another sealed paper, which he put to one side.

Judd Street
New Road,
Hackney, London
2nd February 1821

My dearest Cris and Helena,
I am writing to tell you that I am fading fast. This may

be my last letter to you but be assured we will meet in Heaven.

Praise God for the promise of Eternal Life. I am far from well and know that my time is short. However, there is something I wish to do, and I do not want to leave it to my lawyers or family to arrange. Cris, I have enclosed a bequest for you and your family.

Your ten living children will each receive £10. The girls can use the money as dowry; the boys can build themselves a house or buy land. The £20 is for you and Helena to buy something you have been saving for.

Lad, you were the son I never had but often wished for. You and Helena filled in my lonely years and supported me when needed. You two bolstered me up when everything else was crashing around me. And that darling lad of yours, Jasper, gave me such unconditional love that I wished to do something for him. You and Helena have your farm, as do the other family members, but the children now have a small inheritance each.

When you receive this, I will probably be chatting with Linus in Heaven. I regret not meeting the rest of your children, but I know they are as wonderful as you said.

I find it hard to realise that my little Jasper is now a grown man. I'm glad that he has found his life partner, and with this money, he and Jane can now build their own house.

I had visitors last week. Oliver and Annie Quilpie, better known as the Marquess and Marchioness of Bowbelle, came to see how I fared. Annie is the lass who arrived in the First Fleet with me, and it was through them that Doctor Arthur Bowes Smith's letters and journal changed the Navy's policy on how they treated convicts en route there. They come and see me whenever they are in London.

Do not be too sad, Cris. I have lived a good life. If I only managed to pass the baton of faith to you, Colin, and Nigel, then my life would have achieved its purpose.

I will finally be home, and I pray that my welcome there will be better than my return to England so long ago. I have fought my fight now and passed the baton to others.

My eyes are failing me, Cris. Give Helena and the children a hug from me, and remember me fondly to them all. Colin also received a letter and bequest from me, so he knows about my failing health, so feel free to visit him. Nigel and Connie, too.

I will finish this letter in a way I never have before: I love you, my boy, and I am so proud of the man you have become.

Cris, keep the faith and never fear to side with our Lord. He will see you safe. Remember, Christ is enough. More than enough!

Until we meet in Heaven.
Your affectionate mentor
John Hunter.

Tears dropped onto the paper as he read John's final epistle. Crispin was weeping unashamedly by the time he reached the end. He had lost a dear friend; he knew it and did not wish to read the words in the following letter.

On completing John's letter, he passed it to Lachlan.

Crispin flicked the wax seal on the enclosed paper and unfolded it to find that it contained money in two notes. There were a one-hundred-pound and a twenty-pound note.

The gasp from all but Crispin was audible.

Crispin dug out his oversized linen handkerchief and blew his nose. Then he said, "This is from John for the children. They are to get an equal share. It's for the girls' dowries and the boys to build a house. We are to have the twenty." He handed all the money to Helena.

As the others passed around John's letter and read it, Cris opened the tiny envelope written in a different hand.

It contained a news clipping and a short note. The clipping was an obituary notice from a London paper.

The note was from Penelope.

Crispin remembered her as a tiny, endearing child he had bounced on his lap as they sat in the dining room. William and Eliza often ate at Government House, and their children played together in the garden. Her parents were gone now, too.

Crispin read the obituary clipping and saw how much his mentor had achieved. He passed the cutting to Lachlan.

Judd Street
New Road,
Hackney, London
14th March 1821

Dear Crispin,

I think of you informally, as it was how Uncle John spoke so fondly of you. I only vaguely remember those days in Government House, as I was only small when we left. I write a quick note to say he passed peacefully yesterday, surrounded by his family.

He was eighty-three when he accepted the Lord's invitation. He lived a good life and held his faith firmly until his end. He asked that I let you know the date of his progression to his Eternal Reward, and once again, he wished that I send his love and thanks for your faithful friendship.

Penelope

Everyone remained silent. They watched the emotions cross his very expressive face.

The tears slid unnoticed down his cheeks. Again, Crispin bit his bottom lip then nibbled at his top one. Eventually, he pulled out his handkerchief, wiped his eyes and blew his nose again.

His friends and Helena knew he had reached the end of the sad missive.

Helena reached for his hand. She loved John as much, and they would mourn him together. Their friends, Colin and Aggie, would need a visit soon. Tears welled in her eyes. His passing ended an era. Her family had much to thank John for. He had saved her from a vile horror.

Crispin took a deep breath as a long, hitched sigh and released it slowly. A chapter of his life had now closed. He was not too embarrassed to show the depth of his loss. The lump in his throat was slowly subsiding. He managed to say, "So, he is gone!" He knew he had learned much at John's side. He would ensure the brave sea captain would never be forgotten.

Crispin hardly noticed the conversation around him. His eyes focused blankly on the farmland before him. All this was thanks to John. His few sheep were to keep the grass down. Elizabeth Macarthur insisted that he retain a few of their original crossbreds. Yet Crispin was thinking of the many problems he and John Hunter faced.

He knew he had to tell Eric, Gillian and the others. They, too, had written occasionally but had never been quite as close. They would head over after their visitors left.

He sighed as his breath hitched again, then turned to the compassionate faces of Helena and his friends.

The conversation of the others fell silent.

Crispin said, "When he left here in 1800, he had hoped there would be some sort of welcome for him when he reached London. Nothing! He wrote, and I could read the disappointment in his words by reading between the lines. He never complained about his treatment, I knew his disappointment. I wrote back and told him, 'Sir, there is no welcome home for you, as you are not home yet'."

Helena nodded.

Crispin sniffed. "Well, he is home now, and I bet the Lord gave him a very warm welcome. He will have been greeted by our Lord with 'Well done, my good and faithful servant.' Is this not the welcome we all crave most?"

Lachlan nodded and said, "He had a tough time here as London would not support him. He said he felt he had been 'tossed upon life's billows.' I've seen the sorts of seas he sailed and know them well. He wrote his books because the Admiralty would not give him a platform to tell his side of the story at an inquiry. Well, the tumultuous sea billows will roll John no more. He is now at peace."

The conversation turned to the storms each had faced and how their faith had upheld them.

The Osbornes, Milroys, Kents and Macquaries had lost at least one child. Nigel and Connie had the opposite with the illegitimate birth of Liam. They weathered those storms with the Lord's help. It was John who had turned their eyes heavenward. He had guided each of them through their grief.

Ned Grace was the only one who remained silent. He glanced at Perry, who gave him an almost imperceptible nod of acknowledgement.

Ned was distantly related to John but knew him through his parent's cook and housekeeper. John had visited their home often over his first twenty years of life. He would mourn the great man in private. He swallowed his tears. John met him in London shortly before catching the ship here. John gave him the confidence to have a good life in this land. However, he also challenged him to make himself useful and help the very young convict girls. To find that Perry and Katy were working with the Macquarie's doing that already was wonderful. That had only been two years ago.

Perry and he would reminisce about his cousin tonight. He had to stay quiet about that information as it would reveal his real identity to everyone but Perry. John's two staff, Mrs Peach and Mrs Cowdrey, had been part of Ned's early life, and he adored them both. The dear ladies had become his parent's cook and housekeeper. Mrs Cowdrey had given him many cuddles when a small boy.

~

The visitors stayed for an hour and talked about John and his influence on the colony.

Lachlan admitted that he had sought the wisdom of Arthur Phillip and John Hunter on how to proceed with the settlement. He said, "I learned much from John's books and journals. I was permitted to read much of what he had written in his private journal about his years here. He gave me a starting point. Mind you, having Macarthur absent for my first nine years was a blessing, but the vice-admiral gave me direction on negotiating the issues at hand. They were the admiral's ideas I implemented. He outlined his failures in trusting the wrong people and not setting firmer rules when he arrived. But hindsight is always twenty-twenty. So, I, too, have much to thank him for. Rudi and his idea for coinage also helped, but that's another story. Having our own currency broke the Exclusives' hold over the entire colony. Outlawing rum as a currency quickly followed."

Perry spoke for the first time and said, "Wasn't it John who suggested that you needed to improve the cheese industry here?"

Lachlan nodded. "Yes, and then Jennifer Kellow arrived. God had that in hand, too. She arrived with a letter from a duke." He laughed. "I didn't expect that."

Mark chuckled, adding, "So, God sent you a Cornish milkmaid. Now you have the Kellow Williams dairy, and look at what she's doing. I believe her hard cheeses will be divine if her soft cheeses are anything to go by."

Lachlan grinned but didn't say anything for a few minutes. He then gave a lopsided grin and said, "They are! She is training others, including my housekeeper, Betty Eccles. I took her on as John knew her from his first sojourn here. She was a skilled gardener and married one of her first students. I feel I may soon need a new housekeeper. Betty is obsessed with dairy work. After the ladies have trained enough workers, I'm starting a full dairy industry on the South Coast." With a nod from Lachlan, Ned walked to the carriage.

Ned Grace, a tall blond-haired soldier, was a friend of Perry's from England. Both men admitted they had been at school together and that Perry had been Ned's mentor.

This was hard to believe as Perry was at least six years his senior, if not more. Perry was ten years Ned's senior.

Ned had met Perry when he was eight, and Perry, ten years older, had been in his final year at school. They had lost contact years earlier because of the fire that had scarred Perry.

At Perry's recommendation, Lachlan had taken Ned on as a personal guard, much as John had taken on Crispin. From his speech, manner, deportment and attitude, Lachlan realised that Ned was probably a second or third son of a peer. However, in the eighteen months he had been in the colony, Ned had been drawn into Perry's prayer group with Lachlan.

Ned returned carrying a wooden box. In it were some fresh cheeses that Jennifer had made and sent as a gift for the family.

Lachlan grinned. "We collected these on the way here. Knowing we had sad news, I thought we could end the visit by tasting her new batch of smoked ricotta cheeses. However, Jennifer included some flavoured cottage cheeses and a sample of the new hard cheese she made last year. I confess I have a larger slice, which I have no intention of sharing."

He gave a lopsided grin. "In a roundabout way, these are thanks to Vice Admiral John Hunter."

They noticed a big chunk of the blue waxed cheese wheel was missing.

Perry teased the governor about it.

Lachlan grinned. "Yes, I took that. Trust me when I say you will not regret tasting this one. Jennifer is preparing to send the bulk of the batch back to Cornwall. I shall tell you a secret; King George the Fourth has requested a wheel and intends to grant a Royal Warrant."

Another round of gasps preceded the tasting.

Crispin finally entered into the conversation. "Lachlan, would it be possible to have a memorial service for John sometime? I know you may need to wait for an official notification from London, but I think I would like to have it in Sydney, not here. He chose the site of that church himself, and we measured it out the morning after Richard's church burned down. However, our church here in Parramatta is named after him, so it would be suitable, too."

His friend nodded. "I think that's a grand idea, Cris. After reading his letter, I would like you to do the eulogy. Are you up to that? You knew him better than any of us. We may have memorial services in both churches."

Crispin paused and looked at Helena. Her nod gave him the confidence to turn to the governor and say, "Yes, Lachlan, I think I am. However, Colin Osborne may wish to say some words as well. John mentored him years before we met. I shall ensure that everyone knows the wonderful work John achieved in the difficult situation he was placed into and how the colony benefited from his writings after he left here. The Admiralty had no choice but to believe him. Few here know that he was promoted to vice admiral before retiring. He would say to me, 'When life's billows toss you, turn and keep your eyes on God.' I have tried to do that."

Lachlan chuckled, then smiled. "The Osbornes were some of the first to receive Absolute Pardons from Arthur Phillip because of John's recommendations."

Crispin grinned, nodded, then said, "He was never averse to giving me a loving kick up the nether end when required, but I learned so much from him. So, yes, I shall be honoured to do his eulogy."

He reached out for Helena's hand. Her smile still made his heart jump with adoration. "It was John Hunter who brought us together. After a single meeting in London, he permitted me, a London lamplighter, to enlist. Then, he asked me to become one of his private guards on the journey out here. I treasured that honour, and I still do."

Mark Duffy looked at Lachlan and smiled. "I know that feeling, Cris."

Ned muttered something under his breath.

Perry said, "Speak up, Ned."

The blonde-haired soldier grinned. His dimples popped, and he said, "I arrived with a boatload of convicts. Imagine my surprise to find my old school mentor here. God knew I was alone, and I needed a friendly face. Perry was here waiting, and then the rest of you welcomed me. I was an inexperienced soldier, alone on this side of the ocean. God had already gone before me."

Ned grinned at Perry again. Then, he turned to his boss and said, "Sir, I need to remind you that you have a function tonight, so we must head off."

Lachlan nodded and moved to leave.

As the four men made their *adieus*, Cris and Helena stood on their verandah and bade them farewell.

The remainder of the cheese would be shared with Eric and Gillian later in the day.

Once the carriage was out of sight, Crispin turned to Helena and drew her into his arms. "I remember the day I found you, my sweet, Helena Bella. The church bells were ringing, and you were curled up on the step of my aunt's shop. I thought you were dead, and my heart skipped a beat."

He dropped a kiss on her lips before saying, "I brushed my fingers over your cheek and realised you were alive. My heart jumped with delight. You brought me to life that day. Over that week you were with us, my aunt saw how I was beginning to come out of the melancholy after my father died, which was why she told me to follow you. I was desperate to find you, so I promised her I would hunt high and low. I do not regret a moment of our wonderful life together. I just wanted you to know that."

Helena didn't answer but drew his head down for a long, lingering kiss that reached the very depths of his heart. He was the man she had always dreamed she would find, and he had chased her halfway around the globe. She adored him with her whole heart. She said, "The words 'I love you' are inadequate, Cris. But I do, I wholeheartedly do. We have much to thank both God and John Hunter for."

With Helena beside him, Cris hoped and prayed that life would be smooth sailing. They prayed nightly that there would be no sea billows for them. Not caring that their children were watching, Crispin drew Helena into his arms. Together, they would face the future with happy memories of days of old. They would keep the faith as John taught them and fight the fight for survival.

In loving memory of Governor John Hunter.
29 August 1737 – 13 March 1821
2nd Governor of Australia - 1795-1800

John Hunter by William Bennett, c.1812
National Library of Australia, 2272205

NB Penelope may not have been William and Eliza Kent's daughter, but she was John's niece. Unfortunately, I can find out little about her. She lived with him in Kent and later moved to Hackney and cared for him in his flat in London.

Historical Note:-

Governor Hunter was the first of the governors "The Exclusives" clashed with over the issue of alcohol. Eventually, an anonymous letter was sent to the Admiralty Head Office complaining of the Governor's corruption. However, nothing was further from the truth, and he was absolved of the charge after his return to London. Mutiny had already threatened, but London would not listen. John Hunter was promoted over the following years to Vice Admiral, but the damage had been done.

Following John Hunter, **Phillip Gidley King** became governor, and he, too, fell foul of the same group now known as 'the exclusives.'

Likewise, **Governor Bligh** was involved in a full-blown mutiny, which John Hunter had predicted would occur, but London refused to listen.

Bligh was followed by **Lachlan Macquarie**, who lasted twelve years before resigning, but he too had to face an enquiry on return home.

Thomas Brisbane was also recalled after about four years, as was **Ralph Darling**. Finally, **Major-General Sir Richard Bourke** took office and managed to overthrow the military courts and reinstate civilian government again. His term in office was not without problems, and yet he endeared himself to this same conniving group by declaring the infamous *'Terra nullis"* of our land. He reined in the punishments inflicted on the convicts and reestablished some of Macquarie's ideas. He was reported for sending convict women to Emu Plains to work as prostitutes, but again, these rumours were untrue. He had so many convict women transported and nowhere to house them. He, too, was exonerated.

I won't name the men involved in the backstabbing, but you only have to read Australia's official history to realise who they were. The transcription of these historical documents, which are available online, is slowly revealing these men's names. The governors who followed Bourke had similar issues.

The first rum still.

Robert and Thomas Webb were both crewmen on the First Fleet. Both intended to stay in the colony. Thomas returned to England with Captain Hunter in 1791, and he returned a year or so later with 'goods in kind' instead of the pay they were owed. They were each given land grants, which they farmed. One of the items Thomas brought to New South Wales was a small spirit still imported into the colony. I am presuming that some sort of metal tubing was also available, or else other stills would not have been able to be built. Using this alcohol still as a design, larger ones were soon made, and the brewing and distilling of illicit liquors was quickly a significant problem. A core group of the NSW Corps soon found that the sale and distribution of this illicit spirit brought in much money for themselves.

Characters

Captain/Governor **John Hunter**, b 1737 RN. Governor - 11 Sept 1795 to 27 Sept 1800
Linus Rosedale b 1747 d Aug 1811
m 1773 **Agnes** Armstrong b 1750
Children 15
  1 Gerald (**Gerry**) granted 50 acres - (100 acres shared with Jem)
  2 Jeramy (**Jem**) 23 *Twins M Colleen and Erin* granted 50 acres
  3 **Helena Rosedale (20)** b 1778 - convict on the *Surprize* 1795 (aged 20) granted 40 acres
  (parents Linus and Agnes Rosedale - 14+ siblings) - Arrives in May 1798 on *Barwell*
  M 1795 Private **Crispin Milroy**, b 1772 Mrs Milroy's nephew & soldier in Gov Hunter's
  security detail. *Father, Henry, died in 1792, Aunt in 1793*
      Children 11 (10 living)
      1 Miscarriage -Jesse - Jan 1796
      2 **Jasper** Linus Crispin 3rd Sept 1797   - called John "Guddonor & Captain John"
      3 Jillian Judith (**Judy**) Jan 1799
      4 **John** Henry 29th Aug 1800
      5 Jennifer Agnes 1802
      6 Julien Eric twin 11 June 1804
      7 Janette Elizabeth, twin 11 June 1804FZ
      8 Janice Helen (**Nell**) 11 June 1805
      9 Jonas William 26 Aug 1806
      10 Joanie Constance Feb 1807
      11 Jeramy James Rosedale Milroy, 5th Feb 1808
  4 **Mary** 18 m 3/11/99 **Jonas Thistlethwaite** granted 40 acres
  5 Phoebe 16 m 3/11/99 **Arnold** Kerr granted 40 acres
  6 Nicholas 14 b 1783 eng to a convict girl m Rachel 3 children
  7 Tristan 13 b 1784 eng to a convict girl m Rebekah (Bek) 3 children
  8 Margaret b 86 eng to a soldier, **Harry** (m 1809)
  9 Patience b 88 eng to a soldier, **Algernon Darnley** (m 1809)
  10 **Victoria** b 89 m **Bill** Felton b - George Ellis' friend - retired soldier.
  11 **Katherine** b 91 m **Benjamin** Parker, a saddler on Castlereagh Road, Penrith
  12 **Charlotte** 1793 m **George** Ellis, a tanner & leatherworker, Parramatta (See *Sadlers Song*)
  13 Emily b 1794
  14 Rebecca b 1797
  15 Samantha b April 1798 - youngest died in Dec 1798
Reverend Winchester-Graham Linus's minister in England
Mrs Mildred Milroy - *Domestic Bureau owner*
Gillian Thomas - *Gov Hunter's convict maid,* arrived on the *Boddingtons*
m 1797 **Eric** Bellchambers -Easter - *Crispin's friend arrived on Reliance* with Gov John.
     1 **Caris** b Jan 1798
     2 **Ellen** b March 1800
     3 **John** Eric b May 1801
Mrs **Virginia Cowdrey** - *Gov Hunter's housekeeper - later at Gracemere Castle in Kent.*
Mrs **Priscilla Peach** - *Gov house cook later at Gracemere Castle in Kent.*
Ensign **Jonas Thistlethwaite** *arrived on Barwell May 1798 (Father William Earl of Brightwell,*
Uncle, Charles Phillimont) m **Mary** Rosedale
Arnold Kerr soldiers arrived *Barwell* with Rosedale's m **Phoebe** Rosedale
Travis Garvin soldiers arrived *Barwell* with Rosedale's granted 40 acres - sold to Jonas.
Colin Osborne b 1766 (arrested in 1886 & Transported on the *Charlotte)*
m 1788 Agnes (**Aggie**) Gibbs b 1773
     1 Audrey - miscarriage 5 months 1789
     2 John (**Jonny**) Warren Osborne b Feb 1790
     3 Christine Deidre b June 1793
     4 Helena Agnes b 7th November 1794 twin
     5 William John b 7th November 1794 twin
     6 Constance Marie b in early 1796
     7 Crispin Colin b Oct 1798
Nigel and Connie Bray (nee Waterson)
William (**Wil**) Waterson m Deborah Drummond. (Did/Deb)

Real People

Governor Arthur Phillip

Governor John Hunter b 1737 to William and Helen Hunter.

 Royal Navy *Governor of NSW* -11 Sept 1795 to 27 Sept 1800 *2nd*
John's siblings are William, George, James, Archie, Sarah Mary m Kent, Agnes, Janet, and Margaret.
William Balmain, the doctor who *replaced John White as surgeon in the colony.*

D'Arcy Wentworth, *Assistant to William Balmain as Doctor*

Rev Richard Johnson and Mary, children:- Milbah and Henry (Harry)

Abaroo/Boorong, in 1789 she was 10-15, & a survivor of smallpox. Later married Bennelong.

Bennelong - travelled to London with Gov. Arthur Phillip. He returned with Gov Hunter.

Bennelong's sisters, Benelàng, Munanguri, Wurrgan, Warreweer, Carangarang

Rev Marsden - Richard Johnson's assistant.

Nathaniel Franklyn

Richard Dore, Died December 1800

Phillip Gidley King d a year after returning to England in 1808

Major Francis Grose, d 1814 (a month after 2nd marriage)
 m1 Fanny d 1813   m 2 Elizabeth Paterson 1814

Lieutenant Colonial William Paterson d pre 1814 M Elizabeth

acting Lieutenant-Governor Joseph Foveaux from 1800 on Norfolk Island.

Major Robert Ross

Captain-Lieutenant George Johnston

Sergeant John Sutherland, Corporal Michael Marlborough and Private William Wilford

Bernard De Maliez - Arthur Phillip's French chef. Died 7 August 1789

Major Morrisett

John and Elizabeth Macarthur

George Johnson,

Thomas and Robert Webb

Thomas and Mary Rieby/Raby

James Underwood - convict, brewer and coal merchant

Five Scottish Martyrs arrived on *Surprize* in Nov 1795:- Joseph Gerrard, Thomas Muir, Thomas Palmer, William Skirving and Maurice Margarot.

Three Free settler families - Bowman, McDougall and Smith are all real, as are their skills.

John Baughan built the first treadmill flour mill in Sydney. *John Macarthur's soldiers burned it down.*

James Wilkinson built 2nd treadmill in Sydney - it failed quickly.

<u>Mutineers on the Barwell.</u> George Bond, John Murray, William Hallam, Gregory Belloe, James Nevil, Patrick Welch, John Brown, John Broadbent and Ensign Bayley

HMS Reliance - the ship that brought John Hunter to Australia
Reliance was the first ship to chart the Islands in March 1800. *Reliance* was relegated to harbour service that year, surviving for another 15 years before being sold on 12 October 1815.
Governor John Hunter departed on the *Buffalo* - departed Sept 28th 1800

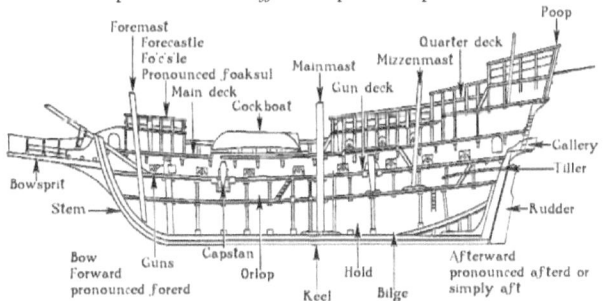

Bibliography

Captain John Hunter Bio
https://adb.anu.edu.au/biography/hunter-john-2213
An Historical Journal of the Transactions at Port Jackson and Norfolk Island
Extract of language from Lieutenant Gidley King's section of the Norfolk Island Journal
https://gutenberg.net.au/ebooks/e00063.html (Language dictionary)
Journals of the First Fleet
https://en.wikipedia.org/wiki/Journals_of_the_First_Fleet
https://collection.sl.nsw.gov.au/record/TN_cdi_proquest_miscellaneous_761031429
John Hunter's Book, vol 1
https://gutenberg.net.au/ebooks/e00063.html
Governors of NSW
https://www.parliament.nsw.gov.au/about/Pages/A-List-of-Governors-of-New-South-Wales.aspx
Gov Hunter's nephew for sale list
https://www.portrait.gov.au/aboutface/2015/05/goods-and-chattels
Bennelong
https://en.wikipedia.org/wiki/Bennelong
The *Surprize*
https://www.freesettlerorfelon.com/convict_ship_surprise_1794.htm
Rev Richard Johnson
https://adb.anu.edu.au/biography/johnson-richard-2275
https://acl.asn.au/resources/richard-johnson-first-chaplain-to-australia/
Ship Departures from Sydney
http://www.ozships.net/ozships/
Thomas & Robert Webb
https://sharpefamilyoffice.com.au/sydney-rum
https://peopleaustralia.anu.edu.au/biography/webb-robert-29848
Webb land grants:- https://peopleaustralia.anu.edu.au/entity/12456?pid=29848
Thomas' death:- https://www.wikitree.com/wiki/Webb-14302
Francis Grose
https://en.wikipedia.org/wiki/Francis_Grose_(British_Army_officer)
https://adb.anu.edu.au/biography/grose-francis-2130
Andrew Thompson
https://en.wikipedia.org/wiki/Andrew_Thompson_(convict,_magistrate)
Phillip Gidley King
https://en.wikipedia.org/wiki/Philip_Gidley_King
First Government House Sydney
https://en.wikipedia.org/wiki/First_Government_House,_Sydney
William Balmain
https://www.visitsydneyaustralia.com.au/william-balmain.html#:~:text=In%20May%201797%2C%20following%20White%27s,entire%20population%20arduous%20and%20frustrating.
John Baughan
https://adb.anu.edu.au/biography/baughan-john-1755
St Phillip's Fire 1 October 1798
http://storage.cloversites.com/stphilipsyorkstreetanglican/documents/A%20History%20of%20St%20Philips_3.pdf
St Phillip's burns down 1/10/1789
https://nla.gov.au/nla.obj-39572890/view?partId=nla.obj-39573902#page/n10/mode/1up
https://nla.gov.au/nla.obj-39572890/view?partId=nla.obj-39573803#page/n9/mode/1up
Colonial Secretary Changes
John Cobly volume 5, 1795-1800 p 272 (Problems with Dore extolling his own virtues)
Many other references.
Nathaniel Franklyn's demise (Chapter 8)
AN ACCOUNT OF THE ENGLISH COLONY IN NEW SOUTH WALES: by David Collins
https://gutenberg.net.au/ebooks/e00011.html
Richard Dore
https://en.wikipedia.org/wiki/Richard_Dore
Darug Dictionary & words
https://dharug.dalang.com.au/language/dictionary?query=duck&type=English&numeric=Exact&dialect=All#
https://www.timeout.com/sydney/things-to-do/10-darug-words-and-their-meanings
Gov Hunter's book, printed 1802
Remarks on the Causes of the Colonial Expense of the Establishment of New South Wales. Hints for the Reduction of Such Expense and for Reforming the Prevailing Abuses
Phillip Gidley King
https://www.ruleoflaw.org.au/education/australian-colonies/governors/philip-gidley-king/
John Cobley - Vol 5 1795-1800
Hard copy edition. ISBN 0207150842

First Fleet Convict Era Trilogy 1788-1800
Gentle Annie Soames

Her dreams lead to unexpected outcomes. An Australian First Fleet story.
A First Fleet story with the descriptions taken directly from the Journal of Doctor Arthur Bowes Smith was the doctor on board the Lady Penrhyn.

Annie Soames is a girl beloved by the community but not afraid to voice her desires. That leads to trouble, illicit love, and a world turned upside down.

Oliver Quilpie, the newly married Marquess, finds his arranged marriage unsatisfactory; he is irresistibly drawn to his wife's companion. Unfortunately, he can't keep his hands off her. In retaliation, Annie copies his every move while riding, dressed as a highwayman. However, she has now fallen in love with him. This ultimately leads to her arrest and banishment to a distant land. After some years, Oliver's wife dies, and his thoughts turn to Annie. He seeks to find her, but she has vanished. He is horrified to discover she was transported to New South Wales as a convict on the *Lady Penrhyn*. Will Annie want to see him?

ISBN 9780645441574   ISBN ebook 9781923097063   LP ISBN 978-1923097346
HC 9798244028607   Draft To Digital 9798233855122
Long-listed in the Historical Fiction Company Competition 2024

The Emancipated Potter

Sydney Cove 1788 to Parramatta 1795
Not all felons are convicts, and not all convicts are felons.

Colin Osborne's serene life as a talented potter is crushed by a self-important peer. A single punch sends Colin across to the other side of the globe. Aggie Gibbs is a young convict girl being hunted by a wayward soldier. The two find themselves in a town of criminals and lecherous men. Captain John Hunter is Colin's mentor, and he paves the way for a new life for his young friends. Then disaster strikes, and he must leave.

Can Colin keep Aggie safe? Will they fulfil Captain Hunter's wishes to build a decent life for the convicts destined to live out their lives in the penal town? Will John ever return to New South Wales?   Paperback ISBN 9781923097476   ISBN ebook 9781923097483
Large Print 9781923097506   HC 9798251872569   D2D ebook 9798233212536

Paternity Unknown

Sydney 1788 - 1800 The Aftermath of the First Fleet landing.
Can forgiveness be that easy?

Connie Waterson is traumatised after she became one of the victims of the attack when the convict women were landed on February 6th, 1788. She finds herself expecting an unwanted child. Along with her friends, she must learn to cope with the challenges of their new environment while protecting the life growing within her.

Nigel Bray is a young convict who almost instantly regrets his carnal actions on the day the prisoners from the *Lady Penrhyn* landed. Knowing that Connie is the unwilling recipient of his base desires, Nigel does what he can to ease her path. He is racked with questions: is the child his? Will she ever forgive him? What must Nigel do to win Connie's trust?

ISBN 9781923097438   ISBN ebook 9781923097445   LP ISBN 978-1923097452
HC 9798251874877 D2D 9798232509286

The Hunter to Macquarie Collection 1795-1822
When Upon Life's Billows

Sydney 1795-1821 - Governor John Hunter
Keep your friends close, and your enemies closer.

John Hunter loved his life at sea. The wind blows where no man knows, and John is caught in a storm. His ship, the *HMS Sirius,* was wrecked in 1790. Five years later, he became the second governor of the rough and filthy penal settlement of New South Wales. From a place he once loved, he now seems to be in the wrong place at the wrong time, trusting the wrong people. Helena Rosedale is not your typical female convict. She fiercely battles to prevent the men from abusing her, earning her the nickname *"Helena the Hellkat."*

Crispin Milroy, alone in the world, serves on the new governor's security detail. Can he win the fair lady's heart? Life in 1795 in Sydney Cove was harsh at best. Food is scarce, and disease often ravages the settlement. Life throws everything at these three, yet somehow, they manage to survive. Why does John trust this young couple when others betray him? What trials must Helena and Crispin endure to make their new lives in this unforgiving town bearable? How can John ease their path?

Paperback ISBN: 9780645783339   ebook ISBN: 9780645783346 Large Print 9781923097513
HC 9798251492620   D2D ebook 9798233358807

The Saddler's Song

London 1790s to Parramatta 1840s
The Strains of Starting Again.

George Ellis is the son of a tanner, living on the outskirts of London. Alone and hurting after a disease takes his family, he seeks a new life, setting up a business in New South Wales. His beloved violin is his most treasured possession, and his talent for making music is hidden from all but a select few.

Ben Parker, a saddler, is also heading to the colony. Combining their skills to start afresh in a new world, the young men find accommodation with a family. Two of the daughters steal their hearts — but how will the business survive in a stock-starved land where access to leather is limited? What is the saddler's song, and why is it so special?

Paperback ISBN: 9780645783353   eISBN: 9780645783360   Large Print 9780645783377
HC 979825105238   D2D ebook 9798233262449

Tuppence to Pass

London 1800s to Parramatta 1820s
An Unlikely Partnership

Josh Callan never expected much from life—just enough to get by in the gritty backstreets of London. But when he's caught stealing from the very man who murdered his father, Josh finds himself branded worthless by a sneering judge and sentenced to a distant, brutal world: the penal colony of Sydney.

Arriving just as Governor Lachlan Macquarie takes charge, Josh steps into a colony on the cusp of change—and into opportunities he never dreamed possible. As he earns the respect of the powerful governor and becomes a trusted confidante, Josh begins to forge a new path not just for himself, but also for his family and his beloved.

Can a boy dismissed as nothing rise to become something more? And what will his unexpected friendship with the governor cost or gain him in the end?

paperback ISBN : 9781923097070   eISBN: 9781923097087   LP 9781923097544
HC 979825188088   D2D ebook 9798233190605

His Majesty's Pageboy

London to Emu Plains, Australia, in the 1800s

Jack Turner, raised in privilege and known as Lord John. However, at age nine, his true identity is revealed. He struggles with society's immorality and shallowness. He finally meets a pure young woman he feels he could love, but because of his chequered background, he is unable to pursue her. Then, his life takes another turn.

Martha Alexander, daughter of a wealthy shipping merchant, met Lord John while at a society ball in London. She is expected to marry well, and she has feelings for John. But her father's drunkenness led to the loss of everything he owned, including Martha, dooming her to a forced marriage. How do these two young people end up as convicts in Australia?

Paperback ISBN 9781923097308   ebook ISBN 9781923097292   LP 9781923097568
HC 9798251886504   D2D ebook 9798233639654

A Fist Full of Holey Dollars

Sydney Cove 1810+
The Holey Dollar and Dump Story

Captain Rudi Greenwood is a solitary man trapped in a job without purpose, in a land where alcohol is the currency and rules are frequently ignored in pursuit of wealth. Rudi's life spins out of control. Will he listen to the minister and turn his life around?

Bethany Edwards is a grieving widow expecting her late husband's child. Rudi's attraction to the lovely widow compels him to reassess his views and contemplate someone new. She seeks Rudi's help and support, but is that all she truly feels? Will he take Reverend Cowper's advice?

When Governor Lachlan Macquarie asks Rudi for help improving the roads, a casual remark alters Rudi's life and affects the entire colony. To tackle the alcohol issue, he proposes creating a new currency. With Bethany by his side, will he rise to the governor's challenges? What actions led to him being despised by the exclusives and free settlers in the colony?

Paperback ISBN 9781923097407   eISBN 9781923097414 Large Print 9781923097537
HC 9798251884937D2D ebook 9798233057052

Far From the Whispering Sheoaks
Set in Australia in 1817+

Fanny Little was in the wrong place doing something she thought was legal. Her actions led to her arrest, trial, and banishment. She was assigned from the female prison to ex-soldier Gordon McKenzie and soon found herself in the despicable and humiliating situation of being sold in the public marketplace. Phil Bentley is a man running from his jealous uncle. He is seeking safety on a secluded farm half a world away. With the community backing them, can Phil save Fanny from Gordon's vile abuse? Why is their relationship destined to spark controversy? And who is Jas? Why does Gordon wish to harm the child? Will they ever escape the shadows pursuing them? Paperback ISBN 9781923097315 eISBN9781923097322 Large Print 9781923097575 HC 9798251893915

Quest for Survival
Sydney 1798-1810 - Between the Governors

Nell Bywater intentionally gets herself arrested after hearing that convicts receive free food and clothing. As a twelve-year-old foundling, life is hard. Her options are few, and most of them are distasteful. She is assigned to Governor Hunter's nephew as a nursemaid for his small children. Then the Kents leave, and she is left alone in an almost empty house.
Aubrey Grey is a young convict assigned to convert the Kents' old house into a new girls' orphanage. There, he meets Nell. Governor and Mrs King oversee the new girls' orphanage, as well as Nell. Mrs King ensures Nell is kept safe, with Aubrey assigned as her caretaker.
As houseparents to more than thirty young girls, both find the security they have sought. However, there is more to life than a roof over your head and food in your belly. What begins as a simple assignment becomes life-changing for both of them when love intervenes.
Coming 2026/7

Bound Down in Iron Chains
An Australian Historical Tale, set in the Boys' Orphanage in Sydney in 1818+
Smuggling, Rum and Ructions
A gripping tale of betrayal, courage, and survival in colonial Australia.

When honest London bookkeeper Howard Marlow is wrongly convicted and sent to New South Wales, he's assigned to the Sydney Boys' Orphanage, where corruption runs deep and the accounts don't add up. There he meets Naomi Buckingham, a convict girl hoping for safety—but facing danger instead. As the two uncover coded ledgers and a smuggling ring tied to the colony's elite, they must risk everything to expose the truth. In a brutal world built on power and fear, can two convicts bring justice to those who have none?
Paperback ISBN 9781923097353 eISBN9781923097360 LP 9781923097551 HC 9798251894677
Coming 2026

Bound Down in Iron Chains
An Australian Historical Tale, set in the Boys' Orphanage in Sydney in 1818+
Smuggling, Rum and Ructions
A gripping tale of betrayal, courage, and survival in colonial Australia.

When honest London bookkeeper **Howard Marlow** is wrongly convicted and sent to New South Wales, he's assigned to the Sydney Boys' Orphanage, where corruption runs deep, and the accounts don't add up. There he meets **Naomi Buckingham**, a convict girl hoping for safety—but facing danger instead. As the two uncover coded ledgers and a smuggling ring tied to the colony's elite, they must risk everything to expose the truth. In a brutal world built on power and fear, can two convicts bring justice to those who have none?
Paperback ISBN 9781923097353 eISBN9781923097360
Coming 2026/7

Buddy's Promise
From the Shadows of London to the shade of the gumtrees

Raised on the streets of London, **Obadiah "Buddy" Jensen** hides a fierce loyalty behind a tough facade. When a dying boy begs him to protect his little sister, **Emily Bolt**, Buddy vows to keep her safe—never expecting she'll become the love he can't have.
Exiled to Australia as a convict, Buddy builds a new life, but when Emily reappears years later, everything has changed. He is married with a child.
She was six when he found her. She was lost when he left. Torn between past promises and present choices, can they find their way back to each other—or will fate keep them apart forever? An emotional historical romance of love, loss, and redemption across the seas.
ISBN 9780645783384 eISBN 9780645783391
Coming 2027

Linen Shirts Aplenty
The first female factory, Parramatta, in the early 1800s.

Biddy Murphy is an Irish girl who caught the eye of an upstart English peer. Convicted and transported as a wanton, she must face the shame of her fallen status.

Major Geoffrey Gilmore is the convict assignment officer in Sydney. His heart goes out to this beautiful but very skilled girl. Can Geoff ease her lot in life, or will their positions in the colony keep them apart? Will the hatred of the Irish mean that Geoff's attraction to this lovely girl be doomed before he can rescue her?

Coming 2027

Unlikely Convict Ladies Trilogy 1792-1840s

Dancing to Her Own Tune
Co-authored by Sheila Hunter and Sara Powter
Sydney 1790s to England 1830s

Annie White is released after serving seven years as a convict in Sydney. She has a visitor who helps her start a baking business. Annie is then asked to assist another ailing man, Sam Corbett. She nurses him back to health, and a relationship blossoms between them. They settle into a life together, barely making ends meet, when she realises she's expecting a child. Sam's past is laid bare, and he must come to terms with the revelations. They both must confront their accusers and discover that the answers to their questions are not what they anticipated. Their life experiences seem to cling to them, and, unable to shake them off, they end up back in England. They must face their ghosts and recognise they are not who they think they are. How can they transform their anger and spite into love and forgiveness? The Dance of Life goes on.

Paperback ISBN 9780645110715   ISBN9780645110722
Large Print 9781923097209 HC 9798763014136 D2D ebook 9798233565748
Long-listed for the Historical Fiction Company Competition 2022

Amelia's Tears
Parramatta 1828 – England 1840s
From Tears of Sadness to Tears of Joy.

Amelia Westaweller awaits her assignment in the Parramatta Female Prison. Forced to leave the relative safety of gaol, she is assigned and now faces her worst nightmare. A foul man claims her and makes her life a living hell. Then, her world goes black. A glimmer of hope arises when she hears from her brother, Jim, who has enlisted a friend to help her. She writes to Jim, pouring out her heart and telling him of the horrors of her new life. He encourages her to stay firm in her faith. All she can do is pray. When Major Ned Grace, her brother's friend, enters her life in Parramatta, he starts to ease her path. Things have changed, as now she has a child in tow. How can Amelia forge a new life for herself? What man could want her with her background and a child at her side? Who is the gentleman who turns her tears of sadness into tears of great joy?

Paperback ISBN: 9780645110739   eISBN: 9780645110746 HC ISBN 9798420617953
Large Print 9781923097216 D2D 9798232247898

A Lady in Irons
England 1800s - Parramatta 1808+

Katy Harrington is mourning the death of her husband after he died in a shooting accident. Barely coping, she awaits the birth of their child. If it's a girl, she must hand the family home to her husband's brother. The day after giving birth to a daughter, she and her daughter are left on the side of a road. She collapses and is found by someone she thought had died in a fire ten years before. Perry White, badly scarred himself, nurses her back to health. They marry and move in with her widowed friend, Mary.

After some years, she discovers her husband and friend in each other's arms. Now living in a love triangle, she flees. Grasping the only straw available, she intentionally gets arrested and is sent to a colony far away. By doing this, her marriage can be annulled.

What happens in the Colony is different from what she expects. Governor Macquarie comes to her rescue, but what of Perry and her children?

Paperback ISBN: 9780645110784   eISBN:9780645441505
Large Print 9781923097223   HC 9798358108141   D2D ebook 9798233855122

The Convict Birthstain Collection 1820-1840s

No More, My Love
Hunter Valley, NSW, 1820s

Jess Elkin is distraught when tragedy ravages her family. Now widowed, she becomes the victim of a carriage accident and is nursed back to health by the driver.

Marcus Ryan, a hard-headed woollen mill owner, was not expecting to fall in love. Yet, when Jess's fortunes suddenly turn for the worse, Marcus must decide how far he will go to pursue her. Years after following her to Newcastle, Australia, Marcus vanishes. Jess is left wondering if he will keep his promise to return to her… Will she ever see him again?

Paperback ISBN: 9780645441536   eISBN 9780645441581

Large Print 9781923097230   D2D ebook 9798233092381

Long-listed in the Historical Fiction Company Competition 2023

The Vine Weaver
Hawkesbury River area 1820s+
New Beginnings and Old Threats

In the 1820s, Joel and Hetty Walker lived on a secluded farm on the Hawkesbury River, which became a haven for the protection of young convict women. A series of events brings Fran Rea to Hetty's attention, and she is taken to the farm. Fran and Hetty develop a cottage industry under the compassionate eye of farmhand Hector Macdougal; Hector's loving words change lives. It is to him that Fran turns when threatened.

The vines now must draw them close to survive the future revelations, and of those, there are many. Paperback ISBN: 9780645441512   eISBN: 9780645441529 Large Print 9781923097247   D2D ebook 9798233189494

Long-listed in the Historical Fiction Company Competition 2023

The story continues in "Scotch at The Rocks"…

Scotch at The Rocks
Glasgow, Scotland, early 1800s to The Rocks, Sydney 1830s

Orphaned children Brodie Stewart and Heather Anderson live on Glasgow's streets. Although hungry, they somehow manage to survive and stay out of trouble. Heather finds a job and looks to be settled; things go pear-shaped for them both. Eventually, they marry by declaration, but even that gets complicated, and they are both arrested soon after exchanging their vows. In 1838, they were transported to Sydney as convicts. Heather arrives within weeks of Brodie, and they are assigned close to each other. They are now living in the docklands of Sydney, known as The Rocks. They now have to forge a new life halfway across the world from their homeland.

Adventures abound, and Brodie gets press-ganged. While he's away, Heather's life changes and soon, she's officially selling Scotch Whisky at a shop in The Rocks.

You can take a Scot out of Scotland, but where did the Scotch come from?

paperback ISBN 9780645441550 ebook 9781923097001 Large Print 9781923097254

Large Print 97810645783377   D2D ebook 9798232122638

Waiting at the Sliprails
The Bathurst Road 1830s
A Convict's Tale

Bea Dawes's term of conviction nears an end, and she has few options other than marriage to a stranger or going on the street.

Jack Barnes, the hired drover, wants a wife. Bea accepts his offer; then, she discovers that he could be gone for months, leaving her alone with Billy and Netty, part of the tribe of an Aboriginal tribe who live on his secluded farm. Bea learns to love her husband and also this wonderful Aboriginal couple. Drought ravages the farm, and Jack must hit the long paddock with the flock. In his absence, a visitor arrives, threatening to destroy everything she has worked so hard for. Can Bea touch her heart? Can she cope? Will the drought ever end? And when will Jack return?

Paperback ISBN: 9780645441543   eISBN 9781923097032

Large Print 9781923097261   D2D ebook 9798233711145

PenCraft Award Winner for Literary Excellence, Christian Historical Fiction 2024

Convict Shadows of the Past
Two Jennifers, two hundred years apart
The colonial history of cheese in Australia

When she discovers her convict family history, eight-year-old Jenny Kellow learns that she was named after a convict from nearly two hundred years ago. Inspired by her grandfather's stories, she delves into her ancestors' convict past. From him, she hears tales of bushrangers, convicts, and life in the early colony of Parramatta. She embarks on a journey to retrace the footsteps of her convict great-great-great-grandmother to honour her. Jenny's quest begins with microfiche in the 1960s, when she discovers a small tin-mining town in Cornwall and the production of a cheese that set London alight. She uncovers that her ancestor, Jennifer Kellow, brought her cheese-making skills to Parramatta, where she taught others the craft. Echoes of the past can still be heard if you know where to listen. Who was the first Jennifer, and what does she have to do with cheese? Why is she so elusive? Did Jenny's ancestor, Jennifer, ever see those two small crosses carved into the bricks of the Female Factory? Would Jenny ever uncover her ancestor's story?   Paperback ISBN: 9780645783315
ISBN ebook 9780645783322   Large Print 9781923097278   D2D ebook 9798233906411

In Defence of Her Honour
London 1800s to Parramatta 1819
Will the real man of quality please stand up?

Bill Miller was raised and educated alongside the family's sons. The youngest, Bert Edison-Browne, had been his best friend. However, jealousy intervenes when Bill's excellent schoolwork begins to curtail their friendship. He wins a scholarship and enters Oxford University. When Bill's father dies unexpectedly, Bert insists that Bill take over as butler, but it's more to oppress him. Bert's jealousy grows and festers. He is now looking for a way to rid themselves of their new butler. A ruckus ensues, and Bill is arrested for assaulting Bert.

Molly Ross, the housekeeper's daughter, will vouch for him. It's too late; Bill has been arrested and is soon to be sentenced and transported. With Bill gone, Molly now fights to defend herself from Bert. After hitting him with a pan, she, too, is arrested and sent to Sydney. Bill and Molly arrive with letters of introduction and compensation from Bert's father. Soon, they will be running the best inn in Parramatta with an endorsement from the governor.
Paperback ISBN 9780645441567   ISBN ebook 9781923097049
Large Print 9781923097339   D2D ebook 9798233129810
Long-listed in the Historical Fiction Company Competition 2024

I Can't Stop Tomorrow
Irish Famine 1840s to Avoca Beach, Australia

Escaping bigotry and prejudice in Ireland, the O'Shane family lives on a secluded farm on the west coast of Ireland. The potato blight soon decimated their farm. It's always darkest before dawn, and the two remaining girls cling to the hope of a new life. With the kindness of strangers, the eldest girls, Clare and Kerry O'Shane, head to their cousin, Sal Lockley, in Parramatta, Australia.   A new, wonderful life awaits them both. Shéamus Connor is the annoying teenage boy who reluctantly draws Clare's affection. However, living in a convict town means ruffians abound. John Moore is a bad-tempered and troubled Irishman who is content to live alone on another secluded farm until he discovers Clare and two other lads need rescuing. Can John protect her from the pain inflicted by an evil world? Can Shéamus find his lost love, who has fled?   Paperback ISBN: 9780645441598   ISBN ebook 9781923097056   Large Print 9781923097421   D2D ebook 9798233594632

Madeline's Boy
England 1830s to New South Wales 1840
The race to protect an Orphaned Boy
All is not straightforward when money and titles are involved.

Orphaned, afraid and on the run, Chip must flee. Madeline was his mother's best friend. Maddie now needs to keep her charge safe and alive. She must give up her life to protect the boy she has loved since birth. Months after Chip's parents' demise, Maddie sets out to deliver Chip to his Uncle Humphrey, who lives in Sydney. Through him, she meets Chip's uncle's friend, Tim, who falls for Maddie. but will they find happiness? The menacing presence soon finds Chip, and Maddie needs to hide him again. They are relocated from hidden farms to secret valleys, ultimately ending up in an Aboriginal encampment. Can Tim find a way to be with Maddie? And if so... Will Chip ever be safe?   paperback ISBN: 9780645783308
ISBN ebook 9781923097094 Large Print 9781923097469 D2D ebook 9798233351396
Long-listed in the Historical Fiction Company Competition 2024

Jam or Marmalade for Tea

England 1820s to New South Wales 1825 (Governor Brisbane Era)

Martha Hamilton is the eldest of four orphans struggling to survive on their own. She is caught stealing, tried, convicted, and transported to New South Wales. With her family gone, she becomes despondent. Life holds no meaning for her, and the ocean waves look inviting. Captain Guy Manning is a frustrated and injured redcoat soldier returning to Sydney for a new assignment. He notices Martha trying to jump overboard and rescues her. How do two cats bring them together? A convict ship is no place for romance, and she's far too young anyway, isn't she? Can Guy save her and forge a life together for them? What connections does he have to try to save her siblings? Why is marmalade important for their future?

Paperback ISBN 9781923097933   eISBN9781923097285
Large Print 9781923097490   D2D ebook 9798224495825
A NaNoWriMo 2023 book winner

A prequel to 'The Lockleys Parramatta' series
Unshackled Lives
Set in England &Australia in the 1800s
Australian historical fiction of early colonial days

Ned Lockley's childhood was a dream, but his adulthood is becoming a nightmare. Following a whirlwind romance that ends in bitter treachery, Ned finds himself adrift in a society collapsing under its own immorality. With his family ties fraying, Ned flees England to preserve his soul and his faith.

The colony of New South Wales is no paradise. Now known as Ned Grace, he is tasked with the gruelling work of placing female convicts, Ned is thrust into a world of grit and shadows. As he struggles to find his footing, he must unravel a dangerous mystery: Who is Charles, and what does he mean for Ned's future?   Print ISBN 9781923097377

eISBN 9781923097384 LP ISBN: 9781923097391   D2D ebook 9798232096021

A 100-year, six-part Australian Colonial series
The Lockleys of Parramatta 1800-1900
Hands upon the Anvil
A blacksmith's life and love are more than work
Parramatta 1830s

Eddie Lockley's parents were transported for their crimes. Can a steadfast lad rise above his origins and guide others to succeed in a land of opportunity?

Ten-year-old Eddie longs to help his mum and dad. Living in a convict town with his family, the keen youngster has been working with the local blacksmith since his sixth birthday. But when a lieutenant doesn't stop abusing his older brother, the young boy yearns for the day when he can stand up and end the torment. Though he's thrilled when his mentor offers to send him off to learn his letters, Eddie fears he won't be around to watch his siblings' backs. But as he takes on the biggest adventure of his life, the brave believer soon discovers that God is looking out for everyone he loves. Does this young man in the making have what it takes to change everything for the better?

paperback ISBN 9780994578235   Ebook ISBN 978-0-9945782-5-9 HC 9798496177368
Large Print 9781923097148   D2D ebook 9798232476335

Out Where The Brolgas Dance
Gold is found, and so is love
Parramatta 1840s
How can a question change so many people?

It's the 1840s, and discoveries across the Blue Mountains continue. Major Mitchell's new road is complete, and towns are planned and being built. Abundant land is available for those who want it. Eighteen-year-old William "Wills" Lockley has laid a solid foundation for a respectable career as a blacksmith, but the Lockley lust for adventure flows deeply within his veins. He dreads the monotony of work at the blacksmith's forge and yearns for adventure in a new frontier. Wills meets six Englishmen (_Coping with what is now known as PTSD_) who have the means to make his dreams come true. What they discover changes the Colony and their lives forever. Gold fever ensues. While in the West, Wills must deal with an uncertain romance. Does Cathy even want him?

ISBN 9780994578242 Ebook ISBN 978-0-9945782-6-6 HC ISBN 9798755445504
LP ISBN 9781923097155   D2D ebook 9798233188794

Diamonds in the Dirt

Diamonds, love and money… but there is much more to life.

Parramatta 1850s

The youngest Lockley son, Luke Lockley, has completed his university education, and his life lacks direction. No job, no money, and no love. Desperately alone, he prays for guidance. How can Luke trust that God has a plan for him if he can't even find a job? He does the only thing he can … he prays. Within a week, life has changed … oh, how it has changed as his brother Wills turns up with a suggestion. Would Luke be interested in joining the expedition with John Evans? Reverend William Clarke needs assistance with a government mineral survey. The challenges, adventures and finds are life-changing for many. However, it gives Luke meaning, purpose and direction. The condition of his heart problems also takes a turn. Can he walk away? Will she wait for him?

Paperback ISBN: 9780994578273 Ebook ISBN: 978-0-9945782-8-0

HC ISBN 979-8788011141 LP 9781923097162 D2D ebook 9798233366239

The Earl's Shadow

Who or what is the 'shadow'? How does it affect so many?

Parramatta 1860s

Charles Lockley, the Earl of Coxheath, spent his youth as a convict in Parramatta, unaware of his noble birth, with limited education and few social skills. Now, after a near-death experience, Charles must decide how to live the rest of his life. He is thrust out of his comfort zone in London. There, Charles discovers his purpose. He delivers a speech in parliament—an action that will reshape the empire. His eldest son, Charlie, shares many of his father's shortcomings. However, the past continues to haunt Charlie.

But how does Jim Leslie, the Cobb and Co. coach driver, fit into their story? And what exactly is 'The Earl's Shadow' that he mentions?

Paperback ISBN: 9780645110708 Ebook ISBN 978-0-9945782-9-7

Large Print 9781923097179 HC 9798836057053 D2D ebook 9798233679209

Once a Jolly Swagman

An old black Billy Can contains the secrets of an incredible life

An Australian Historical Novel Inspired by the songs of The Seekers

Set in 1870s Parramatta and Kent, UK

Rick Lockley, struggling to escape his family's expectations, runs away to find himself. Jack, a jolly swagman, takes him under his care. Even after years together, Rick knows little about the old man. On his death, Jack leaves Rick his precious billy can; the contents reveal Jack's identity. Stunned, Rick must travel to England to finalise Jack's wishes. There, he uncovers Jack's life of love, betrayal and a link to his own family. Rick also discovers there is much more to learn about this enigmatic man.

Paperback ISBN 9780645110753 Ebook ISBN 978-0-6451107-6-0

Large Print 9781923097186 HC 9798353687290 D2D ebook 9798233188794

Jonty's Journey

Gems, Love, Artists and a Golden Lion

Australia and South Africa 1880-1902

Sydney Jeweller Jonty Evans's passion for gems takes him to Africa at a volatile time. There, he finds the diamonds he wants and is given a lion cub. However, Jonty is all but kidnapped. His experiences in the Transvaal plunge him into questioning everything he knows about life. Soon, nightmares haunt him. (This is now known as PTSD.)

Upon returning home, he nearly ruins his chance with Lottie Lockley before it even begins, and he finds adjusting hard. Lottie's father, Luke Lockley from Parramatta, takes him under his wing and directs him to someone who can assist.

Jonty is then called back to Africa as a liaison and reunites with his lion, Chimbu, after saving the life of his security detail. His life journey introduces him to remarkable artists, politicians, poets, rebels, and the scapegoat soldier, Harry Breaker Morant. Can Jonty lay the past to rest and find his lost peace?

Paperback ISBN 9780645110777 Ebook ISBN: 978-0-6451107-9-1

HC ISBN 9781923097124 LP 9781923097193 D2D ebook 9798233808821

$\mathcal{M}$attie

The Story of an Australian Convict Child
An Australian Historical Story inspired by real Life.

An orphaned child, Mattie, is convicted of petty theft, sentenced to seven years, and sent to Australia. She meets another convict woman who, at her death, gives Mattie a chance for a new life. She makes the most of everything that comes her way, earning her freedom, falling in love, marrying, and becoming a mother. But life is not kind to her.

She meets bushrangers, moves to Bathurst's gold fields, and opens a store. Yet, she is the kind of woman who made Australia what it is today. Can she survive alone in a man's world? She is a remarkable woman who breaks down all her barriers.

(Mattie's story continues in The Lockleys of Parramatta - bk 4 & 6)
Woodslane Press Edition 9781925403404 (Brown cover
Paperback ISBN 9781503252370 ebook ISBN 97819023097018
Large Print 978099458204 D2D ebook 9798233382642
(The story continues in The Earl's Shadow & Once a Jolly Swagman) Released 2015

$\mathcal{R}$icky

A boy in Colonial Australia

Ricky English and his mother immigrated from England to join his father in the new Colony of Sydney. Upon arrival, there was no sign of his father. Ricky's mum uses the tiny amount of money they brought to get lodgings in a run-down building. Things go from bad to worse when his mother dies; he is thrown out of the hired rooms, and the caretakers confiscate all their possessions.

Ricky lives on the streets of Sydney Town as a street waif. Ricky finds safe places to sleep and befriends freed convicts who can help him survive. One day, he encounters a lost child and helps reunite her with her family. These people try to help him, but he insists on doing things his way because of his stubbornness. However, he has found a mentor and confidante. The story follows him through his life. He survives and turns his life around, helping others along the way. *(Will's story continues in Jonty's Journey)*

Pacific Wanderland Publications by Woodslane Press 9780994578211 (Brown cover)
Amazon Paperback ISBN 9781500770570 Ebook: 9781923097100
Large Print 9781533472748 D2D ebook 9798233505317

The $\mathcal{H}$eather to The $\mathcal{H}$awkesbury

Four Scottish families brave a new life in a strange land.

Torn from their homeland by starvation, four Scottish families are forced to leave the Isle of Skye and seek a new life in Australia. Mary Macdonald, her husband Murd, and their family, her brother Fergus MacKenzie, sister-in-law Caro MacLeod, cousin Alex Fraser, and all their loved ones are compelled to emigrate from Scotland because of the Potato famine and Clearances.

The story follows these families as they journey from Scotland to the New South Wales colony in the 1850s. Mary struggles to cope with the changes and losses in the first months of settlement. Although the other women rely on her, she is nearly overwhelmed. Mary can't settle in this fierce land and pines for home.

Together, the families endure hardships such as accidents, loss, floods, and relentless work, ultimately forging a strong bond with their new homeland. Trials, tribulations, and triumphs mark their saga as they establish themselves in Australia.

Will Mary ever find peace and contentment where danger and sickness have taken loved ones? Can her love for Murd sustain her through the turmoil of life? And what becomes of the brooch given to Mary as she leaves her mother?

Pacific Wanderland Publications printed by Woodslane Press 9780994578228
Paperback ISBN 9781503251434 ebook 9781923097025 LP ISBN1533473641
D2D ebook 9798223852209

Sara's Author Bio

Sheila Hunter and Sara Powter were a passionate mother-and-daughter team of amateur genealogists. As they collaborated on their family tree, they made many fascinating discoveries. Their most significant finding was the discovery of four convicts whose perspectives on colonial life sharply contrasted with those of the military personnel. Transported to Australia between 1792 and 1814, these four felons lived during the peak of the convict transportation era.

Before her passing in 2002, Sheila adapted some of these histories into enchanting stories, later published as her Australian Colonial Trilogy by Sara. Sheila also left a fourth, unfinished story, inspiring Sara to complete it. Before taking on that task, however, Sara first created the 'Lockleys of Parramatta' series to ensure she could honour her mother's work. She completed the first two books in that series before attempting to finish 'Dancing to Her Own Tune'—for which Sheila had written the first 30,000 words.

Vividly evoking the Colonial Era, these books delve deeper into the theme of overcoming adversity in Colonial Australia, exploring how it emerged, the demise of the Convict system, and the discovery of mineral wealth. Sara skilfully intertwines precise archival data with a captivating narrative to craft a collection of stories about faith, love, loss, and redemption.

Two hundred years after her family arrived in Australia, Sara continues the Australian Colonial stories that start with *Gentle Annie Soames,* a saga about the First Fleet. Her *First Fleet Trilogy* is now complete. Following this chronologically are *The Hunter to Macquarie* Collection, the *Unlikely Convict Ladies* Trilogy, and The *Lockleys of Parramatta*. The *Convict Birthstain Collection*, set in the mid-1800s, follows. All the stories are stand-alone novels.

See Sara's web page to keep up to date with more stories.   Amazon Aus QR

Signed copies are available from:-

https://www.sarapowter.com.au

(Australian Postage only)

Email me at

saragpowter@gmail.com

FACEBOOK

https://www.facebook.com/profile.php?id=100063887262514

Would you like *"Unshackled Lives" for free?*

Download from Book Funnel after you sign up.

FREE Newsletter signup
From my web page.